Robyn Lee Burrow[...] New South Wale[...] since settled on the Gold Coast hinterland. She is a Scorpio, born with the moon in Pisces, and describes herself as emotional, independent and creative. She is married with three sons who refuse to grow up and leave home, and custodian to two cats and a dog. As well as writing, she is a partner in a writing assessment and editing enterprise. In her meagre portion of spare time she enjoys watching good movies, dining out and, naturally, reading. *When Wattles Bloom* is her fourth novel, and seventh book.

Also by Robyn Lee Burrows

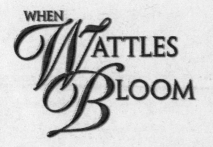

WHEN WATTLES BLOOM

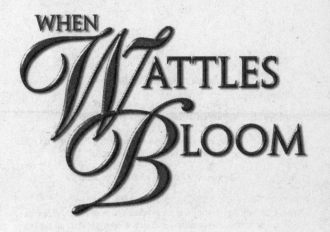

WHEN WATTLES BLOOM

Robyn Lee Burrows

HarperCollins*Publishers*

HarperCollins_Publishers_

First published in Australia in 2000
by HarperCollins_Publishers_ Pty Limited
ACN 009 913 517
A member of the HarperCollins_Publishers_ (Australia) Pty Limited Group
http://www.harpercollins.com.au

HarperCollins_Publishers_
25 Ryde Road, Pymble, Sydney, NSW 2073, Australia
31 View Road, Glenfield, Auckland 10, New Zealand
77-85 Fulham Palace Road, London W6 8JB, United Kingdom
Hazelton Lanes, 55 Avenue Road, Suite 2900, Toronto, Ontario M5R 3L2
and 1995 Markham Road, Scarborough, Ontario M1B 5M8, Canada
10 East 53rd Street, New York NY 10022, USA

National Library of Australia Cataloguing-in-Publication data:

Burrows, Robyn Lee.
When wattles bloom.
ISBN 0 7322 6658 0.
I. Title.
A823.3

Cover illustration by Lloyd Foye
Printed in Australia by Griffin Press Pty Ltd, Adelaide
on 50 gsm Ensobulky

5 4 3 2 1   00 01 02 03 04

dedicated to my grandmother
Elizabeth Annie Barton
(nee McLaughlin)
1894–1972

wattle *n.* Name given to over 800 species of acacia tree growing in Australia. Evergreen. Blooms late winter to early spring with yellow puff-ball flowers gathered in a cluster of globose heads. The blooms are followed by pea-shaped pods that contain seeds. Walls of early colonial buildings were constructed from interwoven branches of the wattle tree sealed with clay or mud, giving rise to the term 'wattle and daub'. Golden Wattle (A. *pycnantha*) is the Australian floral symbol.

CHAPTER 1

Callie stood on the back porch, arms folded, looking down on the garden. Tears pricked her eyes, blurring the sprawling sunlit mass of shrubbery. A leaden feeling worked its way across her chest, settling in the vicinity of her stomach.

Sell the house?

Her mother's words tumbled chaotically in her mind, intertwined with a succession of random images, years old: Rufus, the Irish setter, chasing a stick, his stiff legs moving in an odd stilted way; Alex, her father, pushing the old mower across the lawn while her mother leaned up towards the clothesline, pegging sheets. The recollection was so real, she could almost smell the odour of freshly-mown grass and see the billowing white fabric, could almost hear the way it snapped and flapped in the breeze.

Sell the house?

Callie gave an imperceptible shake of her head, pushing the memories away. Back into the past where they belonged, in some faraway childhood place where dreams had been so bright. Her father had been dead for years, Rufus too.

The house at number twenty-seven Brunswick Street had been built around the turn of the century by Callie's great-great-grandparents, John and

Elizabeth, and their three children were the first generation of Cordukes to be raised there. Thomas, the younger son, had been killed during the Great War. Hannah, Thomas' twin and the only daughter, later married a far-western grazier. Only the eldest, David, Callie's great-grandfather, had stayed, inheriting the property which later passed to his son, Davie, and subsequently to Davie's only son, Alex.

Alex, thought Callie now, remembering her father again. Since his death, Callie's mother, Bonnie, had shared the house with Freya, Alex's unmarried sister.

'No use paying good money to run two households,' Bonnie had said to her sister-in-law after her grief had subsided and her practical nature had taken over once more. 'I'm just rattling around in this big old place by myself. There's room for a whole army here.'

Freya Corduke, who had been experiencing a few cash-flow problems of her own, readily agreed.

That had been almost ten years ago, Callie realised now with a start.

Dejectedly she descended the rear steps and walked through the garden. Though the sun was shining and the day warm, she hugged her arms across her chest, feeling a momentary chill. A huge mulberry tree shaded the yard. The sun's rays danced off its foliage, leaving a muted viridescence and a sense of coolness. Beyond the back fence, a small creek meandered lazily over a rocky outcrop before spilling into a large lily-lined pond.

The garden was Freya's pride and joy. It was haphazard and informal, a wondrous mixture of native trees and traditional English plants: roses,

2

camphor laurels and grevilleas, lilly pilly and bauhinia and conifers, a massive cabbage palm, bougainvilleas trailing above beds of jonquils, pansies and agapanthus. Callie's favourites, however, were the wattles that grew in profusion along the rear fence. They were bare of flowers now, having bloomed during those last cold weeks of winter, months earlier. Now, mid-September, the bright green-tipped leaves seemed a drab replacement for those golden balls of fluff.

Sell the house?

With a deep sigh she turned and glanced back in the direction from which she had walked. Roomy and well-built, the Brunswick Street house was typical of its era. The type, she considered wryly, that people were currently paying inordinately high prices for, and Bonnie would have little trouble finding a buyer.

The layout of the rooms was as familiar as her own heartbeat. A front entry led into a wide central hallway from which opened the main rooms: three large bedrooms, enormous lounge, dining room and the kitchen which still housed the old Aga, though Bonnie seldom used it, preferring the modern electrical hot plates and wall oven that Alex had insisted on installing years earlier.

Callie's great-great-grandfather, John Corduke, had been the local bank manager, and had spared little expense in outfitting the interior. The ceilings were high and the cornices boasted a flower and leaf design. Brass light fittings hung from matching ceiling roses, and the walls were original plaster above a waist-high timber dado. At some stage, during a time before Callie could remember, the rear verandah had been enclosed to form a sunroom, while the front and side verandahs were clad with a variety of creepers: jasmine and honeysuckle and, at the front, a deep-red bougainvillea which seemed to be always covered in a mass of flowers, regardless of the season.

Sell the house?

Sadness settled over her like a cloak as she retraced her path through the garden. It lay in her chest, a heavy twisting mass, causing a ball of nausea to rise in her throat. How could she bear to lose the place? Never walk through the gardens again, never smell the roses?

Her mother waited at the bottom of the steps. 'I know you're upset, love,' Bonnie stated matter-of-factly, slinging an arm around Callie's shoulder, 'and I'm sorry, truly I am. If there was some way we could stay on, we would.'

Callie looked away, staring hard at the garden as she sensed that same leaden feeling in her chest again. She wondered if, at the age of thirty-two, her mother would think it strange if she cried. Silly, she admonished herself. Getting sentimental over an old house. Still, there was something about the place ...

Bonnie gave her daughter a sympathetic smile. 'It's far too big for us, love. We're getting older, Freya and I. We can't keep up the maintenance on the place. And the lawns, the gardens. Freya can't bend like she used to. The arthritis ...'

It was true, Callie supposed, trying to understand her mother's point of view. The two women *were* getting older. Bonnie's face seemed more lined than

4

usual, especially today, with her hair streaked silver at the temples. Freya, jabbing at the bougainvillea as Callie had come through the front gate earlier, had scarcely been able to hold the garden shears in her misshapen hands.

'So where will you go?' she asked dully, trying to keep the despair from her voice and failing miserably.

'We were thinking of a unit.'

'A *unit*! You'd hate that!'

'Well, not so much a unit, but one of those townhouses. There's a new lot going up down by the bayside. Two bedrooms with a nice view over the water and just a tiny slip of a garden. We should get a good price for this place, and we'll have a little left over for a holiday and some new furniture perhaps. We thought we'd let most of this old stuff go with the house.'

Thinking of Davie Corduke's writing desk in the corner of the dining room, Callie shivered involuntarily as other memories dragged themselves from some hidden recess in her mind, flashing disjointedly like old black and white movies at the cinema. Envelopes propped against dark mahogany, the white expanse of blotting paper, pen tray, three-well inkstand, her grandfather's face a picture of studied concentration as his knotted hands struggled to form the perfect copperplate letters. Hands, Callie remembered now, that were stiff and swollen like Aunt Freya's.

A combination of sadness and anger bubbled in her chest. Words of remonstration tumbled from her mouth, and she was powerless to stop them. 'I don't know how you could possibly bear to let this place go. It's been in the family for so long!' She stopped, a sudden thought crossing her mind. Like grasping at straws, she thought wryly. 'If the yard is the only problem then I'll pay someone to come and do the gardening.'

'It's not just the money, dear. It's the house, crying out for someone young.' Bonnie turned and walked up the back stairs.

'Young?' queried Callie as she watched the retreating form of her mother.

'What this place needs,' added Bonnie firmly, 'is a mass of children running through its rooms.'

Michael Paterson slowed the car as it reached the T-intersection. 'Brunswick Street', read the sign that pointed to the left, and he turned the corner, peering curiously ahead.

It was one of those wide leafy streets, uncurbed, with poinciana trees casting a mottled shade along neatly-trimmed footpaths. Only the centre of the road was tarred, leaving a flat stretch of gravel between the bitumen and the lawn. The houses were tucked well back, partly hidden behind thick walls of shrubbery.

He braked and glanced down at the slip of paper that lay on the passenger seat. Number twenty-seven, it read, in his own untidy scrawl. And there it was, the figures painted large and white against the dark green of the letterbox.

Bringing the car to a standstill, Michael let the revs of the engine slow before turning off the ignition. He was expected, having telephoned the weekend before. The woman who had answered the phone, Bonnie, had seemed pleasant enough, though decidedly surprised. 'If I could meet you ...' he had added, pressing the issue.

'Well,' she had replied faintly, 'you'd better come. It all sounds very interesting, though I'm sure I won't be of any help at all.'

They had made the arrangements then. Saturday. Twelve o'clock.

Michael glanced now at his watch, noting that the hands had moved relentlessly forward towards that appointed time. He gathered up his briefcase, opened the car door and swung his long legs to the ground.

The house lay quietly sleeping in the sunshine behind a mass of plumbago, the flowers of which had mostly fallen, creating a carpet of mauve. Along the paved pathway he went, across the wide verandah, coming to a halt at the front door. The paint was peeling, flaking away in small strips, although the timber underneath appeared sound. There was a brass knocker and a bell on the wall beside the door. Deciding on the bell, Michael could hear the melodious tones as they echoed through the house, followed by a thudding of footsteps as the door was flung open.

'Bonnie?' he said, not equating the young woman who now stood before him with the voice on the telephone a few days earlier. Somehow she had sounded much older.

'No, I'm Bonnie's daughter, Callie.'

Another woman appeared behind, older-looking, plump, with short grey curly hair. 'I'm Bonnie.'

Michael held out his hand. 'Michael Paterson. I rang through the week.'

Bonnie stared at him, a blank look on her face. Suddenly her expression softened. She ran a hand through her hair and gave a strained smile, glancing towards her daughter. 'Oh, goodness, what with all the talk of selling the house, I had quite forgotten.'

He hadn't considered that Bonnie might not feel the same interest as himself. She had seemed curious enough on the phone. A wash of disappointment dampened his enthusiasm. 'I can come back another time if it's not convenient.'

Bonnie laughed and beckoned him inside. 'Goodness, no. After driving all the way from the city? Come in. Freya and I were just about to have some lunch. Will you stay, Callie?'

Callie glanced at her watch and grinned. 'Love to. Stuart's not picking me up until one.'

Suddenly Michael felt himself smiling back.

Lunch was an assortment of sandwiches — ham and salmon and chicken adorned with a garnish of parsley — served on the long mahogany table in the dining room. The tablecloth was stiff, as though starched, and delicately embroidered around the edges. Like a family heirloom, Michael thought, wondering at its age. He sat, feeling awkward, and noted his own lack of appetite.

'Well, Michael, you'd better tell us why you're here,' said Freya, the woman Bonnie had introduced as her sister-in-law, as she helped herself to the tray of sandwiches.

They were all watching him, the three women, eyes wide and inquiring, waiting for his explanation. Yet he had none. Not really. This visit was prompted more by ... What? he wondered, for a moment lost for words. A coincidence? A small piece of trivia that he had discovered less than a fortnight earlier?

'A few weeks ago I was sorting through a box of my father's belongings, items that had been kept from his childhood. You know, first pair of shoes, christening gown, baptism certificate, that sort of thing.' Michael rummaged in his pocket, his hand closing over cold metal. He brought it out and laid it on the tablecloth. 'I found this tangled in the fringe of a baby's shawl.'

'What is it?' Callie lifted the J-shaped object, holding it to the light.

'It's a horseshoe,' explained Michael. 'Or, rather, half of one.'

'Funny colour for a horseshoe,' commented Freya dourly.

'It's been silver-dipped. Look near the cut mark. You can see the original metal inside.'

'I'm not sure what an old horseshoe has to do with us or our family,' added Bonnie, looking puzzled.

Michael leant across the table, touching his finger to the metal. 'If you look closely, you'll see the name "Ben" etched on the uppermost side. There's some more writing, along the base. It's very faint, but it looks like, "you always". And on the back, you can just make out the words, "Hannah Elizabeth Corduke, Brunswick Street. 1915".'

Bonnie picked it up, peering closely. 'That's definitely great-aunt Hannah,' she said, tracing one finger across the words. 'We're the only Corduke family who ever lived around here.'

'Who's Ben?' asked Callie, an expression of studied surprise crossing her face.

Bonnie shrugged and replaced the horseshoe on the tablecloth. 'I have no idea.'

'What makes you think there could be any possible connection between this,' Freya paused as she indicated the horseshoe, 'and you, Michael?' Her gaze was frank, her question direct. 'How did your father end up with it? Can't he help you with your enquiry?'

'Well, to be honest, I haven't the faintest idea how it came into my father's possession. And as for asking him — he's been dead for almost two years.'

He hadn't meant to sound so abrupt but the older woman, with her curt patronising tone, had made him defensive. Freya glanced away. 'I'm sorry,' she muttered, clearly embarrassed.

Michael touched her hand, noting the swollen finger joints, and gave her a wry smile. 'Really, there's no need to be. You didn't know him.'

Freya gave a loud disapproving sniff and helped herself to another sandwich.

Michael tapped one finger against the horseshoe, bringing the conversation back to the reason for his visit. 'It was just a surprise finding this, that's all,' he shrugged. 'And I suppose the curiosity got the better of me. How *did* it come to be with my father's belongings? What possible connection could my family have had with yours? I was hoping one of you could shed a little light on it.'

'Perhaps if you told us a little of your family,' prompted Bonnie. 'Did they come from around here?'

'That's the strange thing. My father was an only child, and his parents were getting on in years when he was born. They were all city people, nothing to do with this area at all. I was quite young when my grandparents died and I scarcely remember them.'

Bonnie seemed interested so he told her what he knew, addressing his words in her direction. 'Funny, isn't it?' he ended with a grin. 'Lately I've had an urge to know more about my heritage. When I found the horseshoe, I thought it might be a clue, a shortcut to finding out. I guess I was mistaken.'

Freya listened in silence. Abruptly she held out her hand for the piece of metal, awarding it a cursory glance before dropping it back on the table with a clunk. Her face was an unreadable mask. 'It could have belonged to anyone, and anybody could have put Hannah's name on the back of it, for whatever reason. As far as I can see, it's rubbish,' she snapped. 'Fit for the garbage bin. And as for ferreting around in the past, I don't know why you bother. Muckraking, that's all it is.'

Michael looked up to see Callie staring at her aunt, her grey eyes round with amazement. 'I'm sorry,' he said stiffly, sensing the antagonism in the older woman's voice. 'It was such a strange item to find and I guess curiosity got the better of me. I usually enjoy a good mystery and this one seemed to be handed to me on a plate.'

Bonnie flashed Freya an unmistakable look of annoyance. 'I'm sorry too, Michael. I can't explain how the horseshoe came to be amongst your father's possessions either, but it's impossible that Hannah had any connection with your family. She lived most of her adult life in western Queensland and never had children. So there's no-one else you can ask.'

She pushed the object back towards Michael but he waved it away, feeling disappointed. 'No, keep it,' he insisted. 'If it belonged to Hannah then you should have it.'

'In the bin,' threatened Freya as she noisily rearranged the teacups that were stacked in the centre of the table and began pouring the tea. Bonnie cut four slices from the cake she had brought from the kitchen.

Michael, watching the stubborn expression on Freya's face, wondered what to say next. The questions, dozens of them, that had been bubbling around in his mind had inexorably ground to a halt. Suddenly he wished he hadn't come.

'I'd like to keep it,' said Callie, holding her hand out towards the shoe. 'If no-one else wants it, that is.'

'Humph!' muttered Freya.

As Callie's fingers closed over the metal, the noisy honking of a car horn came from the front of the house. 'That'll be Stuart,' she said, slipping it into her coat pocket. 'Never mind cake for me. Better go, Mum.'

Freya gave an irritated snort. 'Don't know why that boyfriend of yours can't just come inside and tell you he's here like any normal person,' she grumbled irritably, heading back to the kitchen to refill the teapot.

12

'It's been nice meeting you, Michael,' said Callie, rising from the table.

Bonnie gave her daughter a conspiratorial smile. 'Don't mind Freya,' she whispered as she accompanied Callie out of the room. 'She's been a bit niggly lately.'

From the verandah Michael could hear the voices of the two women, low and muted. 'I know, Mum, the arthritis ...'

A laugh. Bonnie's. 'No, actually I believe she thinks she'll miss this old place when we leave. But there's no other way around it, dear. It's just getting too much. Try not to worry.'

Through the open windows Michael could hear the shrill shriek of cicadas and, from further away, the faint drone of a lawnmower. He emptied a teaspoon of sugar into the milky tea, watching as the grains slid towards the liquid, and stirred it absentmindedly. From the kitchen came the sound of Freya banging a drawer shut.

There was another impatient honk on the horn.

'Better go, Mum. Bye.'

With a spray of gravel, the car roared away, taking the corner with a screech of wheels.

Callie lay awake and stared at the ceiling. From the lounge room came the muffled sound of the television. Some spy movie with lots of car chases, enough violence to guarantee nightmares for a week, and the token voluptuous blonde. God, she sighed. She *hated* shows like that. Would have preferred to switch the wretched thing off and put on a CD, some relaxing music to provide a soothing end to what had turned out to be an upsetting day. But Stuart's eyes had been glued to the screen and he'd hardly acknowledged her goodnight.

Sell the house!

Her mind raced as she recalled her mother's words for what seemed like the thousandth time that day. An idea had come to her earlier, surprising her with its simplicity. 'We could sell the unit and buy the house in Brunswick Street,' she had suggested to Stuart after dinner. 'That way, it could stay in the family.'

Stuart, sitting in his chrome and leather chair next to the chrome and glass coffee table, had looked aghast. 'Christ, Callie!' he had yelped. 'You must be joking.'

'No,' she had replied calmly. 'I'm dead serious.'

He had regarded her levelly, eyes narrowed. 'So am I. Live in that mausoleum? No way!'

Michael flicked off the light and slid into the bed, stretching his long legs against the sheets. After the relentless noise of the city, it was quiet in the small motel tucked into the lee of the bay. No rush of traffic, no distant wail of sirens, just the slow lap-lap of the water and the sigh of the wind in the casuarinas.

He stared towards the window, watching the gentle billowing of the curtains. A pale moon had risen, bathing the room with pearly light. Closing his eyes, he let his thoughts settle. Events of the day filtered through his mind, disconnected and random, not appearing in any apparent order. Bonnie with the soft smile, Freya with her tight-lipped mouth and hostile manner. The grey-eyed daughter, Callie, with auburn shoulder-length hair cut in a long bob, and a sprinkling of freckles across her nose. She was pretty in an unusual way, despite a too-wide mouth that turned upwards at the corners when she smiled.

Okay, he thought grimly, dismissing their faces. So the whole day had turned out to be an absolute waste of time. The horseshoe had proved a dud. He had upset the dour Miss Corduke. In short, he had barged into their lives on a whim, achieving nothing.

Despite his thoughts, sleep was descending. He could feel it, was drugged almost by the weight of it. Darkness merging with muted shadows, a blur of walls mottled by the shade of a spreading plumbago. The house in Brunswick Street, he thought groggily, wondering if it were already a dream, noting the way it was set back on the block, like a lazy cat sleeping in the sun.

A beautiful house holding memories of another time, long gone. Who was the unknown Ben? Why was Hannah Corduke's name engraved on the back of the horseshoe? And how did the shoe come to be tangled up in the fringe of a baby's shawl, found miles away, years later?

How mysterious, he thought numbly, his thoughts tumbling in a confused haphazard way. And disappointing because, more than anything, he wanted to be part of it all.

CHAPTER 2

It was Sunday. The main street was almost deserted except for a group of teenagers heading in the direction of the beach, backpacks slung casually over their shoulders. Callie wondered momentarily at their tenacity. It was barely spring and the breeze that whipped in from the bay still held a reminder of colder days. As the group rounded the corner and were lost to view, she gave an involuntary shiver and moved towards the nursery entrance.

She stopped at the large display window, her eyes caught by a splash of yellow: a tub of daffodils. They would be perfect for the balcony, she decided, which was looking decidedly dreary this time of the year. She paid at the counter, waving away the storekeeper's offer to carry the purchase to her car. The pot wasn't heavy, just bulky. Carefully, barely able to see over the top of the nodding yellow heads, she made her way back to the Suzuki which was parked nearby.

'Hello there.'

She turned, awkwardly balancing the pot as she sought the owner of the voice. It was Michael, the man who had come to the Brunswick Street house the previous day.

'Hi.'

He held out his hand for the daffodils. 'Here, let

me carry those.' Easily he hoisted her purchase into his arms, awarding her a wide smile. 'Going far?'

'Thanks. The car's over there,' she added, pointing to the small blue four-wheel-drive that was parked under the shade of a large fig.

'Kellie, isn't it?' he asked.

'Callie, actually.'

He looked puzzled, a slight crisscrossing of lines on his forehead. 'With a C,' she explained, emphasising the letter. They had come to the car and she fumbled in her handbag, searching for the key. 'It's short for Calliandra, which is a bit of a mouthful, so everyone calls me Callie.'

The car door was open at last. He leaned forward and sat the pot on the centre of the back seat. 'There, all safe,' he grinned, as he unfolded himself back out of the vehicle.

For a moment he stood looking at her, a thoughtful expression on his face. 'Can I interest you in a coffee?' he said at last.

Ye Olde Coffee Shoppe was set further back from the road than the neighbouring buildings, creating a small courtyard effect at the front. Wooden tubs contained dwarf ficus and geraniums spilling towards the ground, and the tables were laid with red-and-white checked tablecloths. Michael opted to sit outside. 'Too nice to be indoors on a day like today,' he smiled, ordering two cappuccinos from the waitress.

Out of the direct line of the wind, Callie felt the sun on her face. It gave a gentle warmth, which diffused through her body, relaxing her. Michael

17

settled back in the chair, stretching his long legs, his arms folded behind his head. 'Comfortable?' he asked.

Callie nodded. 'So, how long are you staying in town?'

'I'm not sure. Perhaps a few days. Now that I'm here, I thought I'd poke around the place, get the feel of it.'

'That won't take long,' Callie laughed. 'It's very small — compared to the city, I mean.'

Leaning forward, Michael indicated the nearby buildings with a sweep of his hand. 'Doesn't look as though the place has changed much over the years.'

'Not a lot. The butcher, shoe shop, haberdashery. They've been there as long as I can remember. Clarke's Emporium used to be a little further along, but it burnt down years ago.' She gave a small laugh. 'God, I loved that place when I was a kid. They had wires that ran overhead, which took the money in little metal cylinders to a cashier. I was always fascinated by them, and the loud pinging sound the change made when it came back. But it's all gone now. There are a few new shops, the deli, cake shop — *patisserie*, they insist on calling it — and the supermarket complex on the outskirts of town. But most of the other commercial buildings are probably between eighty to one hundred years old.'

Michael looked pensive for a moment, then changed the subject. 'About yesterday, I hope I didn't upset anyone.'

Callie shrugged. 'Freya didn't seem too pleased. According to my mother, who rang me this morning, she called you a brash young man after you had left.'

'Brash?' An expression of puzzlement crossed his brow. 'I was probably more nervous than anything.'

'I know.'

'Are you usually so astute?' he teased, face relaxing into a smile.

'No, I just know Freya. She can be quite intimidating.'

He laughed. It was a rich sound, deep and warm, and Callie found herself liking this man who sat in front of her. The waitress returned and placed the coffees on the table. As she sipped her drink, Michael told her a little of his job. He was a photographer, he explained, with one of the leading city newspapers, having worked his way up as a cadet, starting with the mayoral openings of new civic buildings, photographing hopeful candidates for the council elections, and so on. That had been twenty years ago. Now he handled the feature shoots, mostly location work, as well as carrying out some freelance assignments of his own. Callie felt a small stab of relief. Somehow she couldn't picture him spending all his working days in some stuffy office. Like Stuart, she thought with a start.

Covertly, over the rim of her cup, she studied him as he spoke. He was dressed in jeans, slightly faded, and a long-sleeved shirt, the sleeves of which were rolled to just above the elbows. Tall, over six feet in height, he had a lean body and sandy-coloured hair that curled in a muddled haphazard way, framing an interesting-looking face. Probably late thirties, she decided, glancing at his hands as he tipped the contents of a sugar sachet onto the white froth of the coffee and stirred it thoroughly. Strong tapering fingers, nails neatly clipped, no rings.

'...it's important, family. My parents are both dead, and there's only me and one sister, Anne. Timothy needs to know his heritage.'

'Timothy?' Deep in thought, Callie had lost the thread of the conversation.

'My son.'

'Oh.' She sensed a vague inexplicable disappointment. 'So you're married?'

'*Was*,' Michael corrected. 'Gaby and I separated several years ago. It was, as they say, a civilised divorce. No messy affairs, we simply grew apart. One day we stopped long enough to realise that the only thing we had in common was our child. We're good friends, which is important for Tim.'

Callie nodded, thinking of the absence of her own father. 'So, you managed to get away from Freya yesterday unscathed? No teeth marks?'

Michael gave a hearty laugh. 'Not a one,' he said, holding out his forearms, which were bare except for an expensive-looking diver's watch, for inspection. 'I left not long after you. Things seemed a bit strained. But that's all right. It was my fault, barging in without any real facts to go on. Next time I'll do my homework properly.'

'Don't mind Freya. I expect she'll have forgotten all about it by next week. And underneath that gruff exterior, she's really quite nice, when you get to know her.'

'Yeah, I'll bet,' Michael grinned. 'Pity I'll never have the chance.'

He has such a nice smile, Callie thought, as she brought the cup to her mouth again.

The next few days passed slowly, without incident. Minolta slung around his neck, Michael roamed the town, taking photographs of the old buildings. Perhaps he would put together a feature article on the area. Six or seven of his best shots, a few hundred words of text. The newspaper editor was always on the lookout for something different.

And this place *was* distinctive, he thought, with its courthouse, bank and pub, their stone façades butter-gold in the sunlight. Gothic, Victorian, old Queenslander: the quaint mixture of styles complemented each other, creating an interesting effect. The local librarian had been most accommodating, showing him several booklets which briefly outlined the history and development of the area.

He felt an odd affinity with the village, with its narrow back streets that wound around the hilly terrain, the snug houses set amongst overgrown gardens, the quiet ambience. Even the shoppers moved slowly, in a leisurely manner, baskets slung over arms. Wandering through the park, he watched the sparrows as they darted through the old bandstand. It must have looked lovely once, he mused. Sunday afternoons, a brass band, couples and families strolling past, children running in mad disarray.

Beyond lay the tennis courts surrounded by neatly clipped hedges, and the war memorial. He stretched out in the sun on the grass, feeling it tickle his back through the thin fabric of his shirt. Overhead the birds made a noisy cacophony in the trees. Tomorrow he would return to the city, leave all this behind. The editor had phoned the previous night to offer several assignments.

That last night, in the small motel room, he listened to the waves rolling ceaselessly towards the shore, lulling him, soothing him with their whisperings, murmured goodbyes. Unbidden, in that grey indefinable area between wakefulness and sleep, his thoughts moved back to the house in Brunswick Street, to Bonnie and Freya, and Callie with the grey eyes. Back to the house drowsing in the sun, and the garden nodding in the midday heat. And the horseshoe, he thought with surprise, remembering how Callie had taken it from the table, lifting it curiously, almost reverently, studying it for a moment before dropping it into her pocket.

But, he reminded himself, an odd sense of disappointment crowding in on him, the horseshoe was Callie's now, gone, and he knew nothing more about it than he had the week before.

The following Sunday dawned fine and clear with the promise of a warm day. 'Thought you might come to Mum's with me for lunch,' Callie suggested to Stuart over breakfast. 'There are a couple of boxes of school things of mine up in the roof of the house. You know, project books, old report cards, texts, that sort of thing. I might need some help getting them down.'

Stuart who, Callie knew, had a loathing of things old, arched his eyebrows. 'Sounds like a load of dusty rubbish to me. Where do you think you're going to put them?'

'In the garage, till I clean them up.'

'Harbingers of creepy crawlies,' he pronounced darkly. Then, 'Sorry, Cal. Rotten timing, I'm afraid. Had a game of squash lined up.'

Callie rose and began to clear away the breakfast plates. Stuart turned and ran up the carpeted stairway, in the direction of their bedroom. After a while he came downstairs again, whistling, taking the steps two at a time, dressed in white shorts and shirt and carrying his squash bag.

'I'll see you later then,' he said, awarding her a quick kiss on the mouth.

Callie felt his lips, cold against hers, and shivered. A feeling of desolation, inexplicable, shuddered through her as he closed the door behind him. And later, setting off by herself in the Suzuki, in the direction of the Brunswick Street house, she felt strangely deflated, as though he had failed her in some obscure indefinable way.

Walking down the front path, Callie could see Freya at the far side of the yard, bent over a tangle of shrubs. She had been pruning, the fact evidenced by the nearby loaded wheelbarrow, clipped pieces of shrubbery protruding over its sides.

Inside, the house was momentarily dark after the brightness outside. Bonnie, hearing the front door bang, called, 'Is that you, Callie? I'm in the kitchen.'

Sunshine slanted through the windows, giving the room a cosy feeling. Delicious smells of cooking permeated the air.

'Mmmm. Something smells good.'

Bonnie bustled around, her back to the door as she took a quiche from the oven. A tray of cold meat and salad sat on the bench. 'I've made your favourite,' she said as Callie came in behind her. Then, turning, 'What's wrong, love?'

'Nothing. Why?'

'Where's Stuart? I thought he was coming too?'

'He'd organised a game of squash.'

'Mmmm,' Bonnie frowned. 'You two don't seem to be spending much time together any more. Everything all right?'

Was it that obvious? Callie wondered. 'Of course, Mum,' she replied, trying to keep her voice light. 'You do get some funny ideas at times.'

Bonnie regarded her thoughtfully for a few seconds, as though not fully convinced, then turned back to the stove.

Freya came in from the garden, amid a fresh bout of grumbling about red-spider mite and an outbreak of aphids on her beloved roses. Callie dutifully kissed her aunt on her leathery cheek and suppressed a smile, then helped her mother carry the trays of food to the table.

Freya, Callie noted with an amused smile, was still grumbling at the events of the previous Saturday. 'Muckraking, that's all it is. Digging into other people's lives. Don't know what good can come of bringing up things long past.'

'Bringing up what?' said Callie, puzzled. 'The horseshoe was just a bit of a mystery, that's all. Michael thought there might be some connection between our families. His own parents are dead; he can't ask them. He has no-one.'

'He has a wife and child,' brayed Freya triumphantly. 'He told us so last Saturday. Isn't that right, Bonnie?'

Bonnie nodded. 'Yes, dear.'

'He's divorced,' interjected Callie. 'Anyway, that has absolutely nothing to do with it. Okay, so the thing with the horseshoe and Hannah turned out to be a dead end. You can't blame him for asking. It was only harmless curiosity. And you needn't have been so rude, either.'

'Callie!' Bonnie gave her daughter a sharp look and Freya pursed her lips and gave a loud sniff.

'Freya and I were planning to go over to the new townhouses after lunch. There's a display unit open each afternoon. Would you like to come?' asked Bonnie, changing the subject.

Callie shook her head. 'There are a few boxes of mine up in the roof. Dad put them up there when I finished school. I thought I'd get them out. Less to clean up later when the house is sold.'

'Good idea,' replied Freya tersely. Callie's earlier criticism obviously still rankled. 'There's a load of old rubbish up there that hasn't been touched for years. Seems to me that if we've gone this long without needing any of it, then we never will. The garbage tip, that's where it all belongs. Perhaps Stuart might give us a hand one day to get it all down.'

After lunch the two women set off for the bayside, Freya firmly gripping the wheel of the lumbering old Vauxhall as it chugged down

Brunswick Street, leaving a trail of blue smoke in its wake. Callie watched them go with a mixture of regret and relief. At least, with the sale of the house, they would be able to afford a new car, one of those nippy four-cylinder numbers to take them down to the shopping centre and Bonnie's craft classes.

With their departure, the house was suddenly quiet. A sonorous silence settled through the rooms like a blanket. Outside, a currawong warbled. The smell of jasmine wafted through the window. Essence of spring, Callie thought, wondering for a moment if it would be their last season there. With a sigh, she finished washing-up and went to fetch the ladder.

The light from the torch did little to illuminate the cavernous underbelly of the roof. Stepping carefully from rafter to rafter, Callie noted how the shadows appeared to dance, swaying in and out of its beam. There was a quietness up there, too, nothing but a soft creaking of old joists and timber bearers, a sense of musty solidness.

Every surface was layered with dust and cobwebs. 'Freya's right. Doesn't look as though anyone's been up here for years,' she muttered darkly to herself, following the words with a loud sneeze. 'Bless me,' she added, then laughed at the absurdity of the one-sided conversation.

The roof was high-pitched, allowing her to stand upright in the centre. Curiously Callie glanced around, memories tugging at her subconsciousness. How old had she been when she'd come up here last? Twelve? Thirteen, perhaps?

It had been a Saturday afternoon, like today. Creeping unnoticed up the ladder, she had discovered the trunks of old-fashioned clothing: dresses with frilly collars and flounces, and huge sweeping skirts, fringed shawls. Another round container had revealed a selection of hats: stiff straw boaters and picture hats decorated with bright ribbons or bunches of silk flowers, a blue Dolly Varden, a pert little cap that was nothing more than wispy fabric with a short veil and a fluff of feathers. At the bottom of a nearby suitcase, she had found an assortment of ladies' boots, the leather stiff and cracked with age.

That was how Bonnie had found her, hours later, parading her discoveries in front of the full-length mahogany mirror, holding them against her coltish body. 'Oh, Callie! Here you are. I've been looking everywhere for you. Your father was *that* worried.'

Inwardly Callie smiled, remembering her mother's astonished expression, the concealed anger that quickly turned to relief.

Now, holding the torch high, she glanced about, seeking out familiar objects. Suddenly she froze as shadows leapt from a dark shape to her right. Then she stifled a giggle. Bonnie's dressmaker's dummy, shrouded with sheets.

She picked her way through the bric-a-brac: two revolving office chairs, broken; a Remington Standard typewriter, its keys barely discernable under a layer of fluff; a set of heavily-patterned kitchen canisters, most without lids. Against one wall sat several Folkestone trunks of varying sizes, old tennis racquets, their strings frayed, and a child's pull-along wagon, once bright red, but now a washed-out maroon.

The room was full of junk mostly, as Freya had said. Callie trailed her fingers over an ornate circular birdcage. It was empty, yet a scattering of seed husks still littered the floor. Behind it stood a high-wheeled perambulator with a torn hood. An old bookcase held an assortment of titles long since out of print.

At her feet was a box containing a selection of jars and tins: Lamb's Linoleum Cream, Nye's Sewing Machine and Bicycle Oil, metal polish, several bars of Colgate & Co Castille soap. She squatted on the floor, sorting through the contents, fascinated by the old-fashioned labels.

As her arm moved, the face of her watch caught her attention and Callie was surprised to see she'd been up there almost half an hour. Right, she thought, letting the soap fall back amongst the long-unopened jars and tins as she rose purposely to her feet and turned to seek out her own belongings.

The boxes were easily located. Tied with string, they bore her name in large lettering on the sides. There was no way Callie could carry them down the ladder, so she took several used supermarket bags from Bonnie's kitchen and manhandled the contents down in portions, eventually repacking them in the now-emptied boxes on the back seat of her car.

As she prepared to descend the ladder for what she considered was the last time, Callie noticed a previously unseen trunk standing in one corner, the dust inches thick on the lid. Curiosity aroused, and her own task completed, she went in search of a bucket of water and a cloth.

The dirt came away to reveal faded red leather. 'I think this is what's called a portmanteau,' she mused as she ran a finger over the grained surface, feeling a rush of unexplained excitement. Kneeling on the bare boards, she leaned forward, pulling the lid upwards.

The hinges were rusty and the trunk creaked open, sounding like a sigh of regret. Callie found herself holding her breath, all at once eager to see the contents. One by one she lifted them out: old recipe books, birthday and Christmas cards, newspaper clippings. There were several school copybooks, invitations to weddings and christenings, books, several eulogy cards — all yellowing at the edges. They smelt musty, and carried the odour of years of disuse. Underneath there were dozens of envelopes, obviously still containing the letters they had borne years previously. There were three separate piles, each tied with pale blue ribbon. Judging by the writing, each appeared to have been addressed by a different hand.

Callie peered forward, deciphering the address on the topmost envelope. *Miss Hannah Corduke. Bright Street, Kangaroo Point, Brisbane*, it read. The postmark was faint, though decipherable. *Bleu. France. 28 November 1916.*

'Hannah,' she whispered, fingers poised over the brittle paper, the memory of the half horseshoe jolting oddly back at her from the previous week. The word echoed insistently within her own consciousness, demanding attention, as she surveyed the crumbling treasured mementoes of her great-great-aunt's life. Slowly she let her hand sift through the contents, weighing them thoughtfully as she remembered Freya's words:

The garbage tip, that's where it all belongs.

Hannah's life crushed amongst the muck and mud, mingled with the lives of other people? 'No!' she muttered, scooping up an armful of papers. She couldn't let Freya destroy what was left.

She worked quickly, half expecting to hear the returning wheeze and chug of the Vauxhall at any moment, not knowing why it was so important that Hannah's belongings be preserved. Once emptied, the trunk was considerably lighter. With difficulty she managed to manoeuvre it down the ladder and onto the back seat of her car, along with the other boxes. Several trips later, the contents had been safely replaced. Bonnie and Freya had not returned, so she stored the ladder in the garage and let herself out of the house, locking the door.

After dinner, Stuart announced he was having an early night. 'Coming?' he asked, trailing one finger down the back of her neck.

Callie shook her head. 'Later. I've a few ideas for the book and I want to jot them down while they're still fresh.'

With Stuart in bed and the television off, the unit was quiet. Carrying a cup of coffee, she went to the downstairs bedroom, which she used as a study, and flicked on the computer.

The machine hummed into life. Quickly she found the file she was working in, and the cursor blinked back at her from a word-littered monitor. There was a movement at the doorway. Oscar came strolling in. He was a big cat, mostly white with irregular-shaped black patches. Casually he jumped onto her knee and settled himself, purring loudly.

Callie stared at the screen. It had been three years since her first novel had been published. Since then there had been several more, all gaining mediocre acclaim from the reviewers and public alike. Enough to provide a moderate, though spasmodic income. But this one, she knew, would be the one to guarantee her success. She had drafted most of the chapters and a detailed synopsis, pleased with the plot and the way the characters had begun to evolve in her mind. It *was* good, she thought. Damned good. Even her agent thought so.

Beginning where she had previously left off, Callie typed a few sentences and then, frowning, deleted them. 'Damn!' she muttered to herself, pushing away the keyboard.

Despite her intentions, her thoughts weren't on the novel. Instead, recollections of the previous week invaded her mind, distracting her. Bonnie's plans to sell the house. Michael's unexpected visit. Hannah.

Hannah! Thinking of her great-great-aunt again, she remembered the trunk. Accompanied by an inordinate amount of grumbling and muttering about the possibility of cockroach or silverfish infestation, Stuart had helped her carry it from the car earlier. Now it sat beneath the study window, a blur of faded leather. She had thought that perhaps, when she had a few spare hours, she might go through the contents more thoroughly, checking for anything of value.

At once the urge to open the trunk again was strong, stronger than the need to write. Without thinking, Callie pushed the cat from her lap and moved towards it, kneeling on the grey carpet as she opened the lid.

The same musty smell came out to greet her. Papers nestled against each other, dry and raspy under her fingers. One by one she drew them out, laying them in neat piles. In one envelope she discovered several photos. World War One snapshots mostly, of a soldier in uniform, and one of a woman with dark hair tumbling around her shoulders, a small blond-haired child perched on her hip, as she smiled uncertainly into the lens of the camera.

At last she had removed everything, except for a battered book that lay at the bottom. Picking it up, she considered its age. Was it a diary? she wondered, noting that there seemed to be something bulky attached to its interior, pushing the pages apart.

Carefully she opened the cover. There, pressed against the paper, was a metal J-shaped object. Remembering the previous Saturday and Michael's visit to the house in Brunswick Street, Callie froze momentarily. Reaching back, she groped in the pocket of her coat, which was casually slung across the back of her office chair, and drew the contents forward, holding the two objects up together.

The word 'Ben' was engraved on the right hand side; on the left, 'Hannah'. Across the curving base of the shoe were the words, faint but decipherable, 'I will love you always', the letters spaced evenly on each side of the break.

A perfect fit, she thought, stunned. The silver horseshoe, now complete, glowed dully in her palm.

CHAPTER 3

August 1914

'Hannah! Thomas! Davie!'

Enid Corduke stood at the top of the back steps of Number Twenty-seven Brunswick Street and smoothed her hands over her dark hair. Outside the day was fading, sunshine giving way to muted shadows. Even the camphor laurels and wattles at the bottom of the garden had dissolved into a faint blur.

All seemed quiet. Hushed. She waited, arms crossed, a frown of annoyance pleating her forehead. Already the air was chill. Glancing back towards the house she noted the yellow glow, promising warmth behind the closed curtains, and shivered.

From the direction of the stable came an abrupt clanking of metal. Ben Galbraith, son of the local blacksmith, was down there, shoeing the last of the horses. Not that the animals were used as much these days, she mused, since her husband David had purchased the Cadillac phaeton a few months earlier.

The breeze shifted, bringing with it the faint sound of chopping from the gully beyond the house. That would be Thomas, David's younger brother, readying another tub of wood for the Aga. Tom had arrived home early this week, on the afternoon train from the city where he had been studying at the university since the beginning of the year. He was a bright lad, well-liked by his peers, and David made no attempt to hide his pride in his brother.

Thinking of Tom, Enid's thoughts drifted to Hannah. How could two children who had simultaneously shared their mother's womb be so different? she wondered. Hannah, the younger twin by fifteen minutes, was the antithesis of her brother. She had no interest in academic subjects, being more inclined towards art and music. Enid considered her sometimes inclined to be dreamy, her thoughts miles away, while she capably executed some composition on the piano that sat in the corner of the parlour, or stirred a pan of custard on the Aga, impervious to the odour of burning milk and the lumps that curdled and formed.

Now, from the direction of the creek came the first faint reply to her summons.

'Coming, Mum.'

Davie's voice, her firstborn. Boyish, shrill.

Enid shivered again in the chill air and hugged her arms to her belly, feeling the solid shape of the child within. The long-awaited baby was due any day now. Another boy would be nice, she considered, another male to carry on the Corduke family name. David had already suggested calling him John, after his father. Grudgingly, Enid had agreed that it would be an appropriate gesture, especially after the trauma of the accident ...

She paused, thrusting her mind away from the memory, from that singularly unpleasant day that had changed all their lives. At her husband's insistence, they had moved immediately into the house in Brunswick Street, herself, David and Davie, trying to bring some semblance of normalcy into Thomas and Hannah's lives. The twins had been sixteen at the time, devastated by the unexpectedness of their parents' deaths.

Two years had passed since then. Two long drawn-out years during which, somewhat unwillingly, she had been forced to accept a measure of responsibility not only for her own small family, but for her husband's siblings as well. She could cope with Thomas. Nowadays he was seldom here, spending the week in the flat in Brisbane, attending to his studies. But Hannah!

She gave an impatient sigh at the thought of the girl, unable to pinpoint exactly what irritated her about David's sister. She was pretty, she admitted grudgingly, with her long dark hair, pale oval face and creamy skin. A mirrored replica of her mother that caused, she knew, a small ball of heartache in her own husband. Often she caught him staring at her, his sister, and she imagined him thinking of how things might have been, had his parents not ventured out in the buggy on that wet windy night. But they had and, in a split second of terror, the course of all their lives had been altered, and Hannah's constant and unavoidable presence in the house seemed an intrusion somehow, an encroachment on Enid's own womanly domain.

Slowly Enid released her arms from her belly, wiping her hands down the side of the apron as she glanced back towards the lighted windows of the house. Inside, the table was set with a new blue-and-white checked tablecloth. There was a plate of cold meat, left over from the midday roast, fresh salad, pickles and a loaf of bread, the latter miraculously still warm from the oven. And, for afters, a pot of jam and a large bowl of cream. The setting of the table was usually Hannah's job, but today she had been nowhere in sight and, in desperation, Enid had tended to the task herself.

The chopping had stopped and Tom would soon be up. '*Hannah*!' she called again, peering ahead into the deepening gloom. Where *was* the wretched girl? David would soon be in from the bank, wanting his tea at five-thirty as usual.

There was no reply. With a further sigh, Enid pulled the cardigan tighter across her chest, closed the door and went inside.

'Come on, Hannah. Just one more kiss.'

Hannah Corduke, her back against the stable wall, raised her face towards Ben's. Up close, she was inordinately aware of his fair hair and the way his skin glowed in the lamplight, the colour of red apples. He smelt nice, she thought, like chaff and sweet molasses, as his arms came round her again and she felt that same soft melting sensation deep inside, like she imagined jelly might feel if it were left in the sun.

It was warm in the stable, cosy, with the big wooden door pulled closed and the light from the lamp playing out across the floor and walls. One of the horses impatiently stamped its hoof and swished its tail. Ben's mouth on hers felt soft, pliable. He moved back and cupped his palms around her

36

cheeks, gazing into her face. His eyes flashed with barely concealed intensity. 'I love you, Hannah.'

'And I love you. I wish we could stay here like this, forever and ever.'

'You'd get very hungry after a while,' he laughed.

'*Hannah*!' Enid's insistent voice, faint and faraway. A muted summons brought by the wind. Suddenly Hannah registered the lateness of the hour. David would soon be home, if he wasn't already, and she had the usual jobs to do. 'I've got to go. *She's* calling,' she whispered, averting her face from his and wrinkling her nose.

'I love you, Hannah,' Ben repeated, taking both her hands. But she had pulled further away until only their fingers were touching. 'Tomorrow, then? There's still old Princess to shoe. I won't get her done today.'

Hannah nodded and bit her lip. She *had* to go. If she didn't, Enid might come in search of her, lumbering big-bellied across the yard, impatient and cross. And what would her sister-in-law say if she found Hannah in the stable with the local blacksmith's son?

She reached up and kissed Ben again on the mouth, brushing one finger against the rough stubble on his cheek. 'Tomorrow, then? I'll dream of you all night.'

As the stable door closed behind her, Hannah was surprised to see how quickly dusk had fallen. She shivered as the cold air swept past, and drew her coat tighter, hugging the fabric to her chest. Ahead lay the house, the many-gabled roof line a dim shape against a dark indigo sky, yellow light spilling from the windows.

Suddenly hungry, she ran across the already dew-damp grass, picking her way through the shadows. Her legs seemed to move of their own accord, taking her past the looming mass of the tank stand and the pile of freshly cut firewood.

At the bottom step she almost collided with her young nephew, Davie. He was panting from his run from the creek, hopping excitedly on sturdy mud-splattered legs. 'Look, Hannah! Taddies!' he cried, holding forward a jar of murky water. 'Hundreds of 'em! Just wait till they all turn into frogs.'

'Not in your mother's house, they won't,' Hannah admonished, thinking of Enid's neat orderliness and stifling a wry smile. 'Leave them over by the tank stand. They'll still be there in the morning.'

He flashed her an injured look. 'Aw, Hannah. Mum won't know if I smuggle them in ...'

In the half-light, Hannah hunkered down on the ground in front of him, injecting the correct amount of authority into her voice. 'Just look at you, young man! Off with you and wash up before tea. *And* before your father gets home, or you'll get us both into trouble,' she added as an afterthought, gently touching his cheek as he passed. It was still child-soft and warm from his exertions. Goodness, he's growing up so fast, she thought fleetingly.

Slowly she turned and followed Davie up the back steps, towards the certain warmth of the house and another strained meal.

Ben untied the mare and led her to the enclosed stall. Then, carefully latching the stable door behind him, he stepped out into the cold. Glancing up towards the house, he saw the outline of figures moving against the curtains. A picture rose in his mind. Enid Corduke bustling around, dishing out the evening meal, her husband presiding at the head of the table. Davie wriggling on his seat, anxious to begin. Thomas saying grace. *Blessed father, thank you for the bounty you have placed on the table this day.* Hannah, eyes closed, dark lashes resting against pale cheeks.

The thought of them as a family caused an odd sensation to flutter up from somewhere deep in his belly. It was a stark contrast to his own existence. The Galbraith home, he knew, would be in darkness. The ashes in the stove would probably be cold, his father lying on his bed, coughing, his face now a permanent shade of grey.

Thinking of his father, Ben felt his forehead muscles contract into a frown. He had known something was wrong for months, long before Harold Galbraith had finally relented and summoned the local doctor. A sudden lack of energy, weight loss, aches and pains, and persistent cough: the first symptoms were similar to a common cold and had been left untreated. His father, in his late forties, was a sturdy man who had never given in to a day's sickness in his life.

'If a man's strong enough he can fight anything,' Ben had often heard him say. In fact, Harold had boasted that the last time a doctor had been in the Galbraith home had been back in '92, the day Ben had been born. That had also been the day, Ben knew, that his mother had died from some mysterious feminine ailment that had somehow been connected with his own birth.

Despite Harold Galbraith's own firm convictions, he did not recover. He regularly broke out in damp sweats. A sudden bout of pleurisy at the beginning of winter finally sent him shivering to bed, his chest afire with pain. The mucous he repeatedly coughed from his lungs was flecked with clots of bright blood.

Tuberculosis. A terrible, insidious disease. The doctor had said it easily enough, the word rolling off his tongue in some unexpected and shocking manner. Ben had watched his father's face and had seen the fear.

'Two years, at best,' the doctor had pronounced, closing his black bag with a snap.

Two years! There was the smithy to run, dozens of jobs already waiting. Now his father would require constant nursing.

'And at worst?' Ben had to know.

'Six months.'

At first he wondered if the doctor had made a mistake, a false diagnosis perhaps. However, during the weeks that followed, he had watched his father's steady decline, reluctantly accepting what he knew could never be changed.

So now Ben was returning to a darkened house. The air settled damply around him as he walked down overgrown back laneways, oblivious to the occasional bark of a dog and the looming shadows of overhanging trees. On the western horizon, above the hills, the remaining slash of red was fading from the sky with a rush. Smoke from kitchen fires lent a woodsy odour to the air.

He washed his hands at the trough beside the back door and went to the room where his father sagged against the pillows, a shell of a man. A lamp lit the room, highlighting the gaunt face, the hollow nothingness of his once-round cheeks, the closed eyes. Was he dead? wondered Ben, a momentary panic fighting its way through his chest.

'Da?'

The eyelids fluttered open in confusion. 'Son?'

It was a hoarse whisper, more like a long drawn-out sigh. Ben went to the window and pulled the curtains against the night, enclosing the room with its mellow light and stale smell of ... What? he wondered. Decay? Impending death? The gradual wasting away of the man who had raised him, cared for him since the day he had been born?

Crushing the thoughts, Ben held a glass of water to his father's lips, watching as a single drop escaped and trickled down his father's chin. 'Won't be long, Da,' he said, heading towards the door. 'I'll just get some supper going.'

In the kitchen a few coals were still warm in the grate, a legacy from the woman he employed to come at lunchtime each day to attend to Harold. Quickly Ben crumpled the remains of yesterday's city paper into several balls, layering them across the smouldering wood. *Thomas Brown and Sons*, read one visible surface. *Importers of General Drapery, Fancy Goods, Tobacconists, Spirits and Grocery*. He watched as the flame caught and held, licking greedily across the inked words.

There was the remains of a beef roast, left over from the previous day. Ben carved several thick slices and divided them between two plates, adding some tomato and cheese. Lastly, he cut two chunks of bread, covering each with a layer of butter. Balancing these on a tray, he carried them to his father's room.

With his son's help, Harold levered himself to a sitting position. Ben noted that he touched little of the food, toyed with it mostly, rearranging it on his plate.

'Mrs Murphy said earlier, while you were out at the Corduke place, that there's going to be a war,' his father said at last, pushing the plate away. 'Said something about a telegram pasted on the wall of the post office, and that there was a big crowd down there, reading it an' all.'

'Is that right?'

There had been talk of war for several months now. Only weeks before, Andrew Fisher, the Labor leader, had made an impassioned speech, promising that Australia would defend England 'to the last man and the last shilling'.

'Just rabbiting on again, I suppose,' mused Ben. Closeted away in the stable with Hannah, he had heard nothing of any telegram.

'No,' Harold insisted. 'She said war had been declared. Reckons we're really in it this time.' He was silent for a while, staring at his food. Suddenly he turned back towards his son, regarding him with dark eyes. 'You won't go? You won't leave your old Da, will you?'

'Of course not.' Ben attempted a smile. 'Couldn't leave you sick like this. But if you were to get better, then I'd have to think about it.'

'Not much chance of that,' Harold replied dourly. Then: 'The doctor was here today.'

'What did he say?'

'He's found a place for me to stay. In the city. It's a sort of hospital. They'll look after me real good there, or so he says.'

'No!'

Harold closed his eyes and, when he opened them again, Ben could see they were bright with tears. Unable to bear the sight, Ben turned his head, watching the shadows as they flickered along the wall. It was one thing to face the inevitability of Harold Galbraith's impending death, but send him away? He could look after his own father. Somehow he would manage.

'Ben?' The voice was insistent, low.

Reluctantly he turned back. 'Yes.'

'I can't stay here. This is madness. You've got enough to do, what with running the smithy, never mind trying to look after a silly old bugger like me. Besides, nursing's women's work, not for the likes of you. I'll get good care in the city. It'll probably cost a few bob, though. Do you think we can afford it?'

Ben pushed his half-eaten meal to one side, his appetite suddenly gone. 'Of course, Da,' he said fiercely, staring into his father's hollow eyes. 'If I have to work double the hours, we'll manage it somehow.'

Still puffing from her hurried sprint across the yard, Hannah slipped into her seat at the table as Tom prepared to say grace. Enid flashed her a curious look and frowned, pursing her lips slightly.

'Blessed father ...'

Hannah gazed down at the blue-and-white checked tablecloth, concentrating her thoughts on the arrangement of the coloured squares, trying to block Ben from her mind. The way he had kissed her, pressing his tongue against her lips, how he had cupped her face with his hands, staring into her eyes. Cool hands stroking her cheeks, stirring sudden heat through her veins, setting her heart thumping on some wild erratic course.

I love you, Hannah.

She wriggled in her seat and felt a sudden ache under her breastbone as she remembered his words. Raising her face, she saw that Enid was still watching her from under lowered lids.

Tom's voice, droning on. 'May we be truly grateful ...'

As she quickly clamped her eyes shut again, squeezing out the vision of David's wife, a sudden idea made her catch her breath. Perhaps she had become transparent and the others could all read her thoughts and see the imprint of Ben's mouth upon hers. At once she felt as though her cheeks were on fire.

'Amen!'

Tom picked up his fork and ladled food unceremoniously into his mouth. Davie poked at his meal, sliding a slice of tomato to one side, trying to hide it under a leaf of lettuce. David and Enid were having some sort of half-whispered conversation at one end of the table. There was a strained expression on her sister-in-law's face.

Hannah stared at her plate. It seemed as though all her senses were suddenly heightened, bringing a new awareness. Mundane items she had always taken for granted, she now saw with new perception, a clarity that stunned her momentarily: the beaded muslin cover of the milk jug, how it sat with perfect symmetry; the indents in the loaf of bread that lay in the centre of the table, random grooves and hollows that ran with no rhyme or pattern. The way Enid's dark hair was swept up into a knot at the back of her head, leaving her throat and neck exposed, white and milky.

A sudden thought. Her brother had probably done those same things: kissed his wife's mouth, her cheeks, her pale neck. Obviously he still did, judging by the swell of Enid's stomach, which even the unflattering tent-like dress did little to hide. Hannah's cheeks burned again with the thought.

'Hannah, you're not eating. Aren't you feeling well?'

The sudden question jolted her back to the present. Her brother was staring at her, a concerned expression on his face.

'Yes,' she whispered as she picked up her fork and automatically placed the food in her mouth, oblivious to the taste.

Tom's week in the city became the topic of conversation, followed by Davie's long and drawn-out account of the capture of his collection of tadpoles. Half-heartedly Hannah listened, not registering the words. After several minutes, David pushed his empty plate to one side and cleared his throat. 'The news came through this afternoon. War has been declared. Apparently in the city, men are already queueing up to enlist.'

War! The word chilled her. It meant guns and fighting and death. Her father's brother, Uncle Thomas, after whom her own brother had been named, had been killed at Mafeking in 1901, during the war in South Africa. She and Tom had only been five at the time, but she still remembered.

Tom's eyes lit up. 'Have I your permission, sir, to join them?'

'Tom, no!' Hannah reached out one hand towards her brother, the other hand covering her mouth.

'You'll do no such thing!' replied David Corduke, his face thunderous. 'I forbid it! Damn fool idea, boy! You've a career to think of now. And you'd do well to consider your family's feelings in the matter.'

'Your brother's right,' added Enid emphatically, her dark eyes flashing. 'We're paying out good money to send you to university. To leave now would be madness.'

Tom ignored her, turning his comment towards his brother. He was, Hannah knew, testing the waters. 'And what if I go without your blessing?'

David's face had turned a dull shade of puce. 'You're under age, Thomas. Nineteen, that's the minimum age they're accepting.'

'I could put my age up and bluff my way in.'

It was said in a jesting tone, but Hannah could sense the friction in the air.

'And you could put your energies into a more worthwhile cause, like your studies, for example,' retorted David. 'Anyway, it's all a storm in a teacup. The whole thing will blow over in a week or two.'

Hannah quickly turned the conversation towards the new play which would open the following night in the town hall, while Enid rose from the table and methodically began to clear the plates and cutlery, her mouth set into a tight, furious line.

It wasn't until later that Hannah found Tom hunched at the table in the kitchen, poring over the daily newspaper after the others had gone to bed. Not wanting to disturb him, she leaned wearily against the doorway, waiting for him to finish.

'Oh, Tom,' she whispered, sinking onto the seat beside him and laying her cheek against the firmness of his shoulder as he carefully folded the pages. 'Why does it have to be like this? If only Mother and Father —'

She stopped mid-sentence, pressing her knuckles against her mouth, stemming the flow of words.

'Well, they're not,' replied Tom brusquely, slipping an arm comfortingly around her shoulders. 'And no amount of wishing will change anything. This is the way it is, Hannah, and we've got to make the best of it.'

'The way Enid carries on, anyone would think it's *her* money sending you to university!' responded Hannah hotly.

Tom nodded. 'I know, I know. It's Father's small life insurance policy that keeps me in the city, pays the fees and the rent on the flat. But if it makes her feel better to think —'

'But she makes out she's so self-sacrificing.'

'Don't, Hannah,' he said wearily. 'It's not worth the heartache getting wound up over it all. Another few years and you'll find yourself some handsome young man to marry and I'll be living full-time in the city. We needn't ever come back here, if we don't want to.'

'You make it sound so simple.'

Though two years had passed, there were still days when she had to remind herself that her parents were gone, and the intervening time had done little to dispel those sudden and unexpected bouts of despair. Despite herself, she felt the hot tears massing at the back of her lids, threatening to overspill and run down her cheeks. 'Oh, dear, I promised myself I wouldn't,' she murmured as Tom foraged in his pocket for a clean handkerchief, eventually dabbing at her eyes, his face a concerned mask.

Composed at last, her thoughts turned back to the dinner-table conversation and talk of the war. 'Why do you want to go?'

He looked at her, surprised. 'Everyone will want to, I suppose,' he replied after some consideration. 'That's all the chaps from the uni have talked about for weeks now, the possibility of war. Perfect chance to see a bit of the world, too.'

'Doesn't it occur to you that you might be killed?'

He gave a chuckle as he straightened, unfolding his lanky frame to its full height, which was just over six feet. 'Killed? Don't be silly, Hannah. We'll walk right over them. Turks. Germans. Have the war won before you can say Franz Ferdinand. Anyway,' he shrugged, turning the conversation away from himself, 'where were you this afternoon? Enid was calling you for ages.'

She regarded him gravely. 'Promise you won't tell?' She had to confide in someone. The knowledge was eating away inside her, anxious for release.

He nodded. 'Promise.'

A wide smile lit her face and she was powerless to stop it. 'In the stable.'

His forehead creased to a frown. '*In the stable*? With Ben Galbraith?' He gave a hearty laugh and slapped his hand against his leg. 'Oh, God! Enid would have your guts for garters if she knew.'

'I know,' she replied, her voice sounding breathless to her own ears, as though she had been running for miles.

CHAPTER 4

The day after war was announced, Hannah expected to feel or see something different, but nothing had changed. As usual, the sun shone brightly. Brunswick Street still looked the same, her brother's car parked on the side of the road, the poincianas overhanging the footpath. Birds shrilled in the surrounding trees as Enid picked the last of the daffodils from under the wattles at the bottom of the garden. Yet she had the oddest sensation that some infinitesimal part of her life had altered, swung away on a different course.

She couldn't shake the feeling. Walking towards the store with Enid's shopping list clutched firmly in one hand, she noticed an enlistment booth set up outside the Town Hall. There, several young hopefuls lounged against the walls, waiting in the sunshine.

'Six-bob-a-day tourists,' grumbled old Mr Parsons, proprietor of the general store, referring to the six shillings that was the going daily salary for soldiers, despite talk of a quick end to the war and the supposition that none of the recruits would ever leave the country, let alone see active service.

Besides Mr Parsons, it seemed everyone was talking of war. Petherbridge, the pharmacist. Miss McKillop, the librarian. Even the butcher stopped to chat, issuing dire predictions that did not necessarily coincide with everyone else's.

Though Hannah waited, Ben did not return to shoe Princess that afternoon as he had promised, nor the day after that. The weekend passed slowly and, by Sunday afternoon, she was frantic at his prolonged absence. After lunch she excused herself from the table on the pretext of going for a walk, and hurried in the direction of the smithy.

It was a bright day, all sunshine and scudding clouds that swooped low across the surrounding hills. Smoke from chimneys spiralled lazily upwards, merging with the blueness above. The town seemed deserted, sleeping. Cats crouched on window ledges, faces turned towards the sun. Dogs dozed on verandahs, barely lifting their heads as she passed.

The smithy had an abandoned air. The lopsided gate was closed and padlocked, the corrugated-iron door propped shut. Weeds sprouted randomly through cracks in the cement path that led inwards from the footpath. Hannah peered through the wire fence, along the side of the building. Ben and his father lived in a small cottage at the rear, but it too appeared deserted. The windows were closed and the curtains drawn.

'Ben?' she called tentatively, hopefully.

There was no reply.

Thinking of her brother's announcement of the war and Tom's reaction two days earlier, a sudden thought crossed her mind. What if Ben had already joined up and gone to the city? No, she shook her head, remembering Mr Galbraith, Ben's father. He was sick. Ben wouldn't go off and leave him.

'Looking for someone, dearie?'

The voice at her elbow caused her to spin around. It was Mrs Murphy, who lived across the road and came to look after Mr Galbraith while Ben was at work.

'I-I was looking for Ben,' Hannah stammered, trying to sound casual. 'He was supposed to shoe Princess, days ago. David was wondering what had happened to him.'

There, she had made it sound as though her brother had sent her, which wasn't true. However it was not a lie, just a careful bending of the facts. David Corduke *had* been muttering all morning about the virtues of reliability and punctualness, especially where the care of animals and one certain local blacksmith were concerned.

'Gone to the city he has,' revealed Mrs Murphy as she touched the brim of her hat. Sunday best, Hannah noted, with a pink silk rose on the crown.

'The city?'

Mrs Murphy leaned closer, confidentially, as though she were about to part with some important secret. 'Mr Galbraith's got the consumption, you know. Ben took him up by train yesterday morning. Some fancy hospital. But he'll not be coming back, if you get my meaning.'

'Who? Ben?'

Impatiently. 'No. Mr Galbraith.' Mrs Murphy seemed anxious to be off, now that her confidence had been shared. She adjusted her spectacles and glanced back towards her own house. 'You come back in a day or so. I'm sure young Ben will be back then.'

Hannah trudged along the road in the direction of Brunswick Street. Back past the crouching cats and dozing dogs, past the closed shopfronts and deserted enlistment booth, past the library and hall and Clarke's Emporium where she had purchased a new pair of boots the week before.

On that lazy Sunday afternoon, the whole world seemed to wait, suspended, basking in the sun. Only her heart was in shadow, cold and lonely.

Walking back along Brunswick Street, Hannah was surprised to see the doctor's buggy parked haphazardly on the gravel shoulder of the road outside the house. Davie was sitting on the front step, a dejected look on his face. 'What's up?' she asked, sitting on the timber plank beside him. 'Is it your Mum?'

Davie raised a miserable six-year-old face towards hers. 'The doctor said there's going to be a baby. Did you know?'

'Yes,' Hannah nodded.

'I hate babies. They cry all the time.'

'If it's a boy, you'll be mates when he grows. Someone to play with.'

Davie's face screwed into an expression of doubt. 'And what if it's a girl?'

Hannah laughed and hugged him close, burying her face for a moment in his still-soft hair. 'You'll always be my favourite number one nephew, no matter what.'

'Promise?'

'Yes. Now, let's go and get a cold drink.'

From her room, Enid heard Hannah and Davie as they moved down the hallway towards the kitchen, their voices growing fainter. At the end of the bed, the doctor fussed over his bag of instruments, rearranging them into a small metal tray with an accompanying clanking sound.

The noise annoyed her, irritated her jangled senses. Go away, she wanted to call, desperately praying for an end to the agonising pain, as another contraction hardened her belly and she felt her body arch upwards in anticipation. Despite her intentions, a low moan escaped her lips as she fought back the impulse to open her mouth and give voice to the scream that was building within.

'Now, now, Mrs Corduke,' soothed the doctor, laying a cool palm on her brow. 'Let's try and remain calm, shall we? Calm and ladylike. Second babies have a habit of arriving without much fuss. An hour or so and it'll all be over, just a memory.'

One hour! How could she survive?

Enid sagged back against the pillow as the pain momentarily passed, biting back a scathing reply as she brought her hands up, covering her face. 'Please God,' she whispered, not caring if the doctor overheard, 'let this child be a boy, so that he will never have to endure this kind of agony.'

It was unexpectedly hard leaving Da at the sanatorium, seeing him propped up in bed wearing the regulation pyjamas, his face almost the same pale shade as the sheets. A sanitised antiseptic odour lingered in the air, causing a small ball of nausea to grow in Ben's belly: the smell of disinfectant, and the imagined stench of death.

It would be the first time they had ever been apart.

'Well, Da,' he said, not knowing how to say goodbye. 'I'll try and get up next weekend.'

'No hurry, son. Just when you get the chance.'

Harold Galbraith held out his hand and Ben grasped it, feeling the dry papery skin beneath his fingers. He sensed a sudden lump in his throat, a tight constriction that made it momentarily difficult to speak. 'Yes, well, goodbye then.'

At the counter in the reception hall, Ben paid two months fees in advance. The charges had been more expensive than he had anticipated, almost emptying his bank account in the process. He had already decided that the money wasn't important. His father's health was the crucial issue. Six months, the doctor had said, or two years. It was precious little time, either way.

He had been saving hard, planning that someday, when he could afford it, he would ask Hannah to marry him. Anyway, he thought now as a sinking feeling washed over him, that was all in the future. There was a war on. His father lay sick, dying. Hannah was only eighteen. When she turned twenty-one, he thought with desperation, then he would approach David Corduke. He had been waiting a year already, so what were three more? Hell! They had the rest of their lives in front of them, didn't they?

Yes, he thought as he walked down the front steps of the sanatorium into sunshine that made him blink. Three years to save and prove to her family that he was the kind of reliable, responsible man who could take care of her.

Ben trudged in the general direction of the station. It was Monday morning. Trams rumbled past, bearing men dressed in their workday clothes: a mixture of overalls and suits, ties and dungarees. He thought of the jobs waiting for him back at the forge, and sighed. It had been easy before Da took sick, the two of them sharing the load. But now . . .

A newspaper vendor on a nearby corner thrust the daily tabloids towards the passers-by. The headlines, Ben noted, were filled with news of the war. What with the events of the past week, the hurried trip to the city and his father's sudden hospitalisation, there had been little time to consider the announcement which had been made several days earlier.

Coming down Caxton Street, he came to a crossroad, the sign informing him he was now entering Petrie Terrace. Queues of men lined the footpaths, joking and laughing.

'What's going on?' he asked, momentarily puzzled.

'It's the war, mate,' said one. 'This's Victoria Barracks and we're all here to join up. Fourteen hundred volunteered already. Gotta get in quick before the quotas are filled. Just waitin' for our medicals now, then we'll be in.'

'Yair,' echoed another. 'Gettin' outta *this* city. Way I see it, it's a chance to travel and have them bureaucrats foot the bill.'

'Too right! South-bloody-France, here we come. Just fancy a holiday on the Riv-i-era.'

The man smiled as he exaggerated the pronunciation of the name, executing a little tap dance on the footpath and waving an imaginary cane. The other men laughed, sharing a camaraderie that he was not part of. Ben moved on, crossing the road, a sense of depression settling on him. Cocky bastards, he thought, wondering at their stupidity. It would be no holiday where they were going.

He strode past the narrow timber cottages that seemed almost to spill out onto the street. Trout's butcher shop. Weetman & Co, the sack merchants. The Bizzy Cycle Works. Military Tent Stores. Along Upper Roma Street.

Finally the railway station loomed ahead, an imposing building. A stream of early-morning trains shuffled in and out. Ben arrived at the platform just as the South Coast Mail pulled in with a shriek and hiss of escaping steam. Patiently he waited until the passengers had emptied through the doors, hurrying away along the platform. Swinging himself up the steps and into the carriage, he almost collided with a shadowy figure carrying a large bag.

'Oh! Sorry,' he murmured, standing aside in the corridor for the man to pass.

The figure halted. 'It's Ben, isn't it? Ben Galbraith?'

He was forced, by the close proximity and the personal greeting, to look into the man's face. Blue eyes stared back at him, a face framed by short black hair that curled at the edges. Blue-black hair, that suddenly seemed familiar. Of course, he realised at once. Thomas Corduke, Hannah's twin brother.

He vaguely remembered Tom, who was four years younger than himself and, consequently, four grades lower, from the small local school, years earlier. Occasionally Tom had brought items to the forge to be mended; however, Ben hadn't seen him around town since the beginning of the year, when Hannah had told him her brother had been accepted into the engineering course at the university in Brisbane.

'That's right,' Ben replied, silently noting the expensive cut to Thomas' shirt and trousers, the casual way he had slung his coat across one shoulder.

'Hannah told me about your father. Mrs Murphy mentioned you had brought him to the city, to hospital.'

'Sanatorium, actually,' replied Ben, remembering his father's waxen face against the pillows.

Tom nodded. 'Hannah said there's no hope ...'

The words had an odd flattening effect upon his spirit and he made a forced reply. 'No. No hope. None at all.'

The station attendant swung along the platform, blowing insistently on his whistle. 'All aboard!'

Hannah's brother slung his bag on the floor and scrabbled in his pocket. 'Look, I know it's not much, but anytime you want to come up, you're welcome to stay. The flat's only tiny, scarcely big enough to swing the proverbial cat, but there's the sofa, if you need a bed. Probably not very comfortable, but at least it's free.'

Ben stiffened at the word. *Free*! Did Tom think he needed charity? He could pay his own way.

From his pocket Tom produced a rumpled piece of paper and a pencil. 'There,' he said, scribbling frantically. 'That's the address. Any friend of Hannah's is welcome.'

'Yes, well, thanks. If I need it, I'll let you know.'

Hauling his bag from the floor, Tom sprinted down the step and was gone. The train jerked forward simultaneously, pulling away with a groan. Ben sank down in the nearest seat and pushed the window up, peering out. Through a sudden gush of steam, he could see Hannah's brother lugging his heavy load along the platform.

The train gathered speed, ticking over the rails, surging forward. Loping along with a rolling motion, past other platforms with uniformed attendants lounging in doorways, past grimy station outbuildings. Eventually it rounded a bend in the track and the station was lost to view. Ben closed the window and stared at the handwritten note. *Flat 3, 21 Wickham Terrace. Come anytime,* it said.

After the city, it felt strange to be back in the cottage. The silence at night unnerved Ben, used as he was to company. Several times during the first few evenings, coming in after work, he almost called out to Da, but checked himself just in time. There was no-one there, he remembered, just infernal silence.

Hannah called into the smithy the following day, anxious for news of his father. He was frantically busy, the jobs mounting up. There was an assortment of machinery waiting for repairs, and several buggy wheels. However, he spared her a few minutes, stopping briefly for the cup of tea which she made in the poky kitchen at the rear of the shop.

'Enid had the baby. A girl. They're going to call her Lily.'

'That's nice.'

'Davie's not impressed. He says if there has to be a baby in the house, then it should have been a boy. At least she doesn't cry much.'

Leaning against the bench as he sipped the hot liquid, Ben was struck by the incongruity of her standing there in a pale lemon organdie dress, talking about babies, in the grimy shop surrounded by the tools of his trade. The blackened forge, bellows lying near the fire, collection of tongs in varying shapes, tue irons, the two-hundredweight steel anvil. In the corner sat the spray outfit that his father had bought before he had taken ill. *F. E. Myers & Bro.*, it read. *Ohio. U.S.A.* Above, the dusty rafters were coated with a layer of cobwebs.

'I ran into Tom at the station the other day. He gave me his address. Said to look him up if I ever needed a bed in the city.'

'And will you?'

Hannah stared at him, her face pale against the darkness of her hair. She looked so vulnerable, so out of place. He had a sudden urge to kiss her but fought it back, thinking of her dress pressed against his dirty work clothes. Instead he shrugged, looking away, almost unable to bear the sight of her, the close proximity.

'I don't know. Probably not. I scarcely know him. I'd feel strange.'

'You shouldn't, you know,' she said, waggling her finger, moving forward. 'Tom wouldn't have offered if he didn't mean it. Besides, he comes home most weekends. You'd have the place to yourself.'

'Maybe.'

Ben considered her words. If he took Tom up on his offer, it meant he could go up to the city most Saturday nights and spend the entire Sunday with his father. 'I'll see,' he replied, setting his empty cup on the bench.

He could sense her breath on his cheek. When he looked back, she was smiling at him, her mouth only inches away. A slow heat, which had been building in his belly, moved down his legs, through his groin.

Leaning forward, careful not to touch her dress, he kissed her briefly, then shooed her out the door. 'I know you're the nicest distraction around here, but I've lots of work and —'

'A distraction?' She grinned impishly. 'Is that all I am?'

'Oh, God, Hannah,' he groaned. 'Just get out of here, will you, before I do something I might later regret.'

Under pressure from Hannah, Ben gratefully accepted Tom's offer. The flat was small, one of four that had recently been converted on the top floor of a rambling house. There was a main room which doubled as a parlour and dining room, an alcove-like bedroom, and a tiny kitchenette. The bathroom, situated at the end of a long hall, was a communal one, shared by the other three tenants. The narrow horsehair sofa, as Tom had predicted, was the most uncomfortable bed he had ever slept on.

That first weekend, Ben planned to spend the entire Sunday with his father. However, after an hour or so he could see that Da was tiring, so he slipped from the room, promising to return later. At a loose end, he prowled the neighbouring streets, getting a feel for the city, finding his bearings. He looked at his watch. Eleven o'clock. The day stretched in front of him, almost empty. His stomach rumbled and he realised that, in the elation of seeing Da again, he had missed breakfast. Fleetingly he thought he might buy a newspaper and a loaf of bread, taking them back to Tom's flat.

As he trudged along the footpath, a sudden clamour of bells claimed his attention. He was passing a small sandstone church, set back from the street, butter-gold in the sunlight. Something about it caught his interest and made him stop. The congregation was hurrying into its interior. Ben glanced along the street. Scarcely a soul was left in sight. The faint strains of the organ reached him, drawing him in.

Inside, there was barely a seat left on the benches. Several men in military uniform stood to attention inside the door as the last of the congregation filed past. The walls were decorated with flags. Ben squeezed into an empty space in the back pew, between a stout woman who wore an absurdly large hat and a small boy who sniffed continually throughout the service.

He glanced around curiously. It had been years since he'd been inside a church. Between the smithy and work at the cottage, there had been so little time. Hannah, he knew, attended every Sunday.

He had felt some sudden urge, some need, to pray for Da. He wasn't certain how he would do this, the idea seeming to lodge in his brain. The eventuality of his father dying was a leaden weight in his mind. With Da gone, there would be no-one left. Except Hannah.

He sang along with the hymn, realising with a start that he didn't even know what denomination the church was. Words danced on the page of the book, unknown yet suffocatingly familiar. He closed his eyes dutifully for the prayer.

The sermon was loud and forceful. Even in the confines of the church, the congregation would not be spared the talk of war. 'I call on God to help us accept our sufferings and sacrifice. Help us overcome the satanic ambitions of Germany,' the minister called loudly from the pulpit.

At last, the final hymn.

God bless our native land;
God's all-protecting hand
Still guard our shore.

And he walked out into the sunlight, blinking.

The weekend visits to the city became a regular event, the late train on Saturday bearing him north towards the random sprawl of houses, shops and factories, and Tom's tiny flat on Wickham Terrace. Though his father still tired easily, Ben thought he looked a little better. There was a faint tinge of colour in his cheeks and his appetite had improved slightly.

Ben often found him in the garden, propped in a chair, a bright chequered rug covering his legs.

Talk was of the smithy and the district's happenings, the latest news of the war. In September, the *Omrah* had been the first troop ship to leave Queensland, carrying the 9th Battalion. Several of the local chaps had been aboard. Ben had attended school with some of them, and played with them on the creek bank during hot summer afternoons. Now they were gone to some foreign place, a place he might never see, possibly never to return.

Sometimes, in a odd self-destructive way, he wished he were part of them. Part of the glorious inconsistency of young men facing needless death, of the careless disregard for life, of the belief that they were invincible. Sometimes he envied Tom, having no money cares. Then, realising what he was thinking, he'd feel so god-damned guilty.

Somewhere along the way he had lost control. His own existence was being pulled in a direction which he would not have chosen for himself. Instead, he felt trapped. Trapped by his father's illness and the mounting medical bills, trapped by a business that financially he couldn't afford to lose.

Even his relationship with Hannah appeared to be stagnant, especially since he had begun spending most of his Sundays in the city.

Hannah! God, he just wished he could marry her!

And, through it all, the constant never-ending talk of war. Ben watched as his father grew morose towards the end of each visit, making Ben promise, yet again, that he would not enlist. Then he would leave his father to the care of the nurse who bore him back to his room for a nap, vowing to return later.

With time on his hands, he roamed the city streets. Once he found himself passing the Exhibition grounds, where rows of white tents dotted the landscape and soldiers exercised on the parade ground. For several minutes he stood watching them, an emotion somewhere between sorrow and envy bubbling under his breastbone.

The months wore on. Christmas had come and gone, accompanied by a spate of hot humid weather which turned the inside of the smithy into an oven. Hannah called by regularly, usually smuggling some offering from the Brunswick Street house kitchen. A pot of casserole, fruit cake, several bottles of home-made ginger beer. But he was hungry only for her, for the taste of her mouth against his. He could feel her breasts as she pressed against him, small and pointed beneath her blouse. Thoughts of her caused him to toss in his bed at night, caused him to wake with the bedclothes damp from perspiration and desire. In his dreams he knew he cried out with the desperate longing, the hot hungry yearning she left behind.

Tom stayed in the city one weekend, ostensibly to finish an assignment but, as Ben later discovered, precipitated by an argument with David Corduke on the subject of Tom's possible enlistment when he turned nineteen later in the year.

Ben and Tom spent the Saturday evening at one of the local hotels, hunched over a small table, debating the pros and cons of the war. Several of Tom's university friends had already joined up. 'I'd go myself, put my age up,' he grumbled, draining the last of another beer, 'but David would have me stopped, I know it.'

They were evicted only at closing time by the publican. Outside, the streets were deserted. Autumn had arrived with a flurry of leaves racing along the gutters. Already the nights were cool. Unsteadily they stumbled towards the flat, Tom loudly protesting the unfairness of his brother's attitude and his lack of understanding. His voice echoed against the houses and blank walls, bouncing back at them like bullets.

CHAPTER 5

Under the pretext of studying for his half-yearly exams, Tom began to stay at the flat in Wickham Terrace most weekends. Ben was surprised to find him there one Saturday evening, sitting morosely by the window, a half-empty bottle of whisky on the table. The room was in semi-darkness, Tom's face and the bottle silhouetted against the faint glow of the lamps on the street below.

Tom turned as Ben closed the door behind him. 'Company. Thank God!' he muttered.

As Ben slung his battered suitcase on the floor next to the sofa, he thought he detected a faint slur to the voice.

'Not going home for the weekend?'

'No!' Tom shook his head, then cupped his chin in his hand, regarding him thoughtfully. 'Fancy a walk down to the pub? This place is driving me crazy.'

'Sure,' Ben shrugged. 'Whatever you like.'

They succeeded in getting themselves very drunk. Ben vaguely recollected the walk back to the flat. There was the image of them stumbling along a dark laneway, arms linked, singing, though later he couldn't remember the song. And preparing to visit Da the next morning, quite late, looking pale and ghostly in the mirror above the washbasin, with a head that pounded like a bass drum.

Tom was conspicuously absent for a few weekends after that. Several times Ben wandered down to the hotel by himself on a Saturday night, though it wasn't the same. The men who breasted the bar were friendly enough but he felt out of place, as though the miles between the city and the smithy separated them.

One Friday evening several weeks later, Tom was waiting at the station as the train pulled in. Ben felt a small stab of pleasure at seeing him there, lounging nonchalantly against a sign that read 'Coates & Son — Premium Gin Distillers'. As the months passed, it became a ritual: Tom meeting the Saturday evening train, supper and a few drinks at one of the many pubs, in the end Tom foregoing entirely his weekend visits to the house in Brunswick Street.

From Hannah, Ben learned of the arguments between Tom and his brother, precipitated mostly by Enid — differences of opinion which seemed to split the family. From Tom, he learned of the lad's frustrated efforts to join his mates who had already sailed for the front, his eagerness to be 'one of the boys'.

In many ways Ben was glad of the weekend company. It lessened his own sense of isolation. During the week he was mostly alone in the smithy or the cottage, with no-one to talk to as the hours ticked slowly past. Sometimes he felt that if he were to open his mouth to speak, no sound would emerge, as though his voice, from lack of use, would cease to function.

He began to look forward to his weekly trips to the city, to the noisy smokiness of the pub, the endless fights and arguments amongst the patrons.

The alcohol numbed his mind and focussed his thoughts away from the daily annoyances, to somewhere warm and fuzzy and intangible. For a while it made him forget about Da, the money, his desperate longing for Hannah.

The blacksmith and the banker's son: underneath it all they weren't so unalike, Ben decided. Somehow, amongst the madness and grog and talk of war, they became friends.

Months passed in a haze, a routine of work and sleep. Saturday nights with Tom and Sundays with Da dissolved into precious snatched minutes with Hannah. Da looked so much better that Ben wondered if, in fact, the doctors had been wrong after all.

Suddenly it was almost Hannah's birthday, and Tom's. Ben had been studying a tray of rings in the window of a jewellery shop he passed every Sunday on the way to visit Da — wishing he had both sufficient money and courage to ask David Corduke for Hannah's hand in marriage — when he let his eyes wander along the display. There, sitting amongst the jumble of estate jewellery, fob watches and bracelets, was a silver horseshoe.

He stood for a long time studying it, noting with dismay that the price on the tag was double what he had planned to spend. However, each time he passed the store, he found himself searching for it. As the weeks elapsed, he made a mental pact. If the shoe were still there by Hannah's birthday, then he would buy it for her. If it were gone, he decided, then she was not meant to have it.

But it *was* there, nestling between a Waltham watch and a tray of gilt brooches. Ben slid the money across the counter and pocketed the now-wrapped parcel, enjoying the solid feel of it rubbing against his thigh as he walked towards the sanatorium. Later, in the privacy of the flat, he took it from its wrapping and studied the letters the jeweller had etched on the silver, to Ben's instructions. On the right-hand side was the word 'Ben'; on the left, 'Hannah'. On the base of the shoe were the words 'I will love you always', the letters spaced evenly on each side of the arc.

As he held it in his hand and admired the perfect symmetry of it, Ben knew he had done the right thing.

Hannah came to the city one Sunday, a few days before her birthday. He took her to the sanatorium where his father greeted her warmly, although Ben could see he was certainly surprised.

'Getting a bit above yourself, aren't you, young man,' Da whispered as they were leaving, 'socialising with the bank accountant's sister?'

Afterwards they strolled in the Botanical Gardens. For months Ben remembered the event as a series of images, linked, yet separate, in his mind, till they blurred with time and ran into others and became jumbled and unclear. A pale spring sky pouring wan sunshine as the brass band played in the rotunda, fractured light spearing through drops of water that sprayed from the fountain. Crowds strolling along the wide pathways and loitering under the palms.

They were in the city, knowing no-one. Ben had brought a tartan rug, spreading it under the shade of a huge fig. He lay there, watching Hannah as she read aloud from a book, unable to take his eyes from her face. Clear pale skin, escaping tendrils of dark hair that curled at the back of her impossibly long neck, the way her eyes followed the lines of text, a small furrow of concentration on her brow. In the end, he forced himself to look away, to close his eyes against the sight of her, as the desperate longing inside threatened to consume him with its intensity.

Later, back at the flat, he gave her the small package. She looked at it in amazement, turning it over and over in the palm of her hand.

'Go on,' he prompted her gently. 'Open it.'

Carefully she pulled back the wrapping, finally holding the horseshoe in one trembling hand. The fading daylight reflected against the silver as a dull sheen.

'Oh, it's beautiful,' she exclaimed, tracing her fingers over the etched words. As she turned back towards him, Ben could see that her eyes were filled with tears.

'Happy birthday, Hannah,' he whispered, touching his hands to her cheeks, kissing away the wetness.

Spring came, then summer. Ben spent Christmas Day in the city with his father, missing Hannah. Da seemed quite lively, looking so much better than the previous Christmas that Ben was momentarily inclined to ask the doctor if, in fact, his father might be well enough to return home.

He was puzzled when he slipped in a side door at the sanatorium a few weeks later, on a grey overcast late January Sunday, to find his father's bed empty.

He'll be out in the garden, Ben thought as he made his way through the shrubbery. But suddenly the day had turned to light misting rain and the chairs that dotted the sweep of lawn were empty. Mystified, he went back to his father's room and sat on the narrow chair beside the bed, holding the brown paper-wrapped parcel containing clean pyjamas, wondering what to do.

On closer inspection, he realised that the bed had been stripped, baring the blue-and-white ticking of the mattress. The pillow was missing its usual cover and Da's few personal belongings had been cleared from the metal bedside chest. A strong smell of disinfectant hung in the air. Ben waited. An occasional nurse rushed along the hallway, intent on some errand. No-one seemed to notice him.

Finally, in desperation, he went to the front reception desk and asked, 'Where's my father?'

Ben had been coming to the sanatorium every week for over a year now; however the woman at the desk was new, he saw, and did not recognise him. 'Harold Galbraith,' he elaborated. 'Has he been moved to another room?'

At the mention of the name, the attendant's stricken face caused some small bubble of unease to rise under Ben's breastbone.

'Where *is* he?' he demanded, leaning forward over the counter, suddenly afraid.

The woman's words tumbled over each other. Faltering, hesitant words that seemed to dance on

72

the periphery of his consciousness. Prancing, sliding words that dipped and swayed alarmingly inside his mind like some diaphanous substance. Ben shook his head, not understanding. It couldn't possibly be true, he told himself. There must be some mistake.

'Da's dead?' he said blankly.

The woman nodded her head, looking distraught. 'I'm sorry. Mr Galbraith ... your father ... passed away last night. Doctor Hastings ...'

She looked hard down the corridor, as though, with the mention of the doctor's name, he might somehow emerge and save her from the uneasy explanation, but there was no-one in sight. 'They tried to contact you, through a neighbour, but someone said you were here in the city, though they didn't know where.'

Legs trembling, almost refusing to support him, Ben sank onto a nearby chair, trying to digest the statement. Head in his hands, he tried to dispel the blankness that threatened his consciousness. 'Da's dead?' he said again, but his voice came only as a whisper.

The woman had rounded the desk into the main corridor, fussing at his side. 'Are you all right, sir? Can I call someone for you?'

Ben shook his head and blinked back the tears, swallowing hard as he rose to his feet. 'No, I'll be all right.'

He was walking now. Past the desk, the front door, down the path that led to the road. Rain splattered against his face, his hair, flinging itself mercilessly like sharp tiny needles. Yet he was impervious to the sting of it. All he could see, shuttered away behind the dull wall of pain, was the blue-and-white ticking of the mattress and the wet empty sweep of lawn.

A tram came clanking along the road, stopped, and disgorged a load of passengers. Unthinkingly, Ben boarded it, not knowing its destination, not caring. There was nowhere he wanted to go. Tom was at the flat. If he returned there, he would be forced to offer explanations, which he was not ready to do. The thought of consoling words was more than he could bear.

He rummaged in his pocket and produced a coin for the conductor, then sat in morose silence as the carriage jolted along the streets. After some time, a tap on his shoulder interrupted his thoughts. He looked up to see the conductor poised over him. 'This's the end of the line, mate. Getting off here?'

Momentarily baffled, Ben glanced through the carriage window. He was in an unfamiliar suburb, the buildings unrecognisable. The tall houses of the inner city had given way to cottages and small farms. Rain sheeted down across the view, partly obscuring it with a misty veil, softening it to a series of pale grey images.

He shook his head, unable to speak.

'Get on the wrong tram, did yer? Never mind. We'll be headin' back in a few minutes. Cost yer another fare, though.'

The journey replayed itself in reverse, though Ben was scarcely aware of the view. Back in the city, surrounded by well-known landmarks, he made his way towards Wickham Terrace. Once at Tom's flat, he would collect his belongings and make his way back to the smithy. He couldn't think of anywhere else to go.

As he waited on one street corner for the line of buggies and trams to pass, a woman walked up to him and pressed an envelope into his hand. He looked up at her, surprised, but she gave a sneer and walked away at a brisk pace. He wondered for a moment if she were a prostitute.

Back in the warm confines of the flat, he thrust his clothes into the small suitcase. Tom was out, so he penned him a brief note, then glanced at his watch. Two o'clock. If he hurried, he would just make the afternoon train. As he replaced the pen on the table, a slash of pale paper caught his eye. The unopened envelope.

It was glued tight. Curiosity now aroused, he took a knife from the kitchen drawer and slid it along the topmost border. For a moment he thought the envelope was empty, as he brushed his hand along its interior. But no, there was something inside. Something hard, yet soft.

Ben froze as he pulled out the contents.

He stood for a long time, weighing it in his hand. The implications were blurred at the edges, indefinite, somehow mixed up with other images: his father's face, Hannah's, the silver horseshoe. A ball of nausea formed in his belly, bringing with it the urge to retch. Slowly, without thinking, he opened his hand and let it flutter slowly to the ground.

That was how Tom found him, hours later.

Standing at the window.

Staring down into the busy roadway.

A white feather lying on the carpet at his feet.

'Come along, Hannah. Time to go.'

Hannah sighed inwardly as she picked up the basket and followed Enid, who was carrying Lily on her hip, down the front steps of the house. The Tuesday Red Cross mornings at the local town hall had become tedious. She hated the constant talk of the war, and dreaded hearing the news, that was slowly filtering through, of the latest casualties. Six local boys had already been killed, leaving grieving families. She remembered one of them, a popular young man with fair hair named Bill, who had been one of Tom's best friends at school and captain of the local cricket team.

The horrifying Gallipoli campaign continued. During late April the first accounts of the landing had appeared in the Australian newspapers. 'Magnificent Achievement' and 'Baptism of Fire', proclaimed the headlines. By the middle of June, the papers were filled with lists of the wounded and dead. Page after page, hundreds — no, thousands — of names printed on white paper, a jumbled alphabet that somehow seemed remote and distanced. Hannah felt sick inside.

Now, sitting in the hall on a decidedly uncomfortable chair, knitting yet another sock, she heard the snatches of conversation humming around her.

'The Hammond boy. That's three they've lost so far ...'

'Young Peter's leaving next week ...'

Indignantly. 'Jim's postcard came from Cairo, but the censor had a fine time with it. Came in little pieces. I was *that* mad ...'

Cape Helles. Ari Burnu. Gaba Tepe. The conversations and names washed over her, pulling her into some kind of numbness. Hannah missed Tom's weekend visits. And with Ben now gone to the city every Sunday, her weeks were fractured, split in two.

She glanced around now, noting the plump faces of the women, baskets of wool, the boxes of finished articles that would be duly forwarded to the Red Cross state branch at the end of the month. Corners of the room were piled high with overflowing cartons containing an assortment of tinned goods, rolled bandages, blankets, mounds of knitted garments. Boxes and faces, conversation, all crowding in on her, leaving her breathless. She had to get out, away from the talk of death.

Enid was deep in conversation. Hannah placed a hand on her shoulder. 'I'm just going out for a while.'

'Are you all right? You look a little pale.'

'I just need a little fresh air, that's all.'

She found herself walking in the direction of the bank. John Corduke had been the local manager before his death. Now, David was the head accountant there, his office next to the one that had been his father's.

After the rain the previous day, it was hot and humid. The sun poured its heat onto the pavement, and a trickle of perspiration rolled down Hannah's back. The footpaths were almost deserted. An occasional shopper hurried past, basket over arm. A dog dozed outside Clarke's Emporium. Finally she reached the old sandstone building. 'Union Bank of

Australia — established 1837', read the sign above the arched entrance.

Hannah stepped through the open doorway into the cool hushed interior. It was mid-morning. A line of customers waited at the counter. Several of them turned and, seeing her, smiled. Beyond, Hannah could see the accountant's office, glass door propped ajar. Nodding in the direction of the head teller, she slipped behind the counter, hoping to surprise her brother.

David Corduke was not alone. Hannah, coming to a standstill in the doorway of the small office, was momentarily stunned to see Tom there. The two men were standing, facing each other across the desk, glaring, unaware of her presence.

Abruptly, Tom leaned forward and his voice, when it came, was furious. 'No, I won't listen. You can't control my life any longer. I don't care what you say! I'm going, and that's final!'

Without warning, Tom flung himself away and ran towards the door, almost colliding with her as he passed, his face grim. David Corduke eased himself onto his chair, his head cradled in his hands.

A dozen thoughts raced through Hannah's mind. What was Tom doing home on a Monday? He was usually in the city at this time of the week, attending lectures at university. And what kind of argument could have produced the reaction she had just witnessed?

'What's wrong?' A sudden fear washed through her as she steadied herself against the door frame, waiting for some reassurance, some sign that the argument was nothing more than a trivial misunderstanding. 'Why is Tom home?'

David Corduke raised his head and regarded her with narrowed eyes. 'Your brother,' he said, bringing his fist down on the desktop with a loud thump, 'against my wishes, has joined the Army. It seems Thomas and young Galbraith from the smithy decided to enlist yesterday.'

Blindly Hannah turned away, heading for the door. Tom, she had to catch Tom! Her brother had said that Ben had joined up too. There must be some mistake. Ben had his father to consider.

She was running now, past the startled customers, down the long length of the bank. The open doorway seemed miles away, swimming in and out of focus. Her chest heaved. A tight band of pain circled her ribs. Through the sandstone archway, down the steps and onto the footpath she flew, blinking in the sunlight as she scanned the roadway.

'Tom!' she screamed, hearing the word pressed back against her ears by the heat.

However, the street was empty.

CHAPTER 6

Callie slept fitfully, the dream repeating itself in her unconscious mind. Over and over the scenes duplicated themselves, like a hi-fi needle stuck in one solitary groove of a record: tortured flickering images of the photos from the trunk intertwined with a silver horseshoe, the house in Brunswick Street and the wattles at the bottom of Freya's garden. Singly they made little sense. Together they formed a kind of bizarre mosaic, a kaleidoscope of form and colour fragmented into a confusing muddle.

She had woken to a room still dark. Five-thirty, proclaimed the bedside clock as it flicked over another of its luminous numbers. Carefully, so as not to disturb Stuart, she eased herself from the bed and padded through the silent unit. In the kitchen she filled the jug and was soothed by the hum of the element as the water warmed. Oscar strolled in, winding himself through her legs, purring loudly.

Callie worked on the novel for two hours, banning all thoughts of the previous night from her mind, until she heard Stuart stir. Then, after breakfast, she rang Bonnie.

Dispensing quickly with the preliminaries, she brought the subject around to the man who had visited the Brunswick Street house the week before.

'I was wondering if Michael left a phone number or an address?'

'No, he didn't. There seemed little point.' Bonnie was quiet for a moment. 'Why, Cal?'

'Oh, no reason,' she replied, perhaps a little too quickly, not wanting to elaborate. What could she say that made sense? I took Hannah's things from the house. I found the other half of the horseshoe. That, in itself, proved nothing. 'I was just curious,' she finished lamely.

The conversation over, Callie sat looking at the piece of paper on the desk in front of her. Michael Paterson, she'd written. She knew nothing about him, except that he came from the city, was divorced and had a son named Timmy. No address. No phone number. Precious little to go on.

'Ring enquiries,' suggested Stuart after she had explained the events of the previous night. He was pulling on a tie, readying himself for work.

Why hadn't she thought of that?

'One 't' or two in Paterson?' asked the impersonal voice on the other end of the phone.

Callie didn't know.

'What address?' the voice persevered. 'There are twenty-four M. Patersons, if you count both spelling variations ...'

Silently Callie replaced the receiver and shook her head.

'Too bad,' Stuart said abruptly. 'Anyway, I don't know why you're so interested in all this. Two halves of a horseshoe do not a mystery make. There's probably a logical explanation and it's not as though you're friendly with this guy or anything. He's a god-damned stranger, for Christ's sake!'

Callie glanced up to see him staring at her from under hooded eyes. 'I'm just curious,' she muttered, for some unknown reason feeling ridiculously close to tears.

Stuart grabbed his briefcase and gave her a quick kiss on the cheek. 'I've got to get going or I'll be late for work. Cheer up. And don't get too hung up over this, hey?'

She nodded and forced a smile to her face. 'I promise.'

Long after he had gone, the smell of aftershave hung in the air, reminding her of Stuart's outburst, the way he had looked at her with an expression akin to ...

To what? she wondered.

Jealousy?

The following morning, after Stuart had left for work, she walked down to the post office and thumbed through the city telephone directory, jotting down the possible telephone numbers. Back at the flat, she rang them all. Half went unanswered. Probably at work, she surmised, so she spent the next few evenings following them up, surreptitiously dialling from the phone in her study while Stuart was engrossed in the television. Finally, after three days, she knew she had come to a dead end.

Stuart was probably right, she thought with exasperation. There undoubtedly *was* a logical explanation to the existence of the horseshoe. Meanwhile, the whole concept of it was bogging her down, taking her mind from her work.

The afternoon traffic was light as Michael made his way back to the city. His Mercedes hummed steadily along the highway, only moving into the overtaking lane as he came up on the occasional slower vehicle.

The car had been second-hand when he'd bought it, ten years earlier. There were a couple of rips in the upholstery, and the engine was almost due for a complete overhaul. However, it was reliable and always started at the first attempt, even on the coldest winter mornings, and he liked the feel of it beneath him, comfortable, like a worn shoe.

The theme to the original *Endless Summer* movie was playing on the radio. 'God,' he laughed quietly to himself as he turned up the volume and the bass notes of the soundtrack filled the car. What year was that?

He tapped the tips of his fingers against the steering wheel, enjoying the nostalgia. The tune stirred something within him, vague memories he could put no form to. The music, though it had been released years earlier, somehow equated with the time he had met Gaby. Careless days at the beach, the sun hot overhead. The smell of wax, salt.

Michael had been fourteen when her family had moved into a nearby house and, instantly, there had been a rapport between them. Gaby, two years younger, had been a real tomboy then, preferring to trail around with the neighbourhood boys. She could throw a cricket ball and climb the trees that overhung the creek as well as the best of them.

He smiled now, thinking how they were then: gangling adolescents eager to take on the world. Full of plans, idealistic beyond belief. Through school they'd been an item, inseparable. Then Gaby had gone on to uni and he'd joined the newspaper.

It was during the spring of '81, halfway through her degree, that Gaby had told him she was pregnant. She was horrified, distraught at the interruption to her studies. 'I want to be a teacher, god-damn it!' she had yelled at Michael, tears tracking a random course down her face. 'Not a mother!'

The memory jolted back at him, surprising him with its suddenness, and Michael found himself gripping the wheel, his fingers stiff with tension. After all these years, he could still picture her hands beating against his chest.

'Hey,' he'd said, raising her tear-stained face towards his own. 'Gaby, this is our *child* we're talking about. A part of you and me. I know we didn't plan it, but maybe it was meant to be.'

Secretly Michael had been delighted. He loved kids, wanted a houseful eventually, though goodness knows how he would support them on his meagre wage. And the eventuality of this child seemed like a wondrous thing, a continuing reminder of the love he and Gaby shared, a part of them projecting into the future, which seemed solid and somehow comforting.

Gaby resigned from her course and they married the following Friday afternoon. Just a small ceremony at the local registry office followed by a quick dinner in the nearby pub for the few family and friends who had come along to wish them well. Gaby in a calf-length cream lace dress looking lovely. Gaby holding his hand tightly, saying 'I do'. The glow of early motherhood on her cheeks, colouring them to a peachy softness, bringing a lump to his throat.

Three weeks later she lost the child.

'Spontaneous miscarriage,' said the doctor after Michael had rushed her to the nearest city hospital. 'Somewhere between ten and twenty per cent of pregnancies terminate naturally. No-one's fault and nothing to worry about. Your wife will have no trouble conceiving again.'

Thinking of it now, Michael thrummed his fingers against the steering wheel in frustration. Had that one singular event become the eventual catalyst for the disintegration of their marriage, years later?

Gaby had pursued a variety of jobs, restless and bored, refusing to take up her uni course again. She blamed herself for the loss of the child. Timmy's birth, seven years later, had settled her temporarily and, for a while, she had been content to stay home and do 'the motherly bonding thing', as she called it. When Timmy started school, she had landed a position as public relations manager for a large city firm.

The changes that had come with the job had happened so slowly that he'd failed to see them in time. In time for what? he wondered now, knowing he would have been powerless to stop the relentless tide of events.

Something had happened to Gaby then. She'd become steely, he supposed, stronger within herself. Less emotional. She had a focus, and it wasn't him. The downhill slide became an avalanche. Michael was travelling constantly with his work. Gaby was absorbed by her job, the demands of her son. It seemed there was so little time to share.

They might have drifted along like that for years; however the divorce had been Gaby's idea. The decision hadn't been made lightly. They hashed and rehashed the possibilities in a strained but civilised manner, Michael feeling awkward and, somehow, out of his depth. It seemed impossible to imagine his life without her. She'd been part of it for so long.

'Hey, first and foremost we're mates, remember,' he had said to her at last. 'No matter what happens between us, Gaby, I'll always love you in a special way.'

He had stood looking at her for a moment, taking in the way her blonde hair framed her face, the resolute set to her mouth. 'Friends?'

She had nodded and turned away, and Michael was certain he had seen the faint glimmer of tears in her eyes.

That had been three years ago. After the divorce, a year later, he had experienced an acute and final sense of loss, as though he had failed them, Timmy and Gaby, in some appalling way. Marriage was supposed to be a permanent thing, wasn't it? Growing old together, sharing? Yet they'd done none of those things. He had felt numb inside, dead.

There had been a few other women since then, casual relationships that had failed to develop into something more. There were days when he felt so lonely, balanced against the time spent with Timmy, when he blessed those years of his marriage and the joy that his son now brought.

The sign announcing the approach to the highway off-ramp, one kilometre ahead, flashed past. The last strains of the *Endless Summer* soundtrack faded and the voice of the radio announcer intruded on the last notes of the music, breaking his thoughts. Michael gave an imperceptible shake of his head and pushed the memories away. It wouldn't do to dwell on them. They were in the past, unchangeable.

Down the ramp and into the heart of the city, stopping at a set of unobliging traffic lights, he felt his thoughts returning to the house in Brunswick Street. To Bonnie and Freya. Feeling that same old bubble of disappointment rise again in his chest. He had so wanted to be a part of them.

And Callie? he mused, easing the vehicle forward as the lights changed to green, merging with the steady flow of the traffic.

He had found his attention turning to her frequently over the past few days. Callie, with a sprinkling of freckles across the bridge of her nose, and those grey, soul-searching eyes. Perky, with a good sense of humour and an easy relaxed manner. An independent woman probably, to a certain degree, but hopefully not neurotic about it. God, he hated those women's libbers. She was about five or six years younger than himself, he guessed, with a boyfriend called Stuart, whom Michael had already decided he would not like.

After several blocks he turned left and eased the car into his own driveway. The grass hadn't been mown for weeks and was ankle high. 'I'll get the Victa out now,' he muttered with determination, sensing the remainder of the afternoon stretching vacantly ahead.

As though on cue, the golden Labrador came lumbering around the side of the house, looking pleased to see him, her tail wagging furiously. Michael crouched down and fondled her ears. 'G'day, Bess,' he said, breathing in the faint doggy smell. 'I'm glad someone missed me.'

Anthony, her agent, rang a few days later. 'How's it going, Cal? The publisher's asking for a synopsis and the first few chapters of the new book. If you can get it together in the next week, I think we can get a good advance on this one.'

'No problem,' she laughed. 'They can have the first six chapters. I'll post them today and you should have them by the end of the week, or the beginning of next, at the latest.'

'Oh, before I forget. Page forty-five, city newspaper. Lift-out section on art, music, that sort of thing. There's an article on one of the local authors up your way. Check it out.'

She promised, then rang off.

The newspaper had been delivered that morning but was, as yet, still lying in its plastic wrapper on the kitchen bench. It was a cumbersome size. Carefully Callie spread it on the table, folding the creases from its pages.

She found the article and read it quickly. It was an editorial-cum-book review, not especially promising. The reviewer, it seemed, had liked little of what he had read, and had gone to great pains to explain why. Characters, plot, even the book jacket, had received a scathing report.

Idly she let her gaze wander across the rest of the page. A sizeable portion was taken up with the recent annual photographic awards. Several of the winning entries were reproduced, with the overall winner topping the page.

It was easy to see why it had won, she thought. A small boy holding an empty cone, ice cream smearing his elfin face. Its simplicity, the look of wonderment on the child's face: something about it touched her in a sad indefinable way.

Callie glanced down, noting the name of the photographer: Michael Paterson. Michael! She pressed her finger against the words for a moment, almost not believing. All at once it came back to her: he worked for a city newspaper. What had he said? Something about starting there as a cadet, years earlier, working his way up to the feature shoots, as well as carrying out freelance work of his own. How could she have forgotten?

A bubble of excitement rose in her chest as she dialled the newspaper's number and asked to speak to Michael, hoping she would catch him at the office.

'Hello. Paterson speaking.'

She would have recognised his voice anywhere. It was deep, almost husky, with a sensual tone to it. For some reason, her hands were shaking.

'This is Callie Corduke. We met at my mother's house. In Brunswick Street.'

'Ah, yes. The niece of the indomitable warlike Aunt Freya. How is the dragon-lady?' There was a teasing, yet kindly tone to his voice, as though he were pleased to hear from her.

'She's fine,' Callie laughed. 'And congratulations on the award. I just saw the photograph in the newspaper. Very impressive.'

'Thanks.'

There was a sudden pause in the conversation. Callie knew she should say something, but the phone call had been spontaneous and she was momentarily lost for words.

'Okay,' prompted Michael. 'What's up? I'm sure you didn't ring to discuss Aunt Freya or my photographic achievements.'

'No,' Callie admitted. 'None of those things. It's about the horseshoe you left behind.'

'The horseshoe?'

She had the sudden sensation that she was taking a conclusive step, a move away from her own compartmented existence, and that the news, once revealed, would change the order of her life in some irrevocable way. What had Stuart said? *It's not as though you're friendly with this guy or anything. He's a god-damned stranger, for Christ's sake.*

Perhaps Stuart was right. She should have dropped the whole issue, not tried to pursue it to some illogical and coincidental ending. But it was too late. The conversation already had a direction which could not now be altered.

She swallowed hard. Then, on a deep breath: 'I found the other half.'

From the earpiece, she heard a quick intake of air. His voice, when it came, was abrupt. 'Where?'

'In a trunk of Hannah's things. It was hidden in a book.' Her words ran on in an effort to be heard. 'I wanted to call you, but I didn't have your phone number. You didn't leave it with Mum, and I couldn't find it in directory services —'

'No, you wouldn't. It's unlisted.'

'So it wasn't until today, when I saw the photo in the paper, that I knew where to find you.'

'So ...' he replied thoughtfully. 'Where do we go from here?'

'I honestly have no idea.'

There was a whispered conversation going on in the background. 'Look, I've got to go,' broke in Michael. 'I've a plane to catch. Assignment out west. I'll be out of town for a week at least. Can we talk about this when I get back?'

On an impulse Callie invited him to dinner the following week. 'Come Saturday,' she said, 'then we can go through whatever's in the trunk. I haven't had time. Perhaps there's something there, some clue. And you can meet Stuart,' she added, almost as an afterthought.

Graciously he accepted the offer. 'That'd be great. Till then.'

'Here's my phone number and address. Call me if you can't make it on Saturday. Otherwise I shall expect you by six.'

Callie, busy writing, had almost forgotten the trunk's existence. By late Friday afternoon the following week, she had finished several more chapters. Now they sat on the table in the entry, wrapped in brown paper and addressed to the Sydney-based publishing company, waiting for collection.

The courier arrived at the same moment that the telephone rang. Firmly she shut the door behind the man and ran to catch the phone.

It was Stuart. 'Look, I'll be held up at work for a

few hours. Don't worry about tea for me. I'll bring something home.'

'Oh.' Now that the work had gone, Callie had thought she and Stuart might go out to celebrate. There was a little steak and seafood place down near the bay. It was relatively cheap, and the food was good too. Then afterwards ... Hell! It was at least a week since they had made love.

'Oh, well. If you're not going to be in I might go over to Jill's for a while.'

'Yeah, fine,' He seemed in a hurry to ring off. 'Gotta go, Cal. Work awaits. See you later.'

'Yes. Later.'

There was a firm click and she brought the phone down against her waist, staring at it, a muted beep-beep coming from the earpiece.

The unit was in darkness when Callie arrived home about ten. She walked through the rooms, flicking lights on as she went. Oscar came down the stairway, miaowing loudly to be fed. Bending down, she scooped him up, resting her cheek against his warm fur.

As she filled his milk bowl, Callie heard the rattle of keys at the front door. Stuart reeled in, clutching a plastic carry-bag, bringing with him the aroma of spices.

'It's Thai,' he said, unloading the take-away containers filled with rice, noodles and something yellow that bore the unmistakable odour of coconut. '*Gaeng Kari*. Curried chicken. Want some.'

Callie wrinkled her nose. 'No thanks.'

He'd been drinking, she could tell. And more

than just the usual two or three Friday-night beers after work. He stopped and regarded her thoughtfully, swaying slightly against the kitchen bench. 'Come on, Cal. Don't be a spoil sport.'

'You're drunk!' she pronounced in disgust as she headed upstairs in the direction of the bedroom.

Callie woke at first light, not surprised to find she was alone in the bed. Stuart's side lay empty, untouched, the bedclothes still smoothed flat.

She lay there, watching through the open window as the sky changed from black-blue to indigo, to the palest of colours, promising a fine day. After a while she padded through the unit, finding him snoring lightly on the sofa in the lounge room, still fully dressed. His dirty plate and glass sat on the coffee table in front of him. Newspapers lay scattered over the carpet and the room had a stale smell, of cigarettes and aftershave and booze.

In the kitchen she followed her early morning ritual. Taking the teapot from the shelf, she automatically ladled in the tea leaves, filled the jug and laid out the cup and saucer. One end of the kitchen bench was littered with remnants of the previous night's takeaway containers and an empty wine bottle. Several puddles of yellow sauce lay cold and congealing on the laminex.

'Just look at this place! It's like a pigsty,' grumbled Stuart, coming up behind her, rubbing the stubble on his chin.

Callie awarded him a cursory glance as she emptied the boiling water into the pot. 'I've been flat out all week with the manuscript,' she replied defensively, taking the milk jug from the fridge. 'You know I've been on a tight schedule. Besides, you live here, too, and this mess isn't mine.'

'No, but it's your job to clean it up.'

Stuart's tone was belligerent, implacable. He'd obviously woken in a foul mood and now he seemed determined to start an argument. Well, she thought with a sigh, perhaps she would give him the satisfaction.

'Who says so?'

Thumping the jug on the bench, she felt a slow anger rise as her heart beat an irregular rhythm in her chest. Certainly, she usually did all the housework, rarely asking Stuart to help. She was home most days and it was easy to slot in around her writing. But just this once . . .

Stuart didn't answer. Instead, he pointed towards the study. 'And how about getting that old trunk out of there? God only knows what rubbish is in it, not to mention the cockroaches and silverfish.'

How like Stuart, she thought, stunned at the sudden realisation, to turn the conversation back to her when cornered!

The trunk! Remembering, Callie felt a rush of surprise. 'Goodness, I almost forgot. I've asked Michael to tea tonight. We're going to sort through whatever's in it.'

'Which won't be much! Anyway, what about the party?'

'Party?' For a moment she couldn't think. 'What party?'

'Miranda's. I told you last weekend.'

A vague memory trailed through her mind. Stuart

had mentioned something about Saturday night, but she had been too absorbed in her work to pay close attention. Inwardly, Callie groaned. Miranda was a flirty blonde who worked in Stuart's office. She gave the most awful parties, cliquey and boring and dull, the guests all standing around trying to talk over inordinately loud music, and Callie seldom knew anyone there.

She put a palm to her forehead, thinking. She could contact Michael, postpone dinner until next week. In consideration, perhaps anything was better than a full-blown argument with Stuart at the beginning of the weekend.

'I could ring him,' she suggested. 'Cancel.' Then: 'Damn!'

'What's wrong?'

'I still don't know his phone number.'

She phoned the newspaper instead, only to be told by an anonymous cultured female voice that Michael was not expected in over the weekend.

'I'm sorry, Stuart. There's nothing I can do about tonight. You'll have to go by yourself.'

He glared at her and stalked off in the direction of the bedroom.

Methodically she cleared his mess from the night before, emptying the containers into the bin, wiping all traces of his meal from the bench. After a while he came back into the kitchen, dressed and freshly shaved.

'I'm going out,' he stated, his voice expressionless. 'I don't need to put up with this shit!'

And he stormed out the door, slamming it in his wake.

CHAPTER 7

Callie had met Stuart while waiting for Jill, her flatmate and best friend, in the downstairs lobby at Jill's office. She had been morose and moody for weeks beforehand, devastated at the recent ending of a three-year relationship. Somehow Stuart had cheered her, made her laugh again.

'On the rebound,' Jill commented darkly, proclaiming dire warnings at the way Stuart had inserted himself into Callie's life so easily. 'It won't last. Besides, you're too different. He wears Armani suits and *Guy Laroche*, for Christ's sake. I don't know how you could even like him, he's so *smooth*.'

He was, too, Callie considered. Smooth and sexy, his body honed by the hours spent each week in the local gym. Also, as she soon found out, he was extraordinarily good in bed.

So they became an item. Stuart and Callie. Callie and Stuart. Slung together, their names made a song in her mind. She doodled his name on pieces of paper when she should have been working. She couldn't think of anyone but him.

After a month she had moved out of the flat she shared with Jill. Stuart had found a unit, new, with a 'For Sale' sign at the front. 'Let's buy it, Cal,' he had urged. 'The repayments are scarcely more that what we'd have to pay in rent.'

Her contribution to the deposit on the unit, matched in value by Stuart, had left a dent in her savings. Luckily, a cheque had arrived the following week for sales from her last book, and Anthony, her agent, had rung with the news that the publishers were delighted with the next manuscript and had offered an almost half-decent advance.

That had been two years ago.

Two years of heaven, and hell.

Ensconced in the unit, Callie had quickly discovered that all was not as it seemed on the surface as far as Stuart was concerned. In a good mood, he was a delight: happy and gregarious, impulsive and indulgent. One dozen long-stemmed roses, boxes of imported chocolates, bottles of French perfume: his generosity knew no bounds. But a sulky Stuart, when things were not going to his own well-laid plans, was moody and irritable and an utter bore.

Like today, she thought with a sigh.

It was at times like these that Callie wondered if she should leave, simply throw her clothes in a bag, jump in the Suzuki, never to return. But where would she go? Jill had another flatmate. Brunswick Street? No, she couldn't go home. Not after being away all these years, having her own sense of freedom. Besides, her mother planned to sell the house, so that wasn't really an option. Anyway, she reasoned, though the temptation was strong, the unit was half hers. Her money had added to the deposit, helped with the mortgage repayments and furniture purchases.

Thinking of the furniture, she wrinkled her nose. It was Stuart's choice really, not her own. Modern, mainly chrome and glass and leather. She supposed it matched the fittings and paintwork in the unit, which were grey. Impersonal. Neutral. Cold-looking. A frugal, simplistic environment. Given the choice, she preferred the rich warmth of timber, the rough feel of Berber carpet, cream or apricot colours surrounding her. The clutter of personal articles.

Callie glanced around the unit with a sigh, thinking of the necessary housework. The furniture was coated with a film of fine dust, though goodness knows how it had managed to find its way inside. The unit was airconditioned and the windows were normally closed. It was only a week since she had cleaned the place thoroughly. However, Michael was coming for dinner and she wanted everything to be just right.

Thinking of Michael again, the anticipation of his visit cheered her immeasurably. 'Stuff Stuart!' she grinned as she flicked the button on the hi-fi system and inserted her favourite *Dire Straights* CD. Turning the volume up, she methodically went through the rooms, gathering dirty clothes as she went, heading eventually towards the laundry.

By lunchtime the flat was sparkling. Chrome shone, tiles gleamed. Seeing her reflection in every glass surface, Callie felt a sudden need to distance herself from the shining correctness of her surroundings, a need to be away from reminders of Stuart and the angry start to the day. Collecting her swimming costume and towel, she hurried out to the car.

The beach was almost deserted, just a few diehard surfers out beyond the breakers and the usual joggers pounding along the compressed sand at the water's edge. The chill of the water momentarily took her breath away; however she waded further in until she could no longer feel the bottom, then headed out with firm strokes. She tried to picture herself from above, from the eyes of the gulls that slid effortlessly through the sky overhead: a solitary figure amongst the waves and white froth and suspended grains of sand.

Treading water at last, Callie looked back at the shore. Along the bay stood the holiday cottages, shut up and sleepy-eyed in the late afternoon sun; the row of almost-finished townhouses; and the public wharf and jetty. Beyond lay the commercial centre and the houses winding their way up into the hills that ringed the township. A spire of smoke rose in the distance.

'I don't care if I don't go to your wretched party!' she called loudly, the words disappearing upwards into the blue emptiness of the sky. Then she laughed at her own silliness.

On the way home she stopped at the supermarket, deliberating over the selection of two thick steaks in the butchery department. Armed with the meat, several fresh bread rolls, fruit, and the makings of a salad, she paid at the checkout and pushed her way once more into the street. Back at the unit she stowed her purchases, then showered, washing the salt from her skin.

Thinking of Michael, she found herself in a good mood, temporarily forgetting Stuart's earlier grumpiness until he returned home later, morose and sullen. He glanced around the clean flat, but said nothing.

From the kitchen, where she was washing and hulling strawberries for a fruit platter, Callie could hear the sound of the shower. After a while he came downstairs, dressed in his good jeans and a pale shirt, clean-shaven and smelling strongly of his favourite cologne. He stood for a moment, looking contrite.

'Sorry about this morning, Cal. Guess I was in a bad mood.'

'I guess you were,' she replied, trying hard to stem the note of sarcasm that threatened to overtake her voice.

'I'll be off then. See you when I get back.'

'Yes,' she nodded, turning towards the bench.

She was surprised to feel a sense of relief as she heard the front door close behind him and his car roar down the street. Slowly her fingers unclenched and her shoulders relaxed. What had she been expecting? she wondered. Another confrontation? Angry words?

Instead, there had been an apology of sorts.

Michael arrived promptly at six o'clock, bearing two bottles of wine. 'Didn't know what was on the menu,' he explained as he placed the bottles on the kitchen bench, 'so I bought both. One red, one white.'

He glanced around as though expecting someone else to be present. 'Stuart's out,' Callie said with a grimace, and then, feeling that some explanation was in order, added, 'A party.'

'Oh! Were you supposed to go, too?'

She smiled. 'He says I have a terrible memory. I forgot completely and I didn't have your phone number.'

Michael slapped his hand against his leg. 'Look, I feel terrible. What if we forget all about tonight and I'll leave, or perhaps I could drop you at the party? It won't matter if you're late, will it?'

Callie gave a wry grin. 'In some ways I was glad of the excuse to stay home. If you knew some of Stuart's friends, you wouldn't want to go, either,' she elaborated as his eyebrows rose in a quizzical gesture. 'Really, I'd rather be here.'

'Well, if you're sure ...'

'Certain,' she smiled. 'Pull up a stool while I put this salad together. And a glass of that wine would be great. White,' she added. 'We'll save the red for dinner. It's steak, by the way.'

'Callie, about the horseshoe ...'

She slid a large manilla envelope along the length of the bench. 'It's in there. See for yourself.'

Michael tipped the pieces of metal onto the laminex bench, aligning them as she had done almost two weeks earlier. He sat for a few moments, studying them, one palm cupping his chin, a finger tapping thoughtfully against the metal. 'Two halves making a whole.'

Callie sliced an avocado in half and deftly removed the seed. 'But what does it prove?'

'Nothing.'

'Yet.'

He glanced up at her, a puzzled expression on his face. 'Well,' Callie went on, 'there's the trunk. Letters. Photos. Books. I haven't had time, but perhaps if we go through them ...' She leaned forward and smiled. 'I love a mystery, don't you?'

He laughed and pushed the pieces of metal to one side. 'Not when there are no clues.'

'But there might be. Do you want to look now or wait till after dinner?'

He raised his eyebrows in a gesture of alarm. 'What a choice! Do you know I haven't eaten since breakfast?'

Michael's sense of good manners, Callie suspected, was overriding his eagerness to see what the contents of the trunk might reveal. In one way, she was glad. It gave them time to feel their way around the newness of the situation, to postpone the feeling of ... What? she wondered, searching her mind for parallels. Standing at the top of a high cliff, wondering what it was like to fall, nothing below to catch you? Swimming across a lake so wide that the other side was lost to view? Or like setting off across unknown lands, with no map or compass for guidance?

The analogies were endless.

Silly! she mentally rebuked herself, laughing inwardly at her own comparisons. Her writer's mind again, embellishing her thoughts.

They made small talk, skirting the issue of Michael's visit. By the time the salad was prepared and the fruit platter laid out, the contents of the first bottle of wine had disappeared.

'Now,' mused Callie, pulling the steaks from the fridge, 'we can grill these inside or light the barbeque on the balcony.'

'Outside,' Michael replied instantly. 'So much better than in.' He held out his hands for the meat. 'I'll do the honours. Cooked some pretty mean barbeques in my time.'

Callie slipped several CDs into the player and flicked the random button, then dusted off the outdoor setting on the balcony. Michael, with a great deal of perseverance, finally managed to light two of the three gas burners. Callie looked doubtfully at the bluish flames. 'We haven't used this for ages. I hope the gas doesn't run out.'

It didn't. Michael deftly turned the steaks on the grid, charring them nicely on the outside. Impulsively Callie ignored the already-set table in the dining room and carried the salad and bread rolls out onto the balcony.

The sun had set and the colour of the sky was deepening, only a slash of red remaining on the western horizon above the tree line. From the direction of a nearby park came the sound of children's voices. In the distance a car horn blared. One short sharp blast, then silence.

The steaks were just as she liked them. Almost black on the outside but juicy and pink within. Michael brought out the second bottle of wine, opening it with practised turns of the corkscrew.

'We never sit out here,' said Callie between sips. 'I don't know why, it's lovely at this time of night.'

A light breeze blew from the direction of the sea, ruffling her hair. She felt it sway about her cheeks, light, like a veil. For a moment she thought of Miranda's party, picturing Stuart in the smoke-filled room, and was glad she hadn't gone.

'How long have you and Stuart been together?' asked Michael as he ladled a spoonful of salad onto his plate.

'Two years.'

'Marriage plans?'

Callie, in the process of buttering a bread roll, pulled a wry face. 'No. No plans.'

'But you'd like to?'

'It's not a priority. I mean, you get married when you have children, right? And that's certainly not on the agenda at the moment . . .'

Her voice trailed away and she was silent for a while, trying to spear a piece of lettuce with her fork, wondering why the thought left an odd fluttery feeling behind.

'You don't want children?' He seemed intent on pursuing the subject.

Callie smiled. 'Actually, I love kids. I've even written a couple of children's books, and illustrated them too. They did quite well but they've been out of print for a while now.'

'Is that what you do, write books? I'm impressed.'

'Silly,' she laughed, feeling more relaxed. 'It's a job, same as any other, but the pay's irregular and the hours are horrific. For some strange reason, my best writing happens between the hours of two and six a.m.'

He gave a mock groan. 'How uncivilised!'

'Yes, it is. But enough of me. Tell me about yourself.'

'Okay,' replied Michael as he refilled their glasses with the last of the wine. 'I'll be thirty-eight next birthday. Divorced two years ago, but you already know that. Timmy, my son, is ten. He's a great kid. Down-to-earth, talkative. I try to spend as much time with him as I can, usually every second weekend. Since the divorce I've been renting a small house in the city. At the time I just wanted to hang loose for a while, not tie myself down. I've got a good job and earn a decent wage. I suppose I should think about buying something of my own but, somehow, I never seem to get the time. House-hunting for one isn't an exercise to get too excited about in my book.'

Callie watched Michael's hands move as he spoke, fluid and expressive. Though he had been a stranger until a few weeks previously, she felt an odd affinity towards him, as if she had known him for years. Silly, she told herself. He probably just reminds me of someone. Wordlessly, she picked up her wine glass and pressed the cold rim against her bottom lip.

Neither spoke for a while, yet the silence was comfortable. There seemed no need for meaningless chatter, dialogue to fill the space between them. The music from the CD player came faintly from within. A colony of bats rose from some nearby trees and went flapping away, silhouetted against a velvet sky.

Michael waved away Callie's offer of more salad. It was dark now, the balcony lit only by the light that spilled from the lounge room. The meal over, empty plates were pushed to one side as they finished the wine. Callie felt a little light-headed, as though drunk on the newness, the strangeness of the situation. As the cool night air whipped past her shoulders, she gave an involuntary shiver.

'You're cold,' said Michael. He rose and collected the plates and cooking utensils. 'Let's go inside. Besides, now that the hunger pains have been dealt with, I'm just about bursting with curiosity to see what's in that trunk.'

Callie deposited two cups of coffee and the fruit platter onto the study desk, while Michael dragged the trunk into the centre of the room. He lifted the lid, staring wordlessly at the mass within. Callie sank onto the carpet beside him, brushing away a stray cobweb. Together they lifted the letters out, laying them to one side. Underneath was a copy of *The War Illustrated*, dated 1917, with a pen and ink drawing on the front page of two infantrymen climbing over the top of a trench.

Recipe books followed, eulogy cards. Pieces of yellowing paper broke away, tiny confetti-like fragments of the past littering the carpet. Torn remnants of other people's lives, long dead. The mustiness again, the smell of decay. An odour of disintegration, and the sense that the mementoes of Hannah's existence were being ground to a crumbling, powder-like form that might blow away on the wind.

The envelope containing the photos was examined. 'Do you know who they are?' asked Michael, pointing to the soldiers and the girl with the dark hair.

Callie shook her head. 'I could ask Mum, I suppose, though she doesn't know I have the trunk.'

Studiously they sorted through the remaining contents of the trunk, Callie unaware of the passing hours as they exclaimed over their discoveries. Together they laughed over the recipes. Calf's foot jelly, blancmange. Dance cards, school copybooks. In particular, one Christmas card, carefully preserved. *To dear Great-aunt Hannah*, read the inscription. *From Alex and Bonnie. 1963.* Newspaper clippings. Wedding invitations. Christenings.

'Hey! Look at this!' exclaimed Callie, extracting one. 'John and Elizabeth Corduke have the honour of requesting the pleasure of your company at the wedding of their son, David —.' She broke off and looked at Michael. 'That's my great-grandfather.'

Towards the bottom of the trunk lay the book inside which she had found the remains of the horseshoe. Handing it to Michael, she went to the kitchen to brew another pot of coffee. When she returned, he was flicking through the pages.

'Look,' he said, holding the pages open for inspection. Inside, written in bold strokes of a pen, were the words: *This diary belongs to Benjamin Galbraith, 11th Field Company Engineers, A.I.F.* 'It's a war diary.'

'The mysterious Ben,' mused Callie. 'Who was he, do you think? Friend? Lover?'

Taking the cup of coffee that Callie held forward, Michael sat, silent for a while, staring at the hot liquid. 'There must be a lot of memories here,' he said softly at last. 'A dance card from 1914. A wedding invitation from 1920. Funeral notices. Events shaping family, friends. It seems strange, doesn't it, that after you're dead, your whole life can be condensed into one small space, and the sum of your whole existence can be reconstructed from scraps of paper.'

He turned and stared intently into her face, one hand unconsciously sifting through the pile of papers, envelopes and clippings. 'Hannah's trunk. Hannah's posessions. But they don't tell you anything about her. What was she *like*?'

Callie shrugged. 'I don't know. After Hannah married Uncle John, they went to live out west. He was a farmer, quite successful, and had a large property. I spent a few holidays with them when I was a child. Of course, Hannah was getting on by then. After Uncle John died, she seemed to go downhill quite quickly. Not long afterwards she had a stroke, and my parents brought her back home to live.'

'To the house in Brunswick Street,' broke in Michael. 'To the place where she'd grown up.'

Callie nodded. 'Mum nursed her until she died. That's why all her things are here.'

'I know you'll probably say it's none of my business, but, quite frankly, I'm curious. Why was one half of the horseshoe stored away in the box belonging to my father? What possible connection could my family have with yours? Or is it simply a coincidence?'

Michael regarded the pile of papers, books and cuttings that lay on the carpet. 'Perhaps,' he mused, 'somewhere amongst all that lie the answers to my questions. I'd like to go through it, if you don't mind, starting with this.' He picked up the diary, weighing it in his hand.

'Look,' said Callie, a sudden idea coming to her. 'Why don't you take the diary home, check it out? Meanwhile, I'll start going through the letters and arrange them in some sort of order. Perhaps you'll be able to get down next week and we can compare notes.'

'You're sure?' he asked. 'Not too boring?'

'No, really, I'd like to. I'm intrigued.'

'I'd better leave you my phone number this time, just in case.'

As she was jotting it down, Michael glanced at his watch. 'Oh, God! One o'clock!' he groaned. 'I promised Timmy we'd go sailing tomorrow. Seven a.m.!'

Callie laughed. 'Well, that's what you get for making rash Sunday-morning promises.'

As she escorted him down the hallway, there was the sound of a key in the lock. It was Stuart, standing stony-faced at the door, looking a little the worse for wear.

'Oh, Stu,' she said, going to him and slipping her arm through his. 'This is Michael. Michael, Stuart.'

The two men shared a reserved handshake. 'Well,' said Michael, stepping back, the diary held firmly in his left hand. 'I'll be off. Keep in touch, Callie.'

Michael was driving through the main part of town towards the highway when he remembered the park and the war memorial. On an impulse he stopped the car, parking it haphazardly against the curb, and took a small torch from the glove box.

Before him stretched a wide expanse of grass which was dew-damp and springy underfoot, muffling his own footfalls. Around him the town slept, dark and silent. The only sound was the distant barking of a dog.

He came to a halt in front of the sandstone memorial. Despite the nearby streetlight, the letters engraved into its wide square base were barely discernible. Flicking on the torch, he ran its beam down the length of stone, peering intently. The words, he knew, *had* to be there.

The air was cold and his breath issued around him as small puffs. The light from the torch was dim, indicating that the batteries were getting low. He had covered three of the four sides before he found what he was looking for.

Silently Michael touched his fingers to the stone. He stood for a few minutes, taking in the shape of the words. *Benjamin Galbraith*: a series of linked letters naming someone who had once lived, breathed. The writer of the diary. Perhaps he had walked through this park, had strolled beneath the old bandstand?

The chimes of a clock carried on the air. One. Two. He hadn't realised how long he had been standing there. An hour's trip still loomed in front of him before he could crawl into his own bed. If he were lucky, he would manage four hours sleep before the promised boat trip. Slowly he retraced his steps across the wet grass.

Wrapped once more in the warmth of his car as it hummed along the highway, Michael felt a stab of confusion, a sense of displacement, an overwhelming feeling that, somehow, he was pushing himself towards events beyond his control. What on earth was he doing, involving himself further? Why had he taken the diary, promising to get back in contact with Callie in a few weeks? He had returned the silver horseshoe to its rightful owners. His job was done. Or was it? he wondered.

Ben. Hannah. The diary. A trunk filled with memorabilia. What drew him to them, to the sleepy town nestled in the bay, to the house in Brunswick Street slumbering behind the wall of plumbago?

Leave it, let it go, said a small conscionable voice inside. But he had come this far, his curiosity aroused, and something within him accepted the direction in which he was travelling. There was no urgent need to move off at other tangents. Not yet.

And Callie, he thought, a series of images suddenly weaving themselves through his consciousness. Callie tossing the dressing through the salad. Callie sitting on the balcony in the half-dark, the profile of her face outlined against the light from inside, hair falling across her cheek. Callie standing at the doorway, a cup of coffee in each hand as he had looked up from the trunk.

Callie, who loved Stuart.

Thinking of that brought a sour taste to Michael's mouth. He had taken an instant dislike to the man, as he had known he would. Why? he wondered. Sixth sense? Vibes unwittingly given off by Callie? He wasn't sure.

God-damn it! He wanted — no, *needed* — to see her again, whatever the consequences.

Outside, the night rushed past: dark trees, an occasional service station brightly lit, the far-off lights of houses. And, stretching ahead, the broken white lines marking the lanes of the road spearing under the car, on and on.

Michael was late, which irritated him, and Timmy was waiting at the front gate, hopping excitedly from one foot to the other.

'Where were you, Dad? I thought you were *never* coming.'

Gaby ran lightly down the steps, looking immaculate as usual in a short floral dress, her legs brown and bare. In her arms she carried a bag.

'Hi,' he said, giving her a quick hug and a kiss on the cheek. 'You're looking as lovely as ever.'

'Flattery will get you nowhere,' she replied with a smile, handing the bag to Michael. 'I've packed a few things for Tim. Change of clothes, a few snacks to nibble on. When do you think you'll be back?'

'Three, four,' he replied, taking a stab at the time.

Timmy was already climbing in the car. 'Let's *go*, Dad. Bye, Mum.'

'Guess I've been given my orders for the day,' Michael grinned. 'No future in arguing with a ten-year-old. Bye, Gab.'

He headed the car southwards on the highway. Traffic was sparse and the sun shone from a clear sky. Timmy chatted incessantly beside him, detailing his week at school, the video he had watched the night before. Michael listened with amusement, one hand on the wheel.

After a while they left the main road and headed east, through canefields and past weather-beaten cottages. The sun was a bright ball ahead. At last Michael pulled the Mercedes into a rough car park.

The boatshed was ramshackle, paint peeling from its walls. Above the door was a faded sign that read 'Smith's Bait and Tackle. Boats For Hire. Hourly or Daily Rates'. He paid the hire on the boat and they stowed their gear on board. Timmy's bag, an old esky that he and Gaby had been given as a wedding present, hats, towels. Carefully he applied a liberal coat of sunscreen to his son's fair skin, rubbing a layer across his own face and arms.

The water was choppy and the tinnie thumped across the small waves, landing with a series of thuds, bringing a cheer from Timmy. 'Go get 'em, Dad!'

It was peaceful out on the water, cruising amongst the chain of islands — Russell, Lamb, Macleay, Coochiemudlo — and weaving around the sandbars at low tide, the sun on their faces, the taste of salt on their lips. At lunchtime Michael pulled the boat up on a sandy beach and they sat in the shade of a stand of casuarinas, where he arranged the contents of the esky onto a hastily laid blanket. Timmy ate the proffered bread rolls, cheese and fruit with a healthy appetite.

It was dark by the time they arrived back in the city. Timmy lay asleep in the front seat, his head lolling against the window. Effortlessly, Michael carried him up the front steps of Gaby's house and deposited him in his bed.

'Good day?' Gaby quietly closed the door on her sleeping son and followed Michael back down the hallway.

'Great.' He rubbed the back of his neck. 'But am I ever *tired*! I'm looking forward to bed tonight, that's for sure.'

Gaby moved behind him, pushing his own hands away, kneading at the muscles on his neck. 'That feel good?'

'Mmmm.' He closed his eyes and leaned his head back, enjoying the feel of her fingers against his skin. Cool. Practised. Efficient. Then: 'Gaby?'

'Yes.'

He turned to face her, pulling away from her touch. 'Do you ever regret it, the divorce?'

'No. Do you?' Arms folded, she tilted her head to one side and regarded him intently. Her mouth had tightened, imperceptibly. For one brief second he felt like shaking her.

Instead, he shrugged and headed towards the door. 'Night, Gab,' he called, before the latch clicked shut behind him.

Home at last, he fed Bess and headed for the shower. Hair wet, towel wrapped around his waist, he prowled restlessly around the house. The fridge yielded little in the way of food so he ate an apple and downed a cold beer. Finally, picking up the diary, he settled himself on the bed.

It was hours later when he woke. The light was still on and the diary had fallen against his chest, a dead weight. Carefully he placed it on the bedside table and clicked off the overhead lamp. Sleep pressed in on him again, pushing him past the years. He felt himself rushing back through time and he was powerless to stop.

In the morning, all he could remember of the dream was a soldier, a horseshoe and a girl with jet-black hair.

CHAPTER 8

It was only the length of her skirt, which seemed to cling damply to her legs, and the overwhelming heat that prevented Hannah from running as she hurried towards the smithy. Sweat trickled down her back. She could feel it, worming a wet path down her spine. Tiny flutters of fear feathered their way through her chest, lodging finally in her throat as she remembered her brother's words.

Thomas and young Galbraith from the smithy decided to enlist yesterday.

What was Ben thinking of? And Tom, going against David's wishes? Recalling the way her brother had pushed past her in the bank, and David Corduke's furious face, she gave an involuntary shiver, despite the heat of the day.

As she rounded the last corner and approached the smithy, Hannah could see the figure of Ben up ahead. He was kneeling at the front wire fence, attaching a large white sign. Coming up behind him, she could see the two words quite clearly: FOR SALE.

'Ben?'

He swung around to meet her, a woeful expression on his face. He was not wearing his usual workday overalls, but looked uncomfortably hot in a dark tweed coat. His arms hung limply by his side.

His shoulders were hunched. Hannah saw the expression of misery in his eyes.

'What's wrong?'

'It's Da.'

He looked bewildered, his eyes unfocused. Behind his voice, she detected a slight tremor, a hint of subdued panic. He brought his hands up, covering his face for a moment before letting them hang by his side again.

Hannah took his arm and steered him into the confines of the smithy. After the bright light outside, it was momentarily dark and she blinked rapidly, letting her eyes adjust to the gloom.

The place was a shambles. Items waiting for repair littered the workbench, and several damaged buggy wheels lay in a pile near the furnace. Tools were scattered on the floor. Ben sagged against the open doorway, staring at her. 'I thought he was getting better,' he said in a broken voice. 'Last week he seemed almost like his old self. Then on Sunday ...' His voice trailed away and he swallowed hard.

'What happened on Sunday?' prompted Hannah gently, taking his hand. His fingers felt cold against hers.

'Da's dead.'

Hannah closed her eyes for a moment against the misery etched plainly across his face. 'Oh, Ben. I'm so sorry,' she whispered.

'He died and I wasn't there.'

'You weren't to know. You said yourself he seemed a lot better.'

Soothing ineffectual words holding no substance, and she immediately wished them unsaid.

Remembering her own losses, years earlier, she understood his grief. Yet how could she begin to comfort him? His pain was such a private emotion, one she could not share.

At a loss what to do next, she put her arms around him, containing the warm solidity of him in her embrace. He was breathing hard, his chest rising and falling in a steady laboured rhythm. He laid his face against her neck and she felt the warm wetness of his tears.

'Da wasn't in his room. I waited and waited, but no-one came. The bed was stripped, all his things gone. I thought they might have moved him to another bed. But they hadn't.'

Slowly she extricated the details. There had been a funeral service the following afternoon. Apart from the minister, Ben and Tom were the only mourners. Then he told her about the white feather, handed to him on the same day he had learned of his father's death, compounding his feeling of despair.

'Father said you and Tom had enlisted,' she said bleakly, when he had finished.

Ben pulled away. 'How can I expect you to understand, Hannah,' he explained in a resigned voice, 'when I don't quite understand myself? Besides you, Pa was all I had. Now he's gone, there's a part of me missing as well. It's as though I'm not a whole person any more. I need to get away, to distance myself from all this. Joining up was the only way I knew how.'

An irrational fury winged its way through her chest. 'So you're giving up all this?' she queried, taking in the contents of the forge with a sweep of her hand. 'Throwing it all away just because a woman you've never met hands you a white feather, and because your father —' She paused, her voice choking with emotion, and swallowed hard. Somehow she had to persuade him to change his mind and stay, if it wasn't already too late. 'Your father worked hard to build up this business,' she finished wildly, a slight hysterical note to her voice, clutching at the first thought that crowded into her mind.

'Don't you see, Hannah?' He swung back towards her, an expression of hopelessness clouding his face again. 'I can't stay here, seeing Da in every moving shadow. There are too many memories, too many years tied up in this place. Too much pain and heartache.'

'What about us?' she asked in a small voice.

'Christ, Hannah. Don't think for one minute that I didn't consider us. You, me. We belong together. And when this war is over, we will be. Married. Man and wife. Not a few minutes snatched here and there. Not some furtive thing. I won't be ashamed of our love.'

'I don't want you to go away. I can't stand the thought of not knowing where you'll be, what you're doing.'

Her voice sounded ominous in her head, the words spinning disjointedly like a far-off shriek echoing down a long tunnel.

'Hush,' he soothed, gathering her to his chest, the fabric of his coat rough against her cheek. Suddenly the roles were reversed and it was Ben offering her comfort. 'Look, we won't be leaving for a while.

First there'll be training in the city, at the army camp. The war could be over by then.'

'Ben,' she said, pulling abruptly away. 'How long do you think you and Tom will be in training?'

The sun had angled itself higher, a beam bursting through a small hole in the wall, higher up. Dust motes hung suspended in its light, tiny wavering specks. Ben shrugged. 'Not long. A month, perhaps two at the most. Why?'

'I could come to Brisbane, too.'

He stood for a moment, as though digesting her words. 'Hannah, be sensible. We'll be in barracks and there'll be little spare time.'

'I don't care,' she replied stubbornly. 'Things will be dreadful at home after Tom goes. I don't think I can bear to think of it. And you —'

'Hush.'

He pulled her roughly towards him and kissed her, silencing the words. She tasted his mouth, sweet, like honey, and took in the faint odour of smoke in his hair, a burnt chicory smell, from the fire.

As her lips moved against his, she felt the rough stubble of his chin. There seemed a sense of urgency in his touch, the way he rubbed one hand at the small of her back with short circular movements, pulling her hips against his. She was aware of the taut hardness of him as his tongue, probing, parted her teeth. Like a drowning woman, she opened her mouth to him, desperately seeking comfort.

I am yours.

The words sung light-headedly in her mind and a mysterious heat pulsed through her veins.

You are mine.

Standing there, feeling the touch of his skin against hers, it seemed they were almost one. Joined, fused by that kiss. Rendered inseparable.

Abruptly he pulled away, turning from her, running his hands distractedly over his face. 'Don't, Hannah,' he groaned, voice ragged. 'Don't *do* this.'

What had she done? Ben had initiated the kiss, encouraged her. Yet, in the end, it had been he who had pulled away, distancing himself from her with a few quick steps. But he hadn't wanted to, not really. She could sense it, the way his chest rose and fell, the wretched expression on his face.

'Do what?'

Another scene came back at her, words and movements dancing disjointedly in her weary mind. Both of them in the forge, alone like today. Ben pushing her away. *Oh, God, Hannah. Just get out of here, will you, before I do something I might later regret.*

He stared at her, the air thick with emotion between them. 'I love you, Hannah. Don't ever doubt that,' he said at last. 'But there are some things that are best left alone. One day you'll be my wife, I promise you that. As surely as the wattles bloom each spring, we'll be together. No war can ever tear us apart.'

He gathered her in his arms once more, holding her close against his chest. Through the fabric of his coat, she could hear the erratic beat of his heart. There seemed a sense of desperation in his words, the way he held her face against the rough tweed of his jacket, holding her as though he never meant to let her go. Yet underneath it all, a feeling of despair bubbled under her breastbone, a sense that she was losing control of all that had been ordinary and commonplace, and a contradictory sense of arriving too late, at a destination that was both foreign and frighteningly familiar.

Later, back at the house in Brunswick Street, Hannah walked into the parlour. The room housed articles that were well known to her. Sofa. Two rocking chairs. The small table that held Enid's bible and David's whisky decanter. Another round table in the corner, on which stood the Manhattan lamp. Along one wall, the Harmonium organ. She waited by the doorway, leaning against the timber architrave, comforting herself by their familiarity, seeing them blindly through a wash of tears.

What was to become of them, her and Ben? Already he was moving away from her, taking routes along which she could not follow. How could she bear to let him go?

... we won't be leaving for a while ... The war could be over by then.

What if he were wrong? What if the war went on for years? What if ...? She stopped, remembering the newspaper casualty lists, not daring to think further.

The queue at Victoria Barracks seemed endless as Ben and Tom waited for their final papers. Painstakingly slow, the men shuffled forward, and it was not until after midday that they reached the head.

They had been joined to the 11th Field Company Engineers, Ben because of his blacksmith's trade and

Tom as a result of his partially completed engineering course. At least they were together, which was almost cause for celebration.

From Victoria Barracks, the men travelled by train to the railway station at Enoggera, where they walked the few miles to the military camp, singing as they went. The day was warm, with scarcely a cloud to mar the interminable blueness of the sky, and the feeling was one of ... Elation? Fear? A sense of moving inexorably towards the unknown; something dark and sinister, yet somehow freeing.

At the camp, which was known as Bell's Paddock, they were issued with clothing, blanket and kit bag. Then they were directed to an area where the ground was covered with stones and small shrubs, which had to be cleared. By nightfall, accommodation was in place: the small white tents Ben had seen earlier on his travels through the city.

A buyer for the smithy had been quickly found. After paying the few last outstanding bills from the sanatorium and his father's funeral expenses, Ben had placed the remainder in a newly established bank account. There was, he told Hannah, little left. 'But it's our wedding fund,' he added, cupping his hands against her warm cheeks and kissing her soundly. 'Maybe it'll pay for a deposit on a little cottage when I get back.'

At night, after the lamps had been extinguished, Ben lay in the tent, staring upwards into the darkness. He tried to imagine them together: a small house with roses growing beside the front path, smoke curling from the chimney. There would be children, little girls with dark curly locks like

Hannah and boys with his own lean long-legged frame and sandy hair.

Sensing sleep descending, he sighed, letting the fantasy merge and blend with his dreams, allowing the image of the house to fade to blank nothingness. And when he woke, it was morning again, a whole new day.

The tension in the house in Brunswick Street was unbearable, as Hannah had known it would be. During those last few days before his departure, Tom had been triumphant, elated to be joining his mates at last. David had been tense, barely speaking. Enid had been disgruntled and vocal, harping long and loud at the ungratefulness of some people and complaining about the interruption to Tom's university studies. Lily, the baby, was fractious, as though sensing the disharmony. Only Davie seemed his normal happy self, lost in his after-school world of tadpoles and the creek that ran past the bottom of the garden.

Almost overnight, Hannah's whole world had collapsed, for the second time. Without Ben the days seemed endless: long drawn-out hours of nothingness that left her drained and lethargic. Red Cross mornings. Comforts Fund parcels. The never-ending talk of war. On and on they went, voices proclaiming the dead, the injured, Enid grumbling about the inconveniences of rationing. To Hannah, everything that was once familiar had now become intolerable, hemming her in.

She missed Ben unbearably. Missed his bright enthusiasm, his ready smile. Missed the way he cupped his hands around her face and kissed her. Unconsciously she walked past the smithy, momentarily surprised to see a strange face at the bellows.

At odd times, the idea she had suggested to Ben the day he had told her of his father's death — that she should follow him and Tom to the city — came back to her. They had been wild words, said without thought in the emotion of the moment. Considering them now, she wondered at Enid and David's reaction if she followed through with them.

A plan formed in her mind, gathering momentum as the days passed, a plan so simple she wondered why she had not thought of it earlier, a plan that would allow her to be with Ben whenever his free time permitted.

Gathering courage, she found Enid in the bedroom, resting, the curtains drawn. Hannah glanced about, seeing the room as it had been when her mother had been alive: double bed, washstand with ewer jug and basin; several favourite pieces of jewellery lying on the dressing table next to the silver-backed brushes and combs, alongside a collection of three silver framed photographs — herself, Tom and David as babies.

Now the photographs were gone and, with them, the sense of family, of unity. But the jewellery was still there, flung carelessly on the dresser, a gold chain tangled about the clasp of a brooch and a turquoise ring. Lily was asleep in her cot in the corner of the room. Enid lay on the bed, the Alhambra quilt turned back to reveal white sheets.

'Are you awake?'

At the sound of Hannah's voice, Enid turned. 'Don't wake the baby!' she hissed, bringing a finger to her lips. 'It took ages to get her down.'

With a swift intake of breath, Hannah raised her head defiantly, ignoring her sister-in-law's words. 'Enid, I'm going to the city.'

'You're what?'

'I have to go,' Hannah went on with a rush. 'I want to be near Tom.' And Ben, she added silently, not daring to say his name aloud. 'They're calling for volunteers to assist with the war effort and I want to help. Not the knitting socks kind of help. I need something more than that.'

For a moment a look of surprise furrowed Enid's brow. Then, realisation setting in, she slid from the bed and caught Hannah around the arm, dragging her into the hallway.

'The Comforts Fund is a very important part of the war effort,' intoned Enid in a flat voice, her fingers digging uncomfortably into Hannah's arm. 'Anyway, David won't let you go. I need you here, to help with the children.'

Since the death of Hannah's parents, the two women had shared an uneasy alliance, and Hannah, thinking Enid would be glad to see her leave, was not prepared for the unexpected resistence. 'My mind's already made up,' she retorted, pulling her arm from Enid's grasp.

'Well, we'll see what your brother has to say about that!' replied Enid, clamping her mouth shut in a tight obstinate line.

A loud wail issued from the bedroom. Lily was obviously awake.

Enid glanced angrily in the direction of the sound. 'Oh, you stupid girl!' she snapped, eyes narrowed with anger. 'Now look what you've done!'

Hannah saw Enid's arm rise, saw it tracking towards her in slow motion, and was momentarily powerless to dodge the stinging blow to the cheek that followed. Shocked, she staggered backwards, bringing a hand to her face as though trying to stem the sudden pain. Tears flooded her eyes and she blinked them away, not wanting Enid to see her discomfort.

The two women faced each other, Enid's face impassive. Slowly Hannah removed her hand, her heart hammering in her chest. Then, fearing what she might say once the words were unleashed, she turned and walked away.

'How dare you, you ungrateful girl! David and I took you in ...'

Enid's accusations followed her, a bitter tirade. But they were half-truths, mostly, and Hannah closed her ears to them. Enid: filled with resentment at the unfairness of having to take two teenage orphans under her wing. Enid: overflowing with anger against them all. Finally allowing the tears to fall, Hannah went to her own room and angrily closed the door, shutting out the tongue-lashing.

She sat on the bed, considering her options. It was obvious she couldn't stay. Not now. The events of the last few minutes had proved that. Too many things had happened. Her uneasy tenuous relationship with Enid had finally been exposed, accusations made that could not be unsaid. She would miss Davie, of course. And Lily: the way her warm plump body snuggled against Hannah, the sweet baby smell. And David.

The decision had been made and there was no point in delaying her departure. The thought of seeing Ben again sent her heart racing. Thump, thump, it went in her chest, beating a steady, excited rhythm. With a sigh, she slid a suitcase from under the bed and began taking her clothes from the drawers.

She was placing the last of her belongings into a suitcase when her brother arrived home early from work. 'Enid said you had an argument,' he said, standing in the doorway to her room.

'You could say that.'

'What's going on?' Cautiously he eyed the suitcase.

'I'm going to the city,' Hannah replied, daring to lift her head with a defiant tilt to her chin.

'Look, I know Enid can be a bit of a tartar,' he said, lowering his voice. 'But this will all sort itself out. By tomorrow she'll have forgotten all about it. Let's not make any hasty decisions.'

Hannah turned to stare at her brother, feeling a surge of anger towards him. 'She hit me,' she replied fiercely. 'And if you were any sort of a man, you'd stand up to her.'

David's gaze slid across the carpet, his eyes not meeting hers. 'I'm sorry, Hannah. I didn't mean for any of this to happen. Enid can be a little forceful sometimes —'

Hannah gave a deprecating laugh, disguising the fact that tears were not far away. 'Forceful! Is that all you can say?'

'Please reconsider and stay. Somehow we'll work it out.'

'No!' she replied, turning back to the suitcase, her back rigid. 'And you can't make me.'

Her voice wavered, but her mind was set. For one brief moment she hated herself, hated David, for what they had become. They had been so close once, back in the past when they had been a family and their parents had been alive. Now they were almost strangers, Enid a wedge between them, she searched for conversation, for words that would link them again, and failed miserably.

'Where will you live? What will you do?' David's voice was faint, scarcely above a whisper.

Irresponsibly, Hannah hadn't thought further than boarding the train to the city and seeing Ben again. Her plans after that were blurred. But somewhere, pushed to the back of her consciousness, lurked the knowledge that she was heading towards unfamiliar territory. She had a few pounds saved. The money would last a few weeks if she were careful, but after that . . .

'I don't know,' she replied miserably.

'Here.' David pushed something hard and cold into the palm of her hand, folding her fingers over the object.

'What is it?' Hannah pulled her fingers back to reveal a key, grey in that soft afternoon light.

'Go to Tom's flat,' he urged, pressing a five-pound note against the key. 'You'll be safe there.'

Resolutely Hannah brought the lid of the suitcase down as she heard her brother's resigned footfalls recede down the hallway.

She supposed there were a few people she should farewell. Old schoolmates, mostly, several friends of her parents. However she couldn't bear the thought of saying goodbye, and the inevitable questions that would follow. Best just to go, she thought. Simply disappear. Avoid any more fuss.

Thinking back, she remembered the remainder of that late afternoon, seeing the long drawn-out minutes of it in slow motion, a blur of black and white, devoid of all colour. Flickering, like the movie reels in the old cinema down by the wharf, a series of disconnected images. Enid crying. David's terse silence towards his wife. Something had happened there, some argument, though Hannah was too tired, too bone-weary to care.

As she dragged her luggage down the hallway, young Davie stood, round-eyed, at the front door, the sky beyond him almost dark. Silently David took the suitcase from her grasp.

'Goodbye, Enid.'

'Hannah.' Enid nodded, as though scarcely able to bring herself to speak. At the last minute, Davie threw himself at Hannah, wrapping his sturdy arms around her legs, while Lily, upset by all the fuss, promptly burst into tears and sobbed inconsolably against Enid's shoulder.

The trip to the railway station was conducted in silence. Sitting next to her in the Cadillac phaeton, David Corduke's face was a frozen mask. 'Please, Hannah. It's not too late to change your mind,' he said as the carriages jerked alongside the platform with a rush of bright lights and a hiss of escaping steam.

Gratefully, she placed a hand on his arm. 'Let me go and be happy. Most of all, please be happy.'

Tears were only a blink away. Turning, she climbed the steps into the carriage, one, two, purposely blinding herself to her brother, refusing to look back. Dry-eyed, she watched as the lights of the township drew away and merged with the darkness. A curious weightlessness mixed with a sense of unrestrained excitement bubbled in her chest. The lighted carriage was a warm safe cocoon bearing her north towards the city, bringing her closer to Ben.

Hannah took a buggy from the station and headed directly to the flat in Wickham Terrace. Arriving late and exhausted, she crawled into the narrow bed that had been Tom's, and slept till the first pale light of dawn lightened the eastern sky.

Looking around the room in the cold hard reality of day, she knew she couldn't stay there. It was too small, cramped. She would go insane. Fine for Tom, who had spent most of his days at the university, only coming home at night. And the loneliness?

A live-in position was what she needed, a means to earn a wage, however small, and provide herself with some company. In a flurry of desperation, she dressed and raced along the footpath until she came to a newspaper stand. There were several advertisements for jobs in the city; however, one in particular caught her eye: a convalescent home for repatriated soldiers required the services of extra domestic staff.

The house, at Kangaroo Point on the south side of the river, was a short ferry ride from the centre of the city. It was set well back from the road on several acres of immaculately kept grounds. Hannah approached the entrance along a wide sweeping circular driveway, the centrepiece of which was a statue of a cherub carrying an urn that spouted a thin stream of water.

Ahead the house loomed, impressive and expansive, the glass windows gleaming brightly in the sun. Several men, some with bandages about their bodies or hobbling with the aid of crutches and walking sticks, moved about on the lawn. A nurse, wearing a starched white veil and pushing a man in a wheelchair, came towards her along the driveway, awarding her a curious stare.

Hannah was horrified to see that the man had no legs. 'I'm here about the position,' she stammered, not knowing where to look, her eyes somehow drawn back to the man's trousers, which were knotted at the knees.

'Front door. Up the stairs. You'll find Mrs Worthington in the study to the left.'

And she was gone, skirt swishing as she moved away, wheelchair wheels squeaking.

Tentatively Hannah knocked at the study door. 'Come in,' was the brusque reply. A woman sat behind a massive desk, grey hair pulled into a severe knot at the back of her head, which was bent over a pile of paperwork. 'Yes?' she rapped, without looking up.

'I'm here about the position advertised in the newspaper,' stammered Hannah again.

'Mmmm.' The woman raised her head and regarded her thoughtfully. 'It's cleaning work for the

131

men,' she said abruptly, 'and we need someone desperately. Downstairs maid, if you want a title. You've had some experience, I take it?'

Hannah nodded, momentarily tongue-tied, hoping she would not be asked for particulars.

'The job pays the usual rates, plus board and keep,' the woman went on in a staccato voice. 'And Sunday afternoons off.' She stood and walked to the fireplace, turning suddenly to face Hannah. 'The welfare of the men is our most important consideration here. They've all been injured in some way. Many are missing limbs, some have suffered the effects of gassing. Several are blind. Our job is to rehabilitate them, although many will never fully recover. What's your name, girl?'

'Hannah. Hannah Corduke.'

'Clare Worthington,' the woman replied, by way of an introduction. 'You'll have your own room upstairs and there's to be no fraternising with the men. You can start tomorrow morning. Be here at eight sharp.'

Hannah almost skipped back to the ferry.

A job! A job!

She had a job!

First parade at Bell's Camp Paddock was at six o'clock every morning. The men stumbled bleary-eyed from the tents, muttering almost inaudible replies to the inevitable roll call, which was followed by physical training, or physical jerks as it was known, then bathing or shaving. Afterwards breakfast was served on the long canteen tables, wolfed down with the aid of cups of hot tea.

There were four of them who formed a group. Ben, Tom, a young potato grower from Toowoomba whom they promptly nicknamed Spud, and Jack. Jack was the sandy-haired son of a grazier from out Roma way. He had never been to the city before and, in his own words, had 'decided to hop over and join up'.

Then there was the fatigue work: erecting tents, route marches, digging trenches. Ben found he took easily to the life, his ability to take orders honed by the years of hard work in the forge.

Marching. Keeping step.

Yes, sir. No, sir.

'Spit in your eye, sir,' muttered Spud, who had no respect for his superiors.

At the end of the second week of training, Ben was surprised to see Hannah waiting by the wire parade-ground fence as they finished drill for the day. It was mid-afternoon, Sunday, and she was standing in the shadows of the straggly gums, her arms raised, fingers hooked through the mesh.

'Hey, Tom,' he called, motioning towards her, as he ran across the level parade ground. 'Look who's come to visit.' Reaching the fence, he reached out and touched his fingers to hers. 'I've missed you,' he whispered as Tom came pounding up behind.

'And I've missed you, too.' She pulled back, her face carefully arranged, artificially bright. Too bright, Ben thought, taking in the paleness of her skin and the dark circles under her eyes.

'Hey, sis!' panted Tom as he threw himself on the grass at her feet, a silly grin dividing his face. 'What are you doing here?'

'I've got a job.'

'You've what?' exclaimed Ben.

'At Kangaroo Point. Mrs Worthington, the lady who owns the house, has turned the downstairs section into a home for repatriated soldiers.'

'You're not a nurse,' broke in Tom.

'No,' admitted Hannah. She was watching his face, Ben noted, as though monitoring some possible reaction. The hint of a smile played at the corners of her mouth. 'Downstairs maid.'

'Downstairs maid!' exploded Ben. 'What on earth do you think you're doing, Hannah? It's one thing to come to the city, but couldn't you have stayed at Tom's flat, done some voluntary work for the Red Cross?'

Tom sat in amused silence, plucking at the blades of grass. 'He's right, sis,' he said at last. 'I don't want you working, either. There's no need. Go back home.'

'No,' Hannah relied stubbornly. She paused and pulled a wry face. 'I thought you'd be pleased to see me.'

'Of course I am,' Ben soothed. 'But look at you. You look worn out already and you've only been at the job for ...'

'Four days,' interrupted Hannah.

Tom clambered to his feet. 'I'll leave you two alone.' He touched a finger to hers through the wire mesh. 'Don't get me wrong. It's good to see you, sis, but not this way. Listen to what Ben says. Go home.'

Ben watched as Tom loped away, then turned back to Hannah. 'What's really going on? What are you doing here?'

'I wanted to be near you,' she replied simply.

'Christ, Hannah!' He stopped and rubbed his hand through his hair, a frown creasing his brow. 'Look, this isn't the place to talk, nor the time. I need to see you alone.'

'I have every Sunday afternoon off.'

He thought for a moment. 'Next Sunday, then. One o'clock. Meet me in the Botanic Gardens. I'll be waiting beside the statue of Queen Victoria.'

'Galbraith!' bawled a voice from the other end of the parade ground. Without looking, Ben recognised the shout of one of the second lieutenants.

'I've got to go,' he said urgently, not wanting to leave her at all. He reached a finger through the mesh, touching it to her cheek. 'I love you, Hannah.'

'I love you, too,' she nodded, and Ben thought she was about to cry. Her mouth had an awkward lopsided twist to it, as though she had lost control of the muscles there. Hannah, who had never done a day's hard work in her life, now labouring like some navvy in a rehabilitation home. Hannah, who couldn't bear to be parted from him, who loved him enough to come to this sprawling city.

'Till Sunday, then.'

He longed to be able to bind her with his arms, to feel the fragility of her. Longed to taste the sweetness of her mouth, to tell her that it didn't matter. But it does, he thought fiercely, pressing away the thought. It *does* matter.

Instead, he turned and walked across the parade ground towards where his superior waited with his hands on hips, not trusting his own emotions to look back.

CHAPTER 9

The house at Kangaroo Point was built on high ground which overlooked the city and river. The upper storey contained several bedrooms and bathrooms, a small converted dining room, billiard room and maids' quarters. The parlour was crowded with stout Victorian furniture and adorned with knick-knacks. A wide verandah ran along the length of the house.

Downstairs, the kitchen was a cavernous area with polished metal surfaces and a gas stove. To one side stood the pantry and scullery, from where stone steps led down to the cellar. A man called daily to refill the ice chest.

The huge ballroom, drawing room, library, study and various sitting rooms had been given over, six months earlier, for the use of the wounded and the medical staff. The act had been one of loving sacrifice, as Hannah soon discovered, and her employer's outward abruptness was, in some ways, a foil. Clare Worthington had been widowed shortly before the outbreak of war and had lost her elder son during the Gallipoli campaign. The family business, a large nearby engineering works specialising in the manufacture of locomotives, still bore the name Worthington & Sons, and was managed by Clare's remaining son, Maurice.

Maurice was a raffish man who had a penchant for boater hats and young female staff. In his mid-thirties, he was engaged to a city socialite, although no marriage had been yet forthcoming. Hannah soon learnt to avoid him, ignoring his remarks and blatant suggestions with a toss of her head. Her every spare thought was of Ben, and Maurice's attentions did not interest her in the least.

Besides the medical personnel, Clare Worthington employed her own staff to attend to the smooth running of the household. There was Mavis the scullery maid, a stable boy and gardener, and Mrs Bonham the cook. Mr Bonham doubled as the groom and Mrs Worthington's chauffeur, and saw to the upkeep of the vehicles that were housed in the adjacent stables, along with the menservants' rooms.

It was Lottie, the upstairs maid, who became friends with Hannah. She was seventeen, a fresh-faced country girl who had already been in the house a month before Hannah's arrival. Astute and discerning, Lottie had her own opinions on everything, from the price of fish to the progress of the war. She knew all the household gossip, the precarious state of the Bonhams' marriage, Clare Worthington's little quirks and Maurice's inclinations. In private, she held the family in disdain, and they were often the subject of her scathing observances.

'They don't mind if there's a war on,' she commented bitterly one evening as she and Hannah inspected the house, checking that all the doors were bolted. 'Good for business, if you happen to own an engineering factory and a fistful of government contracts.'

'What about the son, the one who was killed?' Hannah asked, sliding the latch on the kitchen door. 'No amount of money could ever erase that pain.'

'All I see is some people getting rich on the misery of others,' Lottie shrugged. 'Doesn't seem right somehow.'

'But the house?' Hannah persisted. 'Turning over all these rooms to the soldiers and nurses, closeting themselves away in the cramped rooms upstairs. That's very generous.'

'Trading one thing for another,' proclaimed Lottie heading for the stairs. 'Eases the guilt.'

The following Sunday afternoon, Hannah met Ben in the Botanic Gardens as arranged. Seeing her approach, he ran towards her, arriving breathless and laughing at her side. 'Oh, Hannah, I've missed you!' he exclaimed, his face wreathed in a smile as he kissed her, swinging her up until her feet were off the ground and she had to hold one hand on her hat to prevent it from falling.

'Hello, Ben,' she said when he had returned her to an upright position, feeling a momentary shyness. Here, in the city, there was a sudden, almost indiscernible newness to their relationship. It wasn't Ben the blacksmith, who sometimes wore a tweed jacket and claimed snatched kisses in the middle of the smithy, who stood before her, but Ben the soldier in his new serge uniform. A different Ben. No smell of the smoke from the forge in his hair. No faint odour of horses and burnt metal. A city Ben, clean and shaven. Now, in these new surroundings, she was seeing him through different eyes.

She took Ben's arm and they strolled through the park. He was wearing his khaki jacket and trousers and she felt proud, noticing the admiring glances of the other women as they passed. A band was playing in a many-gabled rotunda. Sailing boats and dinghies crowded the river. The water reflected the sun, millions of dazzling mirrored images bobbing and weaving with the flow of the tide.

They walked towards the city along the water's edge, stopping only to buy an ice-cream from the park kiosk and a newspaper from a stand at the end of Alice Street. A few blocks further along, Ben propelled her into Queen Street. It was filled with horses and drays, buggies, bicycles, and the occasional automobile. Trams stopped haphazardly and people descended to the roadway, wandering amongst the traffic so carelessly that Hannah was certain some terrible accident would befall one of them.

The road was unsealed and lined with blocks of wood, and gas lamps were situated at regular intervals along the footpaths. Yet another tram trundled past, powered from the wires overhead. *Number 30*, read the sign at the front. *New Farm, Ipswich Road*. Comprising a single carriage, it contained no windows and the interior was open to the air. Hannah could see the conductor, wearing a white pillbox hat as he stood at the rear of the carriage and collected the fares.

Ben found a small refreshment room tucked away between a barber shop and a confectioner's. He ordered tea and scones from the white-capped waitress, then settled back in the chair, stretching his long legs.

'I've missed you, Hannah,' he said, taking her hand. He looked earnestly into her face and she was at a loss to explain the expression he wore, etched into the fine lines that radiated from his mouth and eyes. 'Are you lonely here, in this big city, knowing no-one?'

'Oh, no,' she laughed and the effect sounded forced, even to her own ears. She missed the house in Brunswick Street, her own room. In particular, she missed the children, Davie and Lily. 'There's never a spare minute at the Worthingtons', and plenty of company. I especially like Lottie. She's lots of fun.'

'Lottie?'

'Her name's really Charlotte, though she says she hates being called that. She's very pretty, and smart too.'

The waitress arrived with a pot of tea and scones, jam and cream. Thoughtfully, Ben emptied two teaspoons of sugar into his cup. As he sipped the scalding liquid, he stared though the windows at the passing parade.

'Lottie says that the war's good for the Worthingtons' business, that war makes the rich become richer while the poor get poorer.'

'And are they? Rich, I mean.' He turned back towards her, staring unblinking over the rim of the cup.

'Terribly.'

Expressionless, he stared down at his cup. A sudden lull in the background chatter in the tearoom magnified the silence between them. Hannah had an unbearable urge to say something, to fill the void with words that would bind them together, not force them apart. Life in the barracks, the city — already he was moving away from her.

'More money than you or I could imagine. There seems to be no end to it. Maurice has a different suit for every day of the week. Lottie says ...'

She stopped and stared wide-eyed at him, knowing she was babbling. Meaningless chatter, inconsequential words and phrases that told nothing of how she felt, working in that house amongst the legless and coughing. Hallways cluttered with wheelchairs, oxygen masks and bottles, crutches and artificial limbs; beds containing the maimed remains of once-healthy men, their bodies wracked by pain.

Hannah glanced at the scones and felt her hunger dissipate, replaced by a slow sense of unexplained dread. Ben would soon be going to the same far-away places where those men had been. Would he be all right? Would he come back missing an arm or leg, or with his lungs irreparably damaged? Would he even return at all? She couldn't bear to think about it. The possibilities were too awful to contemplate.

In desperation she glanced away, vainly trying to focus her thoughts elsewhere. Sitting in the busy tearoom on that Sunday afternoon, her life seemed disjointed, out of kilter with the rest of the world. The crowd seemed to press around her, strange faces, unknown except for Ben's, and the babble of voices magnified to a dull roar. People were laughing and smiling, eating and drinking, yet she felt her own tears not far away.

She had a sense of not belonging, a feeling of loneliness so acute that the air seemed to leave her lungs. There was a sensation of numbness, too, as though she had been anaesthetised, her mind wanting to close itself off from the constant daily horrors. Mutilated bodies, rationing, lists of dead in the daily papers.

Several more trams passed, bearing signs proclaiming their destinations as Logan Road or Toowong. She watched them, her face turned towards the window, knowing that Ben was studying her profile.

Slowly he reached forward and took her hand, entwining his fingers with hers. She could feel the warmth of his skin, the strength of him. 'Hannah, this is crazy,' he said at last. 'What are we doing here? What are *you* doing here? You should be home, at Brunswick Street, not in this overcrowded city. This war ...'

He paused for a moment and flicked at the crumbs on the tablecloth, pressing them into a neat pile, then gave a bitter laugh. 'You should see the blokes at the barracks, Hannah. And Tom's as bad as the rest. You'd think it was some holiday they're going on. Some god-damn family holiday! They never even think of *dying*!'

'Ben! Don't!' She laid her other hand over his, surprised to find it trembling.

'Silly young fools. They just don't *know*.'

Abruptly he pushed his chair back and stood, running his hands down the front of his uniform. At the counter he paid for their tea, then took her by the arm, steering her into the busy street.

It was late afternoon, the sky hazy already. 'I've got to go,' he said. 'I don't want to, but I must.'

His face was golden in the light, shining with such a soft sadness. He touched the back of one finger to her cheek, trailing it downwards until it came under her chin, and he tilted her face towards his. 'Hannah?'

'Yes?'

'When this whole mess is over, when the world has come to its senses once more, I'm going to marry you and we'll never have to be apart again.'

After several weeks, the company was moved from Bell's Paddock to the Exhibition Grounds, which had the advantage of being closer to the heart of the city. Instead of bare dirt, Ben discovered they now had wooden flooring to sleep on.

'Bloody lovely,' commented Spud hopefully. 'They'll be putting us in hotels next.'

Training became more intensive. The men were issued with rifles and bayonets, and there were route marches through the city, complete with weapons, haversacks and water bottles. Hours of struggling under laden packs.

'Geez, I could do with a beer,' gasped Jack as they struggled along one inner-city street.

'And I'd give anything to be able to have a piss,' replied Spud, screwing his face into an expression of agony, and they all laughed.

There was a tentative camaraderie, of sorts, between the four men. Spud was the dour comic, Jack was a solid type, quieter, who enjoyed a glass or two of Guinness. Tom was his usual rowdy self. Ben found himself one of them, yet separate in some detached way. Used more to his own company than this hearty joking group, he found the familiarity and lack of privacy frustrating at first. Doorless lavatories and showers, communal living quarters, the constant press of people around him: he craved silence, a book, sleep uninterrupted by Spud snoring on the next mattress.

After a few days, leave passes allowing them into the Valley or the city at night were issued. The pubs were crowded with soldiers leaning noisily against bars. Outside, patrols monitored the streets. It was an unreal heady existence.

Hannah was required to stay on duty until nine, after the patients had been settled for the night. There were last-minute bedpans to empty, floors to mop. Occasionally one of the nurses made her a cup of tea and she sat, quietly sipping, listening to the sounds of the ward: incessant wheezing of gassed lungs, the unconscious groans of the men as they relived horrific scenes in their sleep.

Her morning duties were varied and, some days, it seemed she was given every job imaginable. In the laundry she toiled over the hot copper and washboard, rinsing the bed linen in the round iron tubs that had to be filled and emptied by hand, finally wringing the last of the water from the fabric by way of the heavy mangle. Mrs Worthington demanded that everything be ironed, even the sheets, which Hannah attacked with the 'Mrs Potts' iron that was heated on the stove.

The task she enjoyed most was shopping for the men. A new much-needed pair of pyjamas, stationery, tobacco, a pipe. Hannah soon discovered that the best shops were located in the city centre, especially Queen Street. Finney Isles was the largest store. Four storeys high, with an elegantly turreted roof and a sign that said, 'Universal Providers', it ran the whole block between Queen, Edward and Adelaide Streets and sold everything imaginable, including ready-made dresses, underclothing, millinery, shirts and furniture. Compared to Finney Isles, she thought, Clarke's Emporium back home seemed like a corner store.

She was fascinated by Fortitude Valley, or The Valley, as it was known, which was a working-class suburb. The streets had a colourful bazaar-like appearance, with the wares from the various shops spilling out onto the footpaths. The largest store there was Beirne's drapery, which sold fabrics at very reasonable prices.

After life in Brunswick Street, the city seemed a hive of activity, a mixture of old and new. There were many handsome brick or stone buildings, such as the Supreme Court and Treasury, Parliament House, Government House, and the head office of the Queensland National Bank, which had been built to a traditional Corinthian design.

The city was in easy reach of the Worthington house. A short walk along the riverbank brought Hannah to the sturdy wharf from where the P.S. *Hetherington*, a side-paddle steamer, departed every quarter of an hour. The boat trip took mere minutes, yet she enjoyed being on the water, the wind blowing

145

about her face. There was a sense of freedom there, of belonging nowhere.

From the ferry she could see the river baths at the lower end of Alice Street. Beyond lay the breweries, aerated water works and cordial-makers. There were factories that produced jams, bread and biscuits, butter and boots; small foundries, a meatworks, printers, vehicle and carriage manufacturers. Other lives, other existences moving on, caught in the same cycles.

Amongst all this, the rush of the city and the mad demented days of war, Lottie was her only female friend. Lottie, who winked at the men and swung her hips suggestively as she passed them on the lawn, inviting stares and the occasional chuckle. Lottie, the blithe cynic who crept into Hannah's room each night and sat on the end of the bed, her feet tucked under her nightdress, dissecting the problems of the world. Lottie, who wept inconsolably when young Jim, a double amputee and a veteran of the first landing at Gallipoli, died downstairs.

Jim, Lottie explained later, through a wash of tears, had been a childhood friend of her brother, Frank, who had been killed by a Turkish sniper's bullet at Gaba Tepe, six months earlier. In some ways Jim's death was a catharsis, Hannah realised, a means of purging the last remnants of her grief. Lottie was saving hard, planning to buy the memorial headstone for Frank that her parents, poor country folk, could not afford.

Was there no-one, Hannah wondered, who was not touched by the war in some devastating way?

Lottie was an enigma to Hannah, a quaint mixture of naivety and experience, a blend of old-fashioned and contemporary ideas. Her parents' homely teachings conflicted with the death and decay and despair that was inked in every newspaper. There was a touch of recklessness about her, a sense of not caring.

Over the weeks, it was Lottie whom Hannah told about Ben, pouring out her desperate concerns. 'What if he dies? What if he never comes back?' she asked, finally giving voice to her fears.

'You'd cope,' replied Lottie pragmatically. 'Thousands of women do.'

It wasn't what Hannah wanted to hear, but what had she expected Lottie to say? Soothing words filled with hope? Lottie was not that idealistic.

Later she took the horseshoe from her drawer, holding it in her hand, feeling its weight. It was solid, tangible. Proof of Ben's love. She moved a finger over the etched words, feeling the slight indentations.

Hannah.
Ben.
I will love you always.

Slowly she raised it to her face, holding the cold metal against her cheek.

The following Sunday afternoon, she left the house and found Ben waiting on the footpath. The day was warm and sunny, and they had no destination in mind. 'Let's walk,' said Hannah, taking his arm.

They ambled along the riverbank towards South Brisbane, along the low-lying land, past wharves and dry docks. Tucked further back were the chilling works, preserving factories and clothing manufacturers, all closed for the weekend. Nearby were the working men's cottages, poor tenements with common yards. A ship moved downriver, sending a wash slapping against the banks.

To Hannah, the city seemed one of vast inconsistencies, from the mansions at New Farm and Kangaroo Point to these huts that overlooked the river: dwellings standing shoulder to shoulder, cramped and dismal in the sunshine. In the Botanic Gardens, women played tennis in long skirts. Hannah could hear the sounds of their laughter, the lazy plonk-plonk of the balls. Beside her, Ben walked, upright and tall in his uniform. A figure in khaki.

They found themselves at the entrance to the station in Roma Street. Trains shuffled in and out, bearing Sunday afternoon travellers. 'Let's go to the beach,' said Ben impulsively. 'All that salt air and sand. I want to breathe the smell of the ocean.'

The train was crowded with families. Hannah sat opposite Ben, and she could feel his knee brushing hers as the carriage rocked and swayed along the tracks. A humid breeze came through the open windows. Somewhere, further along the corridor, someone played a mouth organ. The journey seemed to take forever, the train stopping at every station along the way. By the time they arrived, Hannah was thirsty and a headache was hovering.

They had come to a sheltered bay where water lapped at the sand in a lazy consistent way. Holiday-

148

makers crowded along the foreshore: women holding parasols, men with their trouser legs rolled up, exposing white ankles. Children splashed through the shallows. At the far end sat the bathing boxes and rows of deckchairs.

Hannah, much to Ben's amusement, removed her shoes. 'You wanton,' he whispered in mock horror and she laughed at his words. The sand was warm between her toes, coarse and grainy. She felt it, soft underfoot, moving and realigning itself as she passed. Down by the water's edge, it was firmer, cold and uncompromising.

Far out, boats dipped and bobbed amongst the waves, their sails outlined brightly against the blue of the sky. Ben led her onto the pier. Standing on the edge, on the bleached wooden boards, Hannah watched as the water swirled away until it merged with the salt spray sky. Sea and sky and salt blending into a shade of blue-grey, meeting at some indistinct line, miles distant.

It was as though she were looking into infinity, into a never-ending abyss that was her own life, hers and Ben's. She had a sudden sense that it would soon end. These Sunday afternoons. Walks along the river. Stolen kisses.

'Word has it that we'll be off in a few weeks,' Ben said, as though reading her mind.

Hannah nodded, not daring to speak, and the uncertainties danced before her like mythical sprites.

'He'll be leaving soon,' she told Lottie that night. 'I don't know what I'll do when he does. I can't even bear to think about it.'

'I suppose you'll go home?'

Hannah shook her head. 'Ben wants me to, but I can't. Nothing's the same any more. It's *all* changed. *I've* changed. I can't go back.'

Lottie nodded. 'It's the war. We think differently, we feel differently.'

They were sitting on Hannah's bed, the covers turned back to reveal white sheets. Lottie had picked up a brush and was drawing the bristles through Hannah's dark hair. The feel of it against her scalp was soothing. She leaned her head back further. 'That feels good. Don't stop.'

'Hannah?' asked Lottie, the brush poised. 'Have you slept with him? You know, had sex.'

She glanced up, stunned into momentary silence by the question. Lottie laid the brush on the bed and lifted her arms, linking her fingers behind her neck, leaning her head back. It was a sensual movement. Her nightdress fell across her chest, outlining the shape of her breasts. She looked small and dark, almost elfin-like. Like a pixie.

'No,' Hannah replied curtly, glancing away, sensing her cheeks colour. It was a private matter, after all, and not open for discussion.

Lottie brought her hands down and hugged her knees, laying one cheek against her arm. It was, thought Hannah, a symbolic gesture of intimacy, of inviting confidences. 'Why not?' she prompted. 'You love him, don't you?'

'Of course I do,' replied Hannah hotly.

'Don't you think about it sometimes, wonder what it's like?'

'Well ...' Hannah swallowed hard and studied

her hands, which were no longer soft but work-worn, with rough callouses beginning to form on her palms.

Sex before marriage? There was a sense of wrong there, a knowledge that it wasn't something that 'good' girls did.

'How does Ben feel?' Lottie went on relentlessly, like a dog worrying at a bone. 'When he kisses you, do you get the feeling that he wants more? All men do, you know. It's a natural urge.'

She had a sudden image of Ben in the forge, pushing her away. *Oh, God, Hannah. Just get out of here, will you, before I do something I might later regret.*

Remembering the responding fluttering sensation in her own body, she blushed again, acknowledging the implication. Of course Ben wanted her, but he would never compromise her in any way. So why was Lottie forcing her to confront the issue?

'The subject hasn't come up, not really,' she said to Lottie instead. 'Besides, I'm certain he wants to wait until we're married.'

'Lots of girls do it, you know, before their men go off to war,' imparted Lottie confidentially. 'Sort of a going-away present, if you like. All that waiting, doing the right thing. Hardly seems worth it if the men never come back.'

'Ben will come back!' retorted Hannah quietly. 'Anyway, there's always the chance of falling pregnant. I wouldn't want to have a baby that way.'

'You can't get pregnant the first time. Everyone knows that,' Lottie divulged in a superior tone.

'How do you know.'

'Maurice told me.'

Privately Hannah thought she would never believe anything that Maurice Worthington told her. He seemed an untrustworthy sort of character, probably the kind of man who would tell a person anything as long as it suited his own intentions. 'You and Maurice talk about . . . ?'

Lottie awarded her a mysterious smile and bounced from the bed. Pausing in the doorway, she turned and gave Hannah a knowing wink.

'Oh, we discuss lots of things,' she replied airily, exiting from the room with a suggestive swing of her hips.

CHAPTER 10

The house at Kangaroo Point was a flurry of activity. Mrs Worthington had organised a dance, which would be held on the following Saturday night. The downstairs patients, who were well enough to attend, were invited, as well as the nurses and several local families.

Delicious smells emanated from the kitchen, where Mrs Bonham was busy at the gas stove. The carpet was lifted in one of the drawing rooms, which had been miraculously cleared of beds and other paraphernalia. Boracic acid was sprinkled liberally on the timber floorboards to make them more slippery for dancing. Trestle tables and chairs were set up along the verandahs, and streamers were strung from the walls and ceilings, lending a festive air.

The band, a quartet, arrived at six o'clock. From the kitchen, Hannah could hear them tuning the instruments and felt a ripple of excitement. She and Lottie had been asked to serve supper at nine o'clock, after which they would be free to participate in the evening's activities.

Slowly the crowd arrived. Cars and buggies crunched along the gravel driveway and the noise in the adjoining rooms grew. The music started. One, two, three. A swinging beat.

'Just listen to them,' grumbled Lottie as she helped Mrs Bonham ice a tray of small cakes. 'All right for some, kicking up their heels. What about us, stuck in the kitchen?'

She had been feeling wretched all day, Hannah knew, suffering earlier from a stomach upset. 'Mrs Worthington said we can join them after supper,' she replied brightly, touching her friend's arm. 'Come on, Lottie, cheer up. No use being miserable. No-one's going to take the slightest scrap of notice, except me.'

Lottie flashed her a reluctant smile. 'I suppose you're right, as usual.' She nodded in the direction of the music. 'All *they* ever think about is themselves.'

Clare Worthington came into the kitchen carrying a large lead-crystal bowl. 'Hannah,' she ordered. 'The cakes and sandwiches can go out now. And Lottie, can you refill this with punch, please?'

Lottie began ladling a fresh supply of juice into the container. Hannah moved away to collect the sandwiches while Mrs Bonham took a tray of hot savouries from the oven. Suddenly there was a loud crash, a sound of shattering glass, and Hannah turned to see Lottie standing round-eyed beside the bench. The front of her dress was wet and stained, and the bowl lay in several pieces on the floor, the contents spreading slowly outwards.

'Oh, you silly girl!' snapped Mrs Worthington. 'Hannah, clear up this mess at once! And Lottie, just look at you! Go upstairs and change.'

As Lottie walked past, she gave Hannah a broad wink.

Hannah ran frantically between the kitchen and the verandah, carrying plates and cutlery. Supper had been consumed and more punch set out in another bowl, yet there was no sign of Lottie.

'Wherever is that girl?' grumbled Mrs Bonham as the mountain of washing-up grew.

'She should have been down by now.' Clare Worthington stood at the kitchen door, her lips compressed into a tight line. 'Hannah, go upstairs and see what's keeping her.'

Hannah untied her apron and laid it on the bench. Up the carpeted stairs she went, suddenly tired from the day's activities. Perhaps she wouldn't stay downstairs after her chores were completed. Her feet hurt, her legs ached. She would be glad, in fact, when her duties were over and she could crawl into bed.

Lottie's room was at the far end of the house, next to her own. Tonight the hall seemed miles long and filled with vague shapes. Beyond, a yellow light from one of the bedrooms spilled out against the carpet.

A faint sound came along the corridor. A laugh, followed by whispered words. Not like Lottie's voice at all, but deeper, masculine. Hannah stopped, puzzled. The party was in full swing and surely no-one but Lottie was upstairs. She shook her head, smiling to herself. Probably voices coming up the stairwell, she thought. In large houses like these, sounds seemed to echo from the most unexpected places.

There was another smothered laugh. 'Sshh!' said a voice that was definitely not Lottie's.

A movement inside Lottie's room sent shadowy images whirling across the hallway carpet. Dual shapes that touched, then moved away, swaying. There was a brief flare of light and the lamp was extinguished, plunging the end of the hallway into darkness.

Instinctively Hannah pressed herself into an open doorway. The voices came closer, moving past her towards the stairs, where they paused. In the light that rose up the stairwell, she caught a glimpse of them: Lottie, her small body pressed suggestively against Maurice; Maurice, trailing one hand along the line of her jaw, down her throat until he cupped one palm against her breast.

They seemed to stay in that same position for an eternity, Lottie looking up at him, her face silhouetted against the light. Suddenly she pulled away, laughing, and Maurice turned and walked past her, disappearing into his own room. Lottie smoothed her blouse and adjusted her cap before descending the stairs. Hannah watched as her head bobbed, lower and lower, until she was lost to view.

Lottie and Maurice! Hannah could scarcely believe what she had witnessed, the explicit sensuality, the way Lottie had appeared to enjoy the way Maurice touched her. Lottie, who was always so disparaging of the Worthingtons, who voiced disgust over the elitist ways of the wealthy.

Scraps of dialogue bounced around in her head. Past conversations, words that had made little sense at the time, now took on new meanings. Lottie sitting on the end of her bed, hugging her knees. *Have you slept with him? You know, had sex.*

Ben in the forge, kissing her, pushing her away. *Oh, God, Hannah. Just get out of here, will you, before I do something I might later regret.*

Dual shadows swaying out against the hallway carpet. Lottie pressing against Maurice. Maurice's hand wandering down Lottie's body, coming to rest finally on her breast.

Lots of girls do it, you know, before their men go off to war. Sort of a going-away present, if you like. All that waiting, doing the right thing. Hardly seems worth it if the men never come back.

Lottie laughing at her, ridiculing her inexperience. *You can't get pregnant the first time. Everyone knows that.*

Obsessively the words jogged back at her at odd moments, causing Hannah to stop whatever task she was involved in. She tried to picture herself as Ben's wife, the war safely over. Pictured Ben coming in the door every night, imaginary children running to meet him. Pictured how she would turn from the stove in welcome, could almost smell the delicious simmering aroma of the supper she was preparing. He would swing her high, laughing as he had done that day in the Botanic Gardens, and she would feel the strength of him supporting her, never letting her fall. Then later, he would carry her to the room they shared and lay her on the bed, slowly peeling back her clothes, kissing her mouth, her neck.

It was there that her imaginings ceased. She couldn't think what would happen next, and the realisation of her naivety caused a bubble of panic to well up inside her, lodging somewhere in her throat.

What if Lottie were right? What if Ben never came home from the war? What if he died never knowing what it felt like to take her to that most sacred unknown place?

She studied Lottie whenever she had the chance, watching the provocative swing of hips as she walked, the obvious flirtations with the men who strolled about the lawns. Even Mr Bonham, invariably found on the wide gravelled driveway at the front of the garages, washing one of the latest Worthington automobiles or tinkering under the bonnet, stopped and watched as she passed, an amused indulgent smile on his face.

It seemed Lottie had time for them all. A cheery wave, words of greeting. The men seemed to look for her, anxious for some sign of recognition. 'Hey, Lottie,' they would call from the lawn below, as she beat the mats against the railing on the upstairs verandah. 'Blow us a kiss, will you?'

And, laughing, she would oblige.

'You're such a tease, Lottie,' grumbled Mavis, the scullery maid, as they sat in the kitchen later, sipping cups of tea. 'Leading them on, that's all you're doing. Some of them blokes have got wives and sweethearts.'

'Well, there were no wives or sweethearts where they've been,' rounded Lottie angrily. 'And most days I don't see too many of them visiting. What about that new chap downstairs, Walter? Just yesterday a letter arrived from his *sweetheart*, breaking off their engagement. Said she didn't see much future in marrying a man with only one arm.'

Mavis gave a deprecatory sniff. 'And I suppose

you'll help ease his broken heart, along with all the others?'

A look of sadness crossed Lottie's face. It was there for a moment, fleeting, and then gone. Hannah remembered Lottie's brother, Frank, dead at Gaba Tepe.

Lottie tossed her head. 'If it makes them happy, then I can't see any problem. Besides,' she added, 'it's just a bit of harmless fun. Don't be an old sourpuss.'

Lottie was a mystery, a curious unpredictable blend of compassion and bluntness. 'I look at the men downstairs and I see such pain, such terror in their faces,' she confided to Hannah later, her own eyes swimming with tears. 'And I see Frank in every one of them. They could easily have been him. Dead on some stinking foreign battlefield.'

She paused and glanced down at her hands which, Hannah saw, were shaking; then she took a deep breath and went on. 'I had a letter from one of Frank's mates, after my brother died. He told me how it happened. How the bullet opened up his face, turning the flesh almost inside out, like a lump of raw meat. Frank died screaming, hurling obscenities. He couldn't see. His eyes were gone, and no-one could get him to a casualty post for morphine. Two hours, it took. Two long horrific hours.'

'How could you bear knowing that?'

'Some perverse part of me wanted to know those nauseating gut-wrenching details. It made my life seem more precious somehow.' Lottie's face tightened imperceptibly, like a veneer wall slipping down, hardening her mouth to a tight line. When she spoke, her voice was hard, too. Hard and unyielding

159

and filled with such hatred. 'I can't comprehend how men could treat each other so. An animal doesn't deserve to die like that. And *those* men,' she thumbed her fingers in the direction of the downstairs wards, 'carry pictures like that in their heads every waking minute. It's a dreadful burden. They can't talk about it. To do so would unleash something terrible inside them.'

'Like what?' asked Hannah.

Lottie shrugged and turned away. 'A sort of demon, I expect. Maybe the very devil himself.'

A week later, Hannah saw Lottie tiptoeing from Maurice's room in the early hours of the morning. Unable to sleep, she had gone to the kitchen and made a mug of cocoa. Coming back along the faintly lit hallway, she heard a muffled giggle and the sound of playful slapping. Backing into the shadows, she had seen Maurice's head peer around the door, looking left and then right. 'All clear. No-one around,' she heard him say. Then Lottie emerged from behind him and sprinted along the carpet runner towards her room.

Ensconced once more in the warmth of her bed and still unable to sleep, Hannah replayed the small scene continuously in her mind: Lottie hurrying along the hallway clutching her robe, the hem of her nightgown flying out about her bare legs; Maurice closing his door behind her with a sharp satisfying click; the hall, so suddenly empty that Hannah wondered, for one brief moment, if she had imagined the whole episode.

But she hadn't, she told herself. It had all been real. Too real. And what was Lottie thinking of? She was always so disparaging of Maurice, so contemptuous of the Worthington money. 'It's not everything,' she had once told Hannah. 'They still don't know how to love.'

So what was Lottie doing in Maurice's room? Thinking of what she had seen, Hannah felt a shiver of bewilderment as her friend gradually assumed new dimensions. It seemed that no longer was Lottie simply her friend, prosaic and asexual and undefinable, but she was now Lottie the woman, the lover. Two years younger than herself, yet evidently much more worldly, she was a sensual creature who obviously knew the ways of men.

With this knowledge came a feeling of disquiet, and a vague accompanying sense of power. Hannah pictured herself standing before Ben, pressing her body against his, as Lottie had done to Maurice. But now it was Ben trailing his fingers down her throat. Ben's hand cupping *her* breast. Hannah herself fleeing down the hallway, running from Ben's room.

What would it feel like, she wondered again as she lay in her bed, stretched rigid and tense against the starched sheets. A heat bubbled in her veins, a slow diffusing warmth that spread through her body. And somewhere beyond it all, past the wondering and imaginings, trod an unfamiliar longing and a sense of aching desperation that she was unable to control.

When she finally slept, she dreamt of darkness — darkness and whirling forces pulling her inwards into some cyclonic abyss. The names and faces tumbled together. Ben. Lottie. Maurice. They lurched past, beckoning her on, a never-ending parade, until she woke to Lottie standing over her, shaking her shoulder. 'Come on, lazybones. It's late and Mrs Worthington will have our guts for garters.'

Word had spread that the company would leave before the month was out, and the fact that the men had been given a full weekend's leave only added fuel to the rumour. Tom decided to return to the house in Brunswick Street to say goodbye to David, Enid and the children. 'It's the right thing to do,' he told Hannah, 'however you might feel about it.' Then: 'Why don't you come home for the weekend, too?'

Hannah shook her heard.

'Come on. What harm can it do? It's only for two days.'

Ben had been at a loss how to spend that weekend. There was no-one to farewell, except Hannah, and the thought of it loomed ominously in his mind. What to say? How? Where? As yet he hadn't even been given a definite departure date.

'Why don't you come back home for the weekend?' asked Tom towards the end of the week. 'There's a dance organised.'

'A dance? A *final*, don't you mean?' said Ben bluntly, referring to the customary practice of holding a farewell dance for enlisting soldiers in the Mechanics' Institute hall.

'Dance. Final. Call it what you will,' replied Tom blithely. 'It'll be a chance to kick our heels up.' Then, accusingly: 'Don't you want to come? I would have thought you'd want to spend a little extra time with my sister.'

Ben sighed. Singing maudlin songs, prolonging the pain; he felt no compulsion to go. Yet Tom was right. It would be a chance to see more of Hannah. 'I might,' he answered warily. 'We'll ring her tonight, see if she can get the time off.'

'And if she can't'

'Then I'll bloody-well stay here.'

In the end Hannah capitulated, bowing to Tom's request. It was his last weekend, after all. And Ben's.

Grudgingly, Clare Worthington allowed her the entire weekend off, from five o'clock on the Friday afternoon. The train was packed with travellers heading towards the southern beaches. Ben and Tom found a compartment with three empty seats, and Hannah sat wedged between a sharp-faced woman and a young schoolboy, trying to think positively about the few days ahead.

Though she had kept in occasional contact by letter, it was the first time she had returned to the Brunswick Street house since that terrible day almost two months earlier. There were bound to be changes. The garden would be bare, piles of mid-autumn leaves falling in banks against the ground. Cooler now, her brother would undoubtedly have the fire going in the parlour. Both Davie and Lily had probably grown two inches, and Enid . . .

Here Hannah's thoughts paused, remembering how she had seen her sister-in-law last, standing in the hallway, hand held to her mouth.

She glanced across at Ben and, in return, he gave her an encouraging smile. Closing her eyes, she swallowed hard. The long hours, the terrible reminders of death in those downstairs wards, the absolute and utter exhaustion as she went to her bed every night: it was worth it so she could be near him. The compensatory hurried afternoons where the hours seemed to rush past, hasty kisses at the Alice Street wharf. Precious snatched moments that were gone too soon. It was better than no contact at all.

The tension in the house was palpable. Enid managed a terse hello, while Davie hugged Tom and Hannah effusively. Lily held back for a few minutes, momentarily shy. 'It's lovely having you both back,' David whispered when Enid was out of earshot. 'Just like old times.'

With a heavy heart, Hannah helped with the decorations at the Mechanics' Institute hall the following afternoon, stringing balloons and streamers along the walls. Ben was ensconced at the local hotel and she hadn't seen him since the train had pulled into the station the previous evening.

'Hey, cheer up,' consoled Tom, leaning from the ladder in the centre of the hall. 'You look like you lost a shilling and found threepence.'

She gave him a wan smile. It was the best she could do under the circumstances. Tom and Ben, two of the people she loved most, were leaving. Already she felt so alone.

She dressed with care, wanting the dance to be special for Ben. He had no family to support him, no-one to make the usual speeches on his behalf. She sat at her dressing table, pulling the brush through her hair, feeling an overwhelming sense of dread. Some part of her wanted nothing to do with the evening. There was a feeling of such finality about it all, an underlying impression that there was no going back, although she wished long and hard that she might have been able to. Instead, she wanted to curl up on the bed and pull the sheets over her head, pretending that the whole wretched war was some terrible nightmare from which she would soon wake.

Consequently, Hannah was late. She found Ben leaning nonchalantly against the wall in a darkened corner, a cigarette in one hand. 'I thought you were never coming,' he whispered, grinding the stub beneath his heel. 'Dance?'

She nodded and he took her hand, leading her onto the polished floor, where they lost themselves amongst the other couples. The nearness of him was both exhilarating and intolerable. His approaching departure kept welling up in her mind. Try as she might, she couldn't rid herself of the unbearable sadness. Tears were only a blink away. She squeezed her eyes shut and gripped her fingers tighter against the tweed of his coat, trying to blank the thoughts. *Let him enjoy this night*, she willed, over and over again.

After several consecutive dances with Ben, she went in search of a cold drink. Enid was at the refreshment table, little worry lines creasing her forehead. 'Hannah,' she said, drawing her aside. 'As Mrs Murphy has just pointed out, you've had three dances with young Mr Galbraith. It's not ladylike, spending all night with the one partner. Now, I'm sure your brother would like the pleasure of your company for a while. And that young gentleman over there ...'

Her voice trailed away and Hannah glanced in the direction of her sister-in-law's gaze. Jimmy

Driver, she noted with a grimace. Tall and gangly, with a pair of horn-rimmed glasses framing an earnest face. Son of the local newspaper owner.

'... well, young James has been trying to catch your eye all evening, Hannah. He's such a nice boy.'

As Hannah swung from partner to partner, she was aware only of Ben watching her, his gaze scarcely leaving her face. What was he thinking? she wondered.

She managed to slip outside after supper. Ben was leaning against the fence, smoking another cigarette. She could see the red tip glowing faintly in the dark, and his face outlined against the light coming from the long windows of the hall. 'Sorry,' she said, raising her eyes skywards in a gesture of helplessness. 'You can blame Mrs Murphy for interfering. She told Enid what a lovely couple we made.'

He caught her to him, pressing her cheek against the rough tweed of his jacket, his mouth on her hair. 'Sshhh,' he whispered. 'Don't talk. I just want to be here. To remember you like this.'

Hannah felt the pressure of his hand, the warmth of him. Inside, the music started again. The slow strains of a waltz came drifting out into the night, sighing away with the wind as it lingered through the trees. Muted sounds of laughter, the cry of a child. A deep rumble, a drum roll of feet against the crow's-ash floor. Thudding, thudding, like soldiers marching, matching the erratic cadence of her heart. 'Oh, Ben, I wish —'

He kissed her then, stopping the flow of words. Pressed his mouth against hers and set her skin on fire, and an odd shuddering sensation pulsed through her belly. A sensation that her body was somehow opening up to him, like a bud opening to the sun, spreading its petals wide.

It seemed as though she were suddenly pliable, made of rubber, and that the heat he generated within might melt her until she dissolved into nothingness, into a steam-like vapour that would disappear into the darkness above, unseen. The thought of it made her light-headed, dizzy.

'Christ, Hannah, I love you.'

Whispered words, yet they meant everything. She nodded her head and he cupped his palms against her cheeks, gazing into her eyes for what seemed a long time.

The speeches had been made, the songs sung: 'Soldiers of the King', 'Rule Britannia', 'Sons of the Sea'. Rousing songs that swelled hearts and stirred fervent patriotic feelings. Songs to make mothers weep, Hannah thought, hearing the voices rising and falling behind a wall of sorrow, like a lament or dirge, a wail for the dead.

It's the soldiers of the Queen, my lads
Who've been, my lads, who've seen, my lads
In the fight for England's glory, lads
Of its world-wide glory let us sing.

'England's glory,' she whispered, stricken. 'Not mine.'

CHAPTER 11

The dance, as Ben expected, had been a maudlin affair. And going back to his childhood town had been another mistake. Everywhere he went, he was smothered by a sense of finality. Familiar landscapes now seemed so strange, so foreign, that they might easily have come from another country. There was a sense of displacement, too, a feeling of not belonging. Da's death, his own enlistment, the subsequent sale of the smithy: it seemed as though, in some final unalterable way, he had relinquished all rights of citizenship to the place of his birth.

Walking past the forge and seeing a stranger at the bellows, the memories of those good times before his father took sick came back, causing a wave of desolation so acute that, for several seconds, he could not breathe, couldn't take a step forward, or back. Instead he stood, his eyes taking in the well-known sights: wagon wheels lying everywhere, a tangle of discarded metal; a buggy lopsided under the straggly pepper tree; the corrugated walls of the building.

From inside came the sound of hammering, breaking his reverie. Taking a deep breath, Ben moved on. A sadness washed over him, a desperate need to see all this preserved: Hannah, the smithy, Clarke's Emporium, the chemist, the butchery, the

168

winding narrow streets that led down to the beach, the house in Brunswick Street. God only knew when he would see them all again.

In such a short space of time, his life had changed irrevocably, moving off at tangents he had never expected. Even his relationship with Hannah seemed to have altered in a subtle way. There was a new intensity about her, a sudden obvious agitation. She moved with a rush of unexplained energy, eyes unnaturally bright, face lit by forced cheerfulness.

Back in barracks, the week passed slowly, the knowledge of their impending departure hanging over him like a weighty cross, unable to be ignored. Each day he expected some word, some hint of when the Company might leave. However, there was none.

He had arranged to meet Hannah the following Sunday, as usual. There was a regatta on the river at Hamilton. Several of the chaps had mentioned it during the week and he thought they might go. Before leaving, he slipped the key to Tom's flat into the pocket of his jacket. He wasn't expected back at barracks until Monday morning. Later in the day, after he had seen Hannah back to the Kangaroo Point ferry, perhaps he'd go back there and spend the night.

At the last minute, Hannah dropped her key to Tom's flat into the pocket of her skirt. It was something she had thought about all week, her emotions seesawing between convention and emotion. As she stood on the ferry, she pressed her hand towards it, turning it over and over in her fingers, feeling the sharp pointed shape.

For almost two months she and Ben had had no privacy, meeting amongst the Sunday afternoon crowds. Nothing more had passed between them than a touching of hands and a few stolen kisses. Now the thought of them, alone in Tom's flat, sent a wash of unrestrained exhilaration bubbling through her. There was something illicit about the idea, forbidden yet tempting. They would be safe there from discovery, too. A letter from David Corduke had arrived the previous day. Tom was expected back at the house in Brunswick Street for the weekend.

Ben was waiting at the Alice Street wharf, pacing along the boards, hands thrust deep in his pockets. He smiled as he saw her walking towards him, a boyish grin that lit his face. A few blocks further along, they caught a tram which eventually deposited them at their Hamilton riverside destination.

Ben had brought a rug. He spread it on the grass before ambling across to the refreshment kiosk, which was doing a brisk trade selling tea and coffee, ice cream and Cadbury's chocolates. Hannah lay back and closed her eyes, listening to the cheering from the onlookers as the boats passed. She felt the sun warm on her face, and sensed the heat of it being absorbed by her skin. Behind her closed eyelids danced a spangle of colours, spinning and re-forming like the beads in a kaleidoscope.

Ben came back bearing two cups of steaming tea, and Hannah sat up and sipped the hot liquid. From her vantage point, she saw the boats return. They were sleek and moved easily through the water. Oars flashed, sunlight catching the sprays of droplets. Dip, dip, dip, they went in unison, spearing into the water with precise timing, while the rowers heaved, muscles straining. Ben sat cross-legged beside her, trailing a long blade of grass across the chequered rug, tracing the outline of the coloured squares.

'I don't know how much longer we've got,' he said at last, turning suddenly in her direction and looking squarely into her eyes. 'We're expecting orders to move out any day now.'

Hannah bowed her head and squeezed her eyes shut, hating the finality of the words and the feeling of hopelessness they evoked inside her. Hated, despicable words, tearing them apart, causing a wash of dread.

Somehow something had to be said, to fill that awful silence between them. 'Do you know where you'll be sent?'

'By all accounts, Adelaide first. We still need more stores and equipment. Tool carts, pontoons, trestle bridges, water carts.'

'You take all that with you?'

'We're an engineering company,' he reminded her gently, knowing she did not know the difference, 'not trench soldiers. Our job is mainly behind the scenes. Reconnaissance, destroying bridges and rail lines, surveying, mapping. That sort of thing.'

'Oh.' She gave a sigh of relief. 'Does that mean you'll be in less danger?'

Ben shook his head. 'We're not expected to be involved in hand-to-hand combat, but that doesn't mean it'll be any less dangerous. Anyway,' he gave a forced laugh and reached out for her hand, 'I'm not

171

planning to tempt fate. Keep my head down, push the enemy back to where he belongs. Then I'll come straight back home to you, my love.'

Words again. Mere words. Hannah looked away, the scene dissolving in front of her. There was a forced quality to the day. The garish brightness of the sun mixed with the high-pitched chirping of the birds overhead, yet a sense of uncontrollable panic tugged at her. She felt a sudden and urgent need, one which she felt powerless to suppress, to run from the people who thronged the park, the foreshore, away from the feelings of joviality and fun.

'Let's go,' she said, standing abruptly.

'Where?'

Hannah grabbed Ben's outstretched hand, pulling him to his feet. 'Let's just walk and see where we end up.'

She knew, as soon as they left the park, that their destination would be the flat in Wickham Terrace. Every step, every footfall, carried her in that direction. Ben walked beside her, not speaking. He seemed preoccupied, distant. Trams trundled past. Eventually he flagged one to a halt and helped her up the steps. Hannah sat next to him, feeling the solidness of his arm as it brushed hers.

They left the tram at Leichhardt Street. The afternoon had cooled, the sky clouded over. White cotton-wool cloud had descended over the nearby hills, promising rain. Hannah shivered. Whether the cause was the cold wind or the excitement that was building inside her, she wasn't sure.

'You're freezing,' said Ben accusingly as he took his coat and laid it across her shoulders, giving her a quick smile. When they came to the corner of Wickham Terrace, he stopped and looked at her, puzzled. 'Where are we going?'

She gave him a knowing look and walked ahead, a quiet purpose to her step, willing him to catch up, not daring herself to speak. She was aware of the fine drizzle that now dampened the pavement, soft feather-light droplets of rain that felt cool against her face. Ahead stood Tom's flat, seconds away. She looked back. Ben was standing several yards behind her, shaking his head.

'No, Hannah.'

'Yes,' she laughed in reply. Suddenly she was running, sprinting towards the front entry of the house, searching for the key in her pocket as she went.

The flat was dark, the curtains drawn. The only illumination came from the hallway, through the still-open door. There was a musty smell, the odour of rooms seldom used.

Ben took a box of matches from the kitchen drawer and went to light the lamp, but Hannah stopped him. 'No,' she said, smiling, the corners of her mouth turning up mischievously. 'Let's have a fire, instead. It's cold enough.'

There was paper and kindling, but no decent-sized logs. Taking a large bucket, Ben headed back down the stairs, towards the rear yard where the firewood was stacked against the fence. For a moment he waited, leaning against the palings, eyes closed as he took several deep breaths. He had the oddest sensation that Hannah had planned, all along, to bring him here. Leading him back from the regatta in a roundabout route, the key conveniently placed in her pocket. The way she had held it forwards, teasingly, as though daring him to follow her into the darkened confines of the flat. 'Let's start a fire,' she'd said, and he imagined the room, all cosy and lit by flames. Oh, hell! Given the opportunity, he wasn't certain he could resist. Once back upstairs . . .

It wasn't what he wanted, he thought, momentarily stunned at the realisation. No, he corrected himself immediately. It was all he had thought about for ages. But not this way. Not making his love for her a furtive illicit thing. He wanted to marry her, for Christ's sake, to make their union holy, blessed by the church.

Taking a deep breath, he tried to organise his thoughts. He'd take the wood back up to the flat, make her a cup of tea, then escort her back to the ferry. He wouldn't permit the chance of something developing, something that perhaps she would later regret.

Quickly Ben placed several logs in the bucket and sprinted up the stairs, taking them two at a time.

'I'm back,' he called as he opened the door of the flat, surprised to see the room bathed in a yellow glow. He peered forward, letting his eyes adjust to the gloom.

The paper and kindling were well alight. Hannah sat on a mat before the fire, her back to him. She was naked, he realised at once. Leaning forward, head bowed, her arms hugged her knees. The pale milkiness of her neck and back was exposed, bathed in that same yellow light. The flames of the fire reflected against the walls and furniture, highlighting the bumps and indentations along the length of her spine, the cleft between her buttocks. Her hair was still pinned up, but stray wisps had escaped, leaving thin dark trails across her neck and shoulders.

Ben stood for a moment, mesmerised by the sight. He was still holding the wood bucket, the door partly open. Slowly she lowered her arms and swivelled towards him. 'Why don't you close the door, Ben?'

Everything seemed to be happening in slow motion, like a movie being shown frame by shuddering frame. He kicked his leg back and the door slammed shut. Jerkily he reached down, placing the bucket on the floor. Something — was it the way her hips curved towards her waist, the convex swell to her belly, or those curling tendrils of hair against the untouched whiteness of her skin? — brought a large immovable lump to his throat. Seeing her like that, the years of pent-up wanting suddenly became an ache, so strong that he thought he might cry out with the pain.

'Hannah, do you know what you're doing?'

He moved behind her and knelt, lifting the strands of hair and teasing his lips along her neck. At his touch, a spasm seemed to pass through her body.

She nodded and took a deep breath, twisting her face, her mouth, towards his. 'Yes,' she whispered. 'I know *exactly* what I'm doing.'

Ben moved his hands downwards, moulding them to the outline of her neck, her shoulders, her waist. She raised her arms, bringing her hands to the back of her head and her breasts lifted with the movement. They were firm and small, and when his palms closed over them, the nipples felt hard, like tiny stones.

Bending, he took her skin in his mouth, flicking his tongue along the exposed flesh. Warm, he remembered thinking later, feeling a sense of urgency flood through him. And there was the feeling, too, that whatever moral reservations he had previously had, whatever personal restraints he had placed upon himself, he and Hannah had already travelled too far to consider turning back.

The kindling in the grate shifted, sending a shower of dying sparks up the chimney. The logs sat in the bucket, forgotten. Ben watched Hannah's fingers moving against the fabric of his shirt as he sank down beside her, slipping the buttons deftly through the tiny holes. He remembered, too, in a distant time and place, feeling the rug underneath, the hardness of the floor somehow in contrast to her own softness, as she drew him into an erotic abyss from which there was no escape.

The room was faintly lit by the lights from the gas lamps on the street below when Ben woke, stiff and cramped, next to Hannah in Tom's single bed.

The process that had brought him there was but a vague recollection, a series of hauntingly exquisite images. He remembered stretching himself beside her on the floor, his clothes gone, Hannah kissing him with abandon, like never before, her tongue exploring the inside of his mouth with short tentative flickers.

All control gone, his resolve fleeing before him like a banished demon, he had sensed the pressure building in his groin. Consciously aware of his own inexperience, he had moved his hand down, caressing her breasts, her belly, fumbling at her, the ache unbearable. All the while, her hands had moved at his face, caressing, kissing, taking him to a place he had never been before, but somewhere he knew he wanted to return to.

Carefully, aware of his weight, he had lowered himself over her, parting her legs gently with his hand, pressing his hardness instinctively against that soft moist opening. At first she had drawn back with a small surprised sob, a momentary pain glimpsed in her eyes.

'I've hurt you!' he had cried, pulling away.

'No! Don't stop!' she had pleaded, cupping her hands around his face, silencing him with her mouth.

Thus encouraged, he had pressed on, urgently now, thrusting himself past that temporary barrier, vaguely disappointed that the first few movements inside her had brought almost immediate release.

Afterwards she had smiled and pulled him close, pressing a warm hand against the small of his back, and he had rested inside her, luxuriating in the aftermath of that unaccustomed intimacy.

Now, as he propped himself on one elbow, she was a vague shape beside him in the gloom, all pale flesh, one arm draped across his belly. With the movement, she stirred. 'What time is it?' she mumbled.

'Oh, Christ! Late!' he replied, trying to move himself out from under the weight of her arm. 'Come on. We've got to get you back before the last ferry.'

But she was holding him back with a firm pressure. 'No. Stay. It's all right. I told Lottie to tell Mrs Worthington that I wouldn't be back tonight.'

I was right, he thought, smiling to himself in the dark. She *had* planned this all along. 'You scheming witch.' He laughed as he trailed his hand across her breasts and down her belly, feeling her hands stroking him towards that familiar hardness once more.

Later he padded into the small kitchenette, filled the kettle and lit the gas ring, watching as the circle of blue flames danced into life. From there he could see Hannah, covered decorously by a sheet, sitting upright, arms hugging her knees again.

'Sorry, it'll have to be black, I'm afraid. There's no milk,' he apologised, pouring the boiling water into the pot. She slid from the bed, wrapping the sheet about her.

Together they sat at the table, sipping cups of tea, Ben unable to take his eyes from her. The drink consumed, he let himself out of the flat and headed down the road towards the small corner store. By the time he returned, carrying eggs, tomatoes, bread and cheese, milk and butter, she was dressed and the fire was roaring in the grate.

Hannah started the makings of an omelette. He offered to cook, but she shooed him away, brandishing a spoon towards him. This is how it should be, thought Ben as he sat at the table, watching her. Hannah, hair loose and falling across her shoulders like a dark cape, her face lit by some inner radiance that he had never seen before.

Hannah, standing at the tiny gas stove, peering doubtfully at the contents of the pan, the expression on her face causing silent mirth to bubble up inside him. And this is how it *would* be, after he returned from the war. He and Hannah, married, alone, no longer needing to hide their love away like something shameful.

His thoughts were interrupted by the heavy pounding of footsteps along the hallway, followed by the grating of a key in the lock. The door was flung open and a figure stood, leaning against the door frame.

'Oh, Tom!' cried Hannah, flinging herself towards him and wrapping her arms around his neck, the omelette forgotten.

Ben rescued the pan from the stove, while Tom took off his coat and poured himself a whisky from the decanter on the sideboard. Hannah had a dozen questions. 'What are you doing here? How are David and Lily? And Enid,' she added with a slight wrinkling of her nose. 'And Davie's tadpoles? It's only a week since I saw him last, but I miss the little devil.'

Tom took a gulp of the whisky. 'All right,' he shrugged. His face had taken on a closed look.

'What's wrong, Tom?'

'The weekend was an absolute disaster, if you must know,' he blurted, setting the empty glass on the sideboard. 'Enid kept on and on about throwing away my studies. We ended up having a terrible row. I didn't want it to be like that. So I came back early. Anyway,' he changed the subject, 'I wasn't expecting anyone to be at the flat. Gave me a surprise to come in and find you two here, the fire going.'

'Stay for supper,' urged Hannah. 'There's plenty.'

Ben saw Tom glance towards the alcove bedroom. From that angle the unmade bed could be clearly seen, sheets and blankets thrown back, pillows thrown in abandonment on the floor. Tom's gaze returned to Hannah. He gave her a hard, scrutinising look. 'No. I don't think so. I see you two are busy. I'll get back to barracks.'

Hannah gave a cry of protest, but Tom was already walking towards the door, pulling on his coat, shoulders hunched as he pulled the sleeves over his arms.

'Night, all,' he muttered, letting himself out the door.

Ben woke about midnight and lay there, feeling the solid reassuring shape of her. Hannah stirred, stretching herself. 'Are you awake?' he asked.

'Yes.' She rolled towards him. He could feel her breasts, her thighs, the warmth where their skin met.

'Are you sorry? About all this, I mean.'

'No,' she whispered, grazing her mouth along the contours of his chest. 'Are you?'

He shook his head. 'Yes, no. I don't know. It wasn't what I planned for us. I wanted it to be right, to be special —'

'Don't say that! It *was* special!' she interrupted vehemently, her voice wavering, sounding perilously close to tears.

Ben shook his head again, a gesture of hopelessness. 'It just seems so furtive, somehow. Sneaking into the flat, Tom finding us like that. He *knows*.'

He was silent for a while, thinking about the events of the afternoon, the night. Caught up in the wonder, the sheer delight of it all, he hadn't considered the consequences. At once he hated himself for exposing her to the risks. 'Hannah?'

She stirred in his arms, draping one leg provocatively over his own. 'Yes?'

'I should have used precautions but I didn't think ... that is ... I wasn't prepared. What if we've started a baby?'

'Don't be silly. Lottie says you can't the first time.'

'Are you sure?'

'Quite,' she replied sleepily, touching her fingers to his mouth.

His arms came around her again, fiercely pressing her body against his. She lay there, her head tucked under his chin, one hand toying with the mat of hairs on his chest.

Ben stared out into the darkness, unable to sleep. He wished that the moment might go on forever, that he would never have to leave.

But that was, he knew, just a fanciful idea.

One night, at the end of the following week, Lottie came running into her room. 'Hannah! There's a telephone call for you in the study.'

'Who is it?'

Lottie shrugged. 'Mrs Worthington said to get you, that's all I know.'

Breathlessly Hannah raced down the stairs and along the wide hallway. Telephone calls, she knew, were like telegrams, giving bad news. Maybe someone at home was sick. David, or perhaps Enid. Oh, no, she thought. Not Davie! Trembling, she picked up the receiver.

'Hannah?'

The voice sounded strained, uncertain. 'Ben, is that you?'

'Yes. I've only got a minute. There must be a hundred chaps here waiting to use the phone.'

The line was all static and she struggled to make out the words. Ben had never telephoned her before, and the actuality of his voice echoing down the line caused an immediate feeling of unease. 'Are you all right? What's wrong? What is it?' Her own voice, she knew, held a slightly hysterical tone.

'We're leaving.'

Two words, expected, yet they sent a chill through her. 'When?' she whispered.

'Tomorrow morning. On the midday train. I'm sorry, Hannah. There's nothing I can do. This is the big one. France, I think. At least that's the rumour, though no-one's saying.'

She could hardly breathe, and a tightness gripped her chest, pressing against her ribs with an unseen force. She thought she had been prepared for this, yet suddenly she found she wasn't. When she tried to speak, no words came.

'Hey, perhaps this will all be over in a couple of months,' Ben continued, his voice forcibly bright. 'Everyone says it can't go on much longer.'

There was silence on the other end of the telephone. For a moment she wondered if they had been cut off. 'Ben? Are you there?'

'Hannah?' His voice sounded far away, a faint

crackle. 'Before I hang up, there's something I wanted to tell you.'

'Yes?'

'On the form, we had to put next of kin, just in case something —'

'No!'

'Please, Hannah, listen. I put your name on the form. That means they'll send my things to you, if anything happens.'

'Nothing will happen!' she broke in fiercely. 'Nothing!' The tears were running down her cheeks, across her mouth, plopping noiselessly onto her collar. The telephone line went to static again. Crackle, crackle. 'Ben?'

There was no answer. Suddenly the line went dead, an empty, echoing silence from which no words came. Slowly she replaced the receiver on the hook. Tomorrow! Midday. Somehow she'd get time off and go to the station. She had to see him, and Tom too, one last time.

The platform was packed, the farewelling throng jostling behind a line of barricades that had been erected near the ticket gate. Hannah threaded her way through the crowd, scanning the platform for Ben's familiar face, but there were hundreds of soldiers pressing towards the carriages, a surging sweeping sea of khaki, each man almost indistinguishable from the next.

Running back up the stairs towards her room the previous night, a sudden idea had come to her. Mr Bonham had lent her a small hacksaw and it had taken almost twenty minutes to cut the silver horseshoe in half. Her hand had ached as she pushed the blade deeper, and she had suffered a sudden pang of guilt as the last fragment of metal was severed and the shoe lay in two equal pieces. The deed done, she sat, momentarily numb. Her actions had been completed in haste, with little forethought, and now possibly were regrettable. What would Ben think, seeing his carefully chosen gift mutilated in such a rough way?

She sat for a while, turning the metal over in her hands, feeling the spiky shards against her palm. No! She shook her head. This shoe was symbolic of their love, and now she was giving him half, her own half, the half that said 'Hannah' and 'I will love', to take with him wherever he might go. He was taking half of *her*, not just the shoe, and he would understand.

She had taken the side that bore Ben's name and placed it back in her drawer. The other half, the one that carried her own name, she now held firmly in her hand, as she surveyed the massing khaki-coloured throng. Where was he? she wondered despairingly, standing on tiptoe near the railway barricades to obtain a better view. And there, as though in answer to her plea, he was walking past, kit bag hoisted over his shoulder, looking straight ahead.

'Ben! Ben!' she called wildly, willing him to turn, but the deafening noise from the crowd drowned out her words. Several people nearby looked in her direction. Heads moved in front, momentarily hiding his face. The thought occurred to her that he might move on, not hearing her at all.

Desperately she pushed towards the barricades, seeing a space through which she might squeeze.

'BEN!' she screamed, and, miraculously, he was standing almost next to her. He turned, staring at her blankly. 'Hannah,' he said, though the sound became caught up with the other surrounding noise and she simply saw the movement of his lips, the way his eyes lit up at the sight of her.

The crowd behind was pressing him on, carrying him away. Vainly she stretched forward her hand, holding the half horseshoe towards him. Their fingers touched, one brief sensation of warm flesh against hers, and then her hand was empty.

'Hannah! Hannah!'

It was Tom, waving madly, a few paces behind. He gave her a smile and a wave, which she returned. The crowd closed around her, momentarily blocking her view and, when she could finally see, all she caught was a glimpse of Ben's retreating form as he passed through the doorway of one of the carriages.

At last the platform was empty of soldiers and the guard strode along checking the doors. Anxious faces peered from the windows as the train gave a tentative lurch. A murmur ran through the crowd, a long dying curve of a sigh, weaving and echoing, linking the present and the past. Around Hannah, there were old men with tears coursing down their faces, women and children holding silent vigil. Hands gripped hers, strangers' hands, holding her tight. Hands bound by love and fear.

They were singing now, the words in unison rising and falling. I must be strong, thought Hannah. I will not cry. She squeezed her eyes shut, blotting out the sight, but the words still came at her, poignant and appropriate.

Should auld acquaintance be forgot ...

Words falling across the pain, the agony of it all.

And never brought to mind ...

Words mixing and blending, sighing like the waves along a stretch of distant beach. I love you, Ben! Don't leave!

For the sake of auld lang syne ...

Hannah whispered the words and they choked like bile in her throat.

CHAPTER 12

During her spare time, Callie turned her attention to the trunk. As she emptied the contents onto the floor for the third time, she was surprised to find they were now familiar to her, like old friends. Idly she glanced through the yellowing pages of a recipe book, grinning to herself at the old-fashioned fare: coddled eggs, jam roly-poly, tapioca pudding. There was an entire section devoted to bottling fruit and pickling meat, and several pages relating to the skinning and boiling of rabbits.

'Yorkshire pudding,' she mused, coming to the end of the index. Bonnie hadn't made that in years, though it had been one of Callie's favourites as a child. Perhaps she would pick up a decent piece of beef from the supermarket later and surprise Stuart with a baked dinner for tea.

She loaded the cards, invitations and newspaper clippings into an old shoe box, planning to go through them later, then replaced the school copybooks in the bottom of the trunk. The pages were brittle, breaking away at the edges, and shouldn't be touched.

It was the letters that interested her most. By the end of the first week she had sorted them into chronological order, using the postmarks on the front of the envelopes as a guide, arranging them in piles on the carpet. They carried three definite sets of handwriting: Ben's, Hannah's and someone called Jack. Jack's letters were distinguishable by his signature on the back. They made only a small bundle, and the postmarks were dated much later than the others, so Callie put them aside and retied them with blue ribbon. That left Hannah's and Ben's correspondence, and she deliberated over which batch to tackle first.

Ben's first letter addressed to Hannah bore a South Australian postmark and return address: Mitcham Camp, near Adelaide. The date was the first week of May, 1916. Curious, she drew out the pages. He wrote:

Dear Hannah,
Training is in place for the whole company while the remainder of the stores and equipment are collected. We have horses at last — not from the remount depot but hacks to train on while we're here, which is a sight worth seeing because they're not fully broken and at the moment we're getting more practice at buckjumping than horsemanship.

Word's out that we'll be gone before the end of the month. Most of the stores are in — tool carts, pontoons (which have just arrived from the Cockatoo Docks in Sydney), and other sundry items, though we've yet to get the Weldon trestles, bridging wagons and water cart . . .

Callie skimmed the remainder of the letter. Several pages in length, it contained information along the same vein, details of the company's technical stores and training, amusing anecdotes of the men. Not until the last line did Ben give vent to any personal feelings. *I miss the soft touch of you*, he had scrawled, before signing his name.

Callie re-read the words, pondering over the meaning. *I miss the soft touch of you.* Were Hannah and Ben lovers? Before he left, had they shared that most private and intimate of unions, bonding themselves to each other the only way time and space had allowed? She shook her head, not knowing, and pulled the next envelope forward.

It contained a postcard that bore a photograph of a ship and carried the title H.M.A.T. A29 s.s. *Suevic*. The writing on the back of the card was cramped and it took several minutes to decipher the words.

My dearest Hannah
We embarked at Outer Harbour on the 31st, along with the 11th Field Ambulance. The blokes are a good bunch and we mostly seem to get along all right. There is a bit of ribbing between the ranks and a few practical jokers on board, too. We had a rough passage through the Great Australian Bight — the worst few days of my life, I think, with seasickness laying low all but the hardiest. At Fremantle the 44th Battalion embarked also, making the living conditions much more crowded. Drill still goes on — two hours per day,
missing you terribly,
love
Ben.
P.S. What do you think of the tub?

Callie turned the postcard over and stared again at the photograph of the ship. The image faced her, not exactly black and white, but varying shades of grainy grey: the bulk of the steel was etched dark against the chop of the waves, three of the funnels — she could count four in total — spewing angry plumes of smoke that trailed away until they faded into the lighter tone of the sky. A white spray enveloped the front of the hull as the vessel made the descent into a windswept trough of water, listing slightly to one side.

Staring at the photograph, she had the oddest sensation of being pulled back through time, of being bodily planted on the deck of that ship as it plowed its way across the sea, decades before. For a brief moment she imagined the taste of salt on her lips, heard the thud of the waves and saw the dark hulking shapes of the men as they moved like ghosts around the deck. Silent ghosts with bleached, fleshless faces, as grey and ethereal as the sky above. A pale haziness shrouded the day, either mist or salt spray, though which Callie wasn't sure. It settled around her, fashioning an eerie veil of white. And over it all, the rotten stench of death, or the imagined threat of it, permeated the air, whirling and pressing its foulness into her nose, her face, until she almost gagged with the smell of it.

'Callie, are you home?'

She started at the voice and the sound of the front door closing, blinked and stared down at the postcard in her shaking hand. s.s. *Suevic*. Silly, she admonished herself as she laid it on the study desk. It wasn't June 1916, but a sunny October day over eighty years later, and the images were merely a product of her overactive writer's imagination. Despite that realisation, and the warmth of the day, her body gave an involuntary shiver.

'Callie?'

The voice was coming closer, more insistent. Stuart, she realised, home early from work. She shook her head, pressing the images into some distant place, bringing herself back to the present.

'Oh, Cal, there you are.' He was bending down beside her, his eyes carrying an expression of excitement, like a child's. 'Do you think you could manage a few days off? A two-day conference is scheduled and there's been a last-minute hitch. The boss can't get away, so he wants me to go instead.'

She stared at him, bewildered. 'I ... I don't know. Where is it?'

'A few hours up the coast. Resort. Five star. All expenses paid. We'd be crazy to pass up the offer. We can drive up tomorrow. I'll be busy on Thursday and Friday with the conference, but I thought we could stay on for the weekend, spend a bit of time together.'

Callie nodded, mentally rearranging her own schedule. There was no pressing work, nothing that couldn't wait. Besides, it would be nice to get away, even for a few days.

'Sure', she said, awarding him a kiss on the cheek. 'Now, if you'll excuse me, I'll just go and pack.'

'Stuart and Callie can't come to the phone right now. If you'd like to leave your name and number, we'll get back to you ...'

Michael weighed the telephone receiver in his hand, listening to the words that came from its interior. He had been trying to contact Callie for two days, leaving messages which had, so far, been unanswered. And now, on Friday afternoon, with the weekend looming, he despaired of finding her at home.

Wearily he pressed the receiver back onto the handset and flicked through the sheaf of photographs that lay on the desk before him, but his mind wasn't on the task. He needed to talk to her, anxious to share the discoveries he had already made from the scribbled notes in Ben's diary.

Gaby he had already told, but she was non-committal and preoccupied with other things. 'That's great, Dad,' Timmy had said; however, Michael knew the details meant nothing to the boy. He felt, coupled with the excitement, an odd sense of deflation, as though he were the only person who was interested. Perhaps Freya had been right when she had said it all belonged in the past. But Callie, he knew, would have wanted to know, if only she would pick up the god-damned phone.

Angrily he stared at the offending instrument and, as though on cue, it emitted a shrill ring. 'Paterson here,' he said tersely, bringing the handset quickly to his ear.

'Hi, Dad!'

It was Timmy. Michael felt himself relax, the tension running out of him like a fast-flowing stream. His son usually had that effect on him, like a grounding of sorts, imparting a sense of perspective.

'Hi, yourself. What are you doing? Shouldn't you be in school?'

'Aw, come on, Dad!' came the amused indignant reply. 'It's almost six o'clock. School finished ages ago.'

Surprised, Michael swivelled in his chair and glanced out the window. In his airconditioned fluorescent-lit office, he hadn't realised the time. The sun had almost disappeared over the western hills, casting long purple shadows over the surrounding landscape. Roofs of houses were darkened blurs. Lights had begun to shine through uncurtained windows, flashing like tiny fireflies in the distance. Wearily he rubbed his hand across his eyes.

'Yeah. Must've forgotten the time. Now, to what do I owe the honour of this call?'

'I've got a project at school and Mum said to ring you.'

Michael stretched back in the chair, crossing his long legs at the ankles. 'That right? What do you need to know?'

Timmy's voice held a tremor of excitement. 'It's a project on gen-e-alogy. Do you know what that means?'

'Sure. Finding out about your ancestors, right?'

'Yep,' replied Timmy importantly. 'Mum told me all about her family. Now I need to know about yours.'

'Well, I'll tell you all I know, but it's not much. Your Grandpa Paterson's name was James and he was born in Brisbane. Grandma was known as Pauline Long, until she married Grandpa in 1953. Grandma died back in 1990. Grandpa died two years ago.'

Michael could hear the studied clicking of Timmy's tongue as he transcribed the information. 'What about Grandpa and Grandma's parents?' he asked at last. 'Our teacher says we're supposed to go back four generations. And we've got to try and get photographs as well.'

Michael tapped his finger against his lips, thinking. His mother's lineage was easy. The Longs had been a large family, involved in city businesses for generations. His sister, Anne, had several large scrapbooks filled with obituary notices and the like. They would surely yield a wealth of information. Of his father's family, though, he knew little.

'Grandpa's parents died when I was very young and I scarcely remember them. Look, what if I ring Aunty Anne? She has all the family stuff. Photos, newspaper cuttings. Perhaps we could go over and see her this weekend.'

'Yeah, Dad. That'd be great. I'm coming over tomorrow, remember? When will you pick me up?'

Michael named a time and said goodbye to his son. He replaced the phone, then picked it up again, dialling his sister's number. When she answered, her voice sounded frazzled.

'Hi, sis. What's up?'

'Oh, you know, the usual. The baby's teething and Tony had to go out of town for a few days. My body's just rebelling against a ration of what seems like three hours sleep each night.'

'Seems like I remember that only too well,' grinned Michael. 'Anyway, thought Tim and I might pop over on the weekend, if that's all right.'

'I'll be in a sleep-induced coma by then,' warned Anne darkly, then laughed. 'You're welcome anytime, you know that. Come for lunch on Sunday. Tony will be back and I haven't seen Tim in a while. I'll rustle up something interesting.'

They made small talk for a few minutes, then Michael replaced the phone in the cradle. He hadn't seen Anne for several weeks and it would be a good opportunity to catch up, see the baby again. Perhaps he would take his camera, shoot a few rolls of film. Sunday lunch would be perfect, he thought, making a mental note to stop by the liquor shop on his way home. A couple of bottles of chablis would ease his sister's fractured mood.

The conference had finished the previous day. While Callie had scarcely seen Stuart since their arrival three days previously, she had easily filled her hours reading, wandering about the mangrove-lined creek that bordered the southern end of the resort and lazing in the shallow water at the edge of the sand.

There had been corporate dinners organised for both previous evenings, to which she had not been invited, though she was happy enough to order room service and eat in front of the television. However, it was Stuart's noisy arrival back at the room in the early hours of the mornings, lurching against the furniture, his hair and clothes reeking of cigarette smoke and alcohol, that disturbed her.

And now, on Saturday morning, with the whole of the weekend looming temptingly ahead, he had been morose and silent, earlier sitting with his nose buried in a newspaper. She had tried to talk to him, to cajole him out of whatever mood he'd found himself in, but he was non-committal, barely acknowledging her existence.

The resort was a collection of modern low-set buildings sprawled across the hillside and overlooking a vast palm-fringed pool. Now, mid-morning, Callie lay on the deckchair, a sarong wrapped over her swimsuit and a book lying unopened on her lap.

Summer was coming and she could feel the growing heat from the sun. Under the layer of protective sunscreen, her skin absorbed it, warming her in turn. Beside her on the grass, Stuart slept, face-down, his skin already a dull shade of pink. She watched his back, how it rose and fell, and the monotonous movement suddenly annoyed her. Any more exposure and he would be complaining of sunburn for the remainder of the weekend, spoiling everything entirely.

Callie leant over and shook his shoulder. 'You'd better cover up or go inside. You're burnt.'

Stuart gave a groan in reply and rolled onto his back, shielding his eyes with his forearm. 'Don't fuss, for Christ's sake. I'm a big boy, remember?'

'Okay, have it your way. I'm going for a walk.'

Shrugging Stuart's mood aside, Callie swung her legs from the deckchair and headed towards the beach. It was almost low tide, the receding water leaving extensive sand flats in its wake. Beyond lay the ocean, the water mirroring the blueness of the sky till they joined and became one, miles distant, in a haze that hid the actual curving line of the horizon from view. A flock of gulls hovered over the waves further out, diving erratically into their dark depths. Several children paddled at the water's edge, stooping now and then to retrieve exposed shells.

She sat on the dry sand near the high tide mark, letting the grains slide through her fingers, gritty particles of weathered rock, shells and dead animal life that moved like silk against her skin. Sitting there, with the sun on her face and the wind pressing against her hair, she watched the ebb and flow of the water as the hours passed. The repetitive flow of the waves, moving in sets towards the shore, lulled her into a reflective mood.

On one hand, life seemed deceptively simple, yet her mind was pulsing with questions to which she had no answers. What was bothering Stuart? He had been so insistent that she come away with him, yet here he was, almost ignoring her. Two years they had been together, and while it was mostly fun at first, lately his moods had been impossible, running hot and cold. He was sullen and irritable, as though sometimes he could scarcely tolerate her presence. Was he bored with her? Perhaps their relationship had run its course? She wanted — no, needed — to discuss these things with him, but he was so uncommunicative at present, so prone to unexpected outbursts, that she was loathe to even raise the subject for fear of another argument.

There seemed no easy solution. With a sigh Callie scrambled to her feet and made her way back to the room. Skirting the main pathways, she came across the lawns and the deck, through the heavy glass sliding door into the living room. Stuart was lying on the lounge, holding the mobile phone to his right ear.

'Better go,' Callie heard him say as she slid the door open. 'Bye.'

'Hi,' she said, with a forced grin. 'I see you've dragged yourself out of those newspapers and the sun. Who was on the phone?'

'Oh, no-one important,' he answered vaguely, waving one hand towards her. 'No-one you know.' Then, accusingly: 'You didn't come back for lunch. I waited for ages then went down by myself.'

Sunlight streamed across the floor. There was a mellowness to the afternoon, a lazy indolence. Yet Callie couldn't shake the feeling that something was wrong. The sense of it gnawed at her, demanding attention.

Slowly Stuart rose from the lounge and came towards her, wrapping his arms around her shoulders, kneading his fingers against the muscles of her back with sure practised movements. His lips brushed her cheek, and she felt his warm breath.

Callie sensed an unexpected surge of desire. He *was* an attractive man, she considered reflectively. And, despite the seemingly increasing bouts of arguments and moodiness, a satisfying sexual relationship was something they still enjoyed.

'I'm going to have a shower. Want to come?' Moving beyond his grasp, she stepped out of her swimming costume, bending down to pick it up and sling it across the chair. A spray of sand followed the arc of her hand, spilling across the grey slate floor, grains catching the sunlight for a moment, tumbling like minuscule prisms through the air.

Stuart watched her nakedness with an indulgent, appraising smile, saying nothing.

'Come on,' she added invitingly.

She was applying the conditioner to her hair when Stuart stepped into the shower cubicle beside her. Soaping his hands, he massaged his fingers across her back and her breasts, kneading at her skin with a skill born of experience. For a moment she leaned back against him, the soap slippery between them, and sensed his own arousal.

Their lovemaking had been satisfactory, Callie decided, as she lay on her elbow watching Stuart while he slept, but not earthshattering. He had seemed preoccupied, far away, as though other things had cornered the bulk of his attention. Perhaps there were problems at work, things he felt he couldn't discuss with her, whatever the reason? That would explain his moodiness of the last few weeks. When they returned home she would call Jill, who worked in the same office block, and investigate it further.

With that decided, Callie slipped from the bed and, pulling on a bathrobe, went to the tiny kitchenette and made a cup of tea. Taking a few biscuits from an opened packet, she made her way into the lounge room. Though she had promised herself a few days' holiday, at the last minute she had stowed a handful of Ben's letters in the bottom of her suitcase. It's like a drug, she mused, flicking on a table lamp and taking up the pile of correspondence. Yet, knowing so little about him, she was desperate to discover more, as though in unveiling Ben's story, and Hannah's, she was somehow filling a void in her own life.

Now she spread the envelopes on the carpet, moving the tips of her fingers across the yellowing paper. Circles, she thought, tracing the swirls and curls of the looped writing. Circles linking us all through time: Hannah, Ben, herself, and all the other Cordukes who had lived in the house in Brunswick Street. Linking them in some vague, as yet undefinable way.

It was almost dark when Stuart appeared, tousle-haired and yawning, at the doorway. 'God, Callie!' he exclaimed. 'You'll go blind trying to read in this light.'

She hadn't realised it was so late. Carefully she folded the letter she was holding and packed the bundle of envelopes into a plastic carry bag. Stuart stood in the doorway, frowning. 'You're not still into those old things?' he asked irritably.

Callie shrugged and levered herself to her feet. Ignoring his remark, she planted a kiss on his nose. 'Come on, I'm starving. Let's get dressed for dinner.'

She had booked a table at one of the resort restaurants. *La Trattoria* specialised in Italian cuisine, and Callie, who had missed lunch, thought hungrily of steaming plates of pasta. 'What do you think?' she asked, wrinkling her nose in deliberation. 'Spinach and ricotta tortellini or a delicious chicken dish dripping with basil sauce?'

In the end they didn't go, settling later for a club sandwich from room service and a selection of liqueurs from the mini-bar. Stuart, leading her back into the bedroom, had pulled her onto the bed and expertly divested her of the bathrobe.

Afterwards, lying beside him, Callie realised with a start that the sex had been the best they'd had for ages. Trailing her fingers absently over his chest, she wondered momentarily if she had been imagining the whole problem. Stuart's moodiness, his lack of understanding — perhaps she had managed to blow them out of context, inflating them in her own mind to worrying proportions. Maybe the whole episode was her own fault? Sitting in front of the computer while she wrote, day after day, she was becoming more and more reclusive, sometimes hating any interruptions to her work.

The writing, her preoccupation with the letters, the sudden and unexpected friendship with Michael: Stuart was involved in none of these. But she *had* offered to include him, she reminded herself hastily, though circumstances had dictated otherwise. Things will change when we're home, she promised. I'll make a bigger effort to involve him, and we'll start spending more time together, too.

CHAPTER 13

To Hannah, it felt strange going back to the Wickham Terrace flat on that following overcast June Sunday. Low clouds scudded above the treetops. An icy breeze whipped the surface of the river into choppy waves. As the *Hetherington* ground to a noisy halt at the Alice Street wharf, she half expected to see Ben pacing the boards, as he had been every other Sunday for the past two months. But the landing was empty except for two boys dangling fishing lines over the edge, and an old man walking with the aid of a cane.

David had written to ask Hannah to meet him at the flat, to help clear Tom's belongings which would be taken back to the house in Brunswick Street. Though her brother's train was not expected into the city until two o'clock, Hannah deliberately arrived early at the flat, drawn by some compulsive need to spend time there alone and undisturbed.

As she walked those last few city blocks, every well-known twist and turn of the road seemed filled with memories, linking her with that other Sunday when she had last been here with Ben. Was it only three weeks ago? Up the front steps and through the entry she went, along the hallway that smelt of cabbage and musty reminders of other people's lives. She could almost see Ben looking at her, puzzled, could almost hear him saying: 'Where are we going?' And herself, dancing ahead, fumbling in her pocket for the key as she went.

Inside, the darkness was depressing and, despite the clutter of heavy furniture, there was an emptiness about the place that seemed almost palpable. Hannah lit the lamp and prowled around the rooms, touching, pressing her fingers tentatively against familiar objects, as though she were seeing them for the first time. Picking up the box of matches that lay on the bench next to the gas rings, she weighed it in her hand, remembering how the blue flame had spurted into life under Ben's careful guidance. On the bench sat two eggs and a tomato, and the wrapped mouldy remains of a loaf of bread, remnants of their shared meal. Like the last supper, she thought desolately, as she scooped them into a paper bag and ran down the stairs, depositing them in the dustbin at the rear of the yard.

Back inside once more, she was somehow drawn to the alcove bedroom. The bed had been made, the sheets and blankets folded smooth. The pillows were flat and bore no trace of the indentations of their heads. She gathered one to her, holding it against her face as she breathed deeply. Perhaps some scent of him remained, some reminder? But there was nothing. No sign that they had ever been there, no trace at all.

Being in the flat again, seeing the stark emptiness of the rooms and exposing herself to the memories of that shared night, the reality of Ben's leaving finally hit her. It was unexpected and abrupt, bringing with it exquisite pain. He's gone, she thought with such finality, and felt the tears as they massed behind her eyes. Hot tears that stung and rolled noiselessly down her cheeks, soaking into the pillowcase. Tears that had been building inside her for weeks, unable to be shed, but now released by some sudden means.

David arrived an hour later, looking tired and drawn. 'Enid insists that the flat be re-let,' he offered by way of an explanation. 'She says we can't afford the expense of letting it sit here empty. I suppose she's right. It *is* a waste.'

'I suppose so,' agreed Hannah bleakly.

'So I thought I'd clear out the contents straightaway. It could be months before Tom comes back.'

Months, thought Hannah dejectedly, watching as her brother threw open the windows, letting the cool breeze blow the curtains about. Seconds, minutes, hours and days, all rolling into an unspecified number of *months*, maybe *years*, until she saw Ben again.

A succession of impressions swayed through her mind, and she caught her breath. Waking next to Ben in that narrow bed. Ben standing at the stove, removing the pan from the flames. Ben reaching out to her at the station, taking the horseshoe from her hand.

'Are you all right?'

She glanced up to find her brother staring at her, a quizzical expression on his face. He held a cool hand against her cheek, which suddenly felt hot by comparison. 'You look pale. You *are* eating properly?'

'Yes,' muttered Hannah, turning away.

After dutifully enquiring after her sister-in-law, and David bringing her up to date on the activities of the children, there seemed little to talk about. Enid separated them, a barrier to that easy familiarity they had shared as children. The silence between them as they packed the few articles of clothing and kitchen utensils was almost palpable.

'I'm sorry about the ways things have turned out,' said David at last, as they were preparing to leave. 'I wondered ... that is, I had hoped, now Thomas has gone, that you might come home.'

Hannah glanced up and saw the expectant expression on her brother's face, the hesitant smile.

'I think we both know that's impossible.'

'If you both tried, made more of an effort,' he said hopefully.

Hannah shook her head, silently dismissing the idea. She couldn't go back. The house in Brunswick Street belonged to another life, to those days before the war, when Mother and Father were still alive, before Enid's intrusion into their lives.

'I can't,' she replied simply. 'I need to stay here.'

Near the memories, she wanted to say, but couldn't.

It was late when Hannah arrived back at the Kangaroo Point house, almost dark. Needing some company, she searched vainly for Lottie, who was nowhere to be found.

'She went out with Mrs Worthington in the car, hours ago,' offered Mrs Bonham, when Hannah cornered her at last in the kitchen. 'And they didn't say when they'd be back,' she grumbled, taking a roast of beef from the oven and basting it with its own juices. 'Don't even know if they'll be wanting their tea or not.'

Taking a handful of biscuits, Hannah went to the large tubs in the laundry and washed her hair. Then, wrapping her head in a towel, she walked upstairs, surprised to see light spilling onto the hallway carpet from Lottie's bedroom.

'Lottie?'

She poked her head around the door. Lottie lay on her side on the bed, curled into a ball, her arms hooked around her knees, keening softly.

Hannah ran to her side. 'What's wrong? Are you ill? I'll go and fetch Mrs Worthington.'

'No!' Lottie's hand flew out, grabbing hers. Hannah could see she had been crying, and her face was pulled into an odd agonising shape.

'What's wrong?' she asked again, feeling a mounting sense of dread. 'Are you in pain?'

Lottie glanced up, staring at her for one long moment. 'They made me get rid of the baby,' she whispered.

Hannah reached across the bed, placing her hands on Lottie's shoulders and giving her an almost imperceptible shake. 'Baby? What *baby*?'

Lottie's face puckered and Hannah could see the skin of her knuckles whiten as she clutched her knees. 'They held me down and pushed something inside me,' Lottie went on, as though she had not heard. 'It was long and metallic, like a pair of curved scissors. I could feel it, cold like ice. And the pain, such pain. I screamed, although they told me not to. "Shut up," they kept saying. "Just shut up." But I couldn't. Then they put something over my mouth and I don't remember what happened next.'

Lottie's voice had dropped to a whisper, barely audible. Hannah eased herself onto the side of the bed and took her friend's hand, pressing it against her cheek. But Lottie was arching herself back, pulling her arm away, a wild vacant look on her face. Her words came with a rush, garbled. 'It was Maurice's, you know. When I told him, he said he didn't want anything more to do with me. Not that I wanted to have a baby to that lying no-good ...'

Exhausted, she sank back against the pillow, her face pale as the sheets.

'Why didn't you tell me?' murmured Hannah, shocked. 'Perhaps we might have found some other way, something other than this.'

Lottie grimaced, her face screwing into an expression of agony. 'Believe me,' she groaned, 'if there had been any other way, I would have taken it. But *they* wouldn't have let me stay here, and I couldn't go back home with some bloke's bastard kid inside me, so I had no choice but to get rid of it.'

'But it was your child, too, not just Maurice's!' Hannah turned her head towards the wall, hoping that Lottie would not see her tears. 'Oh, God,' she whispered. 'What a mess.'

Lottie's voice, when it came, was cold. Unemotional. Detached. 'I told myself that it wasn't really a baby, just a lump of flesh. Anyway, I did what I had to. "Be a good girl and do as you're told, Lottie," said Mrs Worthington. "Don't make a fuss over such a small, silly thing." She gave me five pounds and said I could have a week off work.'

She stopped suddenly, her forehead creased with a frown. 'You won't tell anyone, will you, Hannah? It's against the law, you know. Mrs Worthington said that if anything happened, I was to say I caused the miscarriage myself.'

'It wasn't just a lump of flesh!' replied Hannah hotly. 'It was your child, a living thing. And Maurice had a responsibility to you, whether he wanted to or not.'

Suddenly Lottie looked up at Hannah, tears streaking her pale face. 'You're wondering why, aren't you? Why I'd even let that creep near me.'

'Sshh,' Hannah soothed, lifting the strands of hair from Lottie's damp face. 'Try and sleep. Perhaps you'll feel better in the morning.'

'No! I *want* you to know. So that if anything happens to me —'

'Nothing is going to happen to you!' broke in Hannah.

Lottie gave a self-deprecating grimace. 'It was the money. Remember how I told you I was saving for Frank's headstone? Well, with Maurice's *contributions*, I almost had enough.'

'Maurice paid you to . . . ?'

Lottie began to cry again, long gulping sobs that racked her body. 'Don't say it,' she gasped. 'I'm nothing better than a prostitute. How could I take money from a warmonger and use it for something so sacred as my brother's headstone? Christ, Hannah. I've ruined it all.'

Later, Lottie started to bleed, bright blood that soaked her bedclothes and nightgown. 'I'm scared,' she moaned. 'It hurts so much.'

Hannah sat with her until the early hours of the morning, holding Lottie's shaking body against her chest until the mutilated remains of Maurice's child came away in a bloodied pulpy mass. Gently she washed Lottie and combed her hair, changed the bed linen and helped her into a fresh nightgown. Through all this, there was no sign of Mrs Worthington.

As the first pale light of dawn lightened the sky, Hannah went to her room. 'They don't care! They just don't care!' she muttered to herself as she lay on the bed, unable to sleep. She felt tired, so tired. Ben's leaving. Tom's, too. The loss of Lottie's baby. She felt drained of emotion, almost incapable of caring. Inside her, in a place where her heart might have been, was an emptiness she was certain could never be filled.

Lottie was pale and weak for days after, confined to her bed. Hannah brought her bowls of clear broth and news of the downstairs ward. Mrs Worthington remained in her office, tight-lipped and stern-faced. The announcement of Maurice's forthcoming marriage appeared in the city newspapers.

'Miss Cynthia Frogmeyer,' announced Lottie scathingly, on reading the news. 'Well, I'm sure she's welcome to him.'

Hannah spent her spare time painting. David had forwarded her satchel of watercolours, brushes and paper, and there seemed some therapeutic value in spreading and merging the colours, forming shapes. In the end, there were two she was quite proud of. One was of the front of the house in Brunswick

Street, the other of the wattles in the bottom garden. One day, having saved a little of her pay, she went into the city and had them framed, then hung them on the wall of her bedroom. *Hannah Corduke, 1916*, she wrote on the backing boards in bold letters. They were hers. She had painted them and they reminded her of a house which was no longer home.

Ben enjoyed being on the *Suevic*. Some days the sea was smooth and glassy, stretching away as far as the eye could see, the sun reflected like a giant mirror against its shimmering surface. At other times the water came rearing up like a wild beast, unpredictable, dark and green and laced with foam, and the view was nothing more than the next swamping set of waves. He liked standing on the deck as the ship rose and fell, one minute riding high, the next dipping and plunging into a trough.

They were steaming west across the Indian Ocean into a northern summer, one vessel in a large convoy. From the deck, he caught glimpses of the other ships from time to time, great hulking shapes that seemed to shadow them, spewing dark ribbons of smoke from their funnels. Ships carrying men like himself, bound initially for England, then God-only-knew-where.

Mostly the weather was splendid and they spent hours lying on the decks, reading, yarning and playing cards. Apart from the two hours of rifle and bayonet drill each day, the war, or the threat of it, seemed like a distant menace.

Another round of vaccinations began and the first delivery of mail arrived, courtesy of a White Star boat that had caught up with the convoy several days out to sea. There was a letter from Hannah, which Ben stowed in his pocket till later, until he found a quiet place to open it and savour every word, every sweet phrase she had written. The letters were like soothing balm, his only contact with his former life. Greedily he absorbed them, the small details of Hannah's days, the total normalcy of her existence.

> My darling Ben,
> Lottie is much better and is up and around again. Thankfully that cad, Maurice, has been nowhere in sight. My days go on as usual. In my spare time I have been painting. Just a few watercolours, and I suspect they are very amateurish; however, the task keeps me occupied during my spare time. Otherwise I just find myself missing you. I love you. Come home to me soon,
> all my love,
> Hannah.

He read and re-read the words, taking the letter from his pocket at odd hours. What would she be doing now? he wondered, mentally calculating the time back home. Working in the downstairs ward? Sleeping? Hurrying through the bustling city on some errand for the convalescing men?

He liked to picture her in the flat, as she had been that last morning, all sleepy and soft, her dark hair cascading in waves across the pillow. Pictured her lips moving, mumbling a good morning, sensual. Most of all, he remembered the touch of her, warm and giving, as she had taken him to her that one last time, sealing forever that hauntingly beautiful memory of her in his mind.

The *Suevic* had sprung a small leak. They berthed at Durban, the only natural harbour within 800 miles, until the services of a diver could be obtained for repairs.

The town is very clean and tidy and there are trees and gardens everywhere, Ben wrote to Hannah later. *Everyone travels in rickshaws. They are pulled by big Zulu men who colour their bodies with daubs of bright paint and wear amazing headdresses made from bullocks' horns and ostrich feathers. When Tom offered money for our fare back to the docks, they frisked about like ponies ...*

The further north, and west, they travelled, the more oppressive the heat became. It was like a blanket, Ben thought, as he lay in his bunk each night, the weight of it pressing down on him. At Cape Town the troops were treated to a trip to Cable Mountain, thanks to the Red Cross ladies. A load of coal was taken on at Cape Verde Island; however, the yellow flag was showing and no shore leave was granted, though the troops had a route march through town and a sports meeting.

They anchored for several days in the calm waters off Madeira Island. Viewed from the moorings, the land appeared as one solid mass of green vegetation. During the day, natives brought their rowboats alongside, offering fruit for sale. Tom lowered a bucket and received, for the princely sum of two shillings, a good supply of bananas and grapes. When the *Suevic* steamed out of the harbour, its departure heralded by a piercing blast on the ship's siren, the native boats followed until they were several miles offshore, the vessels bobbing and dancing on the swell.

They were sailing off the coast of Morocco, Ben noted from the worn atlas he carried in his belongings. Marrakech. Casablanca. Strange-sounding names that belonged to cities beyond the eastern horizon. After passing Cape St. Vincent on the south-west tip of Spain, the convoy was met by two British naval destroyers. The remainder of the journey was through the German submarine zone, and the pontoons were brought up onto the top deck for use as emergency lifeboats.

Days passed in a haze of quiet urgency. Eat, sleep, drill, with the thought of the approaching war hanging over them like a grey mist. Some of the chaps, Tom included, were full of bravado.

'We'll show bloody Fritz —' said Spud, waving his rifle, which he was in the process of cleaning, in the direction of the unseen mainland.

'And have them running back where they came from, quick smart,' interjected Tom.

They were either brave words, thought Ben, as he turned away, a frown creasing his forehead, or incredibly foolish. And fear had a strange way of raising itself. Instead, he spent hours scanning the waves, watching for some sign. Of what? he wondered, not knowing. That was the trouble with war. You weren't sure what to expect.

The first sight of England was through a salt haze. As they came closer to the coast, everything looked green, as though freshly washed and prepared for their arrival. They steamed past villages perched precariously along cliff tops. Ben borrowed a pair of binoculars, staring hard at distant red-roofed cottages with sunlight dancing off their whitewashed walls. From his vantage point aboard the boat, they seemed far away, minuscule, like children's toys. He could almost picture the clotheslines filled with washing that snapped and strained in the breeze, children running along the cliff tops through copper-coloured grass, dogs leaping and bounding at their heels, bright paper kites flying, soaring upwards on the wind.

It was that sort of day. Perfect. Too perfect, in fact, like the scene on a picture postcard he might send to Hannah. And he had to remind himself that across the channel a war raged, though it seemed that nothing had touched this land.

The *Suevic* docked at Plymouth to the strains of a local band playing 'Land of Hope and Glory'. It was summer, yet a cold wind whipped across the water, chilling the men as they waited on the wharf for the transport to arrive. Standing there, watching as the gulls swooped low across the waves, Ben had the strangest sensation that he was still aboard the ship, as though the ground were rolling and pitching beneath his feet.

At last, two hours later, after finding what he termed his 'land legs' again, they were entrained for Amesbury. The train stopped only at Exeter, where a group of local women had set up a stall on the platform, serving cups of coffee and sweet buns. As the carriages pulled out, Ben caught passing glimpses of the village, the narrow winding streets, old-fashioned shops and houses with thatched roofs.

From Amesbury, the company marched the two miles to the Lark Hill camp on the Salisbury Plains, along with the 3rd Australian Division. The countryside was green, and Ben was surprised to see the land fenced into large well-kept grazing paddocks. Fields of wheat waved and shimmered in the breeze, and the air was fresh with the ripeness of summer. In the distance rose the dark monolithic shapes of Stonehenge, outlined from time to time against the pale blue sky.

Before training commenced, the company was given four days disembarkation leave.

'So what'll we do?' asked Spud as they stowed their kit bags in the huts.

'Well, I'm not sticking around here if I don't have to,' replied Tom, staring through the open window towards the dismal parade ground.

'I've got distant relatives in Scotland,' mused Jack. 'My Mum said to look them up if I got the chance.'

Spud scratched his head. 'Christ, mate. It'll take you four days just to get up there, the way the trains run around here.'

'So what'll we do?'

'Go to London!' replied Spud and Tom in unison.

And so Ben sat in yet another railway carriage, watching as the outskirts of London slowly came into view. After the wonder of the moving stairs at the railway station, which none of them had ever seen before, their first stop was the Australian

Headquarters in Horseferry Road to collect passes and money. On enquiry, Ben was pointed in the direction of affordable accommodation, and they managed to obtain two double rooms in a cheap boarding house only a few blocks distant.

The city was alive with people pressing past each other like an incoming tide. Footpaths were flowing with men wearing khaki and slouch hats bearing rising sun badges, the trademark of the Australian soldiers. There were female porters at the railway stations and female conductors on the buses, and Ben thought he had never seen so many women working industriously at jobs which had previously belonged only to men.

There was plenty to see: St Paul's Cathedral, Big Ben, the British Museum, Madame Tussard's Wax Works. Starring Oscar Asche, the musical 'Chu Chin Chow' was playing at His Majesty's Theatre. Groups of Australian soldiers, bored by the city, congregated around Nelson's Column, watching the crowds as they passed, streaming from the theatres and pubs.

On the second evening, Ben and Tom were having dinner in a restaurant when a woman sauntered past their table. She was tall and well dressed, and wore bright red lipstick. Her hips swayed as she walked. 'Do you mind if I sit down?' she asked, as she paused and smiled at Ben.

Tom scrambled to his feet and offered his own chair, before taking another from the next unused table. The woman ordered a bottle of champagne and passed around the contents of a packet of cigarettes. Capstans, Ben noted, as Tom took one and held a match towards the woman. She drew heavily on the cigarette and the tip glowed red. Crossing her legs, she leaned provocatively back in the chair and blew a cloud of smoke towards him.

The waiter returned with the champagne. 'Come on, Tom,' Ben muttered, 'we've got to get going.'

'But we haven't ordered yet,' spluttered Tom.

Ben gave him a kick under the table. He felt his foot make contact with Tom's shin, and saw him jerk back with pain. 'We have to be back in camp.'

The woman took another long pull on the cigarette. Her mouth twisted into a bemused smile as Ben scraped his chair back and stumbled to his feet, Tom following with an expression of disbelief on his face.

'What's wrong? What'd you go and do that for?'

'She's a prostitute,' hissed Ben.

He watched as Tom swivelled around for another look, but the woman was already chatting to a group of soldiers who had been sitting at an adjoining table, as though she had forgotten them already.

Work had barely started at Lark Hill when the Company was sent to Brightlingsea, in Essex, for pontoon training at the Royal Engineers depot. The train journey was slow, mostly at night, with frequent unexplained stops. At one stage Ben woke to a darkened stationary carriage. He sat, trying to collect his bearings. Beside him Tom slept, his head lolling against Ben's shoulder. Spud lay stretched out across the two seats opposite, while Jack was a dark hump on the floor.

It was a full moon, and through the window he could see a silver sheen stretching across the fields, merging into darkness where a small wood followed the incline of the surrounding hill. His breath formed a vapour on the glass. Leaning his face against it, feeling the coolness against his cheek, he thought of Hannah. A letter had arrived only yesterday, though it had been posted eight weeks before. *I am well*, she had written, *and I miss you*. His mind lingered on the words, remembering her neat copperplate handwriting.

Without warning, the carriage jerked forward with a hiss of escaping steam. On the opposite seat, Spud gave a groan and curled his legs, rolling himself into a tight ball. Outside, a shower of sparks sprayed out like tiny fireflies, cascading down the embankment. Trees and houses were dark shapes rolling by, materialising for a moment out of the night.

Past the window, the sky glowed silver, the colour of dark metal, and Ben was reminded suddenly of the horseshoe. Rummaging in his coat pocket, he brought it forward, turning it this way and that, the faint light catching on the etched words.

'Hannah,' he whispered, tracing a finger across the bumps and ridges, trying to remember her face.

Slowly the wheels ticked over the track, gaining momentum, pressing them onwards into the night. *I miss you, I miss you*, they seemed to say, over and over, like a never-ending prayer.

The train bore them east, through London, then Chelmsford. At Brightlingsea there was no military accommodation available and the men were billeted in houses within the town. They stayed for two months, the visit extended not only to take in the expected pontoon training, but to include a comprehensive Royal Engineers' course.

On his days off, Ben borrowed a bicycle from his billet and explored the countryside. He enjoyed the feel of the wind in his hair, the sun on his face, the solitude. Out on the narrow winding lanes, peddling hard, his face bowed against the wind, he could have been the only man within miles. And the war might just as well have been a million miles away.

CHAPTER 14

It seemed to Hannah that the city was filled almost solely with women. Women serving behind shop counters. Women staffing street-corner newspaper stands or collecting tickets at railway station gates. Even the greengrocer's cart was manned by two young girls who seemed scarcely old enough to have left school, daughters of the owner who had enlisted several months previously. The men who remained were older mostly, kept at home by age or some physical deformity. The younger chaps still strolling the city streets were regarded as 'shirkers'. Like Maurice, Hannah thought, remembering his callous treatment of Lottie.

Eat, sleep, work. Thinking about Ben, wondering what he was doing, each minute seemed drawn out, stretching into infinity. Yet the days moved slowly on, rolling into one another. Hannah's job continued as before. Cleaning, sweeping, shopping. Repetitious menial tasks that somehow filled her hours and left time for little else.

Exhausted beyond reason, she crawled into bed each night. Sometimes Lottie sat on the end of the quilt as before, chattering away about inconsequential things as she tugged the brush through her long hair. But Hannah sensed a sadness about her these days, a quiet despondency. She seldom smiled, and her face was pale. Even the friendly flirting and chit-chat with the downstairs patients had lessened.

'Are you all right?' Hannah asked one evening, laying a hand on her friend's arm. Besides Clare Worthington and her caddish son, she was the only person who knew Lottie's secret.

'I'm fine, really,' Lottie shrugged off Hannah's concern. 'It was nothing, and best forgotten.'

Yet it seemed Lottie couldn't forget.

In the downstairs ward, Hannah had established a hesitant affinity with the men. The sight of prostheses and crutches, of empty sleeves or knotted trouser legs, of urinals and oxygen masks no longer distressed her as before. She had become hardened, she supposed, to the sight of their suffering, their armless or legless existences. Less vulnerable now, it was as though a wall had come down, closing off her own feelings. The pain of Ben's absence filled her instead, blotting out all else. There was no more room in her heart to care.

She counted the weeks since his departure, crossing the days off the small calender hanging on her bedroom wall. One month, two. Suddenly it was August, and he had been gone for over three months.

Letters arrived sporadically. Sometimes there would be none for a week or more, then two or three would be delivered on the same day, jerking her heart into a mad erratic pounding as she tore the envelopes open, devouring the contents.

He was still in England, training. The letters were cheerful and full of news, detailing the route marches, the shortages and sports meetings.

You should see it here, he wrote. *The countryside is so green, green like emeralds. And as I look out over the water, it's hard to imagine there's a war going on somewhere beyond my line of vision ...*

Tom always sent his love, generally adding a few lines to the bottom of Ben's. At least, Hannah considered gratefully, they were far removed from the fighting in Europe which, according to the newspapers, seemed to be getting worse daily.

Exhibition Day, a public holiday to mark the official opening of the National Association's Exhibition at the showground, approached. Miraculously, Mrs Worthington gave both Hannah and Lottie the day off. 'Be back in time for tea, though,' she cautioned sternly. 'And I'll expect you to make up the extra hours on the weekend.'

Hannah didn't care. It was a chance to escape.

They caught a tram from the city and joined the throng of people surging through the gates. The day was fine with a light breeze blowing. Lottie brushed a hand through her hair, pulling back the escaping wisps. 'Oh, God!' she exclaimed. 'Look at all this! Normal lives going on!'

In the main pavilion there were exhibits of livestock and farm produce, a display of the latest imported machinery, as well as samples of schoolwork and fine art. Hannah and Lottie looked closely at the embroidery and knitting, exclaiming over the tiny exquisitely formed stitches. Hannah paused for a few minutes in front of the watercolour section, thinking she should have entered her painting of the house in Brunswick Street. In the end, Lottie pulled her away, towards the huge doors and daylight outside.

There were trotting and jumping events in the main ring. Fine clouds of dust rose from the animals' hooves, layering a film of white across the scene. The sight of the horses brought a momentary sadness. A sudden image of Ben rose in her mind, and she pictured him in the barn on that long-ago day when war had been declared, bent low, hammering a shoe to an upended hoof, the odour of singed metal hanging in the air. Hannah sighed, remembering. Almost two years had passed. So much had happened since then.

At the far end of the grounds, a wood-chopping competition was underway. Hannah could hear the dull thud of axes and the cheering of onlookers. Meanwhile, Lottie tugged her towards the noise of the sideshow alley. 'Come on,' she urged. 'If we don't get a hurry on, it'll be time to go home and we won't have seen everything.'

Children ran past, clutching balloons. Spielers called from the front of tents, their voices interspersed with the sound of carousel music. In the distance came the strident tones of a brass band. Oom-pa-pa. Oom-pa-pa.

There was so much to see. Outside one tent stood a man shouting the talents of the champion lady boxer who waited beyond the canvas. 'Roll up! Roll up! For your entertainment, ladies and gentlemen, all the way from the Continent . . .'

The words were lost to Hannah as the crowd bowled her along.

There was every ride imaginable. Merry-go-rounds and swinging boats, whirligigs and a little locomotive that pulled tiny carriages around an

223

equally tiny track. The skeletal framework of a Ferris wheel revolved against an impossibly blue sky.

Further along stood an ornate Dutch street organ with a brightly painted exterior, complete with small mechanical figures that moved and swung jerkily to the beat of the music. There was a coconut shy and a stall selling show bags. A phonograph display sent out a stream of thin scratchy music, barely heard above the other cacophony of sounds, beside which stood an exhibition of the latest photographic equipment, dark box-like cameras and tripods and bottles of chemicals.

Under one lean-to awning, an old woman sat at a table, an array of cards fanned across its surface. 'Come and have your fortune told, luvvie,' she called to the girls. Hannah shook her head and moved on. She didn't want to know. In her own mind, the war would soon be over and Ben would be back. Any other alternative was unthinkable.

Delicious smells wafted from bright caravans, reminding Hannah that it was lunchtime. Lottie stopped and bought a bread roll filled with roast meat and gravy, and Hannah laughed to see the thick brown sauce as it ran through her friend's fingers. Try as she might, she couldn't conjure a feeling of hunger. A queasy feeling had settled in her stomach after breakfast, becoming more pronounced as the day wore on. Several times, as the crowd pressed around her, she had fought back a momentary dizziness, a groggy faintness that passed as quickly as it had come. Her eyes stung and a headache threatened, and she longed for a shady patch of grass on which to sit.

'Are you all right?' asked Lottie. 'Your face has gone a funny shade of white.'

Hannah passed a hand across her forehead. 'I'm fine,' she assured her friend. 'Just the heat, I expect.'

Lottie, wiping the last of the gravy from her hand with a clean handkerchief, propelled Hannah towards the far end of the alley where a crowd had gathered. Outside the tent were posters depicting an armless child. A dark-haired man beckoned them forward. 'Come and see,' he urged, touching a fleshy hand to Hannah's sleeve. She pulled back, startled, but he seemed not to notice. 'The eighth wonder of the world. This child writes, paints and eats with its toes.'

Lottie stood, transfixed, staring at the poster and the fleshy stumps that protruded from the shoulders. 'You know,' she began above the hubbub, a look of excitement on her face as she wiggled her finger in the direction of the poster, 'there's hope for them yet'.

'Who?'

'The men in the downstairs ward, the ones who have lost arms. If this child can do all those things, the men could do the same.'

She pulled Hannah towards the tent. 'Come on. I have to see.'

Inside the canvas surrounds, the air was close and musty. A small wooden stage stood at one end. A young boy, perhaps nine or ten years of age, sat on a stool, a bowl on a low table before him. With deft practised movements, he brought his foot towards his mouth.

It seemed such an unnatural action, the leg bending as an arm might, curving up towards the boy's face. As Hannah crowded forward for a better look, she could see the outline of the spoon held between his toes. At each mouthful, the crowd pointed and sniggered.

'It's a freak!'

'A god-damned bloody monstrous freak!'

A small girl began to whimper. 'Mummy, I want to go home.'

Hannah felt sick inside, a slow mounting nausea followed by a sensation of bile burning in her throat. Clasping a hand across her mouth, she raced for the exit, slapping frantically at the canvas flap in her bid for escape. Blindly she pushed past the startled onlookers, until she squatted, gasping and retching in the dirt at the rear of the tent.

Her eyes streamed as another spasm worked its way up her throat, sending her leaning forward again. There was a pressure on her arm. Lottie's voice, low and insistent, softly accusing. 'You're *not* all right!'

Hannah rose shakily to her feet. She rummaged in her bag for a clean handkerchief, wiped her mouth and blew her nose.

'Better?' asked Lottie, taking her friend's arm.

'I think so.' At least the nausea had subsided.

Lottie eyed her suspiciously. 'You were sick one day last week, too. I saw you in the upstairs bathroom. Whatever's wrong?'

'I don't know.' Hannah shrugged and went to move away. 'Just something going around, I expect. It's nothing. I *would* like to go home though.'

'Hannah!'

Lottie pulled her roughly to a standstill. She could hear the brassy tones of the organ pressing through the throng. The sound seemed separate, disjointed and overly loud. Odours of cooking wafted past, caught on some unseen breeze, bringing back the bilious rumblings in her stomach. The crowd seemed to form and re-form before her, a mass of moving and realigning colour.

Lottie stared, round-eyed, small creases of concern wrinkling her forehead. 'Before Ben went away, did you have sex with him?' she asked, her fingers pressing uncomfortably into Hannah's arm.

Hannah looked away as a slow flush crept across her cheeks. She could feel the warmth and was powerless to stop it. 'Yes,' she whispered, mortified at Lottie's scrutiny.

'Oh, Christ!' whispered Lottie, raising her eyes skywards. Then: 'How long since you've had your monthlies?'

She tried to remember, casting her mind back through those long lonely weeks since Ben's leaving. 'I — I don't know.'

'Think!' commanded Lottie, her fingers pressing harder. 'Last month, the month before? Tell me, Hannah. It's important.'

Wordlessly Hannah shook her head.

'Oh, my God! Did it ever occur to you that you might be *pregnant*?'

The word slapped unexpectedly at her consciousness, causing immediate waves of panic. 'It was just one night,' she said wildly, a slightly hysterical edge to her voice. 'You said I couldn't, the first time. Maurice said . . .'

Lottie shrugged. 'I *know* what Maurice said, and

look what happened to me. I wouldn't believe a thing he told me, ever.'

'That's really comforting,' muttered Hannah, thinking it couldn't possibly be true. Pregnancy wasn't an option. Not now. Not with Ben thousands of miles away.

But something *was* wrong. She'd known, no, sensed it for weeks. Sensed, but not admitted it to herself. The sluggish lethargy, the tender swelling of her breasts.

'You should go and see a doctor,' cautioned Lottie, steering her now towards the main gate and the tram line further along. 'Settle it in your own mind. How long since Ben went away?'

'Nearly four months.' Her own voice sounded wooden, compared to Lottie's authoritative tone.

'If you are, there might be still time to do something about it.'

She slammed to a halt, staring at Lottie, shocked. 'An abortion, you mean?'

'Hannah,' said Lottie patiently. 'Be sensible. Lots of girls do it. How could you possibly bring up a child on your own? Ben's across the other side of the world. What if he doesn't come back?'

Hannah sensed the rage bubbling inside her. Scrape Ben's child from her body? She thought of Lottie lying amongst the blood-stained sheets, the pain, the tears. The unspeakable guilt. She couldn't do that.

'I am *not* pregnant,' she hissed, 'but if I were, there's no way I'd go through with what you did. And as far as Ben's concerned, he *is* coming back and don't you dare say otherwise!'

228

And she stormed off towards the tram, which rumbled slowly towards them down the street, leaving Lottie stunned and speechless at the side of the road.

Back at the Kangaroo Point house, Hannah did some quick calculations. Her last period, she remembered, was the weekend of the final dance, eight days before she and Ben had made love in the flat at Wickham Terrace. Four months earlier. She sat on the edge of her bed, her breath coming in ragged waves. Tentatively she moved a hand across her stomach, thinking: 'This can't possibly be true. I won't let it.'

In the end, she closed her mind to the possibility, refusing also to bow to Lottie's insistence that she see a doctor. If she denied the likelihood of being pregnant, she told herself, then she wouldn't be. It was as simple as that.

At David's insistence she went home for a week the following month. It was mid-September, spring, the season for new life. Swallows darted around the eaves of the Brunswick Street house, building nests. Buds were forming on the trees at the bottom of the garden, new shoots pressing tentatively towards the sun. Down by the creek, the wattles had almost finished flowering, the massed clumps of yellow puff-balls looking threadbare and matted.

In the village, fundraising continued at a brisk pace. Red Cross mornings, Comforts Fund afternoons: it seemed Enid, Lily perched precariously on her hip, was constantly running to one meeting or another.

Davie was at school, his father attending to matters at the bank. Alone, Hannah wandered about the house, hearing her own footfalls echoing through the silent rooms. A sense of panic rose and fluttered in her chest, beating its wings relentlessly. No longer could the truth be denied, if only to herself. She stood naked in front of the bathroom mirror, turning this way and that, touching her fingers to her swollen breasts, caressing the tiny mound that was now her stomach. She hugged her arms to the shape. Tears coursed down her face, and she was unable to stop them.

In the privacy of her room, she repositioned the buttons on her blouses, dresses and skirts, gaining the extra half inch of space she now desperately needed. Thankfully the nausea had subsided and, although she was sleeping poorly at night, her skin was glowing. In the bathroom the image stared back at her from the mirror, emitting an inner radiance. Her dark hair shone, circles of pink now coloured cheeks which had been pale only weeks earlier. Enid, racing between her various charities and meetings, had commented one morning that Hannah appeared to be putting on weight. 'Living in the city seems to suit you,' said David.

She felt disconnected, and there was a sense of unreality. This can't be happening, she told herself, over and over again. It was like a nightmare, a dream gone horribly wrong. Endlessly, she wavered between disbelief and confusion.

In wild, reckless moments she wanted to take her brother aside, wanted to let the terrible secret spill from her mouth, but the words wouldn't come. What would David say if he knew the truth? Hannah imagined Enid's furious reaction, almost hearing the words: *You've betrayed us, brought shame to the family.*

She wouldn't, *couldn't* tell. The secret was hers and she would deal with it in her own way.

Lily had grown, amazingly so, and was no longer a baby but a little girl, blessed with a rosy complexion and blonde ringlets. Only Davie seemed unchanged. After school he spent endless hours at the creek. Hannah watched him as he made his way down through the garden at every available opportunity, glass jar in hand, walking with a curious hop and skip. Only once during that week did she see a sadness in the boy's eyes, the day he showed her a postcard from Tom. 'I miss him, don't you?' he asked, a noticeable tremor creasing his mouth.

'Yes, tiger,' she replied, tousling his hair. 'We all do. But he'll be home before you know it. The war will be over soon, just wait and see.'

Was it Davie she was trying to reassure, she wondered later, or herself?

Back in the city, the usual balls and church socials had long since been abandoned — by now there were not enough men left to warrant such an exercise — and were replaced by fairs and fetes and button days. Mrs Worthington had organised a garden party in the grounds of the Kangaroo Point home, and Hannah's arrival back at the house, on the eve of the big event, barely went noticed amongst the fuss.

Mrs Bonham, helped by Lottie, presided over huge trays of coconut ice and marshmallows, toffee apples, sausage rolls and tiny mince pies in the kitchen. The smell of baking hung in the air.

'Where's Mavis?' Hannah enquired after the scullery maid, of whom there was no sign.

'Don't ask!' snapped Mrs Bonham moodily, slamming another tray of confectionery on the bench and pushing a damp strand of hair from her face with her wrist. 'She upped and left last week without so much as a goodbye and thank you. Ungrateful girl! It's been bedlam around here since, what with all this extra work.'

Although she wasn't due to resume her duties till the following day, Hannah took a spare apron from the peg behind the door, meaning to fasten it around her waist, but Lottie was before her, shaking her head. 'Mrs Worthington said you were to go up to her study the minute you got back.'

Hannah arched her eyebrows, an expression of surprise, as she laid the apron on the bench. 'Why? What's wrong?'

Lottie shrugged and turned away. She seemed unable to meet Hannah's gaze.

'Lottie?' Hannah took one step after her friend's retreating back. 'You haven't . . . you didn't . . .'

'No!' she snapped. 'I didn't say a word. But she's been asking lots of questions.'

'Do you think she knows?'

But Lottie had disappeared into the pantry, purposely closing the door behind her.

With a thumping heart, Hannah walked slowly up the staircase in the direction of her employer's study. Mrs Worthington was sitting at her desk, writing furiously in a leather-bound book. 'Come in,' she replied to Hannah's knock, not pausing to look up.

Hannah waited nervously on the thick rug until Mrs Worthington set the pen back in the holder and raised her head. 'Ah, Hannah,' she said, her face expressionless. 'I was wondering when you would be back.'

As the car bowled along the city streets, Hannah sat on the back seat and wondered where they were headed. Past the occasional horse and buggy they went, through the city centre where crowds thronged the footpaths and trams littered the roadway in mad confusion. Ahead she could see the outline of Mr Bonham's grey hair, and the long shiny bonnet of the car.

Beside her sat Clare Worthington, her face revealing no hint as to their destination. 'There's someone I want you to meet,' was all she had said in the study, less than half an hour earlier.

Where were they going? Who was the mysterious person Mrs Worthington wanted to introduce to Hannah? Why couldn't Clare Worthington just come out and tell her? She hated surprises.

At last the car slowed, finally coming to a halt in a leafy avenue. Mr Bonham opened both doors and the women stepped from the car. The houses that lined the footpath were brick, with imposing steps. From what Hannah could make out, most had brass name plates.

Clare Worthington steered her towards one building, dark brick with a freshly painted front door.

'I — I don't understand,' she stammered. 'Why have you brought me here?'

Clare Worthington's face remained impassive. Silently she steered Hannah up the steps and into a small waiting room, nodding at the woman sitting behind the desk.

The woman rose. 'Is this Hannah?' she asked, gathering up a sheaf of papers.

'Yes,' replied Mrs Worthington.

'This way, please. Doctor's waiting.'

CHAPTER 15

Life had a way of reverting easily to the mundane, thought Callie, as she sifted through the photographs of the previous weekend: Stuart stretched out by the pool; herself, squealing as she waded into the surf, arms held high as though delaying the moment of immersing herself fully in the water; the pair of them, smiling, Stuart's arm slung casually over her shoulder, the scene captured on film by an obliging passer-by.

She studied the last one, lingering over the expression on Stuart's face. He was slightly turned away from her, his eyes wide and dark. His smile, she suspected, was wooden, his attention somewhere other than the camera lens. What had he been thinking of? Wishing himself somewhere else?

Sitting there, staring at his well-known face, Callie had a sudden sense of not knowing Stuart at all. Was it possible, she mused, to live with someone and yet be unaware of their emotions, their needs? Sometimes she looked at him and he was a stranger, unpredictable and mercurial.

She closed her eyes, fighting back an overwhelming sense of confusion. Stuart — emotions running hot and cold. Actions and words leading her to vague conclusions that told her nothing and left her in a state of uncertainty. She felt disconnected, out of kilter. Something was wrong, yet she could put no form to it, offer no explanations. It was merely an impression.

Inconsistent — that was the word that described him most, Callie considered with a sigh as she placed the photographs on the table and took another sip of tea. That last night at the resort, they had made wild, impulsive love. She remembered snatches of it, how he had teased her body with his own, finally taking her to unexpected highs. And, driving home the next day, he had been talkative, effusive almost, stopping at a roadside stall to buy an entire bucket of flowers.

'I love you, Callie,' he had pronounced solemnly, handing the red plastic container through the car window, kissing her on the tip of her nose.

Yet this morning he had been morose and sullen, as uncommunicative as ever. 'Stuart, is there a problem?' she had asked, waiting for an expected verbal attack.

Stuart paused midway between popping two pieces of bread in the toaster and regarded her through narrowed eyes. 'What sort of problem?'

'You. Me. We seem on different wavelengths these days.'

Stuart shrugged, the corners of his mouth turning upwards in a lazy smile. 'I don't really understand what you're on about, Cal. It's probably that vivid writer's imagination of yours working overtime again.'

A short exchange that solved nothing. He made it all seem petty, inconsequential.

Stop nagging, implied the tone of his voice.

At odd moments of the day she thought she might ring Michael, bring him up to date on her progress through the letters. But there had been little advancement there, she reasoned, her work all but halted by the few days away with Stuart. And there was the underlying fear, the dread, that she would only have to hear his cheerful voice and she would burst into uncontrollable, unending, unexplainable tears.

After two months at Brightlingsea, Ben's company rejoined the division at Lark Hill. It felt strange to be back. The companies and regiments that had been there previously were long gone, across the channel, and the parade grounds and messes were filled with strange faces. Raw recruits arrived daily, full of bravado and talk of the war. Only the buildings were familiar, and the constant mindless routine. Training in field works, in conjunction with the infantry, began in earnest.

The men were chafing, clearly eager to be away. 'When are we going to see some action?' was the constant gripe. 'Can't win the bloody war from over here.'

But they were engineers, their superiors reminded them. Not common trench soldiers.

In Brightlingsea, it had been easy to forget about the war. Now, back in barracks, the reality was constantly brought home. One morning the men were ordered to line up outside the tents. In groups of twenty, they were taken to a long low building at the side of the parade ground.

'What's going on?' Spud asked one of the captains as they tramped through the doorway in single file into what appeared to be a lecture room containing tables and chairs. Several doors led off to the rear of the room.

'Gas training,' was the terse reply.

The men lined up at a desk where, one by one, they were individually fitted for respirator masks and goggles.

'Four mediums!' bawled the desk sergeant, waving Spud, Jack, Ben and Tom towards a long counter.

'Christ!' exploded Spud, holding his mask in front of his face and choking back a laugh. 'Don't we look the part now!'

'Yair,' added Jack laconically. 'Scare Fritz away, you will. One look and they'll be heading back home like the blessed devil himself was after them.'

The men broke into uproarious laughter.

Ben was handed a small satchel which he tentatively opened. Inside it was divided into two parts, one containing a box and the other a mask. There was also a small repair kit comprising pieces of plaster and a record-of-use card.

Another soldier moved methodically around the room handing out small booklets, while the corporal held up a spare satchel and the whispering fell to a hush.

'Righto, you lot. You've got your goggles and respirators and a copy of the procedures manual.' His eyes scanned the room as though defying any man to dispute the fact. Then, his gaze resting on Ben, he bellowed: 'Your lives are dependent on the maintenance and use of this equipment. It must be carried at all times within three miles of the front line.'

He proceeded to sling the satchel around his neck, the unfastened flap facing inwards, towards his body. 'This is how the satchel must be worn during a gas alert. When the gas hits, there's no time to be fumbling around looking for the mask.' He turned to Tom, pointing his finger. 'Have you ever seen a man that's been gassed?'

'No, sir.'

'No, I didn't expect you had. Bloody awful sight.'

He nodded towards another man standing at the back of the room. 'Sergeant.'

The sergeant came forward. Ben could see he was quite young, only in his early twenties, though he had the appearance of a professional man. 'Today I'm going to explain the different types of gas, then we'll try out the masks. Now, there are two main kinds. Lachrymatory, or tear gas, causes your eyes to water so much you can't see the next step in front of you. Makes a man a sitting target for German guns. Then there's the asphyxiates. Chlorine and phosgene will be the main two you will encounter.'

'Unless the bastards are working on something stronger,' Spud said in a stage whisper and there was a murmured laugh from the men.

'Something you'd like to share with us, soldier?' barked the corporal from his stand at the side of the room.

Spud shook his head and looked suitably chastised.

The sergeant went on. 'Immediate use of the equipment is necessary to avoid damage to either eyes or lungs. Continued exposure to a heavy concentration can cause asphyxia in a few minutes.'

'What's asphyxia?' whispered Spud, looking puzzled.

'Death, you stupid bastard,' hissed Tom.

One of the soldiers held high his pair of goggles. 'What about these?'

'Goggles,' the men were informed tersely by the corporal in a monotone voice, 'are to be used for low dose lachrymatory shelling where only eyes are affected, not lungs.'

'How do you know what sort of gas they're using, then?' asked Tom, puzzled.

'Ah, Fritz'll put up a sign first,' intoned one wit at the back of the room. 'It'll say something along the lines of "Special for this week only. Good quality German phosgene. Only the best grade of ingredients used."'

The men erupted into laughter.

'That's enough!' roared the corporal, glaring around the room.

The devices, as the men soon discovered, were cumbersome. Containing charcoal and soda lime designed to filter the chemicals in the air, the respirator box hung from the neck and was connected by a flexible rubber hose to a closely-fitting mask, which was held against the head by two wide rubber bands.

Although two eye-pieces allowed a wide field of vision, Ben found the mask claustrophobic at first. There was a feeling of being enclosed, his faculties restricted. The use of the nose clip, which was inserted into the face-piece, prevented him from breathing normally. There was a momentary sense of impending suffocation, but he reminded himself to take in air through his mouth, great gulps of it, as he suppressed a fleeting impression of panic. Relax, he told himself sternly, watching the others fumble with their masks.

'Everything all right, Galbraith?' asked Sergeant Hayes, who was circling the room.

Ben nodded. 'Yes, sir.'

Hayes turned his attention to the young lad next to Ben. Will Compton was a thin wiry chap who had also joined the company in Brisbane. He had arrived with a seemingly inexhaustible supply of jokes, a suitcase filled with books, and an enviable knowledge of guns acquired from working on his father's far western property.

'Compton!' thundered the officer, watching as Will fumbled with his mask.

'Yes, sir.'

'Get the blessed thing over your face at once! If this were the real thing, you'd be either gasping or dead by now!'

As the officer moved on, Ben sensed the fear in the young man's eyes. 'It's all right,' he soothed, taking his own mouthpiece away to allow him to talk. 'Look, I'll show you.'

Carefully he adjusted the mask around Will's face, pulling the elastic bands tight over his skull. 'Now, put the nose clip on and breathe through your mouth. Simple.'

Will's eyes widened and his mouth worked, taking in gasps of air.

'See? It's not so bad, is it?'

Will simply nodded, turning his face away.

The men were herded through a door at the rear of the room. Will was hanging back towards the tail end of the group and Ben could see the discomfort on the lad's face. Suddenly he himself was pushed forward by the press of men behind, and he lost sight of the lad.

The lesson took about half an hour, beginning with an ear-piercing shriek that made them all jump. 'That's the Strombos horn,' came the muffled assertion of the sergeant, who was now wearing his own mask. 'That'll be the first warning of a gas attack.'

First they were familiarised with the sight and sound of escaping gas: the hissing noise followed by the unfamiliar white cloud that quickly spread into all corners of the room from an innocuous looking cannister on the floor. The men were urged to move about and talk, to familiarise themselves with the situation and equipment. Will, Ben could see, had stayed at the back of the room, near the door. As Ben approached, he could see the lad had his eyes closed. He was trembling, and seemed to be fighting some inner battle.

'What's wrong?' asked Ben, laying one hand on the lad's arm. 'Are you all right?'

Will gave a muffled shriek and opened his eyes, staring wildly, blankly, into Ben's face. 'Get out!' he shrieked. 'I've got to get out!'

With a sudden movement, he was at the door, reefing at the handle. The door opened and Will slipped through, slamming it behind him. Ben could hear the sound of his boots as they thudded across the floorboards of the room beyond.

'What's going on?' came the thunderous roar. 'Who in hell's name opened that door?'

He's terrified, Ben thought, wondering if he should go after the lad. But Sergeant Hayes was already there, tearing off his mask and fumbling at the handle.

Moments later they were herded back into the front room. Of Will and the sergeant there was no sign.

'Dunno about the masks scaring Fritz away,' intoned Jack with a grave expression on his face. 'Did a good job on young Will though.'

The room erupted into laughter.

'Silence!' roared the corporal, 'or you'll all be on latrine duty for two weeks solid.'

'At least we know we'll be here for another fortnight,' grinned Tom.

Will's absence was noticeable during the next few days. Ben heard through the grapevine that the lad had been given kitchen duty. Spud said no, that he was in solitary confinement, and he'd heard it from a very reliable source. Whatever the punishment, the memory of the lad's face, eyes wide and full of fear, rose up before him at odd moments, reminding Ben of his own shortcomings.

Eventually his thoughts turned to Hannah, as usual. What if something happened and he failed to make it home to her? What if he let her down? For himself, dead in a far-off battlefield, he would be past all care. But Hannah now, how would she cope? There had been no word from her for several weeks. Was something wrong? Had the letters been lost along the way?

The worry of it tore at him. He lay awake at night on his bunk, trying to project his mind forward, into the future. But there were no warnings or clues to be found there, just a blank wall of nothingness.

'Can't sleep?' whispered Tom. His eyes were blobs of white against the darkness.

'No.'

'I reckon we'll be off soon. They can't keep us here much longer. The war'll be over and we won't have done our bit.'

Ben sighed and stared at the ceiling, thinking of Will. 'They say some blokes shoot their own fingers off to avoid going.'

Tom propped himself up on one elbow. Ben could see the blurred outline of him, could hear the creak of the bed as he moved. 'You wouldn't do that, would you?'

Ben gave a forced laugh. 'I'm not *that* bloody stupid. But there's some who are.'

'You mean Will?'

Ben nodded, though he knew Tom could not see. 'He was terrified the other day.'

Will's fear, lapping in waves about his consciousness, creating small ripples circling outwards. One tiny doubt, a pinprick of apprehension. Another man's pain touching some inner core, a part he had never known existed, causing a conflict of emotions. Let the brave fight, he wanted to say, and return the weaker to their homes. Not all men are created equal. He himself had been influenced by a white feather handed to him by a stranger on a city street.

There was a route march from Lark Hill through Chitterne, Westbury, Devizes, Pusey and back to camp. Autumn was upon them, bringing with it light misty showers that shrouded the landscape. The weather was cold, the days colourless, all varying shades of grey. As they marched through the countryside, the rain dampened clothes and packs, leaving a film of moisture on faces.

In a strange way it felt cleansing, the rain. Rain washing away the traces of his former life, preparing him for the new. Rain purging those doubts and sense of dread.

'Look at that,' said Jack, pointing to the mist-shrouded hills as they marched along a muddy laneway. The clouds were low, hanging limply in the valleys, almost obscuring the distant woods. The countryside had a muted beauty of its own, a blurring of green and grey washed into an almost transparent haze. Above, the sun poured cold light through a break in the clouds, and it was as though the scene gave promise of all that was to come.

CHAPTER 16

The woman's shoes made a pronounced clicking noise against the polished floorboards as Hannah followed her along the hallway. To her left and right there were several doors, all closed. To the rear, Hannah sensed Clare Worthington's presence, denoted by the swish of her skirt.

Ahead was one open door and Hannah, having no other choice, followed the woman inside. Behind a large mahogany desk sat a man dressed in a white coat. He was kindly looking, about sixty, with a crop of grey hair and a matching moustache. A stethoscope hung around his neck.

There were two chairs. The grey-haired gentleman waved Hannah and Mrs Worthington towards them. 'Sit down, sit down,' he murmured. Then, 'Clare, how nice to see you.'

'Doctor.' Mrs Worthington nodded. 'This is Hannah,' she added in a commanding voice.

'Ah, yes,' replied the doctor as he rested his elbows on the table, interlacing his fingers and propping them under his chin. 'How are you, my dear?'

'I'm very well, thank you,' Hannah answered in a voice that sounded unnaturally stilted. She sat on the edge of the chair, the hard rim of it digging into her thighs through the fabric of her skirt.

The woman who had accompanied them into the room walked briskly to a low cupboard set against a side wall. From its interior she removed several gleaming metallic objects, setting them with a clang in an enamel basin. Then she walked behind a screen that partitioned off the rear portion of the room. When she returned, her hands were empty.

'It's all ready, Doctor.'

'Thank you, nurse. Hannah?'

The doctor was motioning her towards the screen. 'Get undressed, please. There's a chair for your clothes. When you're done, nurse will bring you a gown.'

'No!'

Three pairs of eyes were focussed on her. She stumbled to her feet, backing away, a sense of fear billowing in waves up through her chest. They know, she thought! Oh, God, *they know*!

'Come along, there's a good girl.'

Her eyes raked the room. The nurse stood, her back to the closed door. The doctor was leaning over his desk towards her, motioning her towards the screen. Suddenly the smile on his face seemed more like a leer. Clare Worthington stared upwards at her, an exasperated expression on her face. 'Don't be difficult, Hannah!' she snapped. 'Do as the doctor says. I haven't all day to waste.'

Hannah's head flew back, as though she had been struck. Dully she moved forward, one footfall after the other, each step taking her closer to the screen, beyond which lay some mysterious process that she would soon be part of. Should she run? Distance herself from this strange house and the accompanying fear?

As a child, she had often hidden from Tom in the shadowy recesses of the stable, or amongst the shrubbery that surrounded the house in Brunswick Street. 'Coming, ready or not,' he would call as she pressed herself back into dark corners or flattened her spine against the ground, under a drooping branch of purple plumbago. Hearing Tom's approaching footfall, she would hold her breath, scarcely daring to breathe, in case it should denote her whereabouts.

But there were no shadows here. No place to hide, to wish herself into invisibility. Simply a brightly lit room and a grey-haired doctor, and a screen looming in front of her. Escape was impossible.

Determinedly she suppressed the instinct to flee and stepped behind the screen, her breath exhaling with a ragged sigh. Against the wall stood a high padded table. Next to the table was a chair and a bench, on the top of which sat the tray filled with shiny instruments. Slowly she eased off her clothes, folding them and laying them on the chair.

First the skirt, which was tight around the waist again. She would have to think about letting out the seams further, not that there was much fabric left with which to work. Slowly she unfastened her blouse, buttons awkward in her trembling hands. Beyond she could hear the murmured whisperings of the doctor and Mrs Worthington.

Low voices, words fading in and out.

'She's been tired lately, and pale ...'

'Mmmm.' The tap-tap-tap of a pencil against the wood-grained desk. Then: 'Is there anything wrong?

You know, some bother with her family? Some problem?'

Clare Worthington's deprecating sniff. 'I really wouldn't know. I don't usually involve myself with the staff ...'

Petticoat. Brassiere. Stockings. Shoes. Lastly, she stepped out of her knickers, folding and placing them topmost on the pile of clothes so recently discarded.

'All done?' The nurse came in, barely glancing in her direction. She was holding out a shapeless garment. It was blue, a colour paler than the sky, with an opening and a single button at the neck.

The garment gave her some initial confusion. The opening was at the back, she realised at last. Gingerly she fastened the button and pulled the fabric closed, enveloping her back, buttocks and legs.

Tentatively Hannah sat on the edge of the table, hugging her arms to her chest. The nurse bustled back behind the screen, bringing a sheet and several towels. 'You have to lie down,' she said, giving Hannah what appeared to be a comforting smile. 'It's all right. The examination will only take a minute or two.'

Hannah clambered up on the table and lay rigid, her legs pressed firmly together. 'Ready, doctor,' called the nurse, taking the tray of instruments and laying them at Hannah's feet.

The next few minutes passed in a dazed blur as the doctor moved behind the screen. He shone a small light into her ears and prodded a wooden stick against her tongue. He took her pulse and listened to her heartbeat with the round flattened end of the stethoscope that dangled from his neck. Through it all, he asked questions that seemed to make little sense. At last, he turned to the nurse and said, 'Thank you'.

The nurse pushed up the gown and placed the folded sheet over Hannah's abdomen and the tops of her legs. Then, reaching under the sheet, she pulled at Hannah's legs, forcing them outwards until her feet were pushed roughly into stirrup-like objects at the sides of the table.

Hannah tried to press her knees back together, but the doctor was already positioning himself at the edge of the table, pulling one knee sideways again, holding it there with his broad shoulder. 'Don't move!' he said abruptly, as he reached under the sheet.

The fabric hid the doctor's hands from view, but she could feel them as they sought their targets. One hand moved high, pushing down heavily against her, while the fingers of the other hand probed into that soft moist place below. Instinctively Hannah felt her body flinch away, her fists clenched into tight balls.

'Relax,' soothed the doctor.

She lay, rigid with fear, watching as the sheet buckled, rose and fell with the movement of the doctor's hands. Felt those same hands invade private spaces. Felt the hot flush of embarrassment as it rose up her neck and spread along her cheeks. So this was her punishment, her shame. Retribution for those forbidden pleasures shared with Ben that last weekend before he had gone.

She stared upwards, towards the ceiling, and blinked back the hot tears that flooded her eyes.

Other thoughts, vaguely threatening, began filtering into her consciousness. Had Mrs Worthington brought Lottie here? Was this the same room where mysterious unspeakable things had been done to Lottie's insides? Perhaps they would do the same to her, take the baby.

The possibility sent a shudder of cold dread through her. They couldn't, could they? Not without her consent. Lottie had consented. They had made her.

They made me get rid of the baby . . .

They wouldn't let me stay here, so I had no choice . . .

No choice . . .

No choice . . .

No, she whispered determinedly to herself, willing the examination over. One suspicious move and she would simply get up and leave. Walk out of there. They couldn't force her to do anything against her will.

There was a clink-clink of metal when the doctor took one hand away and rummaged in the enamel tray at the base of the table. Hannah caught a glimpse of a metallic object. She gave an involuntary shiver as a different memory surfaced. Lottie crying, curled in her bed. Lottie losing Maurice's baby, the blood flowing from her body like an unstoppable tide.

They held me down and pushed something inside me. It was long and metallic, like a pair of curved scissors.

The doctor thrust his hand back under the sheet, his fingers touching her insistently. What was happening? Pain lapping and overlapping, or was it merely a discomfort that she had magnified out of all proportion? Hannah's arms twisted sideways, her hands grabbing at the doctor's, pushing him away.

'No! Leave me alone! What are you doing?'

The doctor stared down at her, frowning. 'How old are you, Hannah?'

'Twenty, next month.'

'Do you know why Mrs Worthington brought you here?'

Mutely she nodded, tears coursing freely down her cheeks.

'You'd better get dressed then,' he said brusquely, disappearing around the other side of the screen.

Hannah sat on the edge of the table, shaking with relief as she pushed the hem of the gown over her knees, barely hearing the conversation at the other end of the room.

'She's almost five months gone, in my estimation.'

'Five months!'

Words washing past her, confirming what she had already known. A baby. Not her secret any more.

'This war, I'm afraid, seems to be sending everyone's morals to the wall. She's the third this week.'

As she hurriedly dressed, Hannah heard the tut-tut-tutting from Mrs Worthington. What about Lottie and your son? she wanted to cry out. Is there one standard for women and another for men?

Knickers, stockings, petticoat, blouse. Hands trembling as she re-fastened the buttons. But it was anger, not fear, that propelled them now. How dare they treat her this way, like an immoral wayward child!

She tossed her head, wiping her hand across her face. No matter what words they used, or the disapproving tone of their voices, she would not let them cheapen the way she felt about Ben.

'The child will be born around the end of January, I would say.'

Hannah pulled on her shoes and walked around the screen. Clare Worthington was sitting in the chair, fanning herself with her hand. 'Oh, dear,' she said vaguely, and Hannah knew her employer was probably calculating Christmas staff levels, wondering if Hannah would be still able to work despite the baby and the fact that it would be due almost four weeks later.

'She could get rid of it, I suppose,' the doctor went on, as though Hannah weren't there, as though she were invisible. 'But five months is fairly advanced. There would be certain risks. I know someone, I could arrange . . .'

'NO!' Kill her own child? Hannah stepped forward, hands flailing, the cry a denial on her lips.

Clare Worthington rose from the chair and walked towards her, placing a hand on Hannah's arm. 'Maybe it would be for the best, dear. One day you'll be married. There will be other babies.'

Frantically Hannah shook her head. 'The war can't last much longer!' she blurted. 'Ben will be back and we'll be a proper family!'

'But what if this Ben of yours doesn't come back?'

Hannah reared back as though stung. 'How can you say that?'

'Be practical, Hannah. You're letting emotional issues cloud your judgement. How can you support a child?'

Hannah gritted her teeth. No matter what argument they used, whatever power of persuasion, she would not surrender this child. It was hers, hers and Ben's. And, if the unthinkable happened, if by some will of God Ben didn't return, then she would still have a part of him to love and cherish, that would be hers forever.

In the car, Mrs Worthington turned to her, her face suffused with anger. 'You stupid, stupid girl!' she cried, shaking her head. 'I would have thought you, of all people, would have had more sense.'

'I'm not Lottie,' Hannah replied defiantly, 'and you can't make me give up my child!'

Clare Worthington sank back against the seat, suddenly defeated. 'All right, Hannah. You've made your point. I don't agree with your decision but I will help, if I can.'

'Then let me stay on at the house. I'll work hard and no-one will know for another month or so.'

'I suppose you could stay on. Just for a while, until you make other arrangements and I find someone to replace you,' replied Mrs Worthington grudgingly.

Back at the house, Hannah went upstairs and sat on her bed. Her mind was numb, filled only with the events of the last hour. No longer could she deny the truth. Her secret was out. Ben's child was growing inside her, temporarily hidden under the unflattering white apron and tightening skirts.

Meanwhile, she had a small sum of money put aside. If she stayed on at the Worthington's until after Christmas and saved and saved, not using a penny of her wages, maybe she would have enough to take a small room somewhere, spend the last few weeks of her pregnancy there. When Ben found out about the child, he'd want to send her something to help out, she was sure of it.

The most pressing task was to tell Ben. Hannah took several sheets of paper from her desk and sat on the end of her bed, chewing the end of her pen. Dispiritedly she sighed. What to write? Where to begin?

There was a tentative knock and Lottie poked her head around the doorway. 'Can I come in?'

Hannah gave her friend a wan smile. 'Of course.'

'Are you writing to Ben?' asked Lottie, settling herself on the bed next to Hannah.

'Yes.'

'Have you told him about the baby?'

Suddenly she found herself crying. Great gulping sobs wracked her body and Lottie wriggled closer, pulling Hannah's head against her chest. 'Sshh,' she whispered. 'It'll be all right. Everything will work out, just wait and see.'

Lottie rocking, soothing her. Back and forth, to and fro. Lulling her into a sense of acceptance. It was done. Nothing could alter the fact. She would have to make the best of it, be strong, for the baby's sake. Somehow, she would manage.

The garden party, the following day, was a great success, with families from miles around coming to enjoy the entertainment. There was a carousel and a painted clown, sweets stalls and a stand selling ice-creams. A brass band played in front of the fountain.

Hannah wandered around the grounds, watching the excitement. I'm going to have a baby, she thought, the words repeating themselves over and over in her mind, until she thought she might go mad with it.

A mixture of emotions juggled for attention. Fear and anxiety intermingled with a vague sense of excitement. And above it all, she wished Ben were there to share it with her. But he was thousands of miles away, on the other side of the world.

CHAPTER 17

By the end of November, the collection of equipment had been finalised at Lark Hill. The required number of horses and mules were taken on, the gas training completed. Excitement was at fever pitch, with each man placing bets as to the exact date of departure and their eventual destination.

Tom won. It was the 24th before the company boarded the train to Southampton, sharing the transport with the men from the Third Division, en route to France. The day was all grey sky and scudding clouds, with an icy wind that rattled at the doors and windows of the carriages as they rocked along. Cold-looking streams flashed past. Branches on trees thrashed about, caught by sudden squalls of wind. Sitting in the comparative warmth of the carriage, Ben hunched himself against the imagined discomfort and tried to project his mind forward.

Nothing came.

France. A land of rolling hills and orchards, according to his geography lessons, years earlier. Of vineyards and woods, and fields ripe with wheat. *Parlez-vous français?* There had been a Frenchman once who had come into the forge. He had spoken with a strange accent, and taught Ben the phrase. How old had he been? Just a kid, yet the words had stuck, coming back to him now with a rush, and he smiled.

'Want to share the joke?'

Ben looked sideways, encountering Spud's puzzled face. 'Oh, I don't know. Just wondering what it'll be like, where we're going. What about you?'

Spud snorted and gave the countryside a scornful glance. It was raining now, a light veil of white that shrouded the distant view. Leaves on trees glistened. Down a nearby lane, an old man wobbled along on a bicycle, his face turned away. 'I've been thinking what a dreary bloody place this is, all rain and cold. As the saying goes, we should give England to the Germans and apologise for the poor state it's in.'

'It could be worse, where we're going.'

'It couldn't!' Spud denied hotly. 'Anyway, I reckon I'll be glad to see a bit of action. That's what we came for.'

'It'll be strange, Christmas coming in the middle of winter,' mused Tom. 'Perhaps we'll see snow.'

Thinking of the possibility, Ben pulled his coat tighter and turned to Jack. 'What do you reckon?'

Jack grimaced. 'My mother had a saying: be careful what you wish for, you might just get it.'

'Meaning?' queried Spud, his chin jutting belligerently.

'Meaning we've had it bloody easy up until now, old chap,' replied Jack easily, ignoring the tone of Spud's voice. 'Don't think it's some Cook's Tour we're going on.'

The group fell into contemplative silence. Jack opened his newspaper while Spud shuffled a pack of cards. Tom laid his head against the back of the seat and closed his eyes. The conversation was over, yet words of it danced through Ben's mind. France. A hellhole, according to some of the blokes he'd spoken to back at camp. Jack was right. Until now it had been easy. Route marches, trench digging, gas mask practice. Nothing life-threatening or dangerous. But where they were going . . .

His thoughts turned to Hannah, as they invariably did. Apart from one delivery two weeks earlier, there had been no mail through for weeks. Was she well?

The not knowing, the uncertainty, drained him. With a sigh he stared out the window. The train, rocking over the rails beneath him, sang a song of its own. Curiously he watched the beads of rain as they trickled down the glass. There was an infinite sadness about them, he thought, the way they merged with each other, losing their identity, becoming one.

We're all like that, he mused. No longer separate individuals, but part of something larger, less definite.

Already the war had changed them.

Accompanied by loud shouts and cheers from the men, the s.s. *Nirvana* docked at Le Havre the following morning. So this was France. Ben glanced about, taking in the scenery. Beyond the dismal docks, several roads wound down to the harbour, lined with cottages of indeterminate age. Above, etched dark against the sky, rose the church spires.

The rain had followed them. It was falling now, spitting from monotone skies that seemed to blend with the grey streets and buildings. Trickles of water ran down necks as the men marched towards the nearby camp. There the tents were sodden, the bedding wet and uncomfortable.

'Bloody hell!' exploded Spud, his face thunderous as he dumped his bag onto the muddy ground.

'Welcome to glorious France, mate,' intoned Jack, trying vainly to keep the smile from his face and failing miserably.

Lunch was their first encounter with field rations. 'Pork and beans,' said Tom, reading the label on the tin before tipping the contents onto a plate. 'Well I'll be buggered!' he exclaimed, delving into the mess with his spoon. 'Someone's pinched the bloody pork!'

They laughed at that, not knowing what else to do as they shuffled their feet and folded their arms awkwardly across their chests. Laughed as much at the wounded expression on Tom's face as at the strangeness they felt, being in a different country, and the unusualness of it all.

'Ah, shit!' exclaimed Spud at last, grabbing a tin of food. 'A bloke could die of starvation around here.'

The following day, the company was organised into four equal lots, each containing about fifty men. Ben and Tom, Spud and Jack were in No. 4 Section, along with Will and a few of the chaps who had joined up in Brisbane. It was a cheerful group mostly, the only sour note being Sergeant Hayes.

Hayes had it in for Will. Following the gas training episode at Lark Hill, he had baited the lad at every opportunity, assigning him the most menial tasks. Several times Ben had tried to intervene on the lad's behalf, much to the sergeant's annoyance. At best, it had only served to increase the problem and, Ben noted, Will soon learned to make himself scarce when Hayes was around.

The next evening the Company marched to the railway station. The train was late — three hours, they were informed by the stationmaster in halting English. There was nothing to do but wait. It was cold standing on the platform and Ben was glad of his coat, which kept most of the chill air at bay. The train finally shuddered into the station about midnight, grinding to a halt with an accompanying hiss of steam. Ben, Tom, Spud and Jack were part of the first group to board. Luckily they managed to secure a compartment.

'Thank Christ for that!' exclaimed Tom, stowing his gear in the rack overhead and throwing himself into the nearest seat. 'The poor buggers who get on last will be standing.'

By the time the carriages pulled from the station, there was little room to move. Soldiers sat or lay in the corridors, and packs and bed rolls littered every available space. As Ben soon discovered, it was a marathon journey just to reach the lavatories at the end of the corridor.

Through the night there were long and annoying delays. The journey was stop-start, the train often rolling to a halt on a side track, waiting while other locomotives went hissing past, spitting cinders along the grassy verges of the tracks. Heaters were non-existent, and the carriages were freezing. At regular intervals they pulled into tiny stations, but the dining rooms were closed. Not even a cup of hot coffee could be bought.

261

Morning found them cold and hungry, but at least they were into the countryside and the train was rocking along at a reasonable speed. The day had turned out fine, blue sky dotted with the occasional ribbon of cloud. Ben stared out the window, taking in every detail of the scenery. Houses with red-tiled roofs flashed past. There were wooded hills and green meadows, and white roads lined with trees, the leaves shiny. Everything appeared washed clean by the rain.

Past small villages and farmhouses they jolted, and through the outskirts of larger industrial towns, chimneys belching dark smoke against the sky. Hasty tasteless meals were served up on station platforms. Porters blew whistles. Doors slammed as the carriages jerked forward again.

His companions slept mostly, heads lolling against seats and windows. Minutes ticked past and became hours, long drawn-out expanses of time where it seemed he might be consumed by his thoughts. Hannah, the forge — it seemed all remnants of his former life were being drawn further away from him, becoming ever more distant.

Thoughtfully he took the remaining half of the silver horseshoe from his pocket and held it in his hand. It was cold against his palm, the etched letters blurring in his tired mind. His thoughts flew back to that last morning together, how he had woken next to her on the bed in Tom's flat. I love you, she had said, stretching herself like a cat in the sun. Hannah: black hair fanned against the pillow; skin pale, almost transparent in that early morning light. He remembered the warmth of her, and it filled him with immeasurable sadness.

With a sigh he replaced the horseshoe in his pocket, folding the flap of fabric over its hardness and re-fastening the button. He could feel the bulk of it against his chest, but it gave him little comfort. Why hadn't he heard from her? Just one letter would reassure him that she was all right.

Stiff and cramped after the rail journey, they reached Bailleul, near the Belgian border, the following morning. The unit, the men were informed, would go to billets at Bleu, south-east of Vieux Berquin, by route march. Kit bags were loaded aboard a grey-painted London bus, which promptly set off, sending a black cloud of exhaust smoke belching along the road. Hoisting his gun over his shoulder, Ben joined the others as they trudged along. He was wearing a hat and greatcoat and, despite the cold weather, was soon perspiring heavily.

The coat was the first to be dispensed with, and he was glad of the water bottle slung around his chest. At regular intervals he stopped and raised the flask to his mouth, savouring the cool liquid. They marched in the shade of tall pines, the needles making a soft carpet underfoot. Narrow two-storeyed houses were set well back from the road, separated from each other by maize-coloured fields and tall hedges. Basking in wan sunlight, the land was flat, sweeping away until it merged with the colour of the sky. From time to time, they were forced to wait on the verge of the road as convoys of motor lorries and ambulances passed, kicking up a layer of dust.

The company stopped for lunch in a grassy field. The fare was bread, obviously fresh from a nearby village, cold meat and tomatoes. Ben ate, although he wasn't hungry. Afterwards, several of the others decided to walk down the hill to the nearby stream, to refill water bottles.

Tom offered to take Ben's. 'No use us both going,' he reasoned. 'You can do it next time.'

Ben lay back, feeling the grass prickle through his shirt. The sun was high overhead, though it carried little warmth. He could have dozed, but he wasn't sure. A shadow falling over him, blocking both the light and the barely felt heat, caused him to open his eyes.

'Monsieur?'

Ben looked up and blinked, trying to retrieve his bearings. He was circled by a ring of faces. A ragged band of children had gathered around, boys mostly, eyeing the guns. They wore long trousers and coats, threadbare and fraying at the cuffs, and berets. Their cheeks were rosy from the cold.

'Hello,' he replied companionably.

The group pushed one of the lads forward. He seemed slightly older than the rest, taller. Obviously he was to be the spokesman.

'You are Australien?' he asked.

Ben smiled. 'That's right.'

'Maman says you have come to save us from the Germans. She says you are very brave soldiers,' the boy went on in halting English.

Most of the boys carried fishing rods, and several bicycles leaned against the nearby wooden fence. Half a dozen fish lay in a cane basket on the ground, scales gleaming cold and grey.

'Here,' the boy said, thrusting two of the largest

onto the grass next to Ben's hand. 'We would like you to have these.'

The other boys nodded in agreement, their heads bobbing earnestly up and down.

'Thank you,' replied Ben, scrambling to his feet.

He stood, hands in pockets, not knowing what to say next. That he, a stranger, should be the recipient of their kindness, had no precedent, and the gesture touched him in an infinitely moving way.

'Thank you,' he said again, the words sounding inadequate to his own ears as the boys ran across the grass, back to their bicycles. Reaching the fence, the eldest turned and waved, and Ben raised his hand briefly.

'What was all that about?' asked Tom, returning with the filled water bottles.

'His mother told him we had come to save them from the Germans,' said Ben quietly. 'So he brought us a present.'

'Fish!' exclaimed Spud, coming up behind. 'You little beauty! Guess what's for supper tonight!'

Several convoys of motor lorries passed as they set off again, resulting in further delays. Storm clouds had gathered on the horizon, bruised and angry-looking; however, it was not until an hour later that the first cold drops of rain began falling.

The men made for the outbuildings of a distant farmhouse. As they neared, Ben saw that the constructions were skeletal, merely blackened frameworks of joists and beams outlined against the darkening sky. There was an accompanying acrid odour of burnt wood. The charred dead remains of livestock lay in the attached stockyards. The rain was coming down harder now, plastering hair to heads and saturating shirts, so they turned their attention to the farmhouse.

It was deserted. No-one came to their knocks or repeated calls, and the sound of their voices echoed through the rooms and hallways. At some time, long past, the windows and doors had been blown in. Jagged splinters of glass were embedded into walls. The roof and most of the upper storey had been razed. Only the lower level remained, a leaking mouldy structure where armies of cockroaches scurried up walls and rats ran along rotting floorboards, sending swirls of dried leaves and newspapers in their wake.

'Well, it's no Taj Mahal but this'll have to do,' pronounced Sergeant Hayes, peering through a glassless window at the worsening rain.

On further inspection, the men found several rooms habitable. They had been service areas once: kitchen, pantry, box room, scullery. Hayes sent Will out into the drenching rain to bring several buckets of water from the well. By the time he was finished, the lad's clothing was drenched.

Ben helped him remove his shirt and trousers, setting them next to the fire which had been built in the remnant of an old fireplace. Steam soon rose from the material, sending out an odour of dampness mixed with scorched fabric. It reminded him momentarily of the forge and the hiss of wet metal. Suppressing the thought, he closed his eyes, letting the babble of men's voices carry him back to the present.

A set of decaying stairs led down to a wine cellar. Spud and Tom took a candle and went to investigate, returning with half a dozen dust-covered bottles. In one of the kitchen cupboards, Ben found an old frying pan, the handle missing. There was no butter to be had, so Jack poured a little water in the pan and poached the fish over the flames.

They ate by candlelight. Fish and tins of Fray Bentos bully beef, and the remains of the lunchtime bread, washed down by local red wine and mugs of steaming tea. Afterwards they curled in dark corners and slept, the silence of the night broken only by the scurrying of rats and cockroaches, and an occasional dream-induced scream.

Ben woke early, cold and cramped. For a moment he lay still, his coat wrapped tightly about him, wondering where he was. In his dream he had been back at the forge, in the tiny quarters he had shared with Da. He blinked and glanced about, seeing Tom's sleeping form nearby. The events of the previous day scrambled back into his consciousness, the fish, the rain, the bottles of wine.

He needed to piss, urgently. There was a pressure in his groin, a sensation almost of pain, and he winced. Careful not to wake the others, he made his way outside, down the mouldy hallway and past deserted rooms, their walls and floors open to the sky.

He came to a door and opened it, finding himself in a walled courtyard. Moss and ivy feathered their way across fallen brickwork. In the centre of it all stood a pear tree. It was stunted, its branches broken. Several rotting pieces of fruit lay amongst the weeds and grass that grew in profusion around the base of the trunk.

Only as he relieved himself against the trunk, after watching the bright stream of urine as it sprayed across the weeds and rough bark, did he raise his face. The rain had gone, stormy clouds from the previous afternoon replaced by a pale sky, cold, like glass. Overhead, birds were dark smudges against the light.

Never, ever, had he felt so alone. Out there, with nothing except the call of the birds and the eye-squinting dawn, it seemed nothing remained. Hannah, Da. All vestiges of his former life gone, eclipsed like a dark moon rising over the sun, blotting out all light. He sat on a pile of bricks, feeling their dampness through the seat of his trousers, and stared skywards. In one desperate moment, he envied the birds. Envied their freedom, their right to choose. Envied their apparent unconcern.

'Ben?'

There was a movement behind him and a voice, making him jump. He turned, seeing only Spud outlined against the house as he undid the buttons on his fly and turned to face the wall.

'Christ, I needed that,' he said at last, walking towards Ben as he fiddled with the buttons once more. 'You know, the further into this place we get, the more I'm enjoying myself. Looking forward to seeing a bit of action now. Give me something to write home to the folks about. Guess they're getting tired of hearing about route marches, hey?'

Spud, the seeker of excitement and action. A man who could not think past that initial blaze of bullets, the trail of destruction he might bring. Did he dream about single-handedly capturing the German army, personally pressing Fritz back into some far-distant corner of the empire?

'Sure, Spud,' Ben grinned. 'When do we start?'

'No time like the present. Let's get those other bastards up and on the road.'

At the camp at Bleu, there was mail waiting. Three whole sacks full, bulging with cards and letters and Comforts Fund parcels from home. Ben was handed a small bundle. Scouting around the other men waiting for their share, he aimed for a patch of grass, where he sat, spreading them on the ground before him.

With a surge of delight, he saw there were several from Hannah. Four in total, almost too much to hope for. But where to start? He examined the envelopes, selecting the most recent by the postmark. That would give the latest news of her, then he would read the others at his leisure.

In his haste, he tore open the flap and his eyes scanned the lines, taking in only every occasional phrase. *Miss you*, she wrote, and his heart soared. *Love you. When are you coming home?*

There was one paragraph, however, that brought him to a sudden halt. Carefully he re-read the lines, thinking he must be mistaken. No. She couldn't possibly be, he thought, his eyes forcibly drawn back to that specific word: pregnant.

The doctor says the baby will be born about the end of January. Oh, Ben, already I love him (or her) as I love you. The child is a part of both of us. But I'm scared of going through this alone. Lottie says she'll help. When you come home, we can be a proper family ...

'Any news?' asked Tom, ambling over, several envelopes in his own hand. 'How's my sister?'

Ben glanced up, for a moment not registering the question. Hannah pregnant? He imagined her body, warm and round with the shape of the child, and a pain bubbled under his breastbone. He was going to be a father. The thought was all-consuming, taking his breath away. A surge of delight, mixed with a tinge of apprehension, coursed through him. And there was a need to share the news, to tell someone, anyone.

Ben handed the letter to Tom. 'You might as well know. You'll find out eventually.'

Wordlessly, Tom read the same lines. When he had finished, he handed the letter back, and stared thoughtfully at the ground, his lips pursed. 'What sort of crazy game were you playing?' he demanded at last, a frown creasing his forehead. 'Didn't you even stop to think what might happen?'

'It wasn't a game, Tom.'

'What was it, then?'

Anger stirred deep in his chest. This was something between himself and Hannah, their concern, and he didn't need Tom reminding him of the stupidity of the whole thing. He'd known, from the start, the possible consequences, yet, when faced with the choice, he'd been unable to stop himself.

'Don't reduce my relationship with Hannah to something cheap and sordid. It wasn't like that. I love her —'

'Haven't you heard of dreadnoughts?' Tom cut in brusquely. 'You know. Condoms, rubbers. For Christ's sake, Ben. It's one thing to muck around with my sister, but leaving her pregnant ...?'

'It wasn't something we planned,' replied Ben tersely.

'So what are you going to do?'

Grabbing the younger man by the shirt collar, Ben drew Tom's surprised face close to his own. 'What do you propose I fucking do? Hop on the first transport out of here? Tell them I have to go home, my girlfriend's having a baby?'

He wanted to shake Tom, but commonsense told him to back off, diffuse the situation as best as he could. Everyone's nerves were stretched tight. It wouldn't do to cause a scene.

Tom stumbled back as Ben released his grip on the shirt collar. 'Steady on, old chap,' he muttered.

'Its not a situation that either of us wanted, but it's happened and we'll have to make the best of it.'

Tom stared at Ben for what seemed a very long time. 'All right,' he said at last. 'If I'm going to be an uncle, I might as well accept it. As long as you do the right thing and marry her as soon as we get back. Still friends?' he added, holding out his hand.

'Friends,' confirmed Ben, taking Tom's palm in his.

The handshake felt of strength and promise, and of a mateship that the days, weeks and years together had not diminished, though the past few minutes had tested its solidity. His relationship with Hannah; Da's death; those first unbelievable days after they had joined up; the terrible uncertainty of it all — Tom had been part of all that. He was also a link to Hannah. Flesh of the same flesh. Blood of the same blood.

And Hannah's child?

Part of him. Part of her. A beautiful blending of them both. Therein lay the future.

Children.

Grandchildren.

Growing old beside her.

CHAPTER 18

'Paterson speaking.'

The voice was abrupt, as though she had interrupted something important. 'Hi, it's Callie,' she said tentatively.

Michael's tone softened. 'Hi, yourself.' Then: 'To what do I owe the pleasure of this call?'

'Sorry to ring you at work. I tried you at home earlier, but there was no answer.'

Callie could almost picture him grimace as he answered. 'Just the usual backlog here. Early start today, I'm afraid.'

Now that the moment had arrived, she was at a loss how to say the words. The thought of revealing the secret, a secret that had been kept from the family for over eighty years, had given her moments of indecision. Would Hannah have wanted this part of her life laid bare? And how would the rest of Callie's family feel?

But Michael wasn't family, she reasoned, merely an interested bystander who had somehow become involved. Besides, Michael *wanted* to know. Hadn't he taken Ben Galbraith's war diary?

'Hannah was pregnant during the war!' she blurted, unable to contain herself further. 'Hannah and Ben had a child!'

There was a momentary silence on the other end of the phone. 'How do you know?'

'The letters. It's all there.'

'When? Where?'

'Brisbane, I guess. There's a letter from Hannah, telling him the news. And one from Ben in return. God, it's weird, reading about all this, years later. Sort of spying, I suppose.'

'You feel guilty, is that what you're trying to say?'

'In a way. It seems so private, this love they shared. And they spelt it all out in those letters. Sometimes I feel as though I'm intruding on that.'

'Perhaps Hannah wanted someone to know,' Michael replied quietly. 'She could have destroyed the contents of the trunk before she died. One small bonfire and the letters and diary would have literally gone up in smoke.'

She hadn't considered that. Hannah's belongings stored away all those years, the fact that they had been left intact. Perhaps she was meant to find them; maybe something beyond her control had planned for this, the final unearthing of secrets long hidden.

'You haven't told me about the child,' Michael prompted, bringing her thoughts back to the conversation.

'As yet I don't know any more. The letters are taking forever to transcribe. The writing's very faded, and rather ornate. But I'm working on it. How's the diary coming along?'

'Slowly, I'm afraid. Work, work, work! That's been the state of affairs around here since I saw you last. Speaking of that, I promised Timmy a trip down your way, to the beach, this Sunday. Interested in joining us?'

She had no plans for the weekend and Stuart usually enjoyed a day at the beach. 'Sounds great. Meet you down there about eleven.'

'See you then.'

There was a click and a monotone buzzing sound that meant the connection had been severed, and Callie replaced the receiver in the cradle.

She picked up Ben's letter again, weighing the pieces of paper thoughtfully in her palm. They were torn-out pages of a field message pad, mostly. The words were scrawled, obviously written in haste, and covered every available space. Sometimes in ink and sometimes in faded pencil, it was as though he had been interrupted in his task several times, and had picked up whatever writing instrument lay close by. A musty odour rose from them, the combined smell of naphthalene and decay.

Carefully Callie refolded the crumbling paper and replaced it in the envelope. Miss Hannah Corduke. Bright Street, Kangaroo Point, Brisbane, it read. The postmark was faint, though decipherable. Bleu, France. 28 November 1916.

'I've spoken to Bonnie and Freya. They both said they knew nothing about Hannah's child.'

Callie lay on the towel, her voice muffled under the broad-brimmed straw hat that covered her face. Michael sat cross-legged in the sand, keeping a vigilant eye on Timmy who splashed in the small breakers with his body board.

'Did that surprise you?'

'No. It just felt a little odd saying something. After all, it was Freya who used such phrases as "ferreting around in the past" and "Muckraking". I know she can be a bit of a tartar at times, but I didn't want to upset her.'

'So what did she say?'

Callie shrugged. 'Not much at all. She seemed pretty stunned, actually.'

'I made it to the corresponding part in Ben's diary.'

'And?' Callie prompted.

'There wasn't much. A couple of lines, and the mention that he had written back to Hannah the same day her letter arrived.'

'November 28, 1916.'

The date, that spidery scrawled address, was etched indelibly in her mind. She rolled onto her stomach, presenting her back to the sun. If she turned her head sideways, she could just see a disjointed view of Michael through the straw hat. Sandy hair, body tanned from the hours spent outdoors on his photographic assignments. Hands, long tapering fingers, reaching for the squat plastic bottle that lay on the towel next to her.

'Sunscreen?'

'Mmmm. That would be nice.'

The lotion was momentarily cold against her skin. She felt his hands move deftly across her back in a caressing motion. *Caressing*? Her own word, she thought with surprise as he slid the bikini straps sideways and massaged her shoulders.

There was something vaguely erotic about the movement, the touch of his hands. Hands that weren't Stuart's. Hands that belonged to another man. Thinking about it, she felt her cheeks flood with sudden embarrassment, and she was grateful for the hat that covered her face.

Earlier in the week she had asked Stuart to accompany them today, but he had already organised a mid-morning game of squash. Then he had politely rebuffed her invitation to join them later. 'I'll probably go on to the pub with the rest of the team for a counter lunch,' he had said and turned away.

'Pity Stuart couldn't join us,' said Michael, his words mirroring the subject of her thoughts as he re-fastened the lid on the sunscreen.

In some ways, Callie thought guiltily, she wasn't sure she had wanted Stuart at the beach and his refusal, in a sense, had been a relief. His moodiness had continued all week and she was uncertain whether it had something to do with herself, Michael, or the business of the letters.

Instead, this had been their special time, her own and Michael's, to talk about Hannah and Ben, and the discoveries they had made. Stuart's presence would have steered their conversation into more neutral topics, and she was forced to admit, if only to herself, that she enjoyed Michael's company.

From under the hat, Callie saw Timmy running towards them, spraying sand and salt water. 'Hey, Dad! Did you see that?' he called. 'I caught the *biggest* wave.'

'I saw,' Michael laughed, handing Timmy a dry towel.

Michael's pride in his son was obvious and Callie had found herself warming to the boy. At ten years of age, he was a miniature replica of his father, not just the physical aspects, such as the lean body and fair hair, but the unconscious mannerisms and the infectious enjoyment of life.

'I'm starving,' the boy pronounced, sliding a fresh T-shirt over his shoulders. 'How about some lunch, Dad?'

'Callie?'

Michael was leaning over her. She could sense his nearness, could smell the faint scent of aftershave mixed with the tang of salt and sunscreen. Lazily she turned over and found his mouth only inches from hers. Unbidden, her heart hammered away in her chest.

'Starving, too,' she admitted with a laugh that somehow sounded forced to her own ears, as she scrambled to her feet and wrapped a colourful sarong over her bikini.

A restaurant specialising in seafood had opened on the esplanade the previous summer. Tables and chairs were strung out along a wooden walkway overlooking the beach. Bright umbrellas provided shade. The mood was casual during the day.

Michael ordered fish and chips for Timmy, as well as a large platter of fresh prawns and bugs. A bottle of ice-cold Sauvignon Blanc complimented the fare.

'Lovely,' said Callie, pushing her chair back as she sipped the last of the wine. 'It's funny, isn't it? This restaurant has been open for almost a year, yet this is the first time I've been.'

'Not crazy about seafood, then?'

'I love it, though apart from the occasional Thai meal, Stuart's more of a steak-and-chips man.'

'Well,' said Michael, calling for the bill and glancing at his watch. Apart from one other group, they were the only ones left at the tables. 'Three o'clock. I suppose we'd better be going.'

The day had been perfect and Callie hated the thought of it ending. Saying goodbye to Michael and Timmy, driving back to the unit alone, the possibility of another argument with Stuart — the thought depressed her. 'Come back to the house,' she said impulsively.

He looked blankly at her. Timmy was dancing, pulling his father to his feet. 'Come on, Dad.'

'The house at Brunswick Street,' she added.

'Look, I don't think that's a good idea. Perhaps another —'

'No! Let me show you over the old place. Properly. I want you to see where this is all coming from. Hannah. Ben. Somehow they're still part of the place. I can feel them there.' She stopped, feeling foolish. 'You probably think I'm crazy, saying that. They were both born more than a hundred years ago and they've been dead for years.'

'No,' he said slowly. 'I don't think you're crazy. Perhaps we all leave a little part of us in places we live.'

'So you'll come?'

'How could I refuse?' he laughed. 'Come on, Tim. We're off to learn some history.'

It seemed silly to take both cars on to the house, so Callie dropped her own car at the unit. Of Stuart there was no sign. 'I'll phone him in an hour or so,' she assured Michael as she climbed into the front seat of his old Mercedes. 'He'll collect me later.'

'Well, if you're certain,' said Michael doubtfully. The expression on his face suggested that Stuart couldn't be relied upon to act predictably if his life depended on it.

They found Bonnie in the kitchen. 'Oh, Callie,' she smiled, giving her daughter a quick hug. 'And Michael, too. How nice to see you again.'

Michael introduced Timmy. Freya ambled in from the garden to see what all the fuss was about, and introductions and greetings were repeated.

'Well,' said Bonnie over a cup of tea, 'Freya and I finally signed the paperwork. As of yesterday, the house is officially on the market.'

Callie looked up to find her mother staring at her, as though waiting to gauge her reaction. She blinked and looked away. It was inevitable, wasn't it? Bonnie had already prepared her, weeks earlier, yet the actuality of it had surprised her. What had she thought? That somehow Bonnie and Freya would muddle through, change their minds, whatever?

'I'm sorry, Cal. It can't be helped, love.'

'I know, mum. There are so many memories here, that's all. It won't seem the same, coming to visit you in one of those new villas.'

'How about showing me through the house?' inquired Michael, breaking the mood. 'I'd love to see it.'

'I'll take you,' said Callie, jumping to her feet, pleased at the chance. 'You don't mind, do you, Mum?'

'Of course not,' replied Bonnie, glancing up at the clock on the wall. 'Actually, it's getting late. Why don't you all stay for tea?'

It was agreed. Michael rang Gaby to let her know Timmy wouldn't be back until later, and they left the boy at the table, helping himself to another glass of homemade lemonade.

There was a sweet familiarity about walking through the rooms once more. Down the wide central hallway, the three large bedrooms: Bonnie's, Freya's, and the room that had once been Callie's own. Bonnie had never altered the furnishings, and every time she walked through the doorway it was like entering a time warp. The same white *broderie anglais* doona with matching valance and curtains, the scattering of pink lacy cushions. A large cane chair and a doll's pram, remnants of a happy childhood.

'Very feminine,' said Michael with a smile and she gave him a playful punch.

'Well, I was quite young when we decorated it like that. Mum uses it as the guest room now, not that there are many visitors.'

Michael admired the high ceilings and rose-and-leaf-design cornices. 'It's a lovely house,' he said as she led him back through the kitchen, into the sunroom and down the back steps. 'Good original condition and well maintained.' Then, out of earshot of Bonnie: 'At the same time, I can see why you don't want them to sell. There *is* a sense of history here. It oozes from the place. The walls, the furniture. If you close your ears to the external sounds of motor cars and lawnmowers, we could easily be transported back fifty, one hundred years.'

Callie shot him a thankful glance. Stuart might think she was crazy, getting sentimental over an old house, but Michael understood.

Down past the mulberry tree they went, ducking under low-hanging branches. Past the wattles and grevilleas, lilly pilly, conifers and palms. A bed of pansies had just come into flower, comical velvet-tipped faces turning towards the last of the sun. The agapanthus were in bloom, too, heavy mauve heads nodding sleepily in the breeze. A riot of magenta bougainvillea cascaded over the back fence.

'It's lovely,' admired Michael. 'Makes my square of unmown lawn in the city look quite drab by comparison.'

'We have my great-great-grandmother Elizabeth Corduke to thank for the garden. She planted most of it out before the Great War.'

'She did a fantastic job. It still looks great.'

'Of course, all the subsequent owners have added to it, but basically it's still Elizabeth's design.'

'I'm impressed, all the same.'

'There was more land surrounding the house then.' Callie pointed to the house next door, its roof just visible over a tall dividing hedge. 'John Corduke kept his horses in stables over there, and the buggy. But my grandfather, David, divided that piece of land off and sold it after the Great War.'

There was a late-afternoon coolness at the bottom of the garden, a sense of stillness, despite the movement of the breeze through the trees. Overhead, a bird chattered, breaking the silence.

'Hey! There's another one!'

From the direction of the creek came Timmy's voice. Callie raised her eyebrows enquiringly towards Michael. 'What on earth's going on down there?'

They peeped through the bougainvillea, careful of the thorns. Ahead, down the meandering length of the creek, were Timmy and Freya. Freya was standing in the middle of the shallow waterway, wearing an old pair of Wellingtons. Timmy was dancing excitedly near her, examining the contents of a small mesh scoop.

'Well, I never!' Callie stepped back and laughed, covering her mouth with her hand in case the noise carried. 'Looks like Timmy's made a friend.'

Instinctively they turned away, retracing their steps until Callie came to a standstill near the wattles. 'I have a painting of these. Did I tell you?'

Michael shook his head.

'Hannah did it, during the war. Seems there were always wattles growing around here, even then.'

The sound of a door opening reached them. They both turned and looked up towards the house. The sloping roof and chimneys were just visible above the mass of sunlit shrubbery. Callie could make out the vague shape of her mother as she stood on the top step and scattered a handful of bread for the parrots that came to feed every afternoon.

Michael reached out, touching a hand to her arm. 'What you said earlier, about your family still being part of this place? I can see what you mean. This solid old house, the wonderful gardens. There's a sense of history here. To be able, years later, to know who planned all this — that's amazing.'

'I can't bear the thought of strangers moving in,' blurted Callie. 'It seems so wrong. I wish I had the money to buy the place myself.'

Michael steered her back towards the house. 'Let's see what Bonnie's up to,' he suggested, changing the topic. 'She might need a hand.'

'I thought we'd cook outdoors,' said Bonnie, back in the kitchen rattling pots and pans. 'There's an old barbeque down the back, though goodness knows when we used it last. Michael, do you think ... ?'

Together they hosed the cobwebs from the lid, and Michael scraped and oiled the plate. It was an ancient wood-burning variety, and he soon had a fire going with bits of kindling and a few logs from the old woodheap.

The sight of the flames leaping under the metal grill brought back a few vivid memories. 'We always used it every weekend,' Callie said wistfully, 'when Dad was alive.'

Bonnie came towards them down the path with an armful of cutlery and plates. With a thump she set them on the garden table. 'Yes,' she said, and Callie heard the same echo of sadness in her mother's voice. 'Now that it's just Freya and I, we never seem to use it. Easier to cook indoors.'

'But so much nicer down here,' Michael grinned.

Her mother's mind, however, was on more practical matters. 'Now, I need to know how many steaks to get out. There's Michael and Tim, Freya and myself. Callie, is Stuart coming over?'

Callie shrugged, realising with a start that she hadn't even given him a consideration. She went inside and dialled the number. He picked it up on the fourth ring.

'Hi, it's me.'

Abruptly: 'I guessed.'

'I'm at Mum's. Come over for tea,' she said. 'Michael and Timmy are here. We're having a barbeque.'

There was a brief silence from the other end of the line. 'No thanks,' came the sardonic reply.

'What's wrong?'

'Nothing. I just don't feel like coming, that's all.'

She knew from experience that he was annoyed. His tone was curt, his words clipped. Well, she thought with a shrug, if that was the way he wanted it ...

'Fine. Don't bother, then. I left my car at the unit earlier, so I'm sure Michael won't mind dropping me home.'

She replaced the phone with a bang and stood looking at it, silent, on the bench. The brief verbal confrontation with Stuart had left her feeling a mixture of anger and relief. Anger at his easy dismissal of her, his unwillingness to join in the family event. And relief that he had declined the invitation. He was obviously in one of his foul moods and his presence would only have strained the relaxed atmosphere.

Stuart wasn't coming, and she hadn't wanted him here.

The knowledge sent tiny ripples of shock coursing down her spine, and she shivered. What was happening between them? This gradual drawing away, the failure of either of them to meet on common ground. Her friend Jill's words, loud in her mind. *It won't last. You're too different.*

But it had been good, in the beginning. 'Opposites attract,' she had assured Jill.

'Wait until the lust wears off,' pronounced Jill darkly. 'Then you'll come down to earth with a thump. Great sex isn't everything. You have to be able to talk to the guy the next morning.'

They had laughed good-naturedly about it then, but the words occasionally came back to haunt her. Had Jill been right? Was the relationship finally grinding to an end?

Pushing the thought aside, Callie descended the back steps. 'He's not coming. Says he doesn't feel like it,' she said, in answer to her mother's raised eyebrows.

'That's too bad,' said Michael, breaking the awkward silence as he relieved Bonnie of the tray of meat. 'Now, let's get this started, shall we?'

Michael attended to the steaks while Bonnie went back up to the kitchen to prepare a salad. Callie sat on a nearby chair, nursing a glass of wine, watching.

'Off to Cairns tomorrow,' he said with a grin, turning towards her. 'Photo shoot for a new range of swimwear. All those golden bodies and miles of female flesh,' he added with a mock sigh.

Callie fought back a faint sensation of inexplicable jealousy. Stop it! said an inner voice, overriding her initial reaction. She was turning into a shrew. Michael had his own life, and was not tied to her in any way. He was free to do as he liked, when he liked. Besides, this was work.

'Bit late in the season for a new range of swimwear,' she said instead, taking a long sip of her drink.

Michael shook his head. 'It's for next year,' he replied. 'They work well ahead in the fashion industry.'

At that moment Timmy bounded from the direction of the creek, Freya following sedately along, boots in hand. The boy was carrying a bucket and water slopped alarmingly from its sides as he ran. 'Hey, Dad, look what I've got. There's snails and taddies, and the littlest fish you've ever seen!'

Michael dutifully inspected the contents of the bucket then sent his son upstairs to wash before tea. Freya, watching him go, smiled. 'Reminds me of when I was a kid,' she said. 'Callie's father, Alex, and I spent hours down in the water.'

Tea passed without incident. Afterwards, with the washing-up done and Timmy looking decidedly weary, Michael suggested leaving. 'I've got an early start to the airport tomorrow and this boy belongs in his bed,' he said to Bonnie. 'Thanks for the evening and the chance to look through the house. It's a lovely old place. I'm sure you'll find a buyer quickly.'

Callie sat in the front passenger seat as the car sped through the streets. Already Timmy was asleep on the back seat, his head lolling against a pillow. Michael, looking straight ahead, had both his hands on the wheel, guiding the large vehicle deftly around the corners.

Finally they came to a standstill against the curb outside the block of units. Glancing up, Callie saw that her rooms were in darkness. Stuart had obviously gone out, or had decided to go to bed early.

Michael walked around the car and opened the door. Callie stood on the footpath, feeling awkward. 'I've enjoyed the day. It's been great.'

'So did I.'

'And thanks for the lift. You've still got quite a drive back to the city.'

'It'll only take an hour at this time of night.'

'Well, goodbye.'

She touched her hand to his, a gesture of farewell, but as she went to move past, Michael caught her by the wrist. She halted, turned towards him, coming up against his chest, feeling the pressure of his hand on hers.

'Callie?' he said, his voice low.

'Yes?'

She raised her face towards his, confused. Suddenly, in that unexpected moment, he reached down and brushed his mouth across hers. Warm lips caressing her own, a brief touch of flesh. She was too surprised to move, the motion completed before she had registered it.

He stepped back, staring at her for one long moment before releasing her arm and walking back to his side of the car. He paused at the open door, facing her. 'I'll be up in Cairns all week and I've promised Tim I'd take him to the Zoo next weekend. Like to come along? It'll mean a trip up to the city.'

'That sounds great. I'll see what Stuart's plans are and let you know.'

'Call me,' he said, ducking into the interior of the car.

The engine revved as Michael let out the clutch and the Mercedes moved down the street, headlights illuminating the trees along the side of the road. Heart hammering, she turned blindly away, heading for the stairwell and her own front door. As she fumbled, trying to put her key in the lock, the door opened with a rush and Stuart stood there, silent and stony-faced.

'What's going on, Callie?'

'What do you mean?'

'He kissed you. I saw it.'

'He's only a friend, for Christ's sake. It was only a goodnight kiss. There was nothing more to it.' She turned towards the bedroom, then, suddenly, turned back again. 'You were spying on me,' she said incredulously.

Stuart shrugged. 'Seems to me you're spending a lot of time with your *friend*,' he replied. 'Perhaps you don't want me around any more.'

He looked so sad, like a lost little boy. Callie put her arms around him. 'Oh, Stu,' she whispered, stroking his hair. 'You don't have to be jealous of Michael. We're sharing an interest in the past, nothing more.'

Stuart stiffened and pulled away, his mouth set into a tight line. '*Jealous*?' he repeated. 'You think I'm *jealous* of that photographer schmuck from the city. You've got to be kidding!'

And, with that, he stormed off to bed.

Callie made herself a cup of coffee and sat at the table, sipping the hot liquid. Despite his hasty and hot denial, it was plain to see that Stuart *was* jealous — though he had no reason to be, she quickly told herself. There was nothing between herself and Michael, apart from one hasty goodnight kiss that

289

had, for some reason, made her heart act like a runaway train. Don't be silly, she silently reprimanded. A man like Michael, tall, good-looking, off on exciting assignments in exotic locations, surrounded by bikini-clad models, was sure to have a bevy of beautiful and available girlfriends.

The remaining contents of the cup of coffee had gone cold. Dispiritedly she swished them down the sink and tiptoed to her bedroom. Stuart lay sprawled sideways on the sheets, taking up most of the room. She thought of sliding in beside him and looked ruefully at the tiny space left on her side of the bed. Suddenly she felt she could not touch his skin, that to do so would raise nauseous feelings inside her.

Instead she went to the study and quietly closed the door. She worked till three a.m., fleshing out a bit more of the plot of the novel and, when she could scarcely see the blinking cursor for tiredness, she pulled a rug and pillow from the cupboard, curled on the sofa and slept.

CHAPTER 19

Michael tipped the contents of the plastic bag onto the kitchen bench. He had collected the relevant articles weeks earlier from his sister Anne; however, this was the first chance he'd had to sort through them.

Timmy had phoned earlier, wanting the necessary information for his genealogy assignment. There wasn't much, Michael thought with a grimace as he flicked through the pile. An assortment of newspaper clippings that had been pasted into a scrapbook, a few handwritten memoirs jotted down by his father before his death, official certificates. Sparse and unexciting, he couldn't help comparing them to the unexpected treasures that had appeared from Hannah's trunk.

The thought of Hannah made him think of Callie and the proposed trip to the zoo. She hadn't rung, as she had promised, and he was loathe to make the first move. Leave it, an inner sense warned. Don't get too involved. She was already in a long-term relationship with another man. He had no right to make demands on her time.

Determined to put her from his mind, he turned his attention to the contents of the bag. Skimming through the scrapbook, he found a few obituaries which provided relevant death dates. His father's memoirs, which he had first read a few years earlier, provided a sketchy outline of his life, growing up in Brisbane during the Depression, his involvement in the war that followed.

We have to go back four generations, Dad.

Timmy needed dates mainly, and information on Michael's grandparents. His father's parents had died when he was very young. Their names, a vague blur in the recess of his mind, would be recorded on his father's birth certificate.

It must be here somewhere, Michael thought, scrabbling through the remainder of the paperwork, impatient to be done. He found it almost at the bottom of the pile. It had been folded several times, the paper thin and tearing along the creases. Carefully he smoothed it flat against the bench before jotting down the relevant details, making a mental note to have it laminated at a future date to prevent any further deterioration.

His grandparents' names were there — James and Cecilia Paterson — their respective ages and places of birth, James' profession. His own father's date of birth, the medical attendant who had witnessed the birth, and the date of registration.

Frowning, he brought the paper further into the light. Strange, he thought, that his father's birth hadn't been registered until over eighteen months after the event, until the fifth of October 1918. He shrugged, the fact unimportant. There was probably a logical explanation, had any of those involved been alive to offer one. At least he had some dates and information for Timmy. He would pass them on to his son when he picked him up on Sunday morning, en route to the zoo.

Callie! Thinking of the planned outing again, without realising it, his thoughts had come full circle. Why hadn't she made contact? The prospect of not seeing her that weekend depressed him. He glanced at the phone hanging on the wall above the kitchen bench. Ring! he silently willed. Ring and tell me you'll come.

But the offending instrument lay silent.

Lifting the handpiece, he listened to the resulting burr for a few seconds before thoughtfully replacing it. At least the wretched thing wasn't out of order.

'Damn!' he muttered, shoving the paperwork back into the bag.

Deflated, he went to the fridge and took out a cold beer, and then sat on the back verandah with the Labrador, Bess. 'Hi, girl,' he said, fondling her ears as she shuffled closer and lay at his feet.

The dog had been Timmy's constant companion during the early years of his childhood, never far from the young boy's side. However, Gaby had moved into a unit after the separation and, out of necessity, the dog had stayed with Michael. At the time he had thought it ironic. Gaby had his son. He had the dog. A slightly unequal division.

Beyond the chirruping of crickets lay a cacophony of city noises: the muted roar of traffic, the occasional siren, a series of honks on a car horn that seemed uncomfortably close. Alien sounds that jarred at his senses. For one brief moment he felt disjointed, out of place. As though he didn't belong.

'This is crazy,' he muttered to the dog. 'Paying rent on this old house. About time we settled down and bought a place of our own. What do you reckon, Bess?'

Gently he fondled the dog's ears and she thumped her tail on the verandah boards in agreement.

Stuart had been called out of town for work for the second weekend in the past month. It was Thursday before he announced the proposed trip, punishing her, Callie supposed, for what had been an innocent, no-strings-attached kiss.

'I'll be back late Sunday,' he cautioned brusquely. 'So don't expect me for tea.'

The weekend loomed temptingly before her. After several days of frosty silence, having the unit to herself would be a relief, Callie considered, as she watched him leave on Friday afternoon.

Several times during the last few days, her mind had replayed the scene on the footpath with Michael. Clearly she remembered the firm grip of his fingers on her wrist pulling her close against his chest, the way his lips had brushed against hers.

It meant nothing, she was certain of that. Just a gesture of friendship, a way of thanking her for an enjoyable day. So why couldn't she stop thinking about it? Why did the images keep revolving in her mind, her memory replaying every small word and gesture?

Considering Stuart's reaction, Callie hadn't mentioned the invitation to join Michael and Timmy at the zoo on Sunday. Call me, Michael had said. Yet she hadn't, not wanting to rock the proverbial boat any further. And now, with the freedom to spend Sunday however she chose, she was reluctant to do so.

Back off, said an inner voice. The friendship was badly affecting her relationship with Stuart. Things really couldn't go on like this. Perhaps it was best to cut the ties now, before she became too involved. She should ask for the diary back, distance herself from this man who elicited strange responses from within, who kissed her on the mouth and caused her heart to hammer, and made her accountable to Stuart.

'No,' she muttered determinedly, awarding the telephone a furious glance. She would not be tempted to call him, however much she might enjoy the day out.

'So,' she said loudly, suddenly hating the silence of the rooms. 'What am I going to do?'

Two whole days of pleasing only herself, not having to dance attendance on someone else. Two days of listening to her kind of music, of reading the old letters, of doing bloody nothing in particular, if she chose. Two days. Forty-eight hours. She was determined not to waste them.

Loading a combination of calming oils into her aromatherapy burner, she stacked her favourite CDs into the player, turned the volume up to a reasonable level, took a bottle of icy cold chablis from the fridge and made chicken stir fry.

The telephone rang about eight o'clock. Callie's hand hovered over the receiver, wondering whether to answer it or not. Commonsense won out. It could be Stuart ringing to let her know he had arrived safely, though she thought it unlikely.

It was Bonnie.

'Hi, Mum. What's happening?'

Her mother sounded tired. 'Not much. We've had a few lookers at the house. Freya's gone to bed. She's spent hours in the yard this week and her arthritis is playing up. What about you?'

'I'm a bachelor girl this weekend. Stuart's away on business.'

'Again?'

There was a slightly disbelieving note to her mother's voice.

'Hey, I don't mind,' Callie assured her. 'Gives me a chance to catch up on a few things.'

'Such as?'

'You know, housework, friends. Michael and Timmy are going to the zoo and he asked me to join them.'

She could have hit herself in frustration. Why had she mentioned that? And why all the questions from her mother?

'Are you going?'

'No.'

'Why not?'

'Mum! This is worse than the Spanish Inquisition!'

'Sorry. I'm just worried about you, that's all.'

Mum worried? She and Freya were the ones facing a major upheaval in their lives. 'Look, I'm fine, really. You sound tired,' she added, deftly changing the subject. 'Why don't you hop off to bed, get an early night.'

'I might do that,' her mother agreed.

They exchanged good nights and Bonnie hung up. Callie poured another glass of wine and changed the stack of CDs, loading in a few old Bob Dylan's that Stuart hated.

She flopped into one of the leather armchairs and closed her eyes. Dylan's raspy voice floated out to meet her, sawing away at her consciousness.

Hey, Mr Tambourine Man, play a song for me.

Words of songs that made no sense.

In that jingle jangle morning I'll come following you.

Jumbled phrases and psychedelic scenes linked with music. Memories taking her back, not forward, to childhood and freedom, and not having to make choices.

When she woke, stiff and cramped, the CD player had turned itself off and the bottle of wine was empty. Wearily, she turned off the lights and went to bed.

On Saturday morning Callie cleaned the unit. Throwing open the wide balcony door, she let the warm breeze blow the curtains about as she vacuumed and dusted and polished. Intermittently she tramped up and down the stairs, inwardly cursing every step, to hang washing on the line. Later, with all surfaces gleaming and the clothing and linen still drying, she loaded hat, towel and sunscreen into the Suzuki. Then she headed down the hill towards the village proper, parking the car in a shady spot under one of the pine trees that lined the esplanade.

The beach was crowded, as it usually was in the last few weeks leading up to Christmas, and the water was momentarily cold, almost taking her breath away. As she headed away from shore with long, even strokes, several children on body boards swept past, narrowly missing her.

It was glorious out there, sun beating down and scarcely a cloud to be seen. She glanced back at the beach, dotted with coloured umbrellas, noting that she was still between the lifesavers' flags. Then, lying on her back and looking skywards, she seemed to be drawn towards infinity, into that same unending blueness that went on and on forever, broken only by the smudged outline of a white seagull hovering high overhead.

Waves came and went, washes of froth and bubbles that died against the sand. She rose and fell with the surge, feeling herself being picked up and carried along. Eventually it returned her to the shore, further along the beach. Stumbling from the water, she headed towards her towel, dried herself, and walked back to the car.

The route took her past the lifesavers' pavilion and the small kiosk that sold pies, drinks and ice-creams. On impulse, as she passed the row of public phone boxes, she dialled Jill's number.

'Hi, it's me. Any plans for the evening?'

Jill had recently ended her latest romance and was, in her own words, 'footloose and fancy free'.

'Are you kidding? Just me and the television tonight, kiddo. I'm beginning to think this being-single caper is for the birds.'

Callie grinned. Despite her intentions, her own evening stretched ahead, lacking promise. 'Feel like coming around? We'll order takeaway and watch a video.'

'Sounds great.'

'Good. I'll pick you up in ten minutes.'

Jill was waiting on the footpath, tapping her foot impatiently. 'About time,' she joked, sliding into the front seat of the Suzuki and depositing her raffia bag onto the floor at her feet. 'Already three gorgeous guys have stopped and asked me if I wanted a lift somewhere.'

'You wish,' grinned Callie good-naturedly.

They chatted as they drove back to the unit, catching up on the events of the past week. Callie told her that Bonnie and Freya had finally listed the Brunswick Street house for sale, and about Michael and Timmy's visit, omitting the part about the kiss and Stuart's reaction.

'Seems you like this guy a lot,' commented Jill when she had finished.

'Yes,' Callie agreed. 'He's nice. A photographer, did I tell you?'

'Twice.'

'Oh, dear,' laughed Callie, pulling into the parking bay at the block of units. 'Tell me if I'm becoming a bore.'

Oscar came to meet them at the door, miaowing loudly. 'Where's Stuart?' asked Jill as she scooped the cat up and walked into the lounge room.

Callie slid open the sliding glass door that led onto the balcony and arranged her wet towel over the railing. 'Away for the weekend,' she called, twisting her head and directing her voice back inside. 'Conference. Something to do with work.'

Jill came to the open doorway and stood looking at her, hands in pockets. 'What, again?'

That same note of disbelief: Jill was starting to sound like Bonnie.

Patiently. 'Yes, *again*.'

'Why didn't you go with him?'

'I wasn't asked.' She went to the kitchen, taking a bottle of wine from the fridge. 'Drink?'

'Yes, please.' Jill took two glasses from the cupboard as Callie wrestled with the cork, which finally came away with a loud pop.

'Is everything all right between you two?' asked Jill as she took a sip of the wine.

'Of course everything's all right. What's with the questions? You're starting to sound like my mother.'

'You don't think', Jill persisted, 'that there's more to all these weekends away than meets the eye?'

'Don't be silly!' snapped Callie, annoyed by the suggestion.

'Okay,' Jill shrugged. 'Let's leave it at that. I didn't come here to argue about Stuart.'

'Me either.'

They stood facing each other, not knowing what to say next. The visit was going all wrong. Jill had never liked Stuart, that much Callie knew. Yet he had never come between them, until now. With a supreme effort she smiled and said, 'What about tea? I'm starving.'

She had somehow missed lunch and the swim had sharpened her appetite. They ordered home delivery Italian: ricotta ravioli for Jill and tortellini for herself, and a large Greek-style salad which they would share. Callie took another bottle of wine from the fridge.

300

Jill, who had barely finished one glass, compared to Callie's two, looked up in surprise. 'Hitting that a bit hard, Cal, old girl?'

'So?' Callie shrugged.

The wine made her feel good and blotted out the events of the past week. Stuart's frosty silences. The misunderstanding about that god-damned bloody kiss.

The delivery boy, according to Jill, was drop-dead gorgeous but a bit on the young side. They laughed over that while they sorted through lettuce, black olives and cubes of fetta cheese.

'So what are you doing tomorrow?' asked Jill, spearing a plump pillow of ravioli.

Callie shrugged. 'I haven't decided. Michael did ask me to join him and Timmy for a day at the zoo.'

She had done it again. Why? Was she waiting for Jill to offer her seal of approval? She had already decided to ignore Michael's invitation, hadn't she?

'And?'

'I'm not going. Definite. Final. End of story.'

'Always Callie the writer,' laughed Jill. 'You're starting to sound like the thesaurus you've always got your nose in.' She put down her fork and settled her elbows on the edge of the table, propping her hands under her chin. 'So what's stopping you?'

'Stuart.'

'But he's not here. While the cat's away ...'

'If only it were that simple,' Callie sighed.

'So there *is* something wrong?'

'Okay, okay,' she said, throwing her hands in the air in defeat. The two women had been friends for too long to be able to hide any real feelings from each other. 'He's so jealous. Not only of the time I've been spending with Michael, but the letters, the diary. He can't see why on earth I'd be interested in them.'

'So you're going to let that jealousy rule your life? You're going to compromise your own happiness for his?'

'Look, I know you don't like Stuart. I'm sorry, but I can't help that, and I won't apologise for the man I chose to make my life with.'

'What life?' interjected Jill. 'Can you honestly tell me you're happy?'

'I don't have to justify my life to anyone,' protested Callie hotly. 'It's just that. *My* life. No-one else's. Can't you leave it alone?'

'All right, have it your own way. But you don't fool me.'

They finished their tea in silence and washed up. Callie produced the video, an old Cary Grant movie that made them alternately laugh and cry. By the end, she was feeling quite magnanimous towards Jill, happy to forgive and forget their earlier disagreement.

Jill phoned for a taxi and the two women waited on the balcony for its arrival. The air had cooled slightly and the stars were out, winking from the dark void above.

'Are you going to ring?' asked Jill, kissing Callie lightly on the cheek as the taxi pulled into the curb below and tooted.

'No.'

'For Christ's sake! You're not doing anything morally wrong. You're not planning to have an affair with this man, are you?'

'Of course not,' retorted Callie, standing back, shocked, folding her arms protectively across her chest.

'No,' laughed Jill. 'I didn't think you were. Good old Cal.'

The taxi tooted again. 'Gotta go,' she said, blowing a kiss. 'Be good. And call him. What harm can it do?'

What harm indeed? mused Callie as she cleaned her teeth and prepared for bed. The wine had made her impulsive and brave. She glanced at the clock on the bedside table. It wasn't late for a Saturday night. Ten o'clock. Michael probably wouldn't be home, anyway. Some hot date, no doubt. Single men didn't spend Saturday nights alone.

Impulsively she picked up the phone and dialled the number. 'If you and Timmy are still going to the zoo tomorrow, I'd love to come,' she blurted when he answered, saying the words quickly before recklessness gave way to commonsense.

They were waiting at the main gate when she arrived: Timmy dressed in shorts, T-shirt and joggers, Michael in faded jeans and loafers, and a pale chambray shirt which was open at the neck to reveal the sprinkling of dark hairs on his chest. Hands in pockets and wearing a wide smile, he looked, as Jill would have said, infuriatingly handsome.

'Hi,' he said, kissing her briefly on the cheek.

'Hello,' echoed Timmy, standing back, suddenly shy. 'I'm glad you could come.'

'So am I,' replied Callie.

She had lain awake for hours the previous night, deliberating the wisdom of her actions. What if Stuart came home early and found her gone? What if her absence started a whole new round of arguments? She couldn't take much more. It would be easier to give in, end her friendship with Michael, play the game Stuart's way.

Michael paid the entrance fee and Timmy ran ahead. 'The elephants are over here,' he called, following the signed path.

'Well,' noted Michael with a grin as they followed. 'Looks like it's this way to the pachyderms.'

It was very hot, a steamy heat rising up in waves from the ground. After an hour Callie was exhausted. Michael steered them in the direction of the cafeteria and ordered cold drinks. Timmy had met up with one of his school friends and ran off to look at the birds, leaving them alone.

'So,' said Michael, stretching his long legs under the table and settling back in the chair. 'How's the book coming along?'

'Great. It's what they call a novella, very short, and I should be finished in a few weeks.'

'Any ideas for the next?'

'Steady on, I haven't got this one off the block yet,' she laughed.

'Just wondering.'

'Actually, I've not said anything to anyone, even my agent, but I do have a few ideas floating around.'

That was Michael's cue to inquire further and he didn't fail her. 'Such as?' he asked, sitting forward, propping his chin on his knuckles.

'Well,' she began tentatively. 'I was thinking about something based on the letters and diary. Hannah's and Ben's story.'

'Sounds good.'

'I wanted to talk to you about it, run the idea past you first.'

'It's your family,' he replied, a puzzled expression on his face. 'Nothing to do with me.'

How could she explain? He was so tied up in all of this, an integral piece. Without his approval, it wouldn't feel right.

'True. But you seem part of it, somehow. In a way you started all this.'

'That's okay. Blame me.' The corners of his mouth turned upwards, caught somewhere between mock indignation and a smile.

She laughed. 'If you hadn't brought the horseshoe back, then my curiosity about Hannah wouldn't have been aroused. I probably wouldn't have even bothered looking in that trunk. So I'm holding you partly responsible and, as such, I need your blessing on the project.'

Michael shrugged. 'It's okay by me.'

'Good. I've done a rough draft, just a few pages. You might like to have a look next time you're over.'

Why had she said that? There was no way she could invite him back to the unit, not the way things stood at present.

'I'd like that.'

Confused by her own thoughts, Callie looked away. A silence loomed awkwardly between them. She needed words to fill it, to tip into that growing void. 'The concepts behind the First World War were fascinating, really, when you think about it,' she said, seizing on the first thought that came into her mind. 'Thousands of Australian men giving up their lives to fight for a country that most had never seen. It wouldn't happen today. We're too selfish.'

Michael frowned. 'That's a rather cynical observation.'

'Perhaps. Would you give up your life for a country you had no connection to?'

'Probably not,' he laughed. 'But don't forget, many of those soldiers had English parents or grandparents, and there was a fierce sense of loyalty towards the place of their ancestors' birth. We're so much more removed these days. Talk of republicanism, of breaking away entirely. Then again, the whole nation's divided on that issue.'

Callie felt herself relax, warming to the conversation. 'I borrowed a few books from the library and they make interesting reading. Did you know that during the war, so many women found themselves pregnant after their soldier boyfriends had gone away that the Prime Minister introduced a marriage-by-proxy scheme into Parliament.'

'Meaning?'

'Meaning a marriage ceremony with only the bride present, and the written consent of the groom. But the churches were against the scheme. Their leaders argued that it encouraged sex before marriage, and the proposal folded.'

'I guess war promoted some strange ideas.'

'It was such an intense time, not only for the soldiers overseas, but for those who stayed at home. The uncertainty of war, the not knowing. People made every minute, every day count. It disrupted the whole system of life back here. Women were forced to take on men's jobs. Families were torn apart.'

Timmy came running up, his eyes shining with excitement. 'Come and see the tigers, Dad! They're huge, this big!'

'Feel up to it?' grinned Michael as he stood and held out a hand to help Callie to her feet.

The day passed quickly. 'Come and have tea with us,' offered Michael as they made their way back to the cars. 'I promised Tim we'd go out for something to eat before Gaby picks him up.'

For a moment she wavered, caught between the possibility of Stuart's early return and not wanting the day to end. Michael, as though sensing her indecision, added: 'It won't be a late night. Unfortunately work beckons early tomorrow.'

She parked the Suzuki behind Michael's Mercedes in the driveway. The yard was overgrown and the lawn needed mowing; however the inside of the house was clean and tidy. The living room boasted a comfortable lounge and a state-of-the-art hi-fi system. Callie sorted through the stack of CDs while Michael changed, and they walked the few blocks to the local pub, where they had a perfectly satisfactory, though noisy, meal.

Someone was waiting at the house when they returned, a sporty white BMW parked behind Callie's own car in the driveway.

'Coming, Mum!' called Timmy, running ahead along the footpath.

So this was the mysterious Gaby, Michael's ex-wife. Blonde hair pulled back into a fashionable knot and wearing a white linen suit and heeled shoes, she was a striking-looking woman. Callie, still in her sun dress and feeling decidedly hot and damp from the day at the zoo, felt drab by comparison.

Michael introduced them and Gaby flashed her a warm smile. 'Pleased to meet you. Timmy's been telling me about your lovely old house.'

Timmy charged towards his mother, face beaming. 'We had a great day, Mum. We saw elephants and lions and ...' He stopped and looked enquiringly at his father. 'What was that type of monkey called again?'

'A baboon,' Michael prompted, standing with his arms folded and smiling in the direction of his ex-wife and son.

Callie had been prepared to dislike this woman who had once been married to Michael and had borne him a son. For weeks she had pondered over the fact, seeing the unknown Gaby in a variety of guises. Cold and aloof. Selfish. Callous. But the Gaby who stood in front of her seemed none of those things. Now, as Callie watched, she unconsciously bent down and gave her son a hug, heedless of the white skirt, which raised Callie's growing estimation of her threefold.

It came to her then, as she stood looking at them, that they were a family. Dysfunctional perhaps, broken, but definitely not bloodied. They had shared things she had only ever imagined, tried to put form to in the pages of her books. Marriage. Parenthood. The pain of divorce. What had Michael said? *We simply grew apart. One day we stopped still long enough to realise that the only thing we had in common was our child.*

She said her goodbyes. Gripping the steering wheel of the Suzuki, she followed Gaby's BMW out of the driveway and down the road, after promising Michael that she would phone him the following week. Reaching the detour towards the freeway, she sped along the on-ramp, finally merging with the other homeward-bound cars.

She was caught in their mass, a surrounding crush of metal and other lives, propelling her own vehicle forward. Suddenly she felt trapped, both physically and mentally. She was committed to Stuart, wasn't she, despite their differences of late. But Michael, intruding on her life . . .

Why did her thoughts keep turning to him at unexpected times during the day? What attraction did he hold for her? There was no denying she found him good-looking, and he felt so comfortable to be around. Yet the feeling that had overwhelmed her as she had watched him with his ex-wife and son earlier . . . She took a deep breath. 'Well, just exactly what did you feel?' she asked aloud. 'Envy? Jealousy?'

She had accused Stuart of the same emotions. Accused and criticised him for that exact response, and realising that, felt a surge of guilt.

Heartsick she stared ahead, watching the lines of brightly coloured cars weave along the road, and felt an enormous sense of loss. Loss for something she had never experienced, perhaps never would. *Admit it*, she told herself. *It's your own feelings you can't trust.*

'I can't ring, I can't!' she said, over and over again, furious with herself. She shouldn't have come today, shouldn't have exposed herself to them, that sense of family. It only served to accentuate her own miserable state of affairs.

She was walking out of the shower, towel wrapped around her wet hair, when Stuart let himself in the door. He was smiling and carrying a bunch of red roses.

'I know I've been a jealous arsehole, but I can't help it,' he said, looking contrite as he held out the flowers. 'I love you, Cal. What's happening to us?'

What motivated him, guilt or concern? Callie didn't know.

Instead she surprised herself by promptly bursting into tears.

CHAPTER 20

With the sudden onslaught of wintery conditions, almost every man in the company had come down with either bronchitis or a cold. Like most of the others, Ben felt lousy. His ears ached. His eyes stung and his head pounded. Never, ever had he felt so miserable.

To make matters worse, the camp at Bleu had proved only temporary and, a few days later, the company marched to Steenwerck. Their task, the men were informed, was to improve the stables and huts for the division.

'And no wonder!' exclaimed Tom, following Ben into the remains of a row of cottages that would provide their own accommodation. 'We're here to fight the bloody war for them and this is the best the French can do?'

Several large rats scurried across the room, diving under the shredded remains of newspapers. There was a stale stench of urine and mildew. Miraculously the roof was intact and the earthen floor dry. At least, they were out of the infernal mud that seemed to surround the town.

The hard work would start the following morning and the remainder of the day was his to do as he pleased. Ben wandered into the main part of the village. Surprisingly, there was a small selection of shops, a bath house and a barber. After a long soak in dirty tepid water and a haircut, he felt more like his old self.

Hands thrust deep in his coat pockets to ward off the cold, he trudged along the footpaths. There was a feed store and a grocer's, café, butcher shop and bootmaker. At the end of the row stood a small haberdashery. The window housed a pretty display of baby clothes. Stepping closer, he could see a fine lacy shawl, a selection of bonnets, tiny jackets and hand-knitted bootees. He pressed his nose against the glass, thinking suddenly that he should buy something for Hannah. Christmas was quickly approaching and, in recent weeks, he had not had the opportunity to make any purchases.

He wandered into the dark interior of the shop. A woman bustled forward, speaking in rapid French, gesticulating with both hands. He shrugged, not understanding. 'Buy something,' he stammered. 'For a lady.'

'Ah,' she replied, smiling broadly, leading him towards a display case and pointing to a pair of gloves. 'Perhaps the *gants* for monsieur?'

Ben strained to make out the words. The woman spoke with a heavy accent and any conversation was obviously going to be awkward. 'Yes,' he said, nodding in affirmation. The gloves were lovely, ivory in colour and beaded around the wrists with tiny imitation pearls. 'I'll take them.'

While she wrapped his purchase, Ben strolled across to the counter that displayed the baby wear. His eyes were drawn to the garments, impossibly small. Tiny openings for necks and arms. Exquisite lace edging the hems.

'You want to buy?' the woman enquired, handing over the carefully wrapped gloves. '*Pour le bébé.*'

In the end he selected several garments, including the shawl. It was white, knitted in an intricate pattern, with a long fringe. Hannah would love it, he was sure.

Feeling buoyed by his purchases, Ben strolled across to the tea room where, for a few francs, he was served a plate of sandwiches and a cup of coffee. Hunched in his coat, parcels at his feet, he sat at the table and sipped at the coffee, which was almost cold.

Past the grimy window a steady parade of soldiers, carts and the occasional lorry trundled by. Two men were picking their way through the mud on foot. They were middle-aged, their backs bent under a load of wood. Behind them trotted a large dog, scrawny, its ribs prominent beneath its mangy coat. As he watched their progress, Ben scrabbled in his pocket for a pencil and piece of paper.

Dear Hannah, he began.

He described it all. The mean poverty of the town, the icy chill that no amount of warm clothing seemed to keep out. The rats, the filthy huts. The almost-cold coffee that tasted of something more, a mixture of the best and worst of this place, of loneliness and an ache for the need of her. Finishing his makeshift meal, he begged some brown paper and string from the proprietress and clumsily wrapped the packages together, slipping the letter inside. Hopefully the parcel would leave with the following morning's mail.

Thankfully they only stayed in the village for a few days, repairing what time and supplies would allow. The mud around the stables and horse standings was horrendous, great slabs caking onto the soles of boots. The rats made sleep fitful, the eternal scurrying and rustling keeping him awake for hours. Already he longed for quiet, for blessed silence. But where they were ultimately headed, he knew, he would find none.

The company moved into Armentières. The town, or what remained of it, sprawled along the banks of the River Lys, two miles from the Belgian border. Two years earlier, it had been briefly under German control. Even now the enemy waited only a few miles distant. As he marched through the streets, kit bag and gun slung over shoulders, Ben could hear the occasional boom of guns.

This was the closest they had come to war and the evidence of it surrounded them. Ben stared about in amazement. Scarcely one glass window or roof remained intact and the streets were pitted with huge shell holes. Entire fronts of buildings were torn away, spilling timber and rubble and the lives of the former inhabitants into the streets. Beyond the windows that still contained glass, the curtains were drawn. No cries of children could be heard, no barking of dogs.

It was a town strangely silent.

The men were billeted at the tram sheds on the northern outskirts of the town. They were huge draughty buildings where the wind blew straight through, sending a moaning sound about the exposed rafters.

'Just look at this place!' Spud complained bitterly. 'We'll all freeze to death in here.'

'Give it a rest,' ordered Jack. 'Jeez, you're starting to sound like those whingeing bloody Poms. What did you expect anyway, the Ritz?'

Tom scratched his head. 'Could be worse, mate. Think of those poor bastards stuck out in the trenches. Least we've got a roof over our heads.'

Spud gave him a dismissive glare. 'It's fucking winter,' he growled. 'Cold enough to freeze the balls off a brass monkey. Do you think we could get those doors shut?'

With much pushing and shoving, they managed to close the huge doors. Spud went off, happy now, to find himself a corner to deposit his belongings. Ben glanced around. Against one wall stood a row of cars. They were covered in dust, their tyres flat.

He tried the handle of one, expecting it to be locked, but it opened easily. Squeezing himself inside, he was surprised that the seats had been removed, leaving a large empty space.

The car became his home. He propped a sign against the windscreen that read Ben's Place, and they all had a good laugh at that. Tom claimed occupancy of the adjacent vehicle, and the others quickly followed suit. A canteen was set up in one corner, and the smell of food soon filled the air.

'God, I'm starving,' said Tom, propping himself on an empty fuel drum.

'What do you fancy?' Ben crawled from the confines of his vehicle after stowing his gear. 'If you could have anything at all, what would it be?'

'Fat juicy steak,' interrupted Jack as he sauntered up, hands in pockets. 'With creamy mashed potato and lashings of fried onions.'

'Na!' Spud was determined to have his say. 'Fresh prawns. Nice juicy crab. Just fancy a bit of seafood.'

'Cook could probably organise a few tins of sardines,' joked Tom. He turned back to Ben. 'What about you?'

Ben thought for a moment, remembering hastily constructed dinners at the forge while Da was still alive. Nothing inspiring there. 'Hannah's sweet pie,' he said at last. 'You know, the lemon one she used to make.'

She had brought him slices after Da had gone to the sanatorium, tasty pieces to tempt him to eat. What he would give for a slice now, her gentle words, the taste of her mouth!

He glanced around at his circle of friends, seeing the familiar faces. All younger than him. No worries, no cares. Their only concern was surviving the war, going home. Yet he had the responsibilities of the world weighing on his shoulders. Hannah, and soon a child.

His heart went out to her, wrenched with guilt. How could he offer any support, thousands of miles away? He could send money, help her financially, but he so desperately wanted to be there when the time came, to hold his newborn child in his arms.

He gave a sigh and turned away, walking blindly towards the car. Nothing was as he had planned. Everything had gone wrong. Spud, Jack and Tom. They were his friends, his mates, yet sometimes he felt alone amongst them.

Although they were not on the front line, there was plenty to keep the men occupied. Existing bridges were being prepared for demolition, and several emergency pontoons required repairs. In his spare time Ben took long walks along the riverbank, pushing his body against the icy wind until he was gasping for breath. Beside him flowed the black sluggish water, chunks of wood and building debris bobbing on its surface, which was cold-looking and oily, and reflected back a rainbow of swirling colours.

In their spare time, Jack and Tom built a spring cart from left-over materials. Spud promptly christened it the Souvenir Cart, and they took it with them about the ruins of the town, collecting salvageable articles as they went. A piece of timber here, a sheet of metal there: useful items that were stored back at the tram shed in an ever-growing pile.

Winter had set in with a vengeance and the accompanying frosts rendered the mud solid again. Security was tight in the town. Guards stood on duty along the lines of breastworks made from piles of sandbags. They nodded as Ben passed, offering the occasional cigarette, grinding out their own stubs on the single row of duckboards — planks chained together to form a path — at their feet.

It was Christmas Eve before the company moved forward to the front line. Reluctantly Ben dragged his kit from the car that had been his home for the past few weeks and joined the line of men marching along the road. The distance was only a few miles, but the day was cold, with an icy wind that bit at his ears and numbed the extremities of his face. His boots chafed at his heel, so much so that he was sure a blister was forming. Rub. Rub. Rub. How much further? he wondered, every step more painful than the last. He raised his face skywards. Everything was grey — clouds, sky, even his mood as he swung along.

The destination trenches were a maze of ditches partly dug into the frozen ground, but mostly built up and sandbagged on the side facing the enemy, to afford protection from bullets and shells. Gingerly they settled in, stowing their gear in an earthen dugout, several of them voicing fears that it might rain.

The weather conditions were still looking unfavourable and, under Sergeant Hayes' direction, the men began carrying out site improvements. The previous engineering company had already begun digging new communications lines behind the main trenches. Thankful for some task that would keep him warm, Ben took up a shovel and went to work.

The going was hard. The ground was frozen almost solid and the tip of the shovel jarred in his hands. He thrust harder, feeling it bite into the soil as he levered chunks of it away. Soon he was perspiring heavily, peeling off layers of clothing until he was wearing only trousers and a sweat-soaked shirt.

As darkness fell, the men were fed and sent into the trenches. There was nowhere else to go. The surrounding land was flattened and desolate, dotted with the shredded remains of tree stumps, shell holes and mounds of spoilings. They sat awkwardly on the wooden duckboards, fifty men wearing gas masks in the alert position, trying to keep their boots out of the pools of water that lay alongside.

During the day, the silence had been broken by sporadic gunfire. Now, under the heavy mantle of night, everything was hushed. No sound of guns. No hiss of approaching gas cylinders. Just infernal bloody quiet.

'Perhaps it's a pre-Christmas cease-fire?' offered Jack, his voice hopeful.

'Yair, maybe Fritz has all gone home for a few days,' added another. 'You know, a bit of festivities, crackers and bon-bons.'

Tom stuck his head over the top of the trench, staring into No Man's Land, the short barbed wire-riddled distance between them and the enemy. 'Can't see a thing,' he said.

Sergeant Hayes promptly pulled him back. 'Get down, you stupid bastard! Want to get your fucking head blown off?'

They sat, looking at each other, not knowing what to do, what to expect. Here they were at the front line. The enemy lay in wait only yards distant. The fact that it was Christmas Eve seemed like a hideous joke.

'You know, I'd imagined something different,' whispered Tom, leaning towards Ben.

'Such as?'

'Lots of noise, shouting, ear-shattering explosions, bright lights.' He glanced about, looking finally up at the sky. The clouds had cleared, leaving the darkness sprinkled with a myriad of stars. 'But it's so quiet.'

From further along the trench came a solitary voice.

Silent night, holy night.

Ben stiffened, turning his head towards the sound. A man was singing, the low melodious notes rising and falling on the cold air.

All is calm. All is bright.

Several others joined in, their voices blending, gruff and slightly out of tune. The song moved towards him, weaving its way through the darkness, arriving before him like an offering. Join me, it pleaded. Be part of what I am.

'Round yon virgin, Mother and Child,' he said, speaking the words self-consciously.

It was Christmas and he didn't *want* to be part of it, in this strange country, singing songs that made him long for home. He wanted to be with Hannah, needed desperately for everything to be the same as it had been twelve months earlier. Da. The forge. Familiar things. The need rose up inside him as an ache. It swept through him in uncontrollable waves, causing him to double over for a brief moment, until the agony passed.

'Are you all right?' hissed Tom, a frown creasing his brow.

Holy infant so tender and mild.

Ben nodded, not trusting himself to speak. They were all singing now. Over fifty men, a varied combination of voices. He pressed his hand against his mouth, willing the words to come.

Sleep in heavenly peace.
Sleep in heavenly —

The words stopped as a flare rose in the sky, illuminating the length of the trench with blue light. Briefly it burned above them, then went out, as though someone had turned off a switch.

'Jesus, what was that?'

'Those bastards are up to something.'

A runner from the Division came pounding through, dodging legs and sprawling bodies. 'You blokes keep your heads down!' he panted as he ran past. 'Looks like Fritz is going to give us a few fireworks tonight, after all.'

Ben's company were engineers, not trench soldiers. Their only means of protection were their Lee Enfield rifles and gas masks. No match for what lay beyond. Suddenly Ben envied the regular chaps with their heavy artillery. At least they could fight back.

As the heavens opened up above, he crouched in the trench, back pressed against the sandbags, willing the ground to swallow him, to take him from the noise and gut-wrenching fear. Was this the time, the place where he was doomed to die?

It was like cracker night, he thought, only on a grander scale. Bigger, louder, more frightening. The stench of cordite filled the air. There were whizzes and bangs that made his ears ring for minutes afterwards as shrapnel shells screamed with mad fury overhead. The far end of the trench seemed to teeter. The force of the explosion rocked outwards, spewing a cloud of black smoke. Earth flew towards him in clods. It showered his face, stinging his body.

Someone was screaming. On hands and knees Ben crawled forward, holding his head low, waiting for another explosion, one that would take him into oblivion.

It was Will. The lad sat on his heels, rocking, his arms wrapped around his legs. His eyes stared straight ahead, unfocused. Shrill animal-like sounds came from his open mouth.

There was a large crater where the walls of the trench had been. One man lay partly buried by the soil. Only his legs were visible, puttees and boots protruding. Ben scrabbled in the clay, frantically digging. 'Shit! Oh, shit! Someone help me!'

But hands were pulling him back, impeding his progress. 'It's no use,' said a voice in his ear.

He couldn't stop. Whoever lay buried had to be pulled free. How many minutes could a man survive without air? He hit out at the hands. Another explosion sent him momentarily down on his knees, his head bent low, arms protecting the back of his neck.

'Leave it!' the voice yelled. Ben glanced up and found himself staring into Sergeant Hayes's face, his mouth close to Ben's ear so he could be heard. 'He's dead. Let's get out of here.'

The noise was still coming out of Will's mouth. Ben crawled across and gave him a stinging slap to the face. Will stared uncomprehendingly. 'Come on,' Ben said, pushing the lad roughly.

They struggled to their feet and, in a running crouch, made for the far end of the trench.

It was the first death in the Company. The body was removed and they all stood to attention as the stretcher bearers struggled past. The wrapped shape had been one of them. Less than an hour earlier, he had been a living, breathing ...

Ben stopped, not wanting to dwell on the possibilities. Later, as one of the sergeants moved through the men handing out packets of Gold Flake cigarettes, everyone seemed quiet, reflective.

'It could have been any one of us,' murmured Jack, holding a match to a cigarette as he took a deep breath. The tip glowed, a tiny pinprick of red illuminated against the night. A wisp of smoke curled around his face.

'Yair, bad luck to be standing where he was. If he was further down the line ...'

'Fate,' growled Spud. 'If there's a bullet out there with your name on it, then you're done for. No matter where you are, it'll find you.'

It seemed a pragmatic approach. Life was cheap on the battlefields. Hundreds, sometimes thousands, dead every day. Unknown names in foreign newspapers, inked words. The actual horror of it meant nothing until you were there, amongst it all.

Christmas morning was spent hard at work on the line. After lunch there was mail, two large bags full. Let there be something from Hannah, Ben prayed silently, as the letters and parcels were handed out along the communications trench in which they were all huddled. And there was. Hungry for news of her, he tore it open, hunkering down on the ground and steadying the pages against his knee.

The paper smelt sweet, like lavender.

If I had one wish for Christmas, it would be that you were here, she wrote. *Every day seems interminable without you. I am keeping well and the baby is growing so big. By the time you receive this letter, I will only have a month to go.*

He closed his eyes and tried to picture her, big-bellied and huge with their child. But the scene that came to him was the usual one, Hannah lying in the bed on that last morning together, dark hair fanned across the pillow, and a wash of love went out to her. Resolutely he pushed the image away and turned his attention back to the letter.

Sometimes I feel so frightened. I'm scared of bringing a child into a world with such an uncertain future. Oh, God, I wish you were here.

There were smudges on the paper and some of the ink had run, the letters watery and blurred, just legible. Had she been crying as she'd written them? he wondered, folding the pages and placing them in his shirt pocket, close to his heart.

After the mail had been distributed, the men were all handed a Comforts Fund box. The parcels were larger than normal and contained knitted socks, cigarettes and tins of 'Invicta' tobacco, handkerchiefs, writing paper and a small tinned plum pudding.

Spud promptly began removing his boots. 'Oh, shit, mate. Not today,' laughed Jack, pretending to hold his nose. 'Put me off the plum pud, the smell will.'

Spud pulled on the new socks and threw his old ones over the front of the trench. 'There you go, Fritz!' he yelled. 'Present for you. Merry Christmas!'

The newspaper reports, which she poured over at every available opportunity, kept Hannah informed of the happenings overseas. The names, foreign to her then, would bring back bitter memories when she heard them repeated, years later: Amiens, Ypres, Verdun. Of Ben's actual whereabouts, she had no clue, other than that he was in France.

According to the doctor, the baby was due at the end of January, one month's time. Huge and lethargic with the onslaught of the hot weather, she counted the days. Mrs Worthington had relieved her of her duties in the downstairs ward two months earlier, when even her large apron had failed to disguise her condition. Instead, she plodded around the house attending to odd jobs for her employer, and helped in the study with the bookwork.

She spent her evenings sitting in her room, knitting or sewing some tiny garment for the child. Occasionally she sat still, her hand curved over the mound that was her belly, feeling the reassuring shape, smiling to herself as she felt the movements — the sudden press of a hand, the thrust of a tiny foot — that never ceased to amaze her.

Her heart hammered with a mixture of emotions: impatience at the slow-moving days as she waited for the child's birth; delight at the thought of finally holding the baby to her breast; and, most of all, fear. She brought her hand to her stomach, feeling it ripple under her touch. What about the pain? What if she cried out and screamed?

The days rolled on, bringing her closer to her time. Some evenings Lottie called in, bouncing on the end of the bed, anxious to tell Hannah of the latest happenings in her life. Correspondence from Ben arrived sporadically, swinging her mood alternately between delight and desolation.

She tried to tell him how she felt, pouring out her heart in the letters. But somehow, re-reading the words before she sealed the envelope and set it on the hall table for the mailman, she felt her emotions had been lost in the translation. How could she expect Ben to understand? He was living under a different fear. Hers was a womanly anxiety.

One evening, as she was preparing for bed, she looked up to see Mrs Worthington standing in the doorway. 'Hannah, I'd like to speak with you a moment,' she said, letting herself into the room and closing the door.

Hannah sat on the edge of the bed and waited.

'How are you?' her employer asked. 'Are you well?'

'Yes.'

'Your baby will be born soon,' Clare Worthington went on. 'Not long to go now.'

Hannah nodded, saying nothing. She wished her employer would get to the point.

'I've been making enquiries. There's a woman who has a house in the city. She's a midwife. A good one, I'm told. Her name is Lizzie. When your time comes, you'll go there.' She walked across to the window, looking down at the garden below. 'You should have a small bag ready, Hannah. Nightgown, underclothes, toiletries.'

'But it's not due for another month!' Hannah blurted.

'Sometimes babies have a habit of coming early, my dear.' Clare Worthington turned from the window, a frown on her face. 'Have you given any thought to what you'll do afterwards?'

'What do you mean?' replied Hannah, surprised.

Her employer's tone was blunt. 'You don't have the finances to support a child. I know someone who could give your baby a good home. It will be loved and well cared for.'

'You mean adoption?'

'No.' Clare Worthington exhaled slowly. 'Not exactly. When the birth is registered, it needn't be in your name. No-one need ever know you've had a child.'

'*I'd* know!' replied Hannah hotly.

Mrs Worthington looked as though she were trying to curb an inner impatience. 'Be sensible, girl! I can't keep you on here with a child. The disruption to the household would be incalculable.'

'I won't let anyone take my baby,' said Hannah quietly.

'There'll be other babies when your young man comes home,' Mrs Worthington went on ruthlessly.

Hannah didn't answer. She tightened her mouth and glanced away, too angry to speak.

Mrs Worthington walked towards the door. As her hand closed over the knob, she turned. 'You've a few weeks left yet,' she said. 'Time for final decisions then.'

'Over my dead body,' whispered Hannah when she was sure her employer had left.

On her next day off, she caught the ferry into the city, planning to buy a small Christmas gift for Lottie. Down Queen Street she went, amazed at the transformation. Pine boughs were strung along the façades of buildings. Small birds flitted amongst the pointed needles of the branches, chirping merrily. Even the shoe-shine boy on the corner had decorated his box with sprigs of pine.

Shop windows were overflowing with a bright assortment of festive wares: toys and clothing, jewellery, scarves and perfumes. In the doorways of grocery shops stood displays of all manner of exotic fare. There were sweetmeats, fruit and bon-bons, souchong tea, jams and mince-meats.

On one corner, the Salvation Army band beat out a lively carol. *Deck the halls with boughs of holly. Tra-la-la-la-la. La-la-la-la.* The pavements were crammed with last-minute shoppers: mothers towing small children behind them, businessmen and bankers, farmers and shopkeepers. Bright-eyed young women jostled each other and called out season's greetings to those they knew. Hannah, head down, hoped no-one would recognise her.

On Christmas morning she was woken by Lottie shaking her shoulder. 'Come on, sleepyhead, wake up. It's Christmas.'

Wearily Hannah rolled over, encountering her friend's beaming face. 'What time is it?'

'Five o'clock.'

'Five o'clock!' Hannah groaned and tried to close her eyes again, but Lottie was pushing something forward.

'Come on, you might have the day off but I've still got to work. I wanted to give you this before I went downstairs.'

Hannah struggled into a sitting position and opened the clumsily wrapped parcel. Out fell a pair of baby's bootees. They were home made, the workmanship atrocious. Obviously Lottie was still mastering her skills with the knitting needles.

'Do you like them?' Lottie asked, smiling hesitantly.

'They're lovely,' said Hannah, throwing her arms around Lottie's neck. 'Just beautiful.'

Hannah held out her own gift, which revealed a packet of scented writing paper and a tin of boiled lollies, Lottie's favourites.

Suddenly she remembered the parcel that had arrived a few days earlier. It had been addressed in Ben's handwriting, with precise instructions on the back that it was not to be opened before Christmas. Lottie fetched it from the top of the dresser and Hannah tore the paper aside.

Inside were two separately wrapped packages. She opened the smallest one first and drew out the pair of beaded gloves. 'Oohh, aren't they lovely!' gasped Lottie admiringly.

Hannah set them aside and tackled the second parcel. 'It's clothes,' she murmured delightedly, pulling them out, one by one. 'Clothes for the baby.'

There were tiny gowns edged with delicate lace, bonnets and singlets, and a beautiful white knitted shawl. Inside the shawl was a letter, which had somehow escaped the censor's attention.

By the time you read this, it will be Christmas Day. I send you much happiness, my love, and wish I could be there to share it with you. I am not much use here to anyone, I'm afraid. All I do is think of you and our baby, and how much I miss you.

I am saving hard. If you need money, let me know. The thought of you and our child is the only thing that keeps me strong . . .

Try as she might, she couldn't stop the tears that rolled down her cheeks. She sensed her face, lopsided, her mouth suddenly uncontrollable. They were tears for Ben and the child, and her own crowding fears. Tears for Elizabeth and John, her parents, long gone. Tears for Lottie, who had lost her own child.

'Don't,' whispered Lottie in a strangled voice. 'Please don't cry.'

Lottie's arms went around her, holding her close. Together they sobbed, their tears washing together, mingling, at the injustice of it all.

CHAPTER 21

Callie and Stuart were invited to the house in Brunswick Street for Christmas dinner. Stuart had agreed, though not graciously, to attend.

'Usual hot boring day,' he grumbled. 'Don't see why we can't spend the day with some of my friends for a change.'

'We could have a few of them over for supper,' Callie offered placatingly. Her own friend Jill had mentioned she might call past after tea. 'We'll be home by then.'

'Don't bother,' was Stuart's terse reply.

Stuart and his moods! She was at a loss what to do. Their presence at Bonnie's was an accepted part of the Christmas ritual. To suddenly stay away would invite all sorts of questions, to which Callie had no substantial answers.

'Well, I'm going, so you can please yourself,' she snapped back, unable to control her temper. 'And while you're at it, at least put a smile on your face.'

Her one concession had been the purchase of a new squash racquet, which Stuart had been admiring in the window of the sports store. In return, he handed her an elongated box. She opened it to find a gold and emerald bracelet nestled on a bed of shot silk. 'Oh, it's beautiful!' she gasped, the argument momentarily forgotten as Stuart fastened it around her wrist.

They were about to leave for Bonnie's when the telephone rang. Callie ran back to answer it, leaving Stuart to reverse the car from the garage. It was Michael.

'Merry Christmas.'

The sound of his voice raised her spirits. 'And the same to you.'

'What's on the agenda for today?'

'We're going over to Mum's. She usually goes the whole hog. Turkey. Baked dinner. Christmas pudding.'

The sharp toot of a car horn broke her concentration. Stuart, no doubt, impatiently waiting in the courtyard below.

'So what are your plans?' Studiously she ignored the summons.

'Oh, just the usual. Gaby and Timmy are calling past to collect me later. We usually have a family day over at her parents' place. Swim in the pool. Too much food. Gaby's mum usually does salads.'

Thinking of Gaby and Michael spending Christmas Day together with their son, sharing the festive spirit, Callie felt a momentary pang of envy. Her own Christmas Day was looming as a potential disaster.

The car horn tooted again, this time a little louder and longer. 'I've got to run,' she said, part of her not wanting to put the phone down at all. 'Stuart's waiting.'

'Ah, the formidable Stuart.'

She wasn't sure what he meant, and there was no time for lengthy explanations. 'Got to go. Bye.'

'Who called?' asked Stuart as she slid into the car.

'Wrong number,' she answered without hesitation.

Bonnie was waiting at the door as they pulled up. 'Merry Christmas,' she called, waving them inside.

During the meal, Stuart appeared edgy, ill at ease. Several times Callie glanced across the table at him, but he did not acknowledge her attention. It was the usual baked dinner: turkey and ham and chicken, potatoes and pumpkin, and Callie's favourite, cauliflower and cheese sauce. Dessert consisted of Bonnie's Christmas pudding, dark and moist and filled with shiny sixpences.

Afterwards Stuart pushed his chair back and got to his feet. 'Lovely meal, Bonnie,' he said. Then he turned to Callie. 'If you don't mind, I'd like to go home. Headache, I'm afraid.'

Bonnie gave them both a questioning look. What's going on? her expression said.

Silently Callie pushed her chair back and went to the lounge room to collect the presents. Without their bright paper, they looked different somehow. Smaller. Cheaper.

There was a movement behind her and she turned. It was Bonnie. 'Is it something I've done, said?' her mother asked, looking worried. 'It's Christmas, Callie. You usually stay for the whole day. What will I tell Freya?'

Suddenly she was tired of the pretences. Why was it always left up to her to make excuses for Stuart?

'Tell her he's pre-menstrual!' she snapped, feeling tears flood her eyes as she turned and ran down the hallway.

Christmas and New Year came and went. To Ben, the days were a blur, a mixture of backbreaking labour and gut-wrenching terror. At regular predetermined hours, the working parties were cleared from the front line and moved back into the reserve trenches. Hunkered there against the icy ground, he kept his head down, hands pressed against his ears as the ground rocked beneath him, the vibrations jarring upwards through his legs and knees.

Familiar hated sounds. Hundreds, sometimes thousands of shells pounding the earth, turning the countryside into a crater-ridden, lunar-like landscape. Whizz-bangs, 5.9s, shrapnel bombs: a never-ending cannonade. Avalanches of mud and debris sliding through the air with a whooshing sound; anguished screaming that seemed to go on and on, like a record stuck horribly in a groove. The thudding of trench mortar strafing and the responding enemy Minenwerfer barrages echoing numbly in his ears long after the attack had ended and the men had returned to their duties.

If there was a hell, this was how he imagined it to be. Dead and wounded men. Limbs missing. Sides of faces torn away. The gasping râles of gas poisoning and bloodied bandages concealing gangrenous, festering sores. These wrecks of humanity passed by, some stumbling on the muddy ground, supported on one side by a mate. Others were carried on stretchers, barely conscious, eyes staring vacantly upwards, each jolting motion bringing another grimace of pain to already tortured mouths.

Mind-numbing, needless. Men killing each other, and over what? Some days Ben couldn't remember. The beginning of all this seemed so far away, another lifetime. And it was, he knew. At night, as he curled in the trench and tried to sleep, he felt as though a blanket had descended, a kind of fog, which would never lift. And always ahead, across the shell-littered barbed wire entanglements of No Man's Land, the hated enemy.

There were daily casualties, trench soldiers mostly, those in the direct line of fire. Somehow, miraculously, Ben's company remained mostly intact. After Christmas the weather worsened. Early morning frosts, thick on the ground, were part of the daily grind. A pale sun shone from cloudless skies, barely warming the frozen ground. For weeks, no digging could be done. The trenches were built up instead, lines of sandbagged breastworks snaking along the ground above the level of the ill-drained land.

Across the plains of Flanders, the wind seemed to blow directly from the North Sea. Ice formed on the men's moustaches and beards. Noses turned blue. Thankfully the quarter master issued an additional ration of clothing — extra underclothes, socks and sheepskin gloves. Particularly welcome were the supply of sleeveless flannel-lined jerkins.

The rations were better than those in the support lines. 'Got to feed the fighting men well,' noted Tom as he unravelled yet another roll of barbed wire. The aroma of lunch cooking wafted from the makeshift kitchen, further back. 'At least the food's all right.'

'Yair,' grunted Spud as he crouched, surveying the breastworks that zigzagged across the level fields.

335

'Fatten a bloke up so he's in peak condition to die. Doesn't seem right, somehow.'

Ben sighed inwardly at Spud's words. The men were all tired. Enemy shells had landed sporadically all night, the noise jerking them awake at odd intervals. Now they were touchy, tempers taut, stretched to breaking point.

They were repairing the previous night's bombing damage to the reserve trenches. At the rear, Ben and Jack were attempting to dig new latrine ditches, but finding the going hard. Fifteen yards ahead lay the main trenches and, in front of them, wire entanglements and lengths of telephone line wound haphazardly along the ground.

Abruptly Jack threw his shovel on the ground. He marched across to Spud, surprising him by grabbing hold of his shirt lapels and yanking him to his feet, pulling his face to within inches of his own. His expression was a mask of fury.

'For fuck's sake, will you shut up! We're not going to die, you stupid bastard! Just cut out the crap talk. We're sick of it, do you hear?'

Spud pulled himself free and stepped back, anger tightening his mouth. His hands had come up defensively, protectively, knuckles white and curled into fists. 'What's so special about you? Invincible, are you? Fight off the Germans singlehandedly?'

'Shut up! Just shut up!'

Crouching, the two men circled each other, waiting for the other to strike.

'Stop it! Both of you! For Christ's sake, stop!'

It was a spontaneous reaction. Ben heard his own voice before registering that the words had come from his mouth. The two men halted and stared at him. 'Ah, fuck,' said Spud, walking away.

Angrily Ben dropped his own shovel and grabbed several handfuls of chloride of lime, sprinkling them into the freshly dug ditch. The dunny trench wasn't the regulation twelve inches deep, but who cared? It was impossible trying to dig in this ground, anyway.

'Going to look for firewood,' he said to Jack, who was staring after Spud's retreating form. 'Coming?'

It was a daily task, scouring the countryside to find the shattered remnants of wood. Tree stumps, branches, old building joists. Picking over the barren-looking ground, if you looked hard enough, you were certain to find something. And the men all looked forward to sitting around the brazier each night, warming hands and feet.

They trudged through the mud in silence. 'What's wrong?' asked Jack at length, after they had wrestled several sticks from the ground, wet but nevertheless prized.

'Wrong?' replied Ben, surprised.

'Something's bothering you. Has been for weeks.'

Was it that obvious, he wondered, the worry about Hannah?

'Have you ever wanted something so bad it hurts?' he asked instead.

'Can't say I have,' Jack shrugged, bending down to tease a partly buried tree branch from its muddy burial place. 'You know me. Easy come, easy go.'

Jack straightened, bringing himself to his full height. 'You still haven't told me what's bothering you.'

Where to start? So far only Tom knew, but he supposed he'd have to tell the others eventually. It might as well be now.

'I'm going to be a father,' he replied simply.

'Well, blow me down!' A smile flickered on Jack's lips. 'A father! I didn't even know you were married.'

'I'm not,' said Ben quietly.

Jack's eyes widened. 'Let me guess. Stray romp in the hay, one last fling before you left home. And now she's up the duff and blaming you. How do you know its yours?'

'No!' He rounded on Jack. 'It wasn't like that. *She's* not like that. I love Hannah. I'd marry her tomorrow, if I could. It was ...'

He stopped, thinking, remembering. Fingers trailing over flesh. The sweet, sweet smell of her. Eyes wide, surprised. Hands around his neck, pulling his mouth onto hers.

The memory was so strong, so real, that it left him breathless. 'Oh, shit. You wouldn't understand.'

He turned away, disgusted at himself, at Jack, precious memories suddenly rendered worthless by the possibility of explanation. It was late January and, any day now, Hannah's baby would be born: a baby conceived in a tiny Brisbane flat, in a bed that was not his own, with a woman who was not his wife. He wanted to be near her, to wait as the miracle that was his child, flesh of his own flesh, slipped from her body. Yet here, in this foreign country, he couldn't bear the not knowing. Son or daughter? Was Hannah well? Mail deliveries being what they were, erratic and irregular, meant he wouldn't find out until weeks later, after everything was over. How could he possibly describe how he felt, the pain that knifed inside him?

'Try me,' suggested Jack, laying a hand on his arm.

He stared into his mate's face, seeing nothing but compassion. 'It's all gone wrong,' he stammered. 'I didn't mean it to be like this. But there's no going back.'

'No.'

A heat was building inside his veins. Words pumped through his mind, fast and furious 'It's my child and don't let anyone say otherwise. Mine and Hannah's. One day I'll get back and we'll be married. There'll be more babies, heaps of them. I always wanted lots of children, did you know that?'

Jack nodded and his mouth parted, as though he were going to respond, but Ben went on.

'I'll get a good job, start another business. Things'll work out just fine, you wait and see.'

The outburst had exhausted him, drained his emotions. He felt them slipping away, and experienced, instead, a feeling of loss, an emptiness that disconcerted him.

'Of course you will.'

Dismissing the conversation, Jack turned his attention back to the buried branch. It pulled away with a sucking motion, accompanied by a little plopping sound. A long bone, putrid streams of flesh attached, came with it. Jack stumbled back as though struck.

It was human, that much Ben knew. He stood staring at it, his eyes drawn to the grainy greyness.

Where was the rest of the body? Buried further down, a rotting decaying mass? He didn't want to look. Didn't want to be reminded of his own mortality, of the frailty, the utter transience of life.

If there's a bullet out there with your name on it ... no matter where you are, it'll find you.

'Bloody hell,' he whispered, sliding his hands over his face, obstructing the view.

But it was too late. The image was already there. Leaning sideways, he was suddenly and unexpectedly consumed by nausea that even several minutes of retching was unable to ease.

Hannah sat at the kitchen table, shelling peas. She had slipped the shoes from her feet and the flagstones were deliciously cold against her skin. Perhaps if she stripped off her clothing and laid her whole body along the floor, she would finally be cool.

She giggled at the thought and Mrs Bonham turned from the stove. Her face was shiny from the heat. 'What's that?' she asked, pushing a stray wisp of hair from her face with the back of her hand.

'Oh, nothing,' replied Hannah wearily. Then: 'I don't know when I've been so hot before. It's like an oven in here.'

'Why don't you pop upstairs for a bit?' offered Mrs Bonham. 'Have a rest. Got to look after yourself and the baby. This heat's enough to knock a grown man out.'

It *was* hot. For almost a week now, the weather had been sticky and humid. Each evening, dark clouds threatened overhead. Thunder rumbled.

Lightning flashed. Yet the storms continually passed, leaving the air charged with unspent energy.

Exhausted, she climbed the stairs, dragging her feet over the carpet runner, thinking only of her bed. She would rest there for an hour, then go back downstairs to the kitchen to help with the final preparations for the evening meal.

As Hannah reached the top step, a pain began, low in her belly. She stopped, holding her hand to the place where it had begun, massaging lightly. She had had little niggles for days now, though the baby was not due for another week. Quiet hardenings of her stomach where the skin felt drum-tight, ready to burst. Small cramps that came and went. Signs, she supposed, that the child was restless to be born.

But this was different. Deeper. More acute. With a thump she sat on the step, her arms cradling the shape of the child through her dress and apron. Warm comforting mound. Solid. As if in reply, the baby gave a kick and she smiled.

As she sat, the pain flooded through her, not unbearable. After a few seconds it passed and she levered herself to her feet and, holding onto the railing for support, walked unsteadily towards her room.

It was steamy in there. She pushed the window open as far as possible and a faint breeze wafted through, barely enough to ruffle the curtains. Lying on the bed, feeling a single bead of perspiration trickle down her neck, she stared at the ceiling.

The baby moved again, thrusting sturdy limbs. Hannah felt the heel of one foot against her hand, a sudden bump that came and went. She stretched, thinking: I'll never sleep. But already her eyelids were closing, her mind far away.

When she woke it was almost dark and the wind had gotten up, blowing the curtains inwards. It was cooler now, with the faint tang of rain in the air. Hannah clambered from the bed and went to the window, inhaling deeply. She could see across the river to the city. A shower of rain was approaching, a veil of white that obscured the streetlights and dark outlines of buildings.

The baby moved, a sudden uncomfortable twist. At once she felt a flood of fluid gushing from her. It ran down her legs and made the fabric of her dress stick damply to her calves. Simultaneously the pain started again, low and insistent.

'Oh,' she whispered to herself, surprised, feeling her way across the room, back to the bed.

What should she do? Call someone? Lottie or Mrs Worthington, perhaps? But the pain had passed again and the rush of fluid seemed to have stopped.

She sat on the edge of the bed, hands wrapped protectively around her belly and waited. The luminous hands of the clock on her bedside table seemed to move very slowly. Finally, after about ten minutes, the pain came again.

It was stronger now, though quite bearable. Outside, the sky was dark. A faint glow from a light further down the hall illuminated the room. A moth hovered, the shadow cast by its wings huge against the wall. She held her breath, counting the seconds until the pain went. One, two three. Concentrate.

It was Lottie who found her, over an hour later.

She stood at the door, peering in. 'Hannah, are you there? Mrs Bonham says to come for supper.'

Hannah, lying on her side, foetal position, gave a small groan in reply. Lottie hovered above the bed. Despite the gloom, Hannah saw her frightened face. Lottie gave a little scream of alarm. 'Oh my Lord! The baby's coming! I'd better fetch someone.' Then she hurried away, the doorway empty again.

Hannah lay in the semi-dark, listening to the muffled sounds of the house below: Lottie's frantic summons as she clumped down the stairs; the slam of a door; voices; the brisk click of approaching footsteps. She was dimly aware of being carried, feeling strong arms under her legs, and sensed the body brace itself against her weight as they descended the stairs. It was Mr Bonham, she knew without opening her eyes, by the faint odour of pipe tobacCo

Downstairs and outside. Fat warm drops of rain on her face. She could smell the sweetness of it in the air. Opening her eyes, she saw only darkness above. Awkwardly, they manoeuvred her onto the back seat of Clare Worthington's car. Cool, cool leather. She twisted and laid her face against it, breathing in the odour. Then the pain descended again as the car pulled away with a series of little jerks.

She remembered little of the journey across the city to the cottage in Leichhardt Street. The motion of the vehicle made her nauseous and, several times, she was certain she would disgrace herself by vomiting all over the fine interior of the car. Then she was being carried again, arms lifting her back into the cool night air.

Distant slamming of a door and cool sheets. She was on a bed. Someone was washing her, stripping the damp clothes from her body and wiping the perspiration and stickiness from between her legs. Surprised, she opened her eyes. Above her hovered a small, plump dark-haired woman. Behind her stood Lottie, a worried frown creasing her forehead.

'Hello, I'm Lizzie,' said the woman, wiping a face cloth across Hannah's flushed cheeks. 'I think we're going to have a fine baby tonight.'

'Yes,' whispered Hannah.

Lizzie dispatched Lottie to bring a cup of ice from the ice chest. 'I need to examine you, see how things are coming along,' she said briskly, once Lottie had gone. 'It won't hurt. Now, legs up here.'

There were stirrups, and Hannah felt her legs being slipped into them. As her belly hardened again with another contraction, she could feel Lizzie's hands probing at her, merging with the pain.

The ignominy, the indignity of it all might have embarrassed her once, but now she was past caring. The safety and well-being of Ben's child, her child: that was the important thing now.

'Good, good, nearly there,' Lizzie was saying as she deftly replaced the sheet and strode to the washbasin on the dresser. 'Won't be long now. About midnight, I'd say.'

Midnight! The hours of darkness had seemed interminable already. What was the time? Dimly Hannah was aware of something cold being passed over her lips. Ice.

'It's almost ten,' added Lizzie, as though in reply to her unspoken question.

344

Hannah grimaced and squeezed her eyes shut, her body automatically tensing again in preparation for the next onslaught.

She had never imagined such pain. It was insidious and agonising, self-focusing, drawing her inwards to some distant place. In jolting waves it shuddered along the length of her belly, cramping low at the base of her spine, leaving her breathless and trembling. On and on it went, until she had lost all sense of time and place. There was barely a break between the contractions now. They rolled over her like waves, huge and suffocating, taking the air from her lungs. From time to time, she felt hands probing and pushing at her, determining the progress of the labour, but the pain separated her from it all, brought up a barrier.

How long had she been there? Hours? Days? Endless spiralling agony seesawing through her body, pulling her downwards into a black bottomless pit. Exhausted beyond all comprehension, she prayed for an end to it all. How could she go on?

Lizzie's hands again. Searching, examining. Hannah's eyes flew open and she saw Lottie sitting in a chair beside the bed. Involuntarily her fingers fluttered upwards and she felt her friend's hand firmly grasp her own. 'It's all right, Hannah. Won't be long now.'

A series of sensations, a shift in focus. A dim awareness of something changing. Pain equalled by an unendurable urge to heave the child from her body. Her hand slid down, touching herself, but there was something strange beneath her fingers, a hard, round bulging dome.

345

She screamed, terrified, snatching blood-stained fingers away, clumsily hauling herself backwards on the bed.

'Hannah? What's wrong?'

Lizzie, walking towards her with an armful of clean towels, came to an abrupt halt. She dropped the linen onto the end of the bed and yanked back the sheet. 'It's coming!' she muttered, nodding, smiling, as she pushed Hannah's nightgown up around her hips and slid her feet back into those hateful stirrups.

Lizzie prying her knees apart.

'Come on, there's a good girl. Baby's on its way.'

A sense of excitement in the room, almost palpable. Hands lifting her shoulders, rounding her forward into a half-sitting position, her belly pressed uncomfortably against her breasts. Legs spread wide.

'Push! Push!'

Obediently she took a deep breath and instinctively bore down. The pressure was unbearable. It shifted and lodged, further down. She could feel it, wedged between her legs.

'Good girl! Now, again!'

She had no reserves of strength. The energy sapped away and she made a half-hearted attempt.

'No, Hannah! You must try harder!'

Drifting away, like a seagull on the wind. Soaring out of reach. Free. Darkness descending, covering everything.

'Leave me alone,' she moaned. 'Take me away from here.' Little girl whimper. 'I don't *want* to be here.'

Brisk little slaps about her face, bringing her back. 'Come on, Hannah. Just a few more pushes and we'll be done.'

The pain was breaking her in two, peeling away the layers of her, like a knife being drawn upwards through her belly. Hands probing. Torturous. 'Go away! Don't *touch* me!'

Someone was shaking her. Lottie's voice. 'Come on, Hannah. If you won't do it for yourself, then do it for Ben.'

Ben! The word transcended everything. Ben waiting in France for news of the child. Ben, separated from her by miles of ocean. Wretched, wretched war taking him away. She had to be strong. Strong for Ben, strong for the child. It hadn't asked to be born, but she would be a good mother. Like Elizabeth. Elizabeth had always been —

'PUSH!'

She gathered the last remnants of her strength. The pressure moved, aided by willing hands, and slithered between her legs. Unbelievably the pain was gone.

'Look, Hannah, look!' Lottie's voice, tremulous with relief.

The baby lay on the sheet. Hannah's hand moved forward, touching skin wet with blood and waxy mucus. 'It's a boy!' exclaimed Lizzie, deftly scooping him up and placing him across Hannah's stomach.

The child lay damp against her skin, staring at her through eyes that seemed a thousand years old. Wise eyes. Blue and unblinking. He gave a mewling sound, like a kitten. Softly, gently, Hannah stroked his arm. She slipped a finger against his palm and his fingers tightened around hers. 'He knows me,' she said, surprised, as Lizzie tended to the delivery of the afterbirth.

She was tired, so tired. A sponge bath and clean nightdress made her feel a little more human. Lottie brought a cup of tea and Lizzie took the baby away. Later she brought him back, washed and dressed. 'Bonnie little chap,' said the midwife, placing him in her arms. 'Eight pounds, two ounces.'

In the early hours of the morning, the sky not yet light, Mr Bonham returned and carried her back to the car. Lottie followed behind, nursing the baby. Sitting on the leather seat as the car moved away from the footpath, the child sleeping in her arms, Hannah felt a sense of quiet peace. This was how it was meant to be. Herself. Ben's child. Only Ben was missing. But he would be home soon, wouldn't he?

The future, that was the important consideration now they were a family. Already the birth was distant in her mind and before the car had turned the corner, the pain of it all had fallen away to a dull blur.

After two weeks, the men were glassy-eyed from lack of sleep. Cheeks were mud-streaked and unshaven. Rank, unwashed smells emanated from bodies. But the expression on their faces was one of victory.

'We made it!' yelled Tom, throwing his hat in the air and catching it deftly, as they made their weary way back from the trenches to Armentières.

'Yair,' growled Spud. 'Those mongrels thought they had us beat, but we showed them, eh?'

They had been to the face of hell and back.

The first thing Ben did after he reached the billets was have a long bath. During the last few days, lice had been a problem, leaving red itchy lines where the seams of his clothes rubbed against skin. Uniforms were sent out to one of the village women to be washed while the men sat around, towels draped decorously about their waists. Luckily the day was sunny and, after a few hours, the garments were returned, cleaned and pressed.

It was an unreal existence, back off the front lines. The men were working but their days were unhurried again, lacking that same degree of fear. Yet only a few miles distant, a war was in progress. Now and then the muffled boom of shelling could be heard, and the intermittent clack-clack-clack of gunfire banged away day and night.

In the town, life went on as normally as possible under the circumstances. The locals, when asked, merely shrugged and smiled. The fighting had become a way of life, a nuisance, but bearable. Besides, the tall good-looking Australians were here to save them, weren't they?

Wine and beer were still procurable from the numerous *estaminets*, a bottle of *vin ordinaire* costing 1.25 francs, and a decent cup of coffee and cheap meals could be bought from several cafés. After work, the purchase of a daily paper at the little shop at the Five Corners and a glass of beer became a ritual. Day-old English newspapers were easily obtainable for the princely sum of twenty-five *centimes*.

January became February. Ben waited anxiously for mail from Hannah, impatient for news of her. Judging by the dates she had given him, the baby should have been born by now. On an average, letters from home were taking six weeks to reach their destination and the anticipation was unbearable. According to Spud, he had become a 'downright touchy bastard'.

It was still bitterly cold. Frost lay on the ground every morning, and the Lys river was frozen so solidly that it could be crossed by horses and wagons. An icy wind howled down chimneys and around corners. Ben felt himself longing for heat and sunshine, and the long hot summer days of home.

One afternoon he borrowed a bicycle and rode away from the town. The wind bowled him along, billowing out his coat. It caught numbly at his ears, his nose. He pedalled furiously, till perspiration dampened his clothes and his breath came in short bursts.

When he finally stopped, he was in a wood. Light ricocheted past the bare branches, slanting across the ground. Rustles came from the underbrush, slight tremors of noise barely heard over the hammering pulse of his heart. Something flapped above him, wings beating against leaves as a flurry of water drops fell to the ground.

It was a bird. He glanced up, watching the outline of it as it hopped from branch to branch. It halted suddenly and opened its beak, thin tremulous notes filling the air.

Ben listened, his eyes straining upwards, neck aching unbearably. The notes rounded and filled out, gaining substance, soaring majestically through the air. Pure, unashamed. A princely calling.

A lark: an unassuming dun-coloured bird with the voice of an angel. Abruptly it finished its song and flapped away, sending a shower of drops around his head. He sighed and turned in the direction from which he had come, wheeling the bike into the wind.

He came to the river. As he walked along the bank, pushing the bicycle beside him, the sun managed to come out for a while, pouring a faint warmth. He walked until it was almost dark, the sky turning from pale blue to deep indigo. As he was about to head back towards the billets, he saw a figure ahead sitting on the bank, hunched against the wind.

It was Will. A rolled copy of *La Vie Parisienne* was clenched in one hand. The other cupped his chin.

'Hello,' said Ben, leaning his bike against a tree. 'Feel like some company?'

Will nodded and looked up. 'If you like,' he replied.

Ben hunkered down, took a packet of Gold Flakes from his pocket and removed two cigarettes. He offered one to Will and the lad took it with shaking fingers. 'Thanks.'

'Are you all right?'

Will shrugged, hands cupped about the cigarette as Ben held forward the match. He took a long draw and exhaled. 'I guess so.'

They talked for a while, general topics mostly. Ben asked Will about his family, his home town. Will answered in a monotone voice, the sound scarcely heard above the wind.

Eventually both men fell silent for a while. The conversation was evidently over. 'Well, I might be off then,' said Ben, hoisting himself to his feet.

Will struggled to an upright position, levering himself awkwardly from the ground. 'I didn't know it was going to be like this!' he blurted, taking a series of rapid puffs on the cigarette.

'What did you think, then?'

Will thought for a while, his forehead furrowed. 'Oh, you know, all that honour and glory bit. For King and country. Support the Motherland!' He took a final puff then bent down and stubbed the remains of the cigarette into the dirt, grinding it down with the heel of his boot. 'My parents are — were English,' he added, straightening up.

There was a certain youthful inflection in his voice. In that half light, he could have been any age.

'How old are you, Will?'

'Sixteen.'

'Sixteen? But how —?'

Will's eyes were white against the dark. 'I look much older, right? They didn't care at the enlistment booth. I was just another number to them. I forged my old man's signature and no-one even raised an eyebrow.'

'And now?'

'Now I'm here in this hellhole wishing I were back home. But it's too late,' he said in a voice that was suddenly hard.

He looked away, blinking rapidly.

He's just a kid, thought Ben. A bloody kid.

CHAPTER 22

Hannah named the baby Nicholas Benjamin Galbraith Corduke.

'Rather a mouthful for such a wee chap,' commented Mrs Bonham, as she fussed over the crib that Mrs Worthington had found in the storage area over the roof of the garage.

Mostly Hannah called him Nick. He was a placid child, eating and sleeping well, as most babies do. Everyone in the Kangaroo Point house cooed and clucked over him, lifting him from his bed every time his tiny face puckered, until Hannah was certain he would be quite spoilt.

She rested for the first day, under strict orders from the midwife, Lizzie. The following morning she wandered down to the kitchen and took up her former post at the table, shelling peas, slicing meat. Anything to earn her keep, while the baby slept alongside in his basket. Mrs Worthington had been kind enough to let her stay on for the first month after Nick's birth.

Mrs Bonham found an old tub, which served as a bath. They all gathered round as Hannah performed the bathing ritual for the first time, tub positioned firmly in the centre of the kitchen table, towels laid out ready. She undressed Nick, who let out a momentary squeal at his sudden nudity, gave an affronted cry as Hannah lowered him into the water, which lapped his chin. Then he relaxed, waving his tiny arms and legs.

Lottie found a large rocking chair in one of the downstairs wards, dragged it up the stairs and deposited it in the corner of Hannah's room. It was here she sat, tucking her feet under her as she held Nick to her breast, watching with a mixture of tenderness and pride as his lips nuzzled her flesh.

The movement of his mouth, that rhythmic tugging, never ceased to amaze her. It calmed her, brought her temporary peace. Watching him, the top of his downy head and his fingers as they curled and uncurled against her skin, she felt both sadness and joy. Joy at the baby who was part of her and Ben, a continuation of them both. Sadness that Ben could not be there to hold his son, to witness the wonder of this, their first child.

She had written a brief letter the morning after Nick's birth. Deliberately she omitted telling him about the agony of it all. Instead she described the elation, the utter relief, that she felt. *He has the required number of fingers and toes*, she wrote, *and I wish more than anything that you could be here. My heart aches for you. The pain is real and won't go away. Come home soon.*

She was woken at varying hours of the night by Nick's demands to be fed. Groggily she slid from her bed and scooped him from his crib, holding him tightly for a moment against her chest, as though reassuring herself he was real. Sometimes Lottie crept in and sat on the coverlet, watching as the child fed hungrily at her breast.

'That could have been me,' she said sadly, the first time.

Hannah glanced at her friend over the baby's nodding head. 'Do you regret it, then?'

Lottie shook her head and attempted a smile. 'Mostly not. Anyway, it's too late for regrets.'

Hannah closed her eyes, taking in the scent of her child. Soft baby smell, of soap and talc. Though mere days had passed since his birth, she couldn't imagine life without him. In part, he fulfilled some insatiable need within her and compensated for Ben's absence. He distracted her, made her daylight hours busy. But at night as she lay in her bed, the tears rolled down her cheeks and she was powerless to stop them. The future loomed ahead, blurred, shadowy. What was to become of them?

Two weeks slid into three. Hannah was constantly tired and still bleeding heavily. Lottie suggested a visit to the doctor, but she was saving hard, putting aside every penny. Mrs Worthington had continued to pay her a small wage, reduced, but nevertheless welcome.

Clare Worthington had been to see her once, taking the baby and carefully looking him over.

'Have you thought about what I said, Hannah? I do know of a young couple who would be happy to take him. He would be well looked after. You need to get on with your own life.'

'This child *is* my life,' she had replied, a pain rising inside her chest at the suggestion. 'The answer is still no.'

She sang to Nick as she fed him, whispered words and snatches of melody, rocking, contented. He lay there, his cheeks flushed, age-old eyes watching her, scarcely blinking. But the knowledge shifted and realigned itself somewhere in her subconscious and became a willing acknowledgement as the days ticked past that life couldn't stay this way. Soon it would be time to move on.

It seemed winter had sent one final onslaught. Back on the front line, the men were faced, either alternately or in unison, with rain, sleet and wind. Ben thought the wind was the worst. It was like a wall of ice, freezing, and almost impossible to walk against. It howled across the desolate land, chilling everything in its path.

Then came the thaw. The water, which lay thigh deep in the trenches, was alive with frogs and plump red slugs. After a few days, the whole area reeked with the stench of rotting decay. Half the company came down with either colds or influenza.

A letter arrived from Hannah in mid-March, revealing the news Ben had waited to hear. Impatiently he ripped open the envelope, hands shaking, eyes quickly scanning the lines. He was a father at last. Sitting on the ground, heedless of the mud, he re-read the words through misty eyes, a mixture of delight and grief washing over him.

Tom came sauntering up, hands in pockets. 'Any news?' He had been asking the same question for weeks now and Ben knew he was concerned for his sister's welfare.

'Yes.' Suddenly his hands were shaking, and it seemed his mouth had a mind of its own. He put a hand against his lips, steadying them. Then he smiled, the news finally dawning. 'A boy,' he said at last, a broad grin creasing his face. 'I have a son. And Hannah's fine.'

'I'm an uncle!' yelled Tom, waving the others over.

Jack brought out a bottle of local wine and Spud went off to the makeshift kitchen, returning with several chipped mugs. Reverently Ben filled them, his hands still trembling badly. 'Christ!' he said to anyone who cared to listen. 'I can't believe it. I'm a father.'

At the first opportunity, he scribbled a return letter. Excitement rendered his words almost illegible, but he didn't care. He enclosed a postal order. She would need money for Nick.

The initial delight stayed with him for days, weeks. At odd hours he remembered, wanting to pinch himself to remind himself it was real, feeling a surge of excitement. Hannah, the child. The thought of them was a promise for the future. Some day the fighting would be over and he would go home. But as he stared at the bleak countryside, at the utter desolation of it all, he knew the war's end to be a dream, nothing more.

Along with the 11th Brigade, the company left Armentières and marched to the nearby Le Touquet sector. The journey was stop-start, the men forced to halt by the roadside ditch as regular convoys of lorries and provisions carts passed.

While he waited, Ben lit a cigarette and surveyed the passing scenery. Though it was spring, there was no sign of change. The earth was bare, with only the occasional remains of a tree trunk spearing towards the sky. Some time in the past the ground had been randomly pitted with shell holes. Graves dotted the sides of the road, mere rubble-filled depressions topped with makeshift wooden crosses. Away to the left, an old woman ploughed a bare field, walking slowly behind the horses as the metal prongs furrowed up clods of dark earth.

The traffic passed and they marched again, a ragged band. Ben hated the constant moving on. He wanted to stay in one place, loathing the upheavals that took him further from familiar territory. There was something unsettling about heading towards unknown destinations and his heart lurched at the prospect. He took the remaining half of the horseshoe from his pocket and stared at it, his step faltering. Slowly he moved one thumb over its surface. A piece of silver-dipped metal etched with words. Some days he felt it was the only tenable link with the past.

The company was billeted at Pont de Nieppe. The accommodation was clean, the stretcher beds free from lice. Though the camp was plagued by bad drainage, there was little time to begin repairs. A few days later the entire area, including Ploegsteert Wood and St Ives Hill, was taken over, and preparations begun for an attack on Messines Ridge, code-named 'Magnum Opus'.

There were trench improvements and extensions to be carried out, and battalion headquarters to be arranged. Ben worked from dawn until dark, tumbling exhausted into bed each night. His dreams were disturbed and distorted, misshapen, filled with images of Hannah. Hannah running across No Man's Land, chased by Germans wearing steel helmets. Hannah lying pale and motionless in a sea of mud at the bottom of a trench. He heard the haunting cry of a child and tried to follow the sound, running through ditches and over desolate fields. On and on he ran, the cry coming no closer. The occasional thunder of shellfire brought him trembling to wakefulness, and he lay there, listening to his own rasping breath, and reminded himself that it was not real.

The month since Nick's birth passed quickly. Apart from the bleeding, which had slowed but not stopped, Hannah felt well, though unbearably tired. On her days off, she propped the baby in an old cast-off pram and went into the city, scouring the 'Accommodation To Let' column in the newspaper.

Closeted away in the Kangaroo Street house, she hadn't realised the cost of housing. At first she thought she might rent a small cottage, somewhere with a square of lawn out the back where Nick might lie on a blanket and kick his chubby legs in the sun. But the price! Quickly she revised her plans. A small flat, then, something with a separate bedroom and a kitchen. But funds were scarce. There was no immediate sign of Ben's return, and her savings and the money he had sent would have to last a few months at least.

Finally she settled on a room in a boarding house in the inner city. It was dingy and run-down, but affordable. Grudgingly the landlady showed her around. 'It's a back room, so it's a bit cheaper. Two weeks rent up front. The bathroom and lavatory have to be shared, and the kitchen. You can use the clothesline on Thursdays.'

Hannah hesitated. The room was tiny and she had seen two cockroaches scuttling across the kitchen floor.

'Well, do you want the room or not?' barked the woman. 'Can't stand here all day yapping. There's jobs to be done.'

The rent was more than she had planned but it was the fourth room she had inspected that morning, and the cheapest. 'I'll take it,' she replied, scrabbling in her bag for the necessary money.

The landlady awarded Nick, asleep in his pram, a scowl. 'I don't usually take children. But what with your hubby overseas, doing his bit for the country, I'll make an allowance just this once.'

Hannah flinched at the woman's easy acceptance of the lie, supported by the purchase of a cheap gold ring which she wore on her left hand.

Mr Bonham brought her few belongings over in the car. 'You be sure to let us know how things work out,' he said, giving Nick a tickle under the chin. 'And look after this little chap.'

Lottie called on her next day off, wrinkling her nose at Hannah's choice of surroundings. 'How you can stay here is beyond me,' she stated. 'Why don't you go home, back to your brother and his wife? At least you wouldn't be wasting all this money on rent.' She held out her hands for the baby, holding him to her chest. 'They wouldn't be able to resist this little scrap.'

David and Enid! She had scarcely given them a thought since Nick's birth, and it had been several months since any correspondence had passed between them. Hannah grimaced as she thought of

Enid's reaction, and acid tongue. 'No,' she replied emphatically to Lottie's suggestion. 'It's not an option.'

The room was minuscule, barely large enough to hold the bed, wardrobe, dresser and Nick's crib, and the window looked out onto a brick wall that scarcely allowed a breeze through. The other boarders were mostly old men who sat in the sun, yarning and smoking. It was a lonely time, just her and Nick and the occasional visit from Lottie. At every available opportunity she set off for the Botanical Gardens and lay on the grass, the sleeping child beside her. Looking upwards at the blue sky, she prayed for an end to all this. No more war. No more senseless killing.

Later, trudging back to her dingy room, Nick clutched fiercely, protectively to her chest, she knew it was wishful thinking, nothing more.

The weather warmed and work went on in nearby Ploegsteert Wood. Signboards and fixed maps were prepared. Gun pits were dug and the cellar of a lodge on the main road was converted to use as a Divisional Command Post. Acres of camouflage netting, laced with strips of raffia and hessian, were draped through the foliage of the trees to hide the gathering troops, artillery and ammunition from enemy planes.

It was there, in that heavily timbered wood, that Ben first heard the soft thudding of shells landing nearby and smelt the whiff of chlorine. Within seconds, the men could hardly see, struggling to pull gas masks over faces while their eyes streamed with tears.

He searched the vicinity for a sign of Will, but the lad was nowhere to be found. 'I think Hayes put him on transport duty,' said Tom, taking the mouthpiece away so he could talk. 'He's back in town.'

The gas stayed in the wood for hours, held low against the ground by the dense foliage and lack of wind. Operations for the day were cancelled and the men returned to billets. Some were coughing and staggering slightly, others suffered vomiting and headaches. For Ben, it was sheer frustration. The end of the war was now an extra day away.

Days of gloriously bright fine weather were little compensation. No rain fell and the mud dried. Preparations went on. The first anniversary of their departure from Australia came and went: twelve months of moving on, strange billets, ever-changing countryside. It was a milestone, of sorts, and he marked the occasion by dashing off a letter to Hannah.

By late May, Ploegsteert Wood teemed with troops. Weeks of sporadic shelling of the enemy lines had already stripped the nearby Messines Ridge of any spring growth. Slowly the landmarks, small dips and gullies, gentle rises, disappeared in a desolate waste of re-formed earth, overlooked by the now shapeless ruins of the village. The wood, with its new duckboard tracks, was no longer a safe place to watch the phenomena of spring. The scent of the wildflowers became lost in the stench of lachrymatory gas, and the note of the lark alternated with the shriek and thud of shells.

It was as though Ben were witnessing the beginning of the end, a terrible monstrosity, the final destruction of the world. Where would it all end? Some days he fought to recall what it was like before the war, struggling to remember a day that was not clouded by choking gas or thudding shells or bullets zinging through the air in search of soft fleshy targets. A hatred rose up in him, mixed with despair. Some days he feared never leaving this place. He would die here, an old man, the bombardments and misery still going on around him. It was already an eternal thing.

On the night before the battle, under cover of darkness, the infantrymen left their billets and marched along dark roads, four abreast. In their thousands, they swarmed towards the front lines. Accompanied by the soft pat-pat-pat of exploding gas shells, they took up positions in the trenches, behind the ribbons of white 'jumping off' tape that lay in the wet grass along the border of No Man's Land. Some gulped thirstily at their water bags. Others curled under greatcoats and tried to sleep.

Ahead in the dark lay Messines Ridge, a black disfigured hump under a full moon. Occasionally a beam of light tailed upwards, bursting into a bright flare. Deep underground, in the maze of damp-walled passages, the British and Canadian Tunnelling Companies set the last of the mines under the German trenches.

Ben, laying out the remainder of the white tape, watched it all in silent horror. Watched the mass of men moving uncomplainingly through the dark towards possible death. Heard the tramp of their feet against the dry earth and the murmur of their voices, and felt a nausea rise in his belly.

'All done?' Spud came sauntering up, hands in pockets.

He tore his attention away and stared blankly at his mate. 'Yes.'

'We'd best be getting back then, before Hayes has the search party out for us?' Spud leaned back against a tree and pulled a packet of Gold Flakes from his pocket, extracting two. 'How about a fag first? Just one, then we'll go.'

The match flared and he held it forward, towards Ben, cupping his hands around the flame. For a moment it highlighted his face, his craggy features. Ben took a puff and the end of the cigarette caught, a tiny red glow in the dark.

Spud laid his head back against the bark of the tree, closing his eyes. 'It'll be a good show tomorrow. Wish we could be around to see the fireworks.'

Ben nodded. Their Company was in reserve during the first stage of the attack and not expected to join in for several days.

'Always the bridesmaid, never the bride,' added Spud, grimacing, and his teeth were a faint smudge of white in the moonlight. 'Seems we get all the dirty work and when the real job's got to be done, where are we? Reserves, for Christ's sake!'

'At least it's safer,' Ben reminded him slowly, nodding towards the lines of trenches. 'We've more chance of surviving this than those blokes.'

'Yair.' Spud grinned. 'But we miss out on all the fun.'

They stood for a while, taking an occasional puff at the cigarettes. 'What will you do', said Ben at last, hating the silence, 'when all this is over?'

Spud considered the question for a while. 'Dunno,' he replied at last. 'All this touring around has given me a taste for travel. Might take off for a couple of years. See the world.' He took another puff. 'Could think of worse things, I suppose.'

'Yes.'

'What about you?'

The answer required no thought. 'I'll be on the first ship out of here,' Ben laughed. 'Can't wait to get back home and see Hannah and Nick.'

'Got it all figured out, then?'

Was there a touch of wistfulness about Spud's voice? 'Yes,' replied Ben slowly. 'I suppose I have.'

'You're lucky,' Spud went on, after some consideration. 'I had a girl, you know, before I joined up. We were pretty serious, or so I thought. But three weeks after I'd gone, she had a new fella.'

'I didn't know.'

'No.'

Suddenly dejected, Ben stubbed out his cigarette. 'Don't know about you, but I'm almost falling asleep on my feet.'

'Go back to camp, then,' said Spud, giving Ben a friendly nudge. 'I'll be along shortly, as soon as I've finished this cigarette.'

Ben moved away. As he looked back, he could see that Spud had moved slightly, now standing in the space he himself had occupied a few seconds earlier. Spud brought one hand up in a farewell salute, just visible at that distance in the pale light of the moon.

There was a crack of rifle fire to his right and ahead, and one brief bright burst of light. Involuntarily Ben flinched and stared in horror.

Outlined against the flare, the scene projected itself towards him like a series of flickering images. A spray of blood. Spud's hand coming up to clutch his throat, clawing at the pulpy mass of flesh. A momentary look of surprise on his face. Body crumpling, folding forward.

There were more shots, loud explosions that echoed dully inside his head. Someone was pulling him back, pushing him in the direction of the camp. 'Run! Run! Get out of here, you stupid bastard, or Fritz'll have you, too.'

It was seconds before he registered that the thudding sound came from his own feet, and the ragged wheeze was his own breath, caught like a gag in his throat.

The thing is, moments earlier, it could have been me. That's the way it is here. A matter of inches separates some of us from life and death. I try to be philosophical about it all, you know, the 'if it's meant to be, then it will be' kind of thinking versus luck, or fate, or simply plain old good timing ...

Hannah folded Ben's letter and put it in her bag, glancing guiltily at the clock on the dresser. David had written, believing that Hannah was still living at the Kangaroo Point house, and Lottie had delivered the letter a week earlier. He would be in the city for the day, to attend to some business for the bank. Surely Hannah's employer would let her take some time off — just an hour or so?

She fed Nick before leaving and settled him in his crib. 'Don't be too long now,' cautioned the landlady who, when offered a few extra pennies, had agreed to look after him. 'Don't want him waking up and making a fuss. Not one for babies, I am.'

Watching over her son as he slept, Hannah had felt a rush of love. Cheeks flushed, chubby fingers splayed against the pillow, his eyelids fluttered, mouth puckering for an instant before flattening again. What were his dreams? she wondered as she tucked the blanket firmly over his shoulders.

Reluctantly she tore her attention from the child and dressed. Pausing in front of the speckled mirror, she surveyed herself critically, turning this way and that, searching for signs of difference in herself. Since she had last seen her brother, she had born a child. Surely there would be some sign, some indication?

Her face was thinner, her cheeks pale. Impatiently she pinched them between thumb and forefinger, bringing an angry line of red to her flesh. Her dark hair was limp; there had been no time that morning to wash it. Deftly she braided it into one fat plait, though wisps of it escaped and fanned about her cheeks. At the last minute, she pulled on a lightweight coat, buttoning it against the drabness of her dress, blew Nick a kiss and hurried out into the street.

There was no sign of David when she arrived at the designated tearoom, so she settled at a table, ordered a pot of tea and took out Ben's letter again.

... We all miss Spud's funny ways and it seems unbelievable that we will never see him again. Any minute I expect him to walk through the door of our shelter, telling us it was all a big mistake. But,

367

of course, that will never happen. I, myself, witnessed his burial. I have written to his folks, telling them ...

The words blurred and Hannah squeezed her eyes shut, blotting them from her vision. What on earth could you say to a parent who has lost a child? What words could possibly ease the pain? As a mother, she now knew these things.

The thing is, moments earlier, it could have been me.

The words, read earlier, jerked back into her consciousness. One bullet carefully aimed in another direction, and she realised she could have been reading a different letter, written perhaps by Tom, outlining the way Ben had died.

Her breath caught in her throat and she feared she might choke. Fighting back a sense of rising panic, she sat for a moment, eyes shut, regaining her composure, willing her breathing to be regular and even again.

After a few moments, she opened her eyes to see her brother advancing across the carpet towards her. 'David ...' she said as she rose. David enveloped her in a hug, leaving his arms around Hannah's shoulders a little longer than usual.

'It's been so long, Hannah,' he said, his face quickly taking on that stern accountant's expression. Brisk. Business-like. 'And I'm late, as usual. Good, I'm glad you've already ordered tea.'

The conversation dawdled along, David grumbling about the lateness and unreliability of trains, his dealings at the bank. Davie's achievements at school were discussed at length, and Lily's somewhat extended vocabulary. What did Hannah think about the progress of the war? When had she last heard from Tom?

Hannah shook her head and listened, not trusting herself to speak. While they talked about Tom, and Enid's involvement in the Comforts Fund and Red Cross, an urgent need to tell her brother about Nick bubbled under her breastbone. Already she had checked herself several times, unconsciously ready to impart some titbit about him. You have a nephew, she wanted to say. He's blond, like his father, and has a smile that can light up the darkest room.

She teetered, caught between the urge, and the fear of her brother's reaction, his conversation blowing through her mind like dry leaves, heard yet not comprehended. Her own words gagged her, dying away in her throat. What to say? How to broach the subject and not cause distress?

She stared at her brother, watched his hands as they moved, emphasising some point. If he notices something, if he starts asking awkward questions, I'll tell him, Hannah promised herself.

But the moment never came. They were interrupted by the waitress and David ordered lunch, a large tray of sandwiches, which Hannah attacked with gusto. It was hours since she had eaten the small bowl of breakfast porridge.

'You're looking pale, Hannah. Are you all right?' David asked, his brow a furrow of concern.

It was almost too much to bear, the lies, the pretences. Tell him, an inner voice urged. But it was too late. If she had been able to confide in him during those earlier days of her pregnancy, it would have been easier, but not now. Too much had happened, too much time had passed.

She glanced at the clock on the wall, alarmed to see that almost three hours had passed. She had promised the landlady she wouldn't be long, and Nick would soon be waking for a feed, demanding her attention.

'I've got to go,' she said, pushing back the chair and rising unsteadily to her feet.

Looking back as she reached the door, she saw David still standing next to the table. He was staring after her, a puzzled expression on his face as he raised a hand in a final farewell. Once out on the street again, she sprinted for the tram.

Back at the boarding house, Nick was crying, red-faced and protesting in the landlady's arms as she paced up and down the footpath, waiting for Hannah's return.

'You said you'd only be a couple of hours!' she bleated accusingly, dumping him unceremoniously in Hannah's arms. 'The brat's been screaming for a feed.'

Mortified, Hannah fled to her room. There, sitting on the bed, she unbuttoned her blouse and held Nick, hiccuping, to her breast. He was quickly soothed, his skin returning to its normal paleness as he curled and uncurled his hands against her skin. Within minutes he was asleep, dark lashes fluttering against his cheeks.

CHAPTER 23

During the first week in February, along with the last of the manuscript to her agent, Callie posted the request for Nick's birth certificate. She watched as the envelope, addressed to the Department of Births, Deaths and Marriages, slid into the dark recess of the post-box, and gave a sigh. Her search for Hannah's past seemed barely begun. So much to learn and she felt she was merely on the brink of it.

Meanwhile, with her latest offering to the publisher finished, she had time on her hands at last. Time to properly clean the flat, she thought with a grimace, bring her accounts up to date, catch up on some outstanding correspondence. Time, she considered with a wriggle of anticipation, to immerse herself properly in the old letters.

But now, she silently admonished herself as she glanced at her watch, it was twelve-thirty. Lunchtime, and a celebratory meal was in order. She would call in at Jill's office on the off-chance that her friend had nothing else planned.

Jill happily offered to forego her prepack of salad and crispbreads. 'My dietary saviour,' she laughed, tossing her lunch box into the cupboard next to her desk. 'Way to go, Cal.'

Callie steered her friend towards *The Red Lobster*, one of the town's more expensive restaurants. 'My shout,' she declared, feeling magnanimous. 'Another book finished, and a few weeks of freedom before I bury myself in the next.'

The waitress led them to a window table that afforded a good view of the street, and Callie requested a bottle of wine. 'You really *are* celebrating!' laughed Jill as the waitress uncorked the bottle and took their orders.

They chatted all through the meal, catching up on each other's news of the past few weeks, waving forks midair and giggling over Jill's latest romance. As the coffee was being placed in front of them, Callie glanced out the window. A steady stream of cars trundled along, while a crowd of shoppers and office workers hurried past. And amidst it all, through a break in the crowd, she saw a familiar figure.

It was Stuart. He was walking briskly away from her, crossing the busy street, weaving his way through the traffic. Halfway across, he raised his hand in greeting. A woman, waiting on the other side, waved in reply. Finally reaching her, Stuart placed both hands on her shoulders and kissed her.

It wasn't a friendly peck-on-the-cheek kiss, but long and lingering, mouth to mouth, the woman's hand coming to the back of Stuart's neck, holding him there. Then, as they moved off, Stuart's hand slipped across the woman's back, downwards, squeezing one buttock. The woman turned her face sideways, towards Stuart, threw her head back and laughed.

Callie stared, unblinking, a wash of numbness settling over her. For one brief moment her mind was frozen, the image of Stuart's fingers burning an imprint in her brain. Fingers pressing in an overly familiar manner, she realised with a jolt, aware suddenly of a pressure against her own hand.

It was Jill. 'Cal, what's wrong? You look like you've seen a ghost.'

Callie nodded towards the window and Jill strained forward, catching a glimpse of Stuart and his companion just as they rounded the corner and were lost to view. 'Oh, Christ!' she muttered, bringing a hand to her mouth. 'Who is she?'

'An architect in Stuart's office,' replied Callie dully. 'Priscilla or Pru — some name like that.'

Her heart hammered erratically in her chest as the scene blurred suddenly before her. She squeezed her eyes shut, willing the tears away. 'Here,' said Jill, thrusting a serviette into her hand. Then, worriedly: 'For God's sake, Cal, don't cry.'

Callie dabbed automatically at her eyes. Her hands seemed to be moving of their own accord, little jerky movements that she was powerless to control. A rush of varying emotions crowded in on her. Disbelief. Bewilderment. Confusion. Shame that Jill should see her like this, reduced to a blubbering mess over some possible infidelity on Stuart's part. *Possible* infidelity? The thought hammered insistently, demanding attention, and she shook her head, pressing it away. He couldn't, *wouldn't* do that to her, would he?

She glanced down. Unconsciously she had been twisting one corner of the serviette around her index finger, pulling the fabric into a tight corkscrew. 'There's probably a logical explanation for what we just saw,' she whispered, her voice suddenly deserting her.

'Cal?' She looked up to see Jill staring at her, a concerned expression on her face.

'No.' She shook her head determinedly. 'I'm fooling myself, aren't I? From what I just saw, they're more than simply good friends. I wonder how long that's been going on?'

Jill looked pensive. 'I've seen them together a few times now. A couple of months, I suppose.'

Hurt welled up inside, forming a tight ball in her chest. 'And you didn't say anything to me? Jilly, you're supposed to be my friend.'

'And what was I supposed to say? Hey, I think your boyfriend's having a fling. Come on, Cal. Besides, I wasn't sure, until now,' she added darkly. 'Bastard!'

One part of her wanted to chase after Stuart, demand an explanation. How long? *Why? Why? Why?* Yet, on the other hand, she was loathe to face him, to hear the truth, knowing it would mean the end of their crumbling relationship. Over two years of loving and living ground into the dirt, flung in her face. A sense of betrayal threatened to engulf her and she stood, swaying against the force of it.

Scrabbling in her bag, she withdrew two fifty-dollar notes and placed them on the table. 'That should cover lunch,' she said.

At once Jill was beside her. 'Let me take you home. I don't think you should drive.'

'No!'

Several of the other diners were staring at them, Callie noticed, swivelling in their chairs to see what the commotion was about. 'Jill,' she said firmly, 'I want to be by myself. I don't need sympathy. I don't want platitudes. I need to think.'

Somehow she found the strength to walk away. Across that seemingly endless expanse of carpet dotted with chairs and tables she went, past the bar area and surprised-looking *maître d'*, until she was standing on the footpath, staring in the direction in which Stuart had disappeared. Through the tears her eyes were drawn to the railing on the old bank building where her great-grandfather, David Corduke, had run the town's finances all those long years ago.

Suddenly she felt sick inside, as though she might vomit. The all-encompassing nausea unsteadied her, made her dizzy.

'Are you all right?' It was Jill at her elbow, laying a comforting hand on her arm.

The solicitude was almost too much to bear. Her heart was breaking, an acute pain that seemed to peel away the layers of her, leaving her vulnerable and exposed. She gave a muffled sob, burying her face in her hands. 'No!'

'Please, Callie, you're in no fit state —'

Stepping back, Callie took a lungful of air. There was an insistent and urgent impulse to flee, though she knew not where, to escape these sudden and frightening feelings.

'I'm sorry, Jill. I can't stay. I've got to get out of here. Please don't follow me!'

Suddenly she was running, along the pavement in the opposite direction to Stuart, around the corner towards her car. She sat there for a while, behind the wheel, catching her breath. Blankly she stared through the windscreen. Pedestrians were blurred moving shapes, scarcely registering, their existence blotted out by urgent, yet less tangible emotions. Hate. Despair. A sense of utter betrayal.

Automatically Callie turned the key in the ignition and steered the car onto the road. She drove randomly, turning into streets she had not ventured down for years, seeing nothing except the road ahead and experiencing a desperate feeling of waste.

Eventually she came to a halt outside the house in Brunswick Street. She stared at the large 'For Sale' sign attached to the front fence. Beyond, the building appeared deserted, the curtains drawn. It was Thursday, she remembered dully. Bonnie and Freya would be at their weekly Senior Citizens meeting. Anyway, why had she come here? What would she tell them? 'I think Stuart's having an affair with someone smart and beautiful and the thought of the deception, the lies, is killing me inside?'

Despondently she headed the car in the direction of the sea, down the narrow winding roads that led to the esplanade, where she parked the Suzuki under the canopy of pines. It was cloudy, with a sou'-easter blowing, turning the waves into choppy whitecaps. The beach was almost deserted during that mid-afternoon period, and only a few surfers waited on the distant line of breakers. Bending, she removed her shoes and stepped onto the sand.

The last time she had been here was with Michael and Timmy. Remembering that happy sunny day, a chill shuddered across her shoulders and she hunched her back against the wind. She walked until she thought her legs might dissolve under her like jelly. Past the occasional fisherman she went, down that long lonely length of beach, surges of froth and water regularly lapping at her feet. The tide was coming in, moving inexorably further up the sand with each successive sweep. When she finally stopped and looked back, the pines and the lifesaver's pavilion were far away, a mere speck.

It was then that the name of Stuart's companion came to her. Not Priscilla or Pru, but Primrose. Stupid bloody name, she thought, remembering Stuart's whispered comment after Callie had met the woman at the annual Christmas party, only weeks earlier. 'They call her Little Miss Prim,' he had said and smiled, obviously at his own deceit.

Now, remembering, Callie sat on the sand, feeling the dampness through her dress, not caring. Nothing mattered anymore. Stuart. The unit. Deception had rendered them both meaningless. Idly she drew her fingers through the sand, back and forth, feeling the gritty grains slide against her skin.

It was almost dark by the time Callie returned home. She let herself in the front door, a feeling of dread settling in the pit of her stomach. A confrontation with Stuart was inevitable, yet unwelcome. Even as a child she had hated conflict.

He was fiddling around in the kitchen, humming. She stood in the doorway, watching him, saying nothing, her mind full of loathsome thoughts.

'Ah, Cal, there you are. I've been wondering where you were.'

Easy words spilling from his tongue. *Cheat, liar*, she wanted to call out, but the accusation was lodged somewhere at the back of her throat. Stuart moved towards her and made to kiss her on the mouth. At the last moment she averted her head, and his lips landed near her right ear. He pulled away, looking surprised.

'What's wrong?'

'That's what I was going to ask you.'

His face assumed an indignant expression. 'I don't know what you mean.'

'I mean High Street today, about one o'clock. Jill and I were having lunch. I saw you with that woman. First you had your tongue almost stuck down her throat, then you put your hand on her *bum*. How could you possibly ask me what's wrong?'

Stuart shrugged and turned back to the kitchen bench. Callie could see that he had been mixing himself a bourbon and ice.

'How long has it been going on?' she asked. 'I suppose I'm the last to know.'

'Well, you're never here!' he exploded, turning back to her with his drink in his hand. 'What am I supposed to do? Sit around twiddling my thumbs until you decide to spare a bit of time for me?'

'I've tried to include you in every part of my life,' she replied numbly. 'You weren't interested.'

Stuart slammed the drink against the bench. Some of the contents slopped onto the laminex. 'If you're not closeted away in front of that computer, you're either running around trying to find out about dead people or sitting with your nose stuck in those old letters.'

He seemed very angry with her, and that hurt. Had she really done all those things he accused her of? Was she really following old ghosts? Callie shook her head, trying to clear her mind. She had only been trying to fit the pieces together.

'They're part of me, my history. If you'd let yourself become involved, you'd see things differently.'

But Stuart wasn't about to be placated, Callie realised as he went on with a rush, his face a mask of fury. 'And Michael. You've been spending a lot of time with him. *Your mate*. Don't think I don't know what's going on there!'

Some sort of pent-up fury seemed to be manifesting itself in his mind and, as usual, he had turned the whole thing around, blaming her. She felt a surge of furious anger. 'There is nothing, absolutely *nothing* between Michael and me! He's a friend, that's all, and I enjoy his company, which is more than I can say about yours for the past few months. You've been moody and irritable and uncommunicative ... and jealous!'

She could see his hand tracking towards her, and felt the force of it as it swung under her jaw, slamming her head back. Her teeth snapped together with a resounding bang. His voice came as a hiss, drawn out, the words tumbling hollowly through her consciousness. 'For Christ's sake, Callie! Get a life!'

He had never hit her before. Had he wanted to? she wondered, the thought sliding randomly into her otherwise numb mind. The act had obviously stunned Stuart, too. His face was a moving kaleidoscope of masks, fury giving way to amazement, then contrition. Suddenly he looked helpless, almost sorry. 'Callie, I didn't mean it. I didn't mean to hit you.'

She could think of no reply.

'For God's sake! Say something! I really am sorry. Something snapped. Things have been getting to me lately. Not just you, but work and —'

'And Primrose?' she interrupted coldly.

She turned and walked away and, thankfully, he made no move to follow. She needed to be alone, wanted no further conversation with this man who had been her lover and who had betrayed her so badly. He hadn't denied the affair, though he had admitted nothing either. But she knew. She *knew*.

Callie was asleep when Stuart came in later, sliding under the bedclothes, and she woke with a start.

'I'm sorry, Cal,' he whispered, bending over her, raining kisses along the length of one arm. 'I didn't mean it. It was just some horrible, horrible mistake.'

'Mistake?' She was fully awake now, pulling away from him. Was he talking about hitting her, or about Primrose, or both?

'Look, it's all over with her.'

So there had been *something*. 'I don't want to talk about it. It's late and I'm exhausted, in case you hadn't noticed.'

'Callie!' He placed both hands on her shoulders and gave her a little shake. 'For Christ's sake, we need to talk. We can't go on like this.'

'No we can't,' she replied tiredly, trying to slide towards the extremity of the mattress.

But Stuart had other ideas. Roughly he pulled her towards him, his hands searching her body. Face, breasts, down the length of her belly, under the oversized T-shirt she had worn to bed.

'Stuart! No!'

She called out and struggled, but he covered her mouth with his and she caught the strong tang of whisky. He was on top of her now, hands probing, fingers urgently seeking. His weight pressed down on her, and she felt his thrusting movements from some faraway place, heard his exultant cries, and felt used. Like a piece of sacking, she realised, and there was such a sense of finality about it all.

Though she tried, Callie couldn't sleep. Later, when she heard Stuart's even breathing, she slid from the bed and crouched under the shower, washing the traces of him from her body. Then, telling herself she had work to do, she went to the study and switched on the computer.

She opened the file that contained the outline of Hannah and Ben's story. Sentences and phrases stared back at her, a jumbled assortment of ideas and quotes from the letters. Blankly she stared at the screen, willing her mind into action, but the words wouldn't come. All she saw was the image of Stuart walking along the road, his hand caressing the woman, and she felt sick inside.

Just after midday Callie answered a knock at the door. It was Jill.

'Only got a few minutes,' she explained. 'Lunch break.' She stopped and peered at Callie. 'Are you all right?'

'No.'

'Want to talk about it?'

Callie shrugged. 'What's to talk about?'

'Tell me how you're feeling? Perhaps it'll help to get things off your chest.'

She tried to smile, but it came out all wrong, her mouth twisting into what felt like a lopsided grimace. 'How am I feeling? That's a laugh? Now, let's see. Hurt, betrayed. Destroyed. How's that for starters?'

'Is that all?'

Incensed now, Callie shook her head. 'There's the way he flaunted this affair in public. What on earth was he thinking of? In a small place like this, there was sure to be talk. How could he let me find out this way?'

Jill walked across the room and sat on the sofa, curling her legs under her, saying nothing, yet watching her intently.

'For Christ's sake, Jill. What am I supposed to do? Forget this ever happened? Put it all behind me like some dutiful ...' Words failed her momentarily and she stood there, tears threatening. 'I've invested so much into this relationship, emotionally, financially. I can't simply walk away!'

'Why not?'

'He says he's sorry,' she replied, the words sounding pathetic even to her own ears. 'I've been neglecting him, leaving him on his own too much. If only I'd —'

'Bullshit! Stuart's redirecting the blame back to you for something *he's* done. Did you force him into the arms of this woman?'

'Of course not!'

'In other words, he did it of his own free will?'

'I — I suppose so. If you put it like that.'

'Callie, I never wanted to be the one to tell you, but this isn't the first time and I'm certain it won't be the last. How can you go on, knowing that?'

Callie turned away, bringing her hands to her ears, as though trying to block out the words, though it was too late and they had already been said. The furniture seemed to sway before her, as though the contents were being sucked into the centre of the room. Was it true? If Jill knew, how many others did, too? Stuart had obviously not been discreet.

The situation clearly required decisions to be made, but she was incapable, her mind spinning. 'I don't know what I want,' she replied in a small voice. 'Tell me, what should I do?'

'Get out,' replied Jill simply, walking towards her and wrapping her arms around her shoulder, making her face the room again. 'Look at this place! This isn't you, all sterile and clinical. Get out and make some sort of life for yourself, before you end up emotionally crippled by this creep.'

Jill stopped and bit her lip. 'I'm sorry, I shouldn't let my feelings influence you. Look, I've never made a pretence of liking Stuart and I'm not about to start now. But for Christ's sake, Callie, I can't stand seeing you like this. Don't fool yourself. Nothing's going to change. Not now! Not ever! He'll always have excuses ready, trying to blame you for his own shortcomings. Can you live like that for the rest of your life?'

That answer was easy. 'No.'

Jill glanced down at her watch. 'I'm sorry, I've got to get back to work. I hate leaving you like this. Will you be all right?'

Callie nodded. 'Thanks for coming over. I guess I've got some thinking to do.'

She was in the bedroom packing a few things in an overnight bag when she heard the sound of the key in the lock. It was Stuart.

'Callie? Are you home?'

Studiously she ignored him, zipping the bag closed as she heard his footsteps bounding up the stairs. He appeared at the door, looking slightly dishevelled, a worried frown on his forehead.

'What's going on?' he asked, his gaze taking in the bag.

'What does it look like?'

It was an effort to talk to him, the words halting and her voice strained. He would want explanations, which she was not ready to give. She shrugged instead, and turned away.

'For fuck's sake, Callie!'

'I'm going now,' she said, trying to keep her voice steady while she hoisted the bag from the bed. He was standing in the doorway, effectively blocking her path. Hopefully he would move. The thought of having to press past him, of any part of him touching her, brought a rush of disgust.

'Where are you going?'

'A motel. I'll be back to collect the rest of my things in a day or so.' The words sounded distant, far-away. A blur of sound. As though uttered by some other mouth, not her own.

She was aware of a sharp intake of breath as Stuart stepped back into the hallway and she was able to move past.

'Callie! Wait! Can't we talk?'

Walking down the stairs, each step leaden and final, she shrugged. It seemed almost an effort to open her mouth, to think of words. What to say? Was there *anything* left unsaid? Worse still, what if she cried? She knew that, once started, she'd never stop.

The sound of his footfalls fell against the carpet, close behind. 'You can't just *leave*. What about us?'

'There's no *us*,' she replied dully, reaching the bottom step. Placing the bag on the tiles, she turned to face him, tired of the pretences. 'There never was. There's you, and there's me. And in the middle there are the other women. God, Stuart! Was I the last to know?'

He had the good grace to look contrite. 'It was nothing. A silly mistake.'

'Don't try and trivialise what happened. I trusted you. How do you think I feel?'

'I love you.'

'No, Stuart. You love yourself. I was just along for the ride.'

'So you're really leaving?'

'Yes.'

'What about the unit?'

'The unit!' She stared at him incredulously. 'You've been having an affair! Our relationship's over — and all you can think about is the unit?'

He shrugged carelessly, lifting his shoulders in an infuriating way. 'We have to talk about it sometime.'

'We'll talk about this when *I'm* ready. It's not something I even want to think about right now,' she added furiously as she fled towards the front door.

She sat in the car for a few minutes, looking up towards the flat. Every light was on, yet she could see no movement behind the drawn blinds. Was Stuart already on the phone, telling Primrose how Callie had callously departed?

Her mind lingered on that thought for a second or two, imagining him dialling the number, his breathless hello. The image flickered and jarred, like an old black-and-white movie. A variety of conflicting emotions jostled for attention, colliding randomly, directing her train of thought at yet another tangent.

She closed her eyes, blocking out the sight of the lit windows, pressing the thoughts away as she stifled a yawn. She was tired, so tired. Too exhausted, she knew, to think rationally. Her priority was to find a cheap motel room, shower and climb into cool sheets, to sleep until morning. Decisions could be made then.

With a deep sigh, she turned the key in the ignition, and the motor purred into life.

CHAPTER 24

From the small village of Romarin, Ben watched as the attack opened at dawn. Even from that distance, he heard the loud muffled boom when the underground tunnels were blown. Ninety-one thousand pounds of ammonal. Nineteen mines circling them in a wide arc.

The earth rocked and buckled beneath his feet, large vibrating shocks that seemed to go on for ages. The distant ridge became liquid red, the colour channelling into crimson fountains that spewed skywards. A mushroom-coloured cloud followed, fanning out as it rose, amidst much cheering from the men.

He had scarcely slept, kept awake by the memory of Spud, the way he had died. When he finally lost consciousness, it had come to him in dreams, every tiny detail distorted, made more horrific, more unreal, until he woke, bathed in a film of sweat.

With a party of attached infantry from the 9th Brigade, the company was in reserve for the first stage of the attack. Two days later they moved into the front lines, relieving the Australian 10th Field Company Engineers. The outgoing men were jubilant as they stumbled past, lugging the heavy equipment. 'Fritz is on the run,' they shouted, smiles creasing tired drawn faces. To Ben, the 'bursting sun' badges on their hats suddenly seemed a good omen, though he wasn't sure why.

The front line again. That same old churning sensation in the pit of his stomach. Moving through the first charred stumpy remains of the wood, past the bloated stinking remains of horses and makeshift crosses hammered lopsidedly into the ground, he heard the familiar soft pat-pat sound, like scattered heavy drops of rain. His nose, sensitive now, caught the first hint of German gas and he fumbled for his mask.

The men were carrying loads of rifles and ammunition. Tools and supplies followed behind on spring carts. It was hard going; the apparatus restricted breathing as they pushed themselves against the lack of oxygen and sleep. The masks also hampered vision and slowed the pace, though Sergeant Hayes was urging them on, hurrying them through the white ghostly drifts of gas that lay about in the artillery areas, amongst the trees and on the ground.

Several of the men at the back of the line pulled the masks from their faces, keeping the mouthpieces between their teeth and clips over their noses. As they passed, dozens of horses and mules were gasping for air, braying pitifully.

There were long stoppages, with much halting and starting. Ben noticed Will towards the back of the line so, over a period of several minutes he dropped back until he was alongside him. The lad was breathing heavily and his shirt was damp with sweat. His eyes, what could be seen of them behind the mask, were wide and dark.

'How's it going, mate?' asked Ben, falling into step beside him.

Will nodded, but seemed either unwilling or unable to speak. He was carrying a large pack on his back, struggling under the weight. 'Here,' said Ben. 'My load's a bit lighter than yours. How about we swap for a while?'

Will nodded again, then stopped, struggling to remove the pack. As Ben slipped his own easily from his shoulders, Sergeant Hayes strode back to see what the fuss was about.

'Come along, no stopping!' he barked, momentarily removing the mouthpiece from his lips. 'No shirkers or bludgers in my company, got that?'

Will ripped the mask from his face. He took a deep breath, gathering air into his lungs, his mouth set in a tight furious line. 'What did you say?' he asked, eyes flinty.

Hayes thrust his face up against Will's. 'I said no shirkers or bludgers! Got that? Now put that mask back on and get going. We haven't got all day!'

Will grabbed his superior by the shirt lapel, thrusting him away. 'I'm not a bludger, you arsehole,' he yelled, dumping his pack and mask on the ground, 'and I've had a gutful of you.'

Before Ben's surprised eyes, the lad was off, sprinting across the ground towards an undamaged section of the wood. Bending down to retrieve Will's discarded mask, he followed.

It was gloomy under the canopy of trees, windless, and clouds of gas hung heavily amongst the vegetation. Will had a head start, and Ben was guided more by the sound of wild thrashing through the underbrush than the faint outline of the lad's body.

389

Over fallen logs they went, through dense thickets of shrubbery. Occasionally, through gaps in the overhead branches, a beam of sunlight ricocheted towards the mossy, detritus-littered ground: near blackness broken by shafts of gold, leaves curling and crackling underfoot. A hoarse wheeze that seemed to shut out all other sounds puzzled him momentarily, until he realised it was his own rasping intake of breath magnified to an unbearable level inside the mask.

On and on they went, an interminable voyage it seemed, through thick clouds of gas. 'Stop!' Ben tried to call, knowing the lad was careless of the poisonous fumes, the real threat of death. But the word came as a ragged whisper, barely heard.

Will was slowing. Ben could see him ahead, barely visible in the half light. He was gasping, staggering from left to right in front of a thick wall of vegetation.

'Will!'

The young lad's white face loomed towards him out of the gloom, arms flailing, pushing him aside. 'Go away! GO AWAY!' he cried, alternately sobbing and raving almost incoherently.

With one supreme effort, Ben lunged forward, tackling him around the waist, bringing him heavily to the ground. He lay there, catching his own breath. Beneath him, Will tried to struggle free. His cries came as a strangled gurgle.

'You stupid bastard,' Ben admonished, struggling to force the mask over Will's nose and eyes, but the lad kept averting his face, yelling and punching at Ben.

Then, quite suddenly, he lay still.

It seemed as though, one by one, Will's limbs had lost their elasticity, folding into limpness. His eyes were streaming, a clear liquid pouring from them, running unchecked down his cheeks. He was gasping piteously, clutching at his throat, his face a strange tinge of blue.

Ben drew back, not knowing what to do. Hayes came running up, accompanied by several of the other men. 'Stand back!' he commanded, calling for help to lift the lad from the ground. 'The stupid bastard's got a lungful of gas.'

Struggling under his weight and their own encumbrances, they took Will to the nearby casualty clearing station, where he was placed in a special tent, the sides of which were rolled up to allow a flow of fresh air.

'He must be kept still,' the doctor cautioned, after Will's eyes were treated with a boric acid solution.

Watching that pale, prostrate form, as a liberal amount of camphor oil was massaged into his heaving chest, privately Ben thought it unlikely that Will was about to indulge in any immediate activity. 'Will he be all right?' he asked instead.

The doctor shrugged. 'Hard to say. Depends on how much gas was ingested. As a rule of thumb, if he survives the next three days then it'll be a good sign.'

Will was given a nip of brandy, covered with a blanket, and propped into an almost-sitting position on the stretcher by several pillows.

As Ben was leaving, an orderly wheeled an oxygen tank next to the bed. The last he saw of Will was the lad's closed eyes, visible over the top of the oxygen mask. 'You'll be right, mate,' he comforted, slipping his hand for a moment onto Will's shoulder. 'We'll have you out of here in no time.'

But Will's eyes remained closed, as though he hadn't heard.

'That gas is a right bastard,' grumbled Tom as he prepared to dismantle his own rifle later. Already small rust spots were beginning to appear along the barrel, and he dipped a swatch of rag into the bottle of oil and rubbed furiously at the offending blemish.

The gas was highly corrosive, causing exposed metal to rust almost at once. The immediate treatment was greasing with mineral oil, though this was only a temporary measure, effective for a day at the most. After that, the machine guns and rifles had to be dismantled and washed in boiling water containing soda.

They were sprawled on the ground a few hundred metres from the enemy lines, an assortment of weapon parts spread before them in varying stages of cleaning. The day was hot, and most had removed shirts, baring skin to the ferocious rays of the mid-afternoon sun.

It had been quiet on the front line that day. The wind, which had sprung up overnight, was a blessing, too, dispersing the remaining pockets of gas and making further attacks impossible. Still the blessed infernal cleaning went on, repetitive and monotonous. The only consolation was that, at that precise moment, the Germans were probably doing the same repairs to their own weapons.

Ben stood, stretching his long limbs. 'Thought I might go over and see how Will is,' he said to Tom.

'Will you cover for me if Hayes comes ferreting around?'

'No problem. Say hello for me while you're at it.'

'And me,' chipped in Jack.

It was about a mile to the casualty clearing station and Ben covered the distance easily. A Red Cross lorry had just arrived and patients were being carried from its interior. He slipped inside the tent, after first clearing it with one of the orderlies.

Will lay propped against the pillows, his eyes shut. His skin was a pale blueish-red. With each intake of breath, a strange rattling sound came from his lungs. From that angle, he looked ridiculously young. Just a kid, thought Ben. 'Hi, old mate,' he whispered, clasping Will's hand.

Will's eyes opened slowly. He was staring directly into Ben's face, yet there was no flash of recognition. Instead, his expression seemed blank and dark with pain.

He tightened his grip on Will's fingers. 'It's me, Ben, come to see how you're getting on. Feeling better?'

At once, without warning, the lad's body folded forward and was wracked by uncontrollable coughing. His shoulders heaved, his face contorted, dark furrows appearing along his brow.

'Does it hurt?' asked Ben, when the spasm finished and Will sagged back against the bed.

'Yes,' Will nodded, moving his hand laboriously to the lower part of his chest. His voice was merely a hoarse rasp.

Ben squatted by the bed, chatting about the happenings in the company since the previous afternoon. Will's face was turned partly away, towards the open canvas flap, and Ben wondered if he was really listening, or caught up in some inner pain of his own.

Suddenly Will sat bolt upright. A spasm seemed to course along the length of his neck, Adam's apple bobbing up and down. He opened his mouth and let out a dry retching sound, then vomited, disgorging a mass of bright yellow froth. It emerged as a projectile, splattering against the end of the stretcher and the floor. Thin streams of it ran down his chin, and across the blanket.

Ben levered himself to his feet, stunned. An orderly, carrying a metal basin and several towels, hurried in and began mopping up the mess. He glanced at Ben and shook his head sympathetically. 'Mate of yours?'

'Yes.'

'Not easy, is it, watching?'

That was an understatement. Words failed him, and he shook his head instead, purposely looking away.

Task completed, the orderly left. Ben followed him outside. 'Excuse me, have you got a minute?'

'Barely,' the man grimaced. 'What's wrong?'

'Why are you keeping him here? Why haven't you sent him on to hospital?'

The man shrugged. 'We haven't the manpower to move terminal cases.'

Terminal? He stopped and stared at the man. 'Will's dying?' he asked, his voice suddenly small.

Two words, yet they seemed somehow momentous, almost unutterable. This was no way to go. Death came from shells and bullets, from mortars and grenades. Mostly it was sudden, a face blown away, a bullet splattering brains and blood against muddy trench walls. Despite what they had been told at gas training, it seemed incongruous that mortality could come from an innocuous-looking white mist that hovered against the ground.

'Look, he's had a particularly bad dose. The air cells in his lungs are affected, producing a kind of pneumonia effect. To be brutal, victims usually drown in the fluid in their own lungs.'

The thought sickened Ben, and his mind railed against it, grasping at possibilities. 'No! He can't die! Not like that. Perhaps there's a chance. Can't *something* be done?'

The orderly nodded. 'Venesection is a last resort.'

'Venesection?' He had never heard the word before, but it sounded barbarous.

'Large amounts of blood are taken from the body, up to a pint and a half. Sometimes it's effective.'

'Can it work on Will?'

The man shrugged and moved away. 'Look, I have to go. I'm really very busy and there are other patients ...' He paused and glanced back at Ben. 'I'm sorry, truly I am. We're not miracle workers.'

Ben walked back into the tent. There was a chair propped nearby and he dragged it to the side of the bed, dropped his weary body into its frame, and waited.

It seemed as though Will slept. His chest rose and fell with short sharp movements. The noise still came from his lungs, dry rattling sounds that seemed loud against the otherwise stillness of the hut. What next? Ben wondered.

Presently the doctor arrived. He nodded at Ben and proceeded to rub the vein on the inside of Will's elbow.

'Would you like me to wait outside?' Ben offered. 'I can come back later, if you like.'

'No need,' replied the doctor brusquely, turning to the orderly. 'Digitalis, please.'

He plunged the intravenous needle deep into Will's buttock, but the lad barely stirred, simply gave a grunt, which started another bout of coughing. A drip was inserted into Will's arm, a bag attached. Sterile salt solution, said the words on its side.

Ben watched as the medical staff moved purposefully around Will's stretcher, automatically taking his temperature and feeling for a pulse. After several minutes had passed, the doctor made a deep incision into a vein in Will's arm. Thick blood bubbled to the surface as he massaged the arm, encouraging the blood to flow.

It seemed the treatment was uncivilised and unnecessarily cruel. Ben rose from the chair and turned away, horrified, a nausea building in his belly. He stumbled outside. It was almost dark, just a faint slash of red on the western horizon. Overhead, a lark was singing, its notes alternating with the distant crash and boom of gunfire. Beyond the trees, an observation balloon was descending, making its way back to earth.

The bubbling memory of dark blood had followed him. Though he closed his eyes, he saw it oozing against Will's flesh, thick and ropey, like glue.

'It's not fair!' he whispered, slamming his hand repeatedly against his palm. 'It's not bloody fair!'

It seemed he stood there a long time. Light from the tent spilled out against the uneven ground. Night noises began: the chirrup of a cricket, the distant call of an owl. How had those tiny creatures survived all this? Ben wondered, marvelling at their tenacity. Men were falling like flies, yet somehow the animal species continued, seemingly unaware of what was happening around them.

After a while he sensed a movement behind him. It was the doctor. 'He's resting now. You can go in, if you like.'

'Doctor, I —'

He stopped, confused. Did he really want to know, or were the words best left unsaid? How could he ask this man to make a prediction?

'You want to know if he'll live,' he said gently, 'and I can't possibly tell you'.

Ben nodded and stared up towards the sky. 'You don't think he's got much of a chance, do you?'

'To be honest, it doesn't look good.'

He's drowning in the fluid in his own lungs.

'What about the *suffering*? Can't you give him *anything*?'

The man shook his head and moved away, unable to meet Ben's gaze.

Afterwards he stood at the end of Will's bed, unable to leave. What if the lad died alone, having no-one close? Oh, the nursing staff were there, but there were so many patients, so much to do. None of then had the time to sit with him, to *be* with him.

He settled in the chair again. The tent was lit by a lamp. After a while he begged a few sheets of paper from a passing orderly and began a letter to Hannah.

As I write, Will is dying — his body filling with fluids after copping a lungful of gas. He could be any one of us, I suppose. His bad luck, our good fortune to be spared, as Spud would have said. But Spud is gone, too. What an awful waste.

The war still goes on, each day much the same as the next. The uncertainty is the worst, not knowing what's in store. Sometimes we sleep in full kit, ready to move out at a moment's notice. Often we don't change boots or clothes for days. Lice are bad, especially when we sleep. Horrible little creatures. When we get a few spare minutes, we strip and pull the wretched things from our clothes. But there are always more.

We are all pretty slow and lethargic at the moment, from lack of sleep, and I think I'm more than a little deaf from the noise.

He paused and glanced through the words, suddenly hating himself. The letter seemed so negative, so wretched, but was there anything good to report? Besides, what was the point of lying to her? He sighed and took up the pen again, finishing in the same vein in which he had begun.

Hannah, I won't glorify war. In truth, I could never have imagined such horror. This is hell on earth. Men die before our eyes and, while we thank God we're still alive, each of us wonders who is next.

*As I re-read these words I have written, I see how
useless they are. How can I express what I see, I feel?
Words fail me. My mind is numb. I love you, Ben.*

He folded the paper, placed it in his pocket and
glanced at his watch. Almost midnight. By rights, he
should have been back from the casualty station
hours ago, yet he was still loathe to leave.

It seemed that Will's condition had deteriorated
as Ben had sat there, writing to Hannah. The boy's
chest rose and fell violently in its struggle for air.
From time to time, he tossed restlessly, throwing his
body against invisible constraints. An occasional
moan issued from between clenched lips, yet his
breathing sounds were faint, scarcely heard above
the chest râles.

Ben took Will's hand and began to talk. Slowly at
first he touched on the daily events of their lives, the
routines, the constant moving on. 'It's a real bugger',
he said, 'not knowing where you'll be sleeping the
next day. What do you reckon, mate?'

Will did not reply.

Desperately Ben went on, pouring forth his
feelings about Hannah and Nick, his longing to see
the child and his plans for his own future. He knew
the topic didn't matter. Will probably wasn't
registering the words, anyway. In many ways it was
an exploration of his own emotions, too, a release of
sorts, a catharsis. A need, a compulsion to speak, to
pour the words from his own mouth as proof that
he, himself, was still alive.

After a while Will opened his eyes. His mouth
moved, dry lips muttering; his eyes were wide and

unfocused. It seemed some kind of delirium had overtaken him.

'Speak to me, Pa! Don't do this, Pa! Speak to me!'

There was an urgency about the words, a sense of unrestrained importance. Between the laboured gasps, the strain showed on Will's face.

'What's wrong, Will?'

'Pa?' the lad rasped, reaching blindly out to touch the unshaven stubble on Ben's chin. In unison, a tear rolled from each eye, slowly tracking a path down each cheek. 'Is that you, Pa?'

'Yes,' replied Ben, stricken, the lie coming easily to him. Besides, what else could he say? It was obviously important to Will, and offered some sense of comfort. 'It's me, lad.'

'I didn't get your letters, Pa. Why didn't you write?'

Will reached out again, his hand closing over Ben's own. His fingers tightened, then went slack.

He slept. Ben watched in fascination the rise and fall of his chest. Finally one of the orderlies came along, shooing him away. 'Go back to camp. Get some sleep,' he cautioned.

Ben stumbled back to his own billet, his mind groggy with tiredness. Sleep, he thought wistfully as he lowered himself onto the bunk. Blessed uninterrupted sleep. It seemed as though years had passed since he had last experienced it.

He closed his eyes, willing unconsciousness, but all he saw behind his closed lids was Will's tortured face. Sleep, it seemed, had deserted him completely.

The evening of the following day, Ben slipped away to the Casualty Station. But the stretcher by the open canvas flap contained another blackened body. Not Will. A stranger.

He was reminded of the day he had gone to see Da, and knew instantly the implication. Blindly he hunkered down on the ground, letting his legs slide out from under him, and buried his head in his hands. Every obscenity imaginable came crowding into his mind. Anger and hate directed at everyone — Hayes, the army, the fucking Germans. He raged against them, giving voice to all he considered shameful and horrific, to the hopeless barbarity he had witnessed.

After a while, when the fury had subsided, he sensed a movement behind him. It was the same orderly who had been on duty the previous day.

'How can you bear it?' Ben asked, struggling to his feet and looking blankly at the man. 'How can you stay here day after day watching all this?' He swept his arm in a circle towards the interior of the tent, indicating the rows of stretchers. 'How can you fucking stay *sane*?'

The orderly looked away, not answering. Ben felt a hand on his arm and turned to stare into a kindly face. It was the company padre — he knew by the clerical collar the man wore. 'Would you like to talk?' the padre asked.

They went outside and the padre offered him a cigarette from a pack in his pocket. 'Smoke?'

Ben nodded, reaching to extricate one. There was a sound of a match striking, the brief flare of flame as he drew heavily and the tobacco caught.

It was cooler out there, a faint breeze blowing and bringing with it the lingering odour of cordite.

High above a distant line of trees, a flickering succession of Very lights lit up the horizon, followed by the muffled boom of the big guns.

'It doesn't seem fair, does it?'

'No!' Ben flicked a column of ash from the cigarette and stared morosely ahead. Spud was gone, and now Will. Who was next? It was as though some superior being was picking them off, one by one. Would he, in some distant time, be the last man left?

'And you wonder if there really is a God?'

'Too bloody right.' He stared up towards the starry sky. 'How could anyone let this all happen? How could God, if he exists, allow men to brutalise each other this way?'

'I have no answer. Nothing I could possibly say could justify what I see happening around me.'

The padre was silent for a while, his head bent. Ben could just make out the profile of his face in the remnant of light that came from the nearby tent. 'Would you like to see where we buried him?' he said at last, taking a step forward.

Ben nodded numbly and the padre went to one of the casualty tents, returning with a lamp. 'This way,' he said kindly, holding it up to highlight the uneven ground.

Ben remembered little of the walk through the field behind the Casualty Station to the small cemetery. Row upon row of crosses dotted the lumpy ground, ragged lines of identical markers. The padre came to a halt at the end of the closest line and nodded to the place where the ground was mounded and still freshly damp.

There was no need for words. Silently Ben hunkered down against the moist earth and said his farewell. Will had been one of them, and the lad's death had stirred up a grief that was unfamiliarly frightening. He wondered for a moment if he himself was close to losing control. What had he written in the letter to Hannah the previous night? *This is hell on earth*. It was not a lie.

Despondently he walked back to his own billet, where he spent yet another night tossing restlessly on his bed.

The following morning, Sergeant Hayes was waiting for him. 'Where in hell did you get to last night?'

'Visiting Will,' came his own tired reply.

'And how is the little bludger?'

'He's dead.'

The anger that might have flared in him once didn't seem to matter any more. Will was gone. Eventually, if the war didn't end soon, chances were that they were all on borrowed time. Next day, next week. When would his own finale come? And, if he could predict it, would he really want to know?

He was put on latrine duty, made to dig new trenches before filling in the old. The ground oozed under the hastily thrown clods of earth, the stench of ammonia coming up to meet him. He didn't care. There was nothing left in this world that disgusted him. He had seen it all. Death. Destruction. In a way, his own eventual demise would be a blessing, wiping him from all this as though he had never existed.

CHAPTER 25

'Well, it's got to stop. I've the other residents to consider. It's not fair on them, a baby crying all hours.'

'I'll do what I can,' said Hannah tiredly, closing the door behind the landlady. She sat on the edge of the bed and stared at her child. He was sleeping now, worn out from hours of night-time whimpering. Hannah would have liked to do the same, simply curl up on the bed and drift off into an uninterrupted sleep, but there were nappies to wash, though technically speaking it wasn't her rostered day to use the clothesline, and the floor to sweep, followed by a quick trip down to the local store when Nick woke.

Nick had been unwell for days now, running a slight temperature and crying for no apparent reason, plucking at his mouth and ears. Hannah had promptly taken him to the local chemist, who diagnosed teething and recommended the use of Palmers Pink Powder. Later, peering in his mouth, she had seen his gum all red and swollen, the pearly white of an emerging tooth still obstructed by several layers of skin. She could feel the small ball-like hardness of it as she probed with her finger. After she put him in his cot, he had grizzled on and off for hours, tossing restlessly. In desperation she had unbuttoned her blouse and held him to her breast, hoping the sucking motion might send him to sleep, but he had pushed her away, pummelling her with his fists, and it had seemed a rejection of sorts.

Now some of the residents had complained, and the pointed stares and frosty silence the next morning as she prepared her breakfast in the communal kitchen said it all. One man ambled up and enquired if Nick was all right. 'He'll be fine, thank you,' she replied stiffly, almost sobbing from a combination of tiredness and the old man's solicitude.

That night she answered a knock on the door. It was the woman who occupied the next room. Impatiently she asked Hannah to keep Nick quiet. 'We've all got to get some sleep around here,' she said. 'Some of us *are* workers.'

Hannah bit back a retort and closed the door in the woman's wake. She couldn't blame the other residents, she supposed. They were entitled to their sleep. In fairness, they had been most patient, but what was she to do?

The following morning, a letter arrived from Ben, accompanied by a money order. It was a fairly large sum and she stared at it, weighing her options. The money would pay several months rent on a larger place, but there would be little left for living expenses. However if she took a job and organised someone to look after Nick ...

She paused, unable to bear the thought of being parted from him, not even for a minute. And what would Ben think, that she could even contemplate leaving their son with a stranger while she went back to work?

The idea gnawed temptingly. Yes? No? Should she move, take a job?

Her resolve wavered, torn between wanting to leave this dreary house and the bleak prospect of a daytime separation from Nick. It seemed a monumental step and not one to be taken without due consideration.

When Nick woke she hurried out and bought a newspaper, and spent the afternoon studying the 'Accommodation To Let' column. Reading and re-reading the advertisements, she imagined herself somewhere else. A small cottage, perhaps, with its own bathroom and kitchen. Not having to share would be bliss. With a pen and a bottle of blue ink, she circled the most likely advertisements, deliberating over phrases such as 'congenial atmosphere' and 'views to the city'. After another two days of fretting over Nick and enduring more pointed silences and grumbling from the landlady, she propped him in his pram and set off, the folded newspaper tucked under her arm.

There were several small cottages close to the inner city. One, in a leafy tree-lined street, caught her attention above the others and after the second inspection, she accepted what seemed like an exorbitant rent.

It was tiny, the layout not unlike Tom's old flat in Wickham Terrace. From the front door Hannah could almost see into every corner. No privacy, was her first thought, but it didn't matter. The only occupants in the foreseeable future would be herself and the child.

A long narrow lounge room led into the kitchen, which in turn led into a minuscule alcove bedroom.

Off the kitchen was a tiny bathroom containing a bath and a wash basin. The lavatory was outside, at the far end of the yard, and the laundry consisted of a set of concrete tubs propped against the back wall of the house, open to the elements. A man would call every second week to mow the lawns.

The furniture was a mishmash of assorted items. The lounge room boasted a hard horsehair sofa and a small round table, while the dining table and four chairs seemed to take up most of the kitchen. Hannah examined the gas rings and the cupboards, finding them surprisingly clean. No obvious sign of cockroaches, no mice droppings in the corners. She gave a laugh and swung Nick around, dancing through the room. 'Do you like this, my pet?' she asked, bobbing her head up and down in front of his until he chuckled and reached out one chubby hand and pulled at her hair.

With a light step she pushed the pram back to the boarding house.

After lunch she had a buggy collect her few belongings: Nick's cot, several suitcases, a box of books and her painting equipment. No-one came to say goodbye. She let herself out the front door, slamming it purposely behind her, climbed aboard the buggy and didn't once look back. It was worth it, she thought, to forego the month's rent she had paid in advance, to be rid of the place.

Nick was tired after his morning's outing. Hannah settled him in his cot, then proceeded to unpack. She stowed the clothes tidily in the wardrobe and chest of drawers, arranged her few pots and jars in the bathroom, and stacked the books neatly on a shelf beside the sofa. Lastly she took the painting of the wattles at the bottom of the Brunswick Street house, and hung it over the bed. Stepping back, she admired her handiwork.

The cottage, though cosy, wasn't much. Scarcely large enough to accommodate both of them, but it was hers. No complaining neighbours, no shared facilities. She could walk around stark naked if she chose.

She giggled at the thought, the idea amusing her in some sad way. Despite her initial elation, there was a lingering sense of wrongness about all this, the setting up of a house without Ben. He should have been there with her, sharing this moment. Suddenly dispirited, she glanced around the room, a feeling of despair overwhelming her.

Nick was sleeping and she was alone, truly alone. The house was quiet, emitting no sounds. No rattle of pots and pans, no chink of crockery. Just an awful deathly silence. A flutter of panic rose in her chest. Who would she talk to? She bent down and peered through the side window, seeing only the weathered palings of the fence. Not even a sign of neighbours.

'Stop it!' she reprimanded herself, pushing the thoughts aside. 'You've got what you wanted, my girl, so you had better get used to it.'

Determined, she took paper and pen and wrote a long account of the past week to Ben. When she had finished, Nick was still sleeping, so she began a brief note to Lottie, giving her new address. Call by and see us when you get the chance, she wrote, fighting back an urgent need to see her friend.

Finished at last, she put the sealed envelopes on the kitchen table and prowled about the rooms.

Soon Nick would wake. She would bath him then prepare supper, and the cottage would be filled with his happy gurgling.

Back in the bedroom her eyes were drawn to the painting of the wattles. She sat on the edge of the bed, staring hard at it. So much had happened since she had put those first tentative brush strokes onto the paper. Ben had just gone away. Nick was already growing inside her, though she hadn't known it then. Over twelve months: so little time, yet so much had happened.

The wattles blurred under her gaze, the greens and golds melting into each other, and she turned away, stricken. What was to become of them?

Herself, Ben, Nick: a shattered triangle.

Would it ever be whole again?

For Ben, life went on, an endless routine. Trucks and mules brought in ammunition, food, water and stores. Under heavy artillery fire, they marked out new trench systems, sank wells, repaired concrete dugouts and made reconnaissance maps.

The weather was uncharacteristically bad for summer. Blue skies turned into monotone grey, saturating the landscape with veils of torrential rain. Shell holes that littered the countryside were brimming with greasy water. The air was foul with the stench of cordite and rotting horses which lay strewn as they had fallen. And over all, the infernal thigh-deep glutinous mud. It clung to clothing and boots, to the lines of duckboards that crisscrossed the countryside. To leave the wooden planking meant certain lengthy delays.

Night, when it arrived, offered little relief. If the wind dropped, the deadly gas came at unexpected hours, sending them scrabbling frantically for their masks. The constant bombardments lit up the sky to almost daylight brightness and the never-ending boom of the guns kept sleep at bay.

Ben was exhausted. His body, weary and sick with fatigue, seemed no longer a part of him. His limbs moved of their own accord, no longer controlled by his brain. His mind churned with a mixture of nervous excitement and dread, the emotions seesawing randomly. For the moment he had lost the ability to think, to reason.

Despite all this, Will's death drew them together: himself, Tom and Jack. Not that Will had ever been a close member of their circle, like Spud, but the lad's sudden and needless end seemed to accentuate Ben's own sense of mortality He had imagined that death, when it came, would be swift. Like Spud, he thought with surprise. One moment of pain, of unguarded fright, then it would be all over. But now he knew first-hand that it wasn't necessarily true.

Just when Ben thought his body and mind could survive no longer, they were relieved from the front and spent a few days leave at the camp at Neuve Eglise. Miraculously the weather cleared. The sun shone from a cloudless sky and the humidity soared. Mud dried, the sour smell of it churning at nostrils.

The barbershop was his first port of call, followed by lunch at one of the small *estaminets* nearby. Here, several miles behind the front line, lives were still going on despite the hardships, and the local proprietor had a ready smile for the

410

hardworking, hard-fighting Australians with the rising sun badges on their hats.

He ate well. Then, several local wines under his belt, he headed for the public baths which were clean and well maintained.

He went there daily. The water, swirling like a tide around his wearied body, healed his fractured spirit. A balm to the soul, it soothed in an odd inexplicable way. If he closed his eyes and concentrated on the flow, it reminded him of home and summer days at the beach before Pa became sick, when it was just the two of them, the sun and the sand, and the never-ending parade of seagulls. It reminded him also of Hannah and those lazy Sundays walking beside the river in Brisbane, the sound of the tennis balls plopping on the courts in the Botanical Gardens.

Then he opened his eyes and found himself there, in that strange town, in a foreign country that maimed and killed. It was early August. In less than a month, summer would begin its slow spiral into autumn. Time was marching on. Some days he thought it might leave him behind, capturing him in a time warp from which he would never escape. He wished — God how he wished! — that he could simply walk away into oblivion.

Orders came through and the company headed towards Ypres, or 'Wipers', as the Aussies called it, across the Belgian border. They came via the Ypres-Poperinghe Road in old motor buses, thankful they were spared the eternal marching under full kit. The road was congested and the going slow. Huge volumes of traffic trickled along in both directions, and the buses soon found themselves part of a long queue, comprising pack animals, ammunition and ration limbers, and wagons laden with the company's own engineering stores.

The journey was stop-start. Tom slept on the seat opposite, his head lolling against Jack's shoulder. From time to time he jolted awake and stared unseeingly around the cabin for a few moments, before closing his eyes once more. Jack read a book. Ben wondered how he had the patience, the bus rolling and pitching along the uneven road like a ship ploughing its way through a storm. For himself, he was content to sit and watch, not anxious to hurry time along, taking in the sights and smells and the sheer magnitude of the exercise.

They passed long convoys of Red Cross cars, marching soldiers and injured men on mules. Leaning dangerously from the windows of the bus, they laughed at the profanities and curses from the other drivers at the bottleneck at Vlamertinghe. The rest of the journey, roads slippery from a sudden downpour of rain, was but an evil memory.

Exhausted beyond all reason, they arrived in Ypres the following morning. As the buses trundled through the streets, the town was just beginning to stir, the first rays of the sun creeping along the sandstone tower of the great Cloth Hall. They passed the allied army stores and camps, a hospital and casualty clearing station. Some time in the past, before the war, the town had been a large fabric manufacturing centre. Now it lay mostly in ruins.

Several black-clad women hurried along the roadway, heads bowed against the stares of the men.

Ben scarcely saw the pair of mangy dogs sniffing hopefully along the pavements that bordered the marketplace, or the narrow, steep-roofed houses that jostled shoulder-to-shoulder along cobbled streets. Instead he longed for sleep, to rest his head on a soft pillow and dream.

The company was billeted in a series of cellars and shelters among the ruins of a home in the southern section of the town. Of the house there was no sign. Merely a few mounds of dirt and rubble remained, and a section of bleached wooden flooring with grass and weeds poking up between. Amongst them lay a series of sandstone steps that led downwards into semi-darkness.

Gingerly Ben descended the steps, twenty in all, which were narrow, with dips and hollows worn into the stone from years of use. There was no handrail and he was so tired, so bone-weary, that he worried he might slip and fall. Reaching the bottom, he glanced around. He was in what had probably been the original cellar. There were signs of recent bombing. Broken bricks were piled haphazardly on the flagstone floor. Archways leaned drunkenly towards each other. Beyond lay a darker, as yet unexplored, maze of dirt-walled tunnels.

Someone had started a fire in the corner and already the smell of cooking permeated the air. 'Bully beef and beans,' growled Jack. 'I'm bloody starving, and that's a fact. What about you, mate?'

Ben shook his head. His stomach was sick with fatigue and threatening to disgorge the previous night's meal. 'Think I'll get some rest,' he said, and walked away.

He made his way along one of the tunnels. It was mid-morning and patches of pale sunlight came through the broken boards overhead. He found an unoccupied corner and spread his coat against the floor. Thankfully, thinking of nothing but sleep, blessed sleep, he lowered himself onto it and closed his eyes.

When he woke, it was dark.

They spent the next few weeks roofing the new ammunitions dump at La Creche. It was hot dusty work and, as Jack repeatedly reminded them, much safer than front-line duty. Apart from the occasional shell which sent them ducking for cover, the days were relatively uneventful.

Then followed a few weeks at the little village of Recquebroeucq on the River Asa. The objective was to rest, train and refit, and the break lasted until late September. The weather remained fine and the locals were friendly. From time to time, farmers called past, bringing eggs and milk, and an occasional slab of bacon.

Comparatively speaking, the accommodation was good. They were holed up in a large rambling house which was a constant source of wonder. Though several shells had left gaping holes in the roof, the structure was relatively undamaged and a glass-roofed conservatory at the rear was untouched. As Ben wandered through the rooms, it was soon clear that the former occupants had left quickly, taking few of their personal belongings. The heavy baroque furniture was still in place. A walk-in cupboard in the laundry yielded vast quantities of sheets, blankets

414

and towels; kitchen cupboards were stocked with crockery and food. Wilted produce lay about the benches, while dirty coffee cups were stacked neatly in the sink. In one particular bedroom there were two chests of drawers full of ladies' clothes: blouses, skirts, petticoats and lacy underwear.

Perched on a small hilltop, the house was large and afforded a good view of the surrounding countryside. The pond in the centre of the circular driveway was full of algae and several dead fish floated on its surface. Stretching away, down the slope, the garden was overgrown, impenetrable, a tangle of branches. Roses and poppies dotted the vegetation, bright daubs of red, white and pink.

A rear garden yielded a strawberry patch, overgrown with weeds. Seemingly unaware of their neglect, the plants had produced masses of ripe fruit, undetected so far by the others. Ben bent down and picked several, popping them into his mouth. They were plump and juicy, sweet, not tainted with the sourness of war.

He was glad of the respite, pleased with the quiet countryside, making the most of the opportunity to write long letters to Hannah. His missives of late had been hasty scribbled affairs, scarcely more than a few lines to let her know he was all right. Now he sat and poured out his heart to her.

It was also a time for talk and making plans. He and Tom went for long walks beside the river, picking their way along the overgrown banks where cows had once grazed. After the war: that was the usual topic. They made no mention of that other awful possibility, that they wouldn't survive. To do so would give voice to their fears, perhaps lessen their chances of coming through all this unscathed.

Mail arrived, bearing a welcome letter from Hannah and a photograph of herself and Nick. Ben held it out, into the light. Hannah stared back at him, wisps of dark hair curling around her face, lips curving into a tremulous smile. He thought she looked thinner than he remembered, her face even paler, though it could have been the quality of the reproduction. Nick was perched on her hip, reaching one chubby hand towards the camera. He was blond, a pretty child, Ben considered, with an inquisitive expression on his face.

He sat, studying the photograph for what seemed like a long time, scrutinising every small detail. Hannah's hand against Nick's upper thigh, the other pressed against his belly, holding him tight. Holding him, he thought with a desperate surge of love, as he himself wished to, feeling the solidity of his son in his own arms. The photograph was a miserable substitute.

Tom threw himself down on the grass, a handful of letters clutched in his fist. One was open, the paper scrunched in his hand. 'I wish it didn't have to be like this!' he blurted, laying the letter aside.

'Like what?' asked Ben, glancing up.

'He scarcely ever writes, and when he does, his letters are so cold. He makes me feel so god-damned *guilty*.'

The letter was obviously from David Corduke. Furrows of anger twitched at Tom's brow. His mouth was set into a tight line.

'Does it ever occur to you,' asked Ben as he lowered Hannah's letter, 'that your brother might not be able to write the things he feels? Some men can't put their emotions into words. You know, stiff upper lip, that sort of thing.'

'That's all very well,' Tom retorted defensively. 'But *this*?' He threw the pages on the grass. The wind ruffled the paper, threatening to blow it away, and Tom made no move to restrain it. 'If only he could have wished me good luck, stood up for me. Things would be so different. I don't think he'll ever forgive me for joining up.'

'He'll come round eventually. Just give him time. When the war's over, he'll be so glad to have you back that all will be forgotten.'

'Sounds too good to be true. You don't know David. And Enid's worse. If she gets a bee in her bonnet about something, then she never lets up. I'll be hearing about this for years, if not the rest of my life — how I deserted my family and my studies.'

'You're lucky to have family at all,' replied Ben. 'I'd give anything to be in your shoes, forgiveness or not.'

'I suppose,' mused Tom gloomily. He scooped up the pages and shoved them unceremoniously into his pocket. '*After the war*. Seems such a long way away. Do you think there'll ever be an end to it?'

'Of course.'

Did he? Ben didn't know. But he had to remain positive or how could he summon the strength to go on?

'I'll go back to uni, of course. Finish that degree. Get a job. That might bring David around.' Tom shielded his eyes with one hand and gazed out across untilled fields. Then: 'What about you?'

Lying on his back in the grass, the sun warm on his face, Ben pondered the question. He had a family to support now, and a decent wage was a necessity.

'Well, the forge has gone, but I guess I could start up again somewhere else. I think I'm a pretty fair tradesman —'

'You're the best,' broke in Tom with a grin. 'Only one who could ever shoe Princess without getting a kick in his shins for his trouble.'

'Horses! By the time we get back, they'll be almost a thing of the past. Automobiles are the transport of the future and, if we think otherwise, then we're only kidding ourselves.'

'So many changes.' Tom rolled onto his stomach and regarded Ben with serious eyes. 'When all this is over, do you think anything will ever be the same again?'

'No.'

Tom was silent, obviously waiting for further elaboration. 'Well, it can't, can it?' Ben went on defensively. 'We've all been through so much, *seen* so much. Do you think we can just walk away and go back to our ordinary lives?'

Tom shrugged. 'I plan to give it a bloody good try.'

'Yair.'

'And Hannah and Nick?'

Ben smiled. 'The first thing I'm going to do when we get back is marry her, whether your brother agrees or not.'

That night, as he lay in his lonely bed, he thought of her, as he had done hundreds of times, on that last night in Tom's flat. He remembered the sheen of the fire against her skin, the warm smoothness of her. He thought of all that had happened between them, intimacies not normally experienced outside the sacred bonds of marriage. What he would give to be able to reach out and touch her! But so many things had changed.

War. It had snatched all that was loving and familiar to him, and set lives on different courses. It had pushed him beyond the boundaries of normal endurance. It had taken everything, leaving just the memories and scant hope for the future.

Too soon the break ended and they were on the move again, back to Ypres. It was late September and already the leaves on the few remaining trees were turning gold and russet. The days were mellow and felt of ripeness, of summer's end. The smell of wood smoke permeated country laneways. Mornings found a heavy dew on the grass, drops glittering like jewels on a tiara.

They were delayed at Poperinghe on the night of the harvest moon, holed up in a deserted farmhouse. Through the hours of darkness, they huddled against the floor, vainly trying to sleep as Allied machine guns chattered hysterically at enemy planes droning overhead.

They completed the journey under the cover of nightfall. In the dark, Ben heard the tramp of feet and snatches of conversation laced with song. Every so often they stopped for a break while the men relieved themselves at the side of the road. Matches flared and cigarettes were nothing but red pinpricks. Ben's legs were chafed and his feet blistered, rubbed raw against the heels of his boots, and he remembered thankfully the pot of Zambuk ointment he'd had the foresight to stow in his kit bag.

There was a movement beside him, and something was being pressed against his hand, something rectangular with blunt corners. 'I want you to take this,' said a voice which was Tom's.

'What is it?'

'It's a letter to my brother. If anything happens —'

'*Nothing* is going to happen!' broke in Ben fiercely, pushing Tom's hand away.

But Tom was reaching out to take Ben's hand in his own. Against his will, Ben felt the envelope between his fingers. 'If nothing happens,' replied Tom calmly, before walking away, 'then you won't have to send it.'

Sergeant Hayes came along, hurrying everyone to their feet. With shaking hands, Ben tucked the envelope into his coat pocket. As he moved off, he imagined he could feel the leaden weight of it, dragging him down, slowing him, and he wanted to tear it to shreds and throw the pieces to the wind. A sweep of bitter fear filled him.

Nothing would happen.

Nothing *could* happen.

Nothing. Nothing. Nothing.

CHAPTER 26

Callie had already looked at six tiny and overpriced units by the time she arrived at the flats in Bay Street. Constructed of red brick, the building was in a handy location, half a block from the small cluster of convenience shops that lined the foreshore, and directly across the road from the beach.

When she stepped from the car, a brisk wind caught her hair, sending it in mad disarray about her face. As instructed by the receptionist in the real estate, she knocked on the door of one of the ground floor flats. She could hear noises behind the closed door. A radio, the muffled hum of a vacuum cleaner. After a few seconds the door was flung open.

'I'm here about the flat,' Callie explained. 'The real estate said to speak directly to you.'

The woman shook her head, looking apologetic. 'They weren't supposed to send anyone around for at least two weeks. The painter can't come until Friday and the carpet needs shampooing. I'm sorry you've had a wasted trip.'

Another dead end. She had already spent two sleepless nights in the motel and had been counting on finding a suitable place today.

'Seeing I'm here, you don't suppose I could have a look anyway,' Callie asked hopefully.

'I'm afraid it's a bit of a mess,' the woman replied doubtfully, shaking her head again. 'The previous tenant ...'

But Callie's mind was racing ahead, considering her options. The flat *was* in a good location and the rent was reasonable. She would have to be frugal until the balance of the advance for the recently completed manuscript arrived. But if the premises were suitable, perhaps she could bum a bed at the house in Brunswick Street for a few days, or perhaps Jill's sofa?

'Please? Just one look. If I decide to take it, it'll save you being bothered again.'

The woman gave her an amused smile. 'Oh, all right,' she relented. 'I suppose it won't hurt. Just wait while I get the key.'

It was on the top floor, up two flights of stairs. 'Its hard getting good tenants in these old places since they started building those modern townhouses over the other side of the bay,' the woman said as they trundled up the steps.

'I thought this would be a really popular location here, right opposite the beach.'

They stopped at the door and the woman produced the key, turning it in the lock. 'Oh, it's popular all right. But not with the sort of people the owner wants living here.' The door swung open and she ushered Callie inside. 'No good getting top rent but finding the place trashed after the tenants have gone, usually owing a month's back rent. But don't listen to me. You'll see for yourself.'

The rooms *were* a mess, as the woman had said.

Dirty marks randomly covered the walls. The bath and shower had not been cleaned, and the grouting around the tiles sprouted black mould.

'The last tenants were a couple of young guys. Don't think they did a day's work while they were here.' She indicated several oil stains that dotted the carpet in the centre of the lounge. 'Spent their time pulling down one of their motorbikes.'

Despite all this, the flat showed promise. As in most older-style buildings, the rooms — living room, separate bedroom, kitchen and bathroom cum laundry — were large. The stove, though filthy, seemed to be in good working order, the hot plates glowing obligingly as Callie tested each one in turn. The walls would look as good as new with a coat of paint, and a thorough wash would freshen up the grubby curtains. A professional steam clean would bring most of the carpet back to its original condition and, she thought with sudden surprise, realising she was warming to the place, a colourful mat would hide the stains.

The particular feature of the flat that swayed Callie in its favour was the huge floor-to-ceiling window in the living room. Besides allowing lots of natural light to flood the room, it overlooked the beach. A perfect place to set up her work desk.

She swung the balcony door open and stepped outside. From that elevation she had an uninterrupted view along the esplanade. Huge pine trees flanked a walking track. Further back, a pale expanse of sand fringed blue water. Out amongst the far line of breakers sat several surfboards, their riders waiting patiently.

She closed her eyes and took a deep breath. The tang of salt was in the air. Somewhere overhead a seagull screamed.

'I'll take it,' she said.

Over the next half hour, and several phone calls to the owner, the deal was done. Callie had immediate access to the flat, as well as a month's free rent, on condition that she repaint the walls and have the carpets steam cleaned. Apart from the cost of the paint and brushes, carpet cleaning, a few bottles of disinfectant and cleanser, which she estimated to be equal to two weeks rent, the rest would require nothing more than a considerable amount of elbow grease and time. Now that the latest manuscript was finished, the latter was something she had plenty of.

Once the deal was completed, she hurried down to the electricity company to arrange a power supply account. Back at the motel, a further three phone calls organised the telephone, carpet cleaner and a furniture removalist for the following day. Then, taking a deep breath and picking up the phone again, she rang her mother.

'Hi, it's me, Callie.'

'Hello, love. I tried to ring you this morning but there was no answer. Been out?'

Another deep breath. 'You could say that. I've been flat hunting.'

There was a moment's silence on the other end of the line. Please, don't give me the third degree, Callie begged silently. She wasn't ready for in-depth questioning on the state of her now non-existent relationship with Stuart. It was all too new, too raw, to discuss.

'I don't understand,' prompted Bonnie. 'What do you mean, *flat hunting*?'

Maybe this would have been better face to face, Callie considered, but it was already too late. And Bonnie *should* know what was going on. What if Stuart rang the house in Brunswick Street, wanting to know where she was? What if he had already rung? Bonnie would have been frantic with worry. But her mother hadn't mentioned that. Stuart had obviously been keeping a low profile.

The news had to be told. Spell it right out, said a determined inner voice. Tell her straight, no beating about the bush. 'Apart from Jill, you're the first to know. Stuart and I have decided to call it quits, and I've moved out.'

She heard Bonnie's sudden intake of breath. 'Where are you staying? With Jill? I'll come right over.'

'No, please. I'm all right. I've been at the Lodge Motor Inn for the last two nights.'

'Why didn't you come home?'

Her mother was hurt. Callie could sense it in the reproachful tone of voice. And why *hadn't* she? There had been several good reasons at the time, though they had all deserted her now and her justifications sounded lame. 'Well, you and Freya have been busy, packing and getting the house in order. Besides, I didn't want you involved in something that could have been quite messy.'

'And was it?'

Thankfully. 'No. At least, not yet. Look, I'm not

ready to get into all this right now. Can we just leave it?'

'Sure, Cal.'

There was a pause, a silence which she felt bound to fill. 'I found a flat. It's down by the beach. Bring Freya over on Sunday night and we'll have dinner.' Hopefully she would have the place cleaned up a bit by then.

'We'd like that.'

Callie gave her mother her new phone number and address, and they exchanged goodbyes. Sitting on the motel bed, receiver in hand, she gave thankful praise. Bonnie had never liked Stuart, though her mother had taken considerable pains to disguise the fact, especially over the past few months. And the last thing Callie needed to hear now was 'I told you so'. But the conversation had been minimal, lacking in accusations and recriminations. What had her mother's last words been? *I hope you'll be happy now, Cal.*

Happiness — that was what life was all about, she thought morosely, though she hadn't seen too much of that lately.

Stuart had long since gone to work by the time the removalist truck arrived at the unit the following morning. He had been her last phone call the previous evening. 'Take what you want,' he had snapped brusquely. 'It's half yours.' Then he had hung up.

She had almost expected him to be there, but the garage was empty, simply containing a few dry leaves that swirled around in the wind. With a hammering heart, she unlocked the front door and stepped inside.

The interior of the flat smelt musty as she walked down the hallway into the kitchen. There was a piece of paper on the breakfast bar. A note from Stuart perhaps? What would it say? Don't go? Please reconsider? Casually she picked it up and glanced at the words. Nothing but a reminder to collect the dry cleaning before the end of the week.

'Shit!' she whispered, crushing it in her palm.

She had wondered how she would feel, coming back. Now, standing in the kitchen, there was nothing except a sense of detachment. Stuart, the unit: they all belonged to another time, now past. Things had changed. *She* had changed. Already, in her mind, it was his place. Not hers.

She prowled through the rooms, seeing them as though for the first time. Nothing seemed different since she had left, but what had she expected? Sudden alterations to the interior of the unit?

A movement behind her caused her to swing around. It was one of the removalists. 'Okay, love. Show us what you want taken and we'll get this show on the road.'

Where to start? As Stuart had so magnanimously stated, she supposed half the contents of the flat were hers; at least her money had gone to pay for them. However she baulked at the glass and chrome furnishings, knowing they were more his taste than hers. The burly removalist man stood waiting for her instructions.

In the end, she took the contents of her study, the sofa bed, computer, Hannah's trunk, office chair and desk. The men helped pack the contents of the bookcases before carrying them downstairs. She deliberated over the fax machine, but it was an ancient thing, cumbersome and inclined to be temperamental, and, in the end, she waved it aside.

Quickly she went through the kitchen cupboards, pulling an assortment of utensils onto the breakfast bar. In the lounge room she bypassed the television, stopping in front of the hi-fi system. It had been an expensive purchase almost twelve months earlier. 'I'll take that, too,' she told one of the men.

The small bar fridge in the laundry would come in handy, as would the casual table and chairs on the balcony. Stuart wouldn't miss the setting. After a small deliberation, she instructed one of the men to load the gas barbeque as well.

In the bedroom, she flung her clothes from the dresser drawers, shoving them unceremoniously into a spare box. Stockings and knickers, bras, shorts, tops and jeans. A jewellery case. Scrabbling at the back of one drawer, she brought forward the carefully wrapped package containing Davie Corduke's fob watch and chain, given to her by her own father, Alex, before his death.

Clothing hanging in the wardrobe fitted neatly into several specially designed removalist boxes. Another soon held an assortment of bathroom toiletries and cosmetics. Glancing up, above the bedhead, Callie spotted her great-great-aunt Hannah's watercolour of the wattles. Carefully she lifted it down and set it aside for packing.

After the men had left for the flat on Bay Street to disgorge their load, she made one last sweep through the rooms. Back in the kitchen, she found two ceramic cats she had made at craft class a couple of years earlier.

The cat! How could she have forgotten?

Oscar was nowhere to be found. She prowled around outside for a while, calling his name. Through the gardens she searched, eventually finding him asleep under a hedge. At the sight of her, he opened one lazy eye and began purring loudly.

'There you are!' she exclaimed, pleased beyond all reason as she scooped him into her arms. Inside, in the laundry, she bundled him into the cat cage. 'Sorry, mate. I can't have you taking off on me. I'd never find you again.'

He gave an affronted miaow, then settled on the towel she had used to line the bottom of the cage, and proceeded to wash himself.

The carpet cleaning company had been and gone by the time she returned to the flat. The floor coverings were clean, though slightly damp. Only a slight stain remained where the oil had been spilt. There was a fresh smell to the place, lemony, replacing the musty odour.

After the removalists had left, she let Oscar out of his cage, laughing as she watched him prowl around the rooms, swishing his tail. A few minutes later, he leapt onto the sofa where he sat, watching her balefully. 'I know, it's a strange place, but you'll soon get used to it,' she admonished with a smile. 'I already have.'

In reply he closed his eyes, ignoring her completely.

She sat on the sofa, absent-mindedly stroking the cat. This was the first time ever she had lived alone.

When she had first left the house in Brunswick Street, she had flatted with Jill, then moved in with Stuart. Now, unused to the solitude, she found the silence almost palpable. Restlessly, she strode across the room, flinging open the large window. Sounds of the sea crept in, the gentle swish of the water against the sand, the scream of the gulls. Along the esplanade, traffic murmured. In the distance, a car horn sounded.

The furniture and boxes sat in the centre of the room. There was no point unpacking until she had cleaned the kitchen and bathroom. Determinedly she picked up a bucket containing disinfectant, cleanser and brush.

It was dark by the time she had finished. Her back was stiff and her legs ached, but the bathroom tiles gleamed again and the kitchen positively glowed. Even the upright stove, stripped of its layers of grime, shone. Stretching, she prowled through the rooms, admiring her handiwork. Already the place seemed different. Her own, she thought with surprise.

She fed the cat, rang for takeaway pizza and had a shower. Hair freshly washed, she sat on the balcony, on the office chair, hungrily devouring the 'Reef and Beef', and watched the lights along the foreshore. There was a certain peace there, a sense of timelessness. A tranquillity that lulled her, soothed her fractured spirit. 'We're going to like living here,' she said to the cat as he strolled out to meet her. 'Just you and me, buster. Okay?'

As if in reply, he rubbed his whiskers along her leg.

She woke to the sound of seagulls. Propping herself upright on the sofa, Callie stared around the room. Disorientated, she took in the grubby walls, boxes and furniture, wondering for a brief moment where she was.

Then she remembered.

She had left Stuart. She had finally left!

Now, in the cold light of morning, it seemed so final, so irrevocable. The past two years of her life now lay dissolved, voided by her own actions: leaving the unit, walking out on all that had been familiar to her. For the first few days in the motel she had wavered, wondering if she had done the right thing. Stuart's words, accusing, had strung themselves through her consciousness, pulling her this way and that.

You're never here! If you're not closeted away in front of that computer, you're either running around trying to find out about dead people or sitting with your nose stuck in those old letters.

Then the image danced before her again: Stuart walking along the road, his hand caressing another woman; that same hand tracking towards her, head slamming back, teeth snapping together. And, despite the ever-present tears and nagging uncertainty, no matter how much it hurt, no matter how much her instinct was to forgive him, to rush back and resume that comfortable other life, she knew she had done the right thing. There would be no going back.

Then, in another mad erratic moment, she remembered the hurtful words and silences, the hateful innuendoes, and wondered why she had stayed with Stuart so long. Everyone else — Bonnie, Jill, probably even Michael — had seen Stuart in other lights, not in the rosy glow of her own complacency. How could she have been so stupid, so *gullible*?

At other times she felt winded, almost breathless with self-doubt. A mantle of suppressed grief washed around her, numbing her. Over two years of her life had gone, amounted to nothing. Or had they? she considered later, feeling stronger, more positive. During that time she had consolidated her writing skills. The books were selling well. She had a definite career path mapped out.

And Stuart? Well, she could learn from the experience. I don't need a man to make my life complete, she told herself. I have my writing, I have Hannah's letters. I have friends.

I have my independence.

No sharing. No bowing to other people's wishes. I can bloody-well please myself, she thought, with a bubble of unexpected pleasure. Never, ever, will I let someone control my life again.

Spirits momentarily buoyed, she made her way to the kitchen and made a cup of coffee. Then, dressed, she set off for the hardware store.

It seemed as though every possible hue imaginable was represented by the rows of colour selection cards in the paint department. Finally she decided on a pale primrose for the walls and a grey-blue for the architraves, doors and skirting boards. The cans went into the trolley along with sandpaper, masking tape, brushes, a roller and tray.

Callie decided to paint the bedroom first. She carefully masked the door frames and window sills before tackling the walls. During the course of the afternoon the phone rang several times, but she was in no mood to answer it. Perched on top of Bonnie's ladder and covered in paint, she studiously ignored the shrill tones. It might be Stuart. He may have rung directory services, obtained her new number, and she didn't want to spoil her otherwise pleasant day.

It was painstaking work and the bedroom took the best part of the day to finish. But standing back, the room miraculously transformed, she felt a certain sense of achievement. In that light the walls glowed, the primrose turning to gold. And the blue matched perfectly the colour of the waves, seen through the window in late afternoon shadow.

'Well,' she addressed the cat. 'That's that. Tomorrow we tackle the living room.'

After a long relaxing bath, she walked along the esplanade to the fish shop. The phone was ringing again when she returned, the shrill sound echoing down the stairwell. She *should* answer it, Callie thought crossly, annoyed at the possible interruption to her day. Maybe it was Bonnie, saying they couldn't make it on Sunday night.

But as she turned the key in the lock and hurried to lift the receiver, the ringing stopped.

Michael had tried Callie's number for three days in a row. There was no reply, no telltale click to signal the fact that she had picked up the receiver. Instead, the repetitive burr-burr echoed in his ear, an unwelcome sound. Just the insistent buzzing of the phone, not even the answering machine.

On the fourth afternoon, Stuart answered.

'Callie?' he said, sounding surprised. 'Don't you know? She moved out.'

'When?'

'Earlier in the week. I don't know.' A hesitation, then: 'What day is it?'

What a strange question! Had Stuart been drinking? There was a slurred edge to his words. 'It's Friday,' Michael replied firmly.

Stuart paused for a second, as though considering that fact. 'Yep, that's right. Must've been Tuesday when she went.'

A mad erratic sense of hope slid through Michael's chest. Callie had left Stuart. Three whole days had passed since then, and she hadn't returned. And, more importantly, Stuart had obviously made no attempt to contact her. He was quiet for a moment, and the silence became too much for Stuart.

'Look, I don't know where she's gone. She didn't leave any contact number or address, if that's what you're after. Perhaps she didn't want you to find her, either.'

It was a needless jibe, but still it rankled. 'Perhaps she didn't,' he replied abruptly, thinking: I should hang up on this creep and not give him the satisfaction of a reply.

But Stuart was already one step ahead. 'Try Bonnie,' he advised. 'She'll know.'

Bonnie answered on the fourth ring. 'Callie?' she said, sounding surprised to hear Michael's voice. 'She and Stuart have had a parting of the ways. She's moved out.'

'So Stuart has just informed me.'

'Oh, dear,' Bonnie sympathised. 'Between you and me, I think it's been coming for a long time.'

'Is she all right?'

He could imagine Bonnie's shrug. 'I've only spoken on the phone. She says she needs time to be by herself.'

They chatted for a few minutes. Bonnie went off for the scrap of paper on which she had written Callie's phone number and address. 'But I'm sure she'd like to see you,' she offered in parting. 'She's really been enjoying going through that old trunk of Hannah's. Stuart wasn't interested, you know.'

He sat for a while after Bonnie had hung up, staring at the telephone number she had given him, remembering. He'd never forgotten how it felt the day Gaby had left, taking Timmy and all that was important in his life. He'd never forgotten that sense of desolation, the utter hopelessness that had swamped him. Nothing could have prepared him for that, he was certain. And now, years later, it was Callie going through those same motions.

He'd wanted to closet himself away, not talk to anyone. Was Callie feeling that same response? Or did she need company, voices and laughter, to help her over those first terrible days and weeks? Michael didn't know.

Then there was the dilemma of what to say, when he finally did contact her. Explanations of the conversation with Stuart, the ensuing phone call to Bonnie. Should he even mention Stuart at all? *Hi, Callie, I hear you finally came to your senses and left that arsehole!* Inwardly he suppressed a wry grin as, unbidden, the words jostled into his consciousness.

I'm sure she'd like to see you, Bonnie had said and, in the end, it was those words that swayed him. Tentatively, he dialled the number, but there was no reply. He couldn't stop thinking about her, alone in her new flat, and felt frustrated at being unable to picture her there. At various times of the afternoon he re-dialled, but there was still no answer. He tried before he left for home, while he was preparing tea, and afterwards.

Still nothing.

The need to see her gnawed persistently. She was okay, wasn't she? A vague sense of apprehension clouded his rationale. People did crazy things following relationship break-ups. But Callie wasn't 'most people', he quickly reassured himself. She was clever and talented and, underneath a very feminine exterior, undoubtedly a very strong woman.

The only solution was to drive down the coast the following morning, Saturday. Five minutes, that was all he'd stay. Just long enough to see for himself that she was all right. Make some inconsequential conversation about the letters and Ben's diary, enquire if there were anything she needed, make an effort to offer some sort of condolence on the breakdown of Callie's relationship with Stuart.

Effort! That was an understatement. As far as Michael was concerned, Stuart could move to Outer Mongolia, and that would still be too close.

Callie had already begun the day's preparations for painting when she heard the knock the following morning. With a sigh, she covered the paintbrush in plastic wrap and threw open the door.

It was Michael.

'Hi', he said, leaning nonchalantly against the door frame. 'Just driving by, so I thought I'd pop in.'

She stood, confused, one hand gripping the door handle, staring at him. A surge of annoyance swayed at her. She had wanted to be alone, hadn't she? Didn't want to talk to anyone, didn't want to dissect the reasons behind her actions of the last few days. It was too soon, her own emotions too shredded, and his arrival at her front door, uninvited, felt like an intrusion of sorts.

'I guess you'd better come in, then,' she said drily, stepping back to allow him access.

He regarded her thoughtfully, not moving. 'I was concerned about you, Callie. I've been trying to ring, but no-one seems to be answering the phone. But if you want me to butt out, then just say so.'

The phone! The unanswered phone calls hadn't been from Stuart, after all! Simply Michael, concerned for her well-being. And here she was being ungracious, almost brusque. Ill-mannered, that was what Freya would have called it.

Conscience-stricken, she bit her lip, mentally assembling some sort of an apology. 'Look, I'm sorry,' she stammered. 'I didn't mean to be rude. It was a surprise, that's all, seeing you here. Besides,' she awarded him a wan smile, 'it's been one hell of a week and I guess I haven't felt like talking.'

'I'll talk then, and you listen,' he said, pulling one hand from behind his back and holding out a bunch of flowers. 'But let's get the formalities out of the way first.'

Her mood lifted at the sight of them. They were roses mostly. Tight blood-red buds, petals unfurled, they curled like babies' fists against a bed of green leaves. The perfume of them rose up to meet her — sweet, she thought, surprised, like honey or wine.

'You shouldn't have.'

The words were out before she could stop them, and she cringed inwardly, wishing them unsaid. But it was too late.

'Perhaps I shouldn't,' he agreed, nodding, his face expressionless. 'But as I did, perhaps you'd like to put them in a vase of water before they expire.'

Callie wasn't sure if she had offended him, or if he were simply playing along with her. She glanced back at him and suddenly he smiled, his face creasing into a broad grin.

'Oh, dear,' Callie apologised, trying to stifle a laugh, the remnants of her annoyance fleeing. 'And how rude of me to keep you standing in the doorway! Come in. As you can see, I'm in the throes of painting.'

She felt a certain awkwardness. How much did Michael know, and was there a need to explain? And how had he discovered her phone number and address?

'I rang Stuart,' he said, in answer to her unspoken question. 'He told me you had moved out. Bonnie passed on the relevant details.'

He stepped inside the door, closing it in his wake. For a moment his eyes lingered about the room. Oscar jumped down from his perch on the sofa and wound himself through Michael's legs, purring loudly. 'You're my first visitor,' she laughed. 'And it looks as though he's giving you his seal of approval.'

'Callie?'

He had come to a halt in front of her. The roses were between them at chest height, a barricade of sorts, and she was unduly aware of the sweet musky scent of them.

'Yes?'

'I've been worried about you,' he said simply.

'No need. As you can see, I'm fine.'

'Really?' He gave her a long look. 'I've been through a relationship break-up, remember. I know how traumatic it is. One minute you're going along, thinking life is wonderful, and next minute you feel as though you've been kicked squarely in the stomach.'

'I thought you and Gaby had an amicable parting of the ways?'

'We did. But ...' He stopped for a moment, as though considering his words. 'The severing of a relationship is still the end of something more indefinite, and infinitely sad, no matter how it happens. It's the finalisation of unfinished plans and comes with a sense of failure, I suppose, however small.'

'It *has* been a terrible week,' Callie admitted, suddenly overcome by his concern, feeling ridiculously close to tears. 'And one I'd much sooner forget.'

She studied the roses, surprised to find her hand shaking. 'Well,' she said briskly, changing the subject, 'I suppose I'd better find a container for these.'

Finding a vase in one of the unpacked boxes, she went into the kitchen to fill it with water. When she returned to the living room, Michael had tipped a quantity of yellow paint into the tray. 'Seeing I'm here,' he said, brandishing the roller, 'I might as well make myself useful.'

Callie continued masking the timber door and window frames, while Michael began rolling the paint onto the walls. Watching him out of the corner of one eye, and remembering her aching arms from the previous day, she thought he made it seem so effortless. And despite her initial misgiving at finding him at her door, she soon found herself grateful for the company.

The morning rushed past, broken by several coffee breaks, and suddenly it was lunchtime. Callie put down her brush, washed the worst of the paint from her hands, and headed down the road to the delicatessen.

When she returned, Stuart's car was parked outside. With a sinking heart, she headed up the stairwell. The two men were inside, talking. They stopped as she entered. Stuart looked angry, his mouth set in a petulant line. Small furrows creased Michael's brow. She came to a halt just inside the door, trying to make sense of the scene.

Had they been talking about her?

'I'll just pop into the bathroom,' said Michael, giving her a tight smile. 'Wash this paint off before lunch.'

Callie steered Stuart towards the door and down the stairs. 'How long's *he* been here?' Stuart demanded loudly, not making any effort to speak quietly.

'I don't think that's any of your business.'

'What's he doing?'

Don't cause a scene, her inner sense warned. Just send him on his way. 'Helping me paint.'

'Didn't waste much time.'

'What's that supposed to mean?'

They were on the footpath now, standing in front of Stuart's car. He gave her a slow meaningful smile. 'I should think it's pretty obvious. He's still hanging around. Perhaps he's hoping to climb into your pants.' He brought his face close to her own, and the smile turned into a sneer. 'Perhaps he already has!'

'You're disgusting!'

She stepped back, fighting away an urge to slap him across the face. But he had already turned and was lowering himself into the front seat of the car.

'Can't handle the truth, Cal, old girl?'

Couldn't he leave her alone? This constant harping over Michael was driving her insane. She bent down, bringing her head into alignment with his own through the passenger window. 'Stuart, you are no longer a part of my life and whom I choose to spend my time with is really no concern of yours. Now, if you don't mind, it's lunchtime and I'm starving.'

'Yeah, so's Michael.'

She walked away, not giving him the satisfaction of a reply. Let him have the last word, for what it's worth, she fumed. Don't lower yourself with some cheap retort. As she neared the door of the flat, she heard the familiar screech of tyres spinning down the street.

The fresh rolls, cheese, ham and tubs of salad were on the kitchen bench where she had left them. 'Sorry about that,' she said to Michael as he emerged from the bathroom. 'I guess it had to happen sooner or later.'

'How did he find out where you were? He had no idea of your whereabouts when I phoned yesterday.'

Callie shrugged. 'This is a pretty small place. Word had to get out sooner or later. Or perhaps he rang Mum.'

They picnicked on the balcony, mugs of coffee and plates strewn before them on an old blanket. The day was warm and the sharp tang of salt lay in the air. People wandered along the beach: families, singles, the occasional arm-in-arm couple.

'More salad?' asked Callie, glancing up, finding his plate empty.

Michael shook his head and smiled. 'You're very pretty with your hair pulled back. You should wear it like that more often.'

'Am I?' she asked, surprised. He was staring intently at her, a slight frown on his forehead. 'I bet you say that to all the girls.'

'No.'

She bent and furiously stirred a teaspoon of sugar into the coffee, trying to hide the slow flush that crept along her cheeks. What should she say? Something flippant, perhaps? But Michael's face had been serious, not carrying the hint of a smile.

Goodness! she reprimanded herself. Accept the comment graciously and stop acting like an adolescent schoolgirl. Men had paid her compliments before and none had affected her like this.

She mumbled a reply and fled to the kitchen, bearing the empty plates. When she emerged, he had resumed painting.

442

It was almost dark when they finished. Michael cleaned the brushes and rollers in the laundry tub and they stood back to admire their handiwork. 'Looks great,' said Callie. 'Almost like a different place. Thanks for helping.'

'That's okay. I enjoyed myself.'

'About Stuart ...'

'Forget it. I already have. He's not worth the energy.'

'No, you're right. You're perfectly right.'

He glanced at his watch. 'Sorry, I've got to run.'

'I was going to ask you to stay to dinner,' she said lightly. It was all very well thinking about solitude and independence, but she had enjoyed his company, and the promise of a lonely evening loomed uninvitingly before her. 'My chance to repay you for all the hard work.'

'I can't. Previous engagement, I'm afraid. Promised Tim I'd take him to a movie. Can I take a raincheck, though? Perhaps next Saturday?'

'That'd be great. I might have this place back to some semblance of normalcy by then.'

He rested a finger against her chin. 'Callie, if there's anything you need during the week, anything at all, promise me you'll call?'

His mouth was only inches away. Without warning, Callie's breath caught in her throat as she resisted a sudden impulse to put her fingers there, along the line of his lips. She glanced away, inordinately aware of him. Not as a friend, but something more. 'Yes, I promise.'

He cupped her chin, turning her face back towards him. 'Callie ...'

She felt his breath against her cheek and the fleeting pressure of his mouth on her forehead. It was as though her whole being was rushing towards him, uncontrollable. Her legs felt like jelly. He held her for a moment against his chest. 'I worry about you,' he said. 'Take care.'

She stood at the window, watching as he walked towards his car on the street below. At the last minute, before sliding into the driver's seat, he turned and waved, and she waved back. The car moved off slowly, then turned the corner. Suddenly the street below seemed empty. All that was left were the people still walking along the beach and the gulls, wheeling high above the waves, as she fought back the abrupt and inexplicable urge to cry.

CHAPTER 27

Suddenly it was spring. The weather warmed with a rush. Buds appeared on bare branches. Small dun-coloured sparrows foraged in the grass for the breadcrumbs that Hannah threw from the kitchen window.

Those first few weeks in the cottage were happy ones. Nick loved crawling about the garden, clutching at the occasional leaf or flower. He was over eight months old now and bright as a button. Inside, he dragged himself around the furniture, balancing on unsteady feet, challenging her with a proud mischievous grin. Look at me, his eyes seemed to say.

'You're a smart boy,' Hannah beamed at every small milestone. 'Your Papa will be so proud.'

But they were empty words, lacking promise.

As the casualty lists in the newspapers grew, there were times, mainly at night after Nick had gone to bed, when she wondered if she would ever see Ben again. His absence seemed such a permanent part of her life. Their only contact was the letters, which arrived at irregular intervals, often containing money orders. *Buy something for the boy*, he would write. *Or treat yourself to something nice*. But there were no treats, no little surprises. The money was never enough and she needed every penny to survive.

In desperation, she found a neighbour who offered to care for Nick while she went back to work. Molly was in her mid-twenties, with two young children of her own. Her husband was in Palestine, part of the Australian Light Horse contingent. Molly thought he was still alive, though she hadn't received a letter for five months. 'Bloody sod,' she had grumbled to Hannah the first time they had met. 'Thinks I can live on thin air.'

The money for looking after Nick, she said, would help pay her own bills.

At least Nick will have company, thought Hannah, as she left him that first morning and set off for work. She had managed to find a job in a laundry. The premises were several suburbs away, necessitating a twenty-minute tram ride and a lengthy walk. It was hot arduous work, labouring over the steaming tubs. Her back ached. Her head throbbed from the constant heat. By evening, when she collected Nick and struggled back to the cottage, she was exhausted, barely able to stay awake long enough to prepare supper.

Afterwards, with Nick grizzly and tired, she took him into her bed and unbuttoned her blouse, soothing him with whispered words. The morning and evening feeds were all that remained after her busy schedule. Already she could see Nick growing away, no longer so dependent on her, and she missed the closeness, the bond between them. He was her child and she craved his dependency.

Watching as his mouth moved drowsily at her breast, she felt a momentary contentment. Suddenly her daily absence from him ceased to matter. They were together then, for that small fraction of time — though it wouldn't last, she told herself bleakly. Already her milk was almost gone, the last vestiges of it depleted by the daily grind at work and the sheer, all-consuming tiredness.

Lottie came to visit, bringing several old curtains that Mrs Worthington had ordered into the rag bag. Together they tacked them across the windows. They weren't much, but at least the fabric afforded some privacy.

The following weekend Lottie returned, bearing a chocolate cake. 'Mrs Bonham sent it,' she divulged. 'Said she wished you'd come by and bring the baby.'

Between work and the cottage chores, Hannah had little spare time. 'That's nice,' she replied wearily. 'Tell her I said thank you, and I'll bring Nick over one day soon.'

Lottie gave Nick a piece of cake on a plate. Tentatively he poked a few crumbs into his mouth; then, deciding he liked the taste, proceeded to smear it over his face. They laughed at him, girlish giggles that sent Nick into explosions of mirth.

'I haven't seen you like that for a long time,' said Lottie soberly, when they had finished cleaning the child's face and hands.

'I haven't felt much like laughing.'

'No, I suppose not.'

Lottie looked at her for what seemed like a long time. 'You're not eating properly, are you?' she asked, concern showing in her eyes.

Hannah glanced away, uncomfortable. 'I'm all right. Money's a little scarce right now, that's all.'

After Lottie had gone, she took the remaining cake and cut a huge slice. Nick watched, curious, as she wolfed it down. How long was it since she had tasted something sweet? God, it tasted good!

She helped herself to another slice, and another. There was so little left. She should keep a piece for Nick for tomorrow.

Feeling sick, she pushed the plate away. Lottie's astuteness worried her. Was it that obvious? In truth, between rent and travel costs, not to mention Nick's expenses, there was little left for food. But she always made certain Nick had enough to eat.

After Lottie left, she fed her son, holding him protectively in her arms. He felt warm there, his rounded body snuggled against hers, his eyes heavy with sleep. One hand lay against her breast, fingers opening and closing in rhythm to the tugging movement of his mouth.

'Sshh,' she whispered, slowly rocking. But when she glanced down, he was already asleep.

Hannah's last ritual before tucking herself into bed was to re-read Ben's latest letter. No matter how tired she was, or how miserable, his words never failed to cheer her. How he could remain so optimistic, in the face of all he witnessed, was amazing.

Now she smiled as she took the pages from the envelope, her eyes quickly scanning the words. She knew them all by heart, but the sight of them gave her comfort, and a sense that some part of him stayed with her during those long hours of darkness, watching over her.

Finally, the last page:

And so, my darling Hannah and Nick, she read. *Before you go to sleep tonight, look up at the brightest star in the sky. For one moment, imagine I am on the other side of the world, thousands of miles away, looking at the same star, although we know that's impossible. It's day here while it's night over there, but we can pretend, can't we? The thought of you and Nick is all that keeps me going. Some days I'm so tired ...*

She sighed and folded the paper, inserting it back into the envelope. She knew what tired was. Tired was slaving over a hot laundry tub all day, then coming home to a baby and cooking dinner, and cleaning, and washing nappies and ...

She stopped, at once hating herself. Compared to Ben, she had little to complain about. She was safe, she never feared for her life. But Ben was in constant danger.

She slid from the bed and walked across the room to Nick's cot. He was sleeping, dark lashes resting against his cheek. Bending over, she kissed him on the forehead, taking in the baby smell of soap and talcum powder. For a moment he stirred, stretched, then his face relaxed again, his breathing even. A tenderness came welling up inside her. He was her son, his existence a mixture of heartache and hope, sorrow and laughter. And she knew that whatever happened, whatever the future had in store, at least she would always have him.

As their second winter in France approached, the company was back on the front lines. The men came through Ypres, shocked at the further deterioration of the town in only a few weeks. Recent bombing had destroyed virtually all that had been left of the buildings. Solitary walls stood amidst the rubble. Most of the townsfolk had gone. The place was teeming, instead, with British, French and Australian soldiers.

They were billeted at Zonnebeke, working in the battle zone north of the railway line. The area was utter wasteland, with not a green leaf in sight, and recent falls of rain had reduced the low swampy ground to a quagmire. The trails that crisscrossed the wilderness of shell holes and mud had to be marked with tapes, stakes and lamps, then duckboarded.

Causeways were built over the worst of the swamps. Roads were patched, and concrete dugouts repaired and made habitable. Lastly, cursing the war, the Germans and the glutinous mud with every foul expletive they could muster, the men turned their attention to digging new trenches.

They were constructed in a zigzag pattern, with twists and turns at random intervals, to reduce the effects of shelling. The going was hard. Mud stuck to shovels. It caked on the soles of boots. Splatters of it dripped from puttees and shirts. Worst of all, it stank.

As they dug, the men were inundated with a mishmash of foul smells: the stench of stagnant swampy soil, overflowing latrine buckets, chloride of lime, rotting sandbags and half-buried corpses. From their own clothes came the odour of stale sweat, and fear.

For Ben, the days passed in a haze: work, eat, and precious little rest. Often, when he couldn't sleep, when the lint stuffed in his ears failed to muffle the constant noise of shelling, he made his bleary way to the Salvation Army lean-to, where he received hot coffee and, if the supply lorries had managed to get through, a handful of sweet biscuits.

Built of sandbags and camouflaged with the remnants of broken branches, the Salvos' lean-to was liable to be hit at any time by long-range shells. But sitting there, watching the passing traffic as his hands warmed against the mug, Ben felt a certain safety. Safety in numbers? he wondered, smiling, despite himself, at the misconception. German bombs could not differentiate between a hundred soldiers and two.

Even during the darkest hours of the night, there were always people coming and going. Relieving troops, those being relieved, supplies, Red Cross vehicles: lines of them moved along the roads, crawling at an interminable pace, a ceaseless parade. At sporadic intervals, flares went up from the nearby trenches, bringing almost daylight brilliance to the scene for a few seconds. Bodies outlined against its bluish-white glare became hulking shapes casting momentary shadows along the ground. The occasional bomb roared overhead, leaving a fine fleecy cloud of shrapnel in its aftermath. It scarcely caused a ripple of alarm, so used were they to the noise.

As dawn approached across the waste that was No Man's Land, the dark outlines of shattered trees and farmhouses grew out of the dark. Figures moved silently — were they German or Allied? — crouched low, running. In the trenches, fat rats fed off dead men, their beady eyes reflected in the pearly light.

The constant shellfire meant little sleep for days on end. Each night, exhausted, Ben flopped on the ground, curling himself under a bush or in a handy trench. But often sleep still refused to come. At odd hours he thought of Hannah and, remembering in a mechanical way, took the horseshoe from his pocket. It seemed a lifetime ago since he had given it to her. It *was* a lifetime ago. So much had happened since. Thousands of miles separated them. The horror of war had drawn them apart. Yet she was an integral part of him, the very core of his being. A future without her was unimaginable.

After three weeks, they were taken off the front lines, marching back into Ypres via the Menin Road. On both sides of the roadway, the usual flattened landscape stretched away, no longer surprising him with its bleakness. Shell craters dotted the charred plain. Tree trunks, stripped of branches and leaves, were shattered poles reaching towards a leaden sky. A steady stream of passing wagons and lorries, limbers, horses and soldiers along the narrow rutted track provided an entertainment of sorts. That ceaseless moving mass of men again. Would he ever be rid of it?

Beside him, Jack and Tom strode on. Jack whistled a popular tune that he could not put a name to. Tom stared morosely ahead. He had been quiet of late, uncommunicative to a degree. They were changing, all of them. Growing apart or closer? Ben couldn't be sure.

Blindly he stared out across the reeking tufted land. 'If there is a God,' he whispered, 'I fear he has deserted this place'.

'What's that?' asked Jack, turning, a grin creasing his face. 'Thinking about getting to town, are you? Hot bath, hair-cut. Wouldn't say no to one of those pretty little French girls, myself.'

How could he explain? They had all been through the same experiences, lost loved ones, yet they were all emerging differently.

'Nothing,' murmured Ben, the words dying in his throat. 'Nothing at all.'

They came in across the remains of the ancient ramparts that surrounded the town, through the Menin 'gate', though no structure remained that could be so termed. There was simply an opening, a gap of sorts, guarded on each side by a pair of stone lions. Ben smiled to himself as he marched through, remembering the oft-repeated, but impossible request amongst the soldiers: will the last one through please shut the gate?

They entrained for Recquebroeucq, marching the last few miles to the rest camp. Exhausted, he collapsed on the grass outside the billets, letting his face soak up the last of the day's sun. A sudden itch sent him scratching unconsciously at his shoulder, near the seam of his shirt. He closed his eyes against the scudding clouds, thinking of a cold beer, but the itch was spreading, setting his skin on fire. Frantically his hands moved from hip to leg, to belly, then to arms. Finally, in desperation, he tore the shirt from his back.

'Did you know that lice carry typhus and trench fever?' said Jack, watching him with a grin.

'Thanks, mate,' muttered Ben. 'Got any suggestions on how to get rid of them?'

But Jack was busy removing his own shirt.

It was good to be back off the front line, back in a familiar place again. Since Ben's last stint at the camp, the previous engineering company had erected a canvas bath shed with, miracle of miracles, twelve showers. There were pumps and a heating apparatus, and no apparent lack of water. They rested and refitted until early November, when they went into the reserve lines near Wulvergem. Pipe burying and drainage kept them busy and, when the weather was fine, the daylight bombing raids carried out by German aeroplanes had them running for cover.

They were snowy white, those German Taubes, looking for all the world like seagulls sailing on some unseen current of air as they passed by, so close sometimes that Ben feared they would graze the trees overhead. As the allied guns opened fire, shrapnel burst high in the air, floating outwards like soft white cotton-wool clouds long after the planes had gone. At other times the aircraft were high overhead, tiny dark dots almost lost against the infinite blueness of the sky, their droning barely heard.

There were numerous nearby *estaminets* where the usual array of local wines, eggs, chipped potatoes and even fresh meat could be purchased. Ben found a shop that sold cotton singlets and promptly bought three. Someone had told him they were less likely to harbour lice.

Then it was back to Armentières. Though the town was much changed since the previous visit, it was like coming home to an old friend. Except for a few remaining locals, the townspeople had mostly left, driven out by enemy shelling and gassing. The tower of the church still stood, although the roof was gone. All that remained of the stained glass windows were coloured shards of glass lying in the sooty mud, the colours caught by the pale watery sun.

December was upon them and the weather freezing. Although the billets were comfortable, there was a shortage of fuel and the fire gave out little heat. Alongside the nearby boiler house were three large coal piles, vigilantly watched over by the factory caretaker. Notices saying 'Not to be touched' were everywhere, in French and in English, but each of the men picked up a lump when passing, which kept the stove going.

In his spare time, Ben took long walks, pushing himself against the piercingly cold wind. Despite his coat, it seemed to penetrate every part of him, and he welcomed it. Along roads that were merely quagmires he strode, scarcely noticing the bleak landscape and bare winter trees and, in unexpected places, the clusters of graves marked by plain crosses.

He was punishing himself, though for what he wasn't sure.

One afternoon he came to a farmhouse to beg a glass of water. There was a girl at the well, drawing a bucket of water. When she turned, he could see that she was quite young, only about fourteen or fifteen.

She turned to walk away from him. 'Please,' he called out, 'I only want water.'

He accepted the pannikin, staring in surprise at the swell of the girl's belly under the sack-like dress.

As though sensing his gaze, she moved her hand there, pressing it against the fabric.

'Helene!'

A man came from the rear of a nearby shed, shooing the girl back towards the house. 'You Australian?' he asked, jabbing the cigarette he held between thumb and forefinger in Ben's direction.

'Yes.'

'You see Helene, my daughter?'

Ben took a sip of the water, not knowing what to say. 'She's very pretty,' he offered at last.

'She having baby.'

'I guessed so.'

He took another sip and stared about. Along the edge of the nearest field were the remains of an old orchard hedge. The garden surrounding the house must have been lovely once, but now had a neglected air. Roses rambled across the skeletal remains of an old shed, which was lopsided under the weight. Someone had picked a few, fat and blowsy and white, shoving them unceremoniously into a tin; petals had fallen onto the rough wooden table that stood in the middle of the yard. A few ragged chooks pecked in the dirt.

The man leaned forward, his face distorted by anger. 'She was raped by German soldiers. Not just one, but three. Three of the pigs! They threw her down on the floor, like an animal, and made us watch.'

He stopped and spat at the dirt, then went on. 'Bastards! Now her mother sits and cries. She is not the same any more.'

Ben drained the last of the water and handed the glass back to the man, words failing him. 'I'm sorry,' he said and moved to go.

The man grabbed him by the sleeve of his coat. His voice, when it came, was urgent and filled with hate. 'Do you know what we will do with the baby?'

Ben shook his head.

'Firstly, I am hoping it will be born dead.'

'And if it is not?'

Did he really want to know? A bubble of nausea rose in his chest and he swallowed, wishing it gone.

'Then I will hold its head in a bucket of water until it is. German filth!'

He spat again on the dirt and Ben backed away. He could see the girl, standing round-eyed on the steps of the house, arms wrapped protectively around her belly. 'I'm sorry,' he repeated. 'I'm sorry for your daughter and I'm sorry for your wife. I'm sorry for the whole *fucking* mess!'

He stumbled away, sickened by what he had heard. It was two days short of Christmas. What had happened to the festive cheer, the goodwill unto men? Yet, he wondered, how would he feel if the girl had been Hannah?

He found himself in a wood. At some time in the past, the trees had been poplars, proud lines of them flanking the road. But now they were splintered, shattered, like broken matchsticks. Beyond lay flat water-logged country, and a deserted lorry, bogged to the axles in mud.

When he thought he could walk no more, when his breath came in ragged sweeps, tearing at his lungs, Ben hunkered down against the damp leaf-littered soil and wept uncontrollably. He wept for the girl and her child. He wept for Hannah and Nick. And, last of all, he wept for himself, caught up in this inescapable nightmare that was not of his own making, that had somehow become his.

It was late by the time he reached the outskirts of the city again. Outside the billets at the tram sheds, he passed a group of Australian soldiers washing at large wooden tubs. 'Come and have a drink,' offered one.

'Yes, mate,' joined in another. 'It's Christmas.'

Christmas: a season for celebrating the birth of a child.

Somehow he couldn't get the young girl from his mind. The thought of her danced there in his consciousness, standing big-bellied, watching, listening with horrified eyes on the steps of the farmhouse, the rambling roses providing an incongruous backdrop.

In his mind she was mixed up somehow with Hannah and Nick. Blindly he thought of them, a faraway dream, and their names echoed hollowly in his mind, like a steam train speeding down a darkened tunnel. A pain filled the place where he imagined his heart was, an ache that almost made him cry out with surprise.

Numbly he sat amongst the men and had one drink, then another. The grog beat a fiery path through his chest. It warmed him and sent a rosy glow through his frozen body. After a while it blotted his pain, reducing it to a watery blur.

It was almost Christmas again. Decorations were strung along the city streets. Shoppers ambled along footpaths, arms laden with purchases. The aroma of mince pies and fruit puddings wafted from bakeries as Hannah hurried past on her way home from work.

She had been feeling unwell all day and the manager had called her into his office after lunch, offering to send her home. 'No, I'm fine, really,' she had protested. The few hours of missed work would result in a drop in wages, which she could ill afford.

But, to her dismay, he had insisted. 'Go home to bed. You'll feel better in the morning. You're no use to anyone like this.'

Gathering up her bag and hat, she set off down the street towards the tram stop, a fifteen minute walk away. The day was hot and, from time to time, she felt dizzy, stopping once to sit on a low fence that edged a footpath. Fearing she might faint, she put her head between her knees.

The woman of the house came out, offering a glass of cold water. 'Are you all right, dearie?' she asked. 'Shouldn't be out in the heat on a day like this.'

Hannah thanked her and gratefully drank the water.

The tram was ten minutes late. Once aboard, she leant her cheek against the cool leather of the seat, wishing the journey over. At Molly's, the front door was locked. From inside she could hear the sound of a child crying. She thumped on the door, but no-one answered.

Picking her way along the overgrown side path, Hannah found the back door propped ajar. 'Molly?' she called, but there was no reply. She found Nick standing in his cot, screaming, hanging onto the metal bars. His face was red, his cheeks streaked by tears. At the sight of her, he held out his arms, waiting to be picked up.

'Hush, hush!' she cried, hugging him to her. His nappy was wet and soiled. Deftly she changed him, stopping once to lower her head again as the dizziness passed.

Of the babysitter there was still no sign. Clutching Nick she stepped outside the back door again, into the yard.

One of the neighbours was taking in washing from the line. 'Have you seen Molly?' Hannah asked, supporting herself against the palings on the fence.

'You'll find her down at the pub, no doubt. Goes there every afternoon.' The neighbour nodded towards Nick. 'That your boy?'

'Yes,' replied Hannah, holding him tight.

'You'd do well not to bring him back here again,' said the woman. 'Molly can't even look after her own kids properly, never mind yours.'

She stumbled home, slamming the front door behind her, and lay on her bed. In her arms, Nick hiccupped, nestling his face against her shoulder. She coaxed a smile from him with an arrowroot biscuit and, after a while, he went off to sleep.

What was to happen to them? There was no way she could take him back to Molly and, without a reliable babysitter, she could not return to work. Without money she couldn't pay the rent and provide food. The small amount Ben sent was never enough. Even if she wrote, asking him for more, it would be months before she would receive it.

She cried a little, then blew her nose. It was three days until Christmas. There was scarcely enough money to buy food for the next week. And to make matters worse, she discovered later when she went down the back to the lean-to lavatory, the bleeding had started again.

CHAPTER 28

Hannah was sick for a week. Some days she was barely able to leave the bed, such was the dizziness that overtook her. She tended to Nick as best she could, thankful for Lottie's arrival on the third day.

It was Christmas. One glance at Lottie, who came bearing gifts, and she dissolved into tears. There had been no time, and certainly no money, to purchase any of her own.

'Never mind,' comforted Lottie briskly, passing a handkerchief to Hannah to wipe her eyes. 'Nick's too young to know the difference. Besides, Aunt Charlotte's here now.'

Without a murmur of complaint, she washed nappies and hung them on the line. Then she tackled the kitchen, preparing a tasty meal which Hannah promptly pushed away. Although she hadn't eaten in days, the sight of the food made her nauseous. It was only Lottie's threat to call the doctor that prompted her to attempt a few spoonfuls, though she mostly rearranged it on the plate with the fork.

On Lottie's fourth visit in as many days, she found Hannah up at last, her face having taken on some of the colour it had lost, playing with Nick at the kitchen table. 'I went down to the laundry today, explained what had happened,' Hannah said, over a cup of tea.

The story came out haltingly, with much prompting from Lottie. The boss had turned her away, saying he'd already found a replacement. She had been given the wages that were owing. 'I used the last of it for food and there's none left for rent. It's due next Friday.' Sick with worry, she bent down and picked up Nick, burying her face in his hair.

'You'll get another job,' replied Lottie optimistically.

Hannah shook her head. 'I can't find anyone to look after Nick. And after the problems with Molly, I'd be too scared to leave him with just anybody.'

'So what are you going to do, sit here and starve to death?'

'No,' she replied slowly. Nick was wriggling in her arms, demanding to be put down. She lowered him towards the floor and he took off across the room, crawling furiously, his little bottom wiggling as he went. 'I've been giving it a great deal of thought. I'm going to give up the cottage. There's a children's home, privately run, in the next suburb. They have a vacancy there for Nick.'

Lottie stared at her incredulously. 'You're going to give up your child?'

'I'm not giving him up!' she cried, tears springing into her eyes. 'This is not some spur-of-the-moment decision. I've thought long and hard about it. I'm doing what's best for my son.'

'That's rubbish, and you know it!'

'For God's sake, Lottie! Don't make me feel worse than I already do!'

'He's a baby, Hannah. He'll forget who you are.'

The thought of that brought fresh tears. 'He won't,' she hiccupped. 'It'll only be for a short while, just till I get on my feet financially, or Ben comes home. I'll look around for a live-in position. The money won't be as good but, apart from Nick's expenses, I'll be able to save every penny. I'll see him every weekend and I know he'll be well cared for.'

Her mind was made up and Lottie could not budge her from her decision. She had already written to Ben, posting the letter that very morning before she had lost heart.

'Well, if you've decided then,' said Lottie, 'you'll be interested to know that the girl who took over your job on the downstairs ward is leaving to get married. Mrs Worthington always said she wasn't a patch on you. If you asked, I'm sure you could have your old job back.'

It was settled. Mrs Worthington offered Hannah the position, and arrangements were made to bring Nick to the children's home at the end of the weekend. She moved her few things back to the Kangaroo Point house, back into the familiar bedroom she had left ten months earlier.

The day of Nick's departure dawned and her determination almost deserted her. If it hadn't been for Lottie's support, her words of encouragement, she would have scooped him up and run, though to where she wasn't certain.

'It won't be for long,' Lottie soothed, sensing Hannah's distress. 'Look, I'll come with you, if that'll make it easier.'

The tram ride seemed to take forever, jolting along while Nick tried to wriggle from her lap onto the grimy floor. Hannah held him tight, savouring the chubby firmness of him.

At last they arrived. Standing before those formidable gates, gazing up at the bleak building, her courage almost deserted her. Lottie steered them up the long driveway, offering to wait outside until Hannah returned. 'You can do it,' she said, giving Hannah a small push.

Nick's small suitcase in one hand, her son on the other hip, Hannah walked up the steps with a sinking heart. At the door she was met by a young nurse. 'This must be Nick,' she said brightly, holding her arms towards him. Nick went willingly.

Hannah faltered, not knowing what to do next. She turned and looked back at Lottie, who nodded encouragingly. 'Why don't you say goodbye now?' suggested the nurse. 'It might be easier that way. Next week when you visit, he will have settled in. You can come up and see his room then.'

Hannah nodded and bit her lip. Mutely she handed over the suitcase. 'Till next week, then.'

She kissed Nick on his warm cheek and he swivelled towards her, a puzzled expression on his face. As she took one step backwards, his arms went out. The corners of his mouth turned down. His lips trembled.

Her own tears were but moments away. 'Don't,' she whispered, reaching forward and placing one finger on her son's rosebud mouth. 'I can't bear it if you cry.'

The nurse turned, bearing Nick away from her. He struggled in her arms, levering himself up over the woman's shoulder, eyes searching for Hannah.

His face fell, features screwed into a tight mass. His screams echoed into every corner of her consciousness. The nurse turned the corner and suddenly they were gone, leaving one last lingering image of Nick's hand reaching out towards her.

She was powerless to stop the tears. Blindly she walked back to Lottie, sensing her friend's comforting arms around her as she sobbed out her heartache.

Oh, God. What had she done? In the distance, she could hear Nick's cries moving further away. It's only temporary, she reassured herself. I have a job. Nick will be well cared for. Ben will be home soon. But she felt empty, like a shell containing no substance. Nick was her present, her future. Without him, she felt barely alive.

In desperation she raised a tear-stained face to Lottie. 'Tell me I'm doing the right thing,' she whispered.

She woke that night, not knowing for a moment where she was. In the dark she listened, ears straining for the sound of Nick's even breathing in the cot beside her bed.

Then she remembered.

Nick was in his own bed, suburbs away, and the only sound was her own ragged breath.

The following day was agonising. Unconsciously, at every turn, she expected to see Nick crawling towards her. But there were only rows of beds filled with the rejects of war, an endless supply of bedpans to be emptied, and floors that never seemed to stay clean, no matter how often she washed them.

Lottie came to Hannah's room that first night. 'Listen to me,' she said pragmatically. 'This is the worst it will get. Every day from now on will be easier.'

Hannah nodded. 'I know what you're saying is right, but I can't help missing him.'

'Of course you can't. No-one expects you to. He's been part of your life for almost a year now. It'll take time to adjust.'

She missed his smiling face and his happy disposition. She missed the way he held out his arms, waiting to be cuddled. But most of all she missed those quiet times when he lay against her, nuzzling her flesh. Her breasts, though they were almost devoid of milk, ached for him. Her arms longed to enclose his solid frame. Inside she felt an emptiness that was almost tangible, a pain almost crippling.

Each Sunday morning she set off, catching the Kangaroo Point ferry, followed by a lengthy tram ride. Nick seemed happy enough to see her, though his cries each time she left seemed to shred her resolve. On the third Sunday, the week of his first birthday, he came wobbling towards her on unsteady legs, arms outstretched. Walking! He was walking, she thought with amazement, and she hadn't been there to see his first tentative steps.

A letter arrived from Ben, the contents disturbing her in some small way. His words seemed harder than before, less forgiving. War, she thought, was changing them all in unexpected directions.

The men took a German trench, he wrote, apologising that they had been on the move and it was the first chance he'd had to write for a week.

The enemy huddled against the wall and cried like babies to see our soldiers. They called for mercy, but there is no mercy here. Here it is either kill or be killed. There's no middle road.

Fritz keeps all sorts of things in his trenches. Some of the chaps take mementos from the dead or captured Germans — badges, buckles, helmets, rifles and watches — although the penalty for looting is death. Not me. I will not need anything to remind me, years down the track, of the ghastliness of this war. I carry the pictures in my head, the pain in my heart, indelibly etched. I imagine they will never go away.

Our dead and wounded lie on the ground outside the trenches. We must wait for darkness to bring them back, or face German snipers. They call for water, only there isn't any. Not where they are. We can hear their cries from inside the trenches, and the sound sickens me.

She couldn't read any more. Hastily she refolded the letter and crammed it back inside the envelope. But the words, already read, danced inside her brain that night, imagined flickering images, long after she had extinguished the light.

Towards the end of January, the company took over a system of trenches and shelters west of the river, which had previously been held by the Germans. Ben was quite comfortable in the small concrete dugout he and Tom had claimed as their own. It contained two beds and a table. Boxes doubled as seats and, miracle of miracles, there was a good supply of army-type blankets, one of which they nailed across the open entrance to keep out the wind. There was even a fireplace of sorts, ventilated by a makeshift chimney, and it was here they crouched at every available opportunity, trying to keep warm.

The smell of mould and damp garments permeated every corner of the room but, for now, it was home. Rats and mice were constant company and Ben could hear them at night, scrabbling against the walls. By the light of the fire he could make out their beady eyes as they scuttled to and fro, searching for stray crumbs.

The company remained there for the duration of the winter, moving at the beginning of March. Ben was glad to be gone. By this time the thaw had set in on the front lines, and No Man's Land between trenches and enemy lines was a sea of mud and bodies, halting progress on both sides.

On the southward hillsides, winter gave way to spring with a rush. Days were all glorious sunshine. The fields greened. Trees seemed bare-branched at a distance, but up close Ben could see the tiny green shoots spearing outwards towards the sun. The sound of bombs was just a distant memory.

The time was spent productively, overhauling stores and equipment. It was almost two years since they had left home and the remaining men were weary. Dozens had died or been repatriated back home. Replacements were young, too young, thought Ben, noting their fresh faces and outspoken scepticism about a war which was almost three years old.

The distant throb of gunfire was the first hint of a new German offensive. Within days they were on the move again, entraining at Lottingen while the attached transport went on ahead by road. News from the battle area in the south filtered through by word of mouth: the Germans were advancing through the Somme region and the town of Albert had been taken.

Four days of travel was almost Ben's undoing. Transport was whatever was available: cattle truck for the first stage, then motor bus. He woke at odd hours, thirsty and badly needing to pee, wondering where on earth he was, while the countryside rolled past.

The hills of Picardy were a change after the flat plains of Flanders. Pise and thatch cottages basked in the sun along the white chalk roads, equally white dust rising behind the long lines of convoys that passed. Children stood in yards and waved, calling: 'Vive Les Australiens!' In the fields, old men with scythes were cutting hay. One looked up and shielded his eyes with his hand, then waved. Then he turned back to his task, head bent.

They halted at a crossroads to let the regiment of another division pass, Royal Scots Fusiliers, Ben thought, judging by their braided uniforms and tall busby-like hats. At noon the lorries pulled onto a grassy verge of the road, and they lunched under ramrod-straight poplars. Here, white daisies and blood-red poppies grew haphazardly in the ditches along the roadside, masses of them stretched as far as the eye could see, waving and dipping and dancing in the breeze. Clouds of butterflies darted about the flowers. The occasional blue dragonfly hovered, wings incandescent in the sunshine. Above, two birds were dark specks against the cobalt sky.

470

It could have been a pleasant picnic anywhere, thought Ben, laying back and feeling the sun warm on his face, except for the clusters of small white crosses on the hillsides and the occasional sound of distant bombing.

During the last part of the journey, old disused trenches were a tangle of white lines on the surrounding hillsides. They passed tiny villages nestled against shredded foothills. At some time in the past, the houses had probably been quaint, with gardens lovingly tended by residents. Now most were reduced to rubble.

The *Maire* had organised billets in the schoolhouse and attached barns. The rooms were clean, with fresh linen on the beds. The windows afforded a view across the valley. In the yard below, several fruit trees were in blossom.

'Holy shit!' exclaimed Tom as he dumped his kit bag on the floor and rolled back the bedspread. 'Sheets! I must have died and gone to heaven!'

Ben flung himself on the bed, noting the solid springs. 'Can you believe this?' he asked.

Jack, sticking his head around the door, added, 'Think I'll just stay here for the rest of the war. You blokes'll have to go on without me.'

The following morning, Ben was surprised to find several of the local girls waiting at the front door. 'The *Maire* has sent us,' one of them explained in halting English. 'We do your laundry.'

'How much?' asked Tom. Experience had taught them that offers of help were not always free.

'Ten *centimes* per garment. You provide the soap and soda, and we will work for you. We do good job.'

They were young mostly, barely out of their teens. One girl in particular smiled at Tom, who returned the attention with a broad grin.

It felt strange listening to the chattering of the women at the laundry tubs as they went about their work. Later, when his own clothes were washed, Ben hung them along the fence that bordered the yard and went for a walk.

It was mid-morning. As he headed towards the main part of town, he heard a shout behind him. 'Hey, wait up!'

It was Jack. Together they strode along, hands in pockets. 'Wouldn't mind a beer,' said Jack, 'if we can find one of those funny little bars.'

Down rubble-filled streets they went, past the remains of houses with no front yards. Ahead lay a large squarish building. There were several shell holes through the roof and the bricks lining the rims of the windows were blackened.

'What's that?' asked Ben, pointing to the building, as one of the local men wobbled by on a bicycle.

'It is the orphanage, monsieur,' the man replied. 'The Germans raided and set fire to it before they left. There is no-one there now.'

'Come on, let's go,' said Jack, touching a hand to Ben's shirt sleeve, obviously anticipating the longed-for beer.

But something drew Ben inside.

Along narrow corridors he went, glancing into deserted rooms. There had been a fire, all right. Black soot lined the walls and ceilings, and the odour of smoke hung in the air.

'Christ, mate,' said Jack, following gingerly along behind. 'This is weird in here. And the bloody stink ...'

A beam above shifted and creaked, then was still. Ben glanced up, then continued on his way.

'And we're liable to get killed, if that lot decides to come down,' Jack added darkly.

They were in some kind of a dormitory. Rows of metal cots and beds lined the walls. There were bars on the windows, though the glass was shattered. A beam of sunlight speared through, dust motes caught in its brilliance.

Ben reached in his pocket for the letter that had arrived the previous day, thrusting it towards Jack. 'Read this,' he instructed.

Jack finished the letter and handed it back. 'Shit, mate. That's rough,' he sympathised.

'Nick's living in a place like this. Hannah couldn't afford to keep him with her.'

'He's in capable hands,' reassured Jack. 'The letter says so.'

'My son's living in an institution, and there's nothing I can do while I'm stuck here in this godforsaken place.' Ben pounded a fist against his palm as he glanced around. 'Christ, it's like a prison in here.'

Something caught his eye: a small hump in the cot in the far corner. Warily he stepped forward.

'Jesus, what is it?' stammered Jack.

It was a baby boy. He was naked, his belly swollen grotesquely and blackened limbs already stiff. Gently Ben lifted the tiny body and stumbled outside.

'What are you going to do?'

'Bury him. If you want to help, you could look around for a shovel.'

Ben said a prayer over the grave while Jack waited, hands linked behind him, looking visibly shaken. 'Don't you ever feel guilty?' he asked at last, laying aside the shovel.

'Why?' Jack shifted uncomfortably.

'Because we're alive and so many have died.'

In the trees behind them, the larks were singing. From high above came the faint drone of an aeroplane. Hedges and trees, or what was left of them, were budding. In a nearby field, a farmer was sowing wheat. When Ben finally looked upwards, the aeroplane seemed like a white cabbage moth outlined against the interminable blueness of the sky.

'Doesn't this seem strange?' He lowered his gaze towards the freshly placed mound. In his mind he could still feel the weight of the child in his arms, the substance of it.

'What does?'

'That after what's happened here, after the absolute horror of it all, the seasons are still going on in an endless cycle.'

'Too right,' Jack replied soberly. 'You'd think the whole fucking world would have ground to a halt by now.'

Too soon they were moving back up to the front lines, passing small towns and villages: Franvillers, Heilly, Pont-Noyelles. Much of the travelling was done at night. It was raining softly and there was no moon. Progress was slow, with enemy aircraft making random overhead sweeps. From time to time they were forced into the ditch at the side of the road, crouching in the dark, hands held over heads. It was a useless gesture, Ben knew, but there seemed nothing else to do. The hands offered the only protection he could muster.

It was night, too, when they finally went into the trenches. A raid was in progress. The Vickers guns ripped and roared, bullets zipping and humming against the sandbags. In a half-crouching, half-standing position, Ben followed the shape of the man in front, feeling the claustrophobic closeness of the trench's earthen walls with his outstretched hands. A splattering of stars reflected in the pools of water that lay alongside the duckboards. Random shells burst above, turning night momentarily into day. Past the gunners he ran. They were stripped to their waists, gas helmets slung around necks, sweat shiny on their bodies as they peppered the darkness. Rat-a-tat-tat.

He fought back the impulse to clamp his hands over his ears in a vain attempt to block the noise. A faint unease was stirring in his belly, though for what reason he was unable to say. Was this his time to die? Did that leaden sinking feeling constitute some kind of premonition?

Daylight brought more work. New rows of trenches replaced the old, floored by lines of clean duckboards. It was backbreaking labour, under the range of the German guns. As the days passed, there were constant casualties from snipers or bombs, and gas was a never-ending threat.

After the trenches came the job of laying out the rolls of barbed wire in No Man's Land. It was dangerous work, usually undertaken at dawn, when the mist mostly hid the German trenches from view. Often the front lines were less than twenty yards apart. Across the still air they could hear the Germans talking, rapid bursts of words in deep guttural accents, the gist of which Ben was unable to follow. Of one fact he was certain; if he could hear them, then it followed that they heard him also.

The dawn of the third day started as usual. Ben went to unload the replacement rolls of barbed wire from the lorry, while Tom and Jack assembled the metal pickets needed to support the wire. Sergeant Hayes detained him at the truck for several minutes, discussing arrangements for repairs to one of the dugouts which had collapsed the previous night. By the time he returned, Jack was hoisting the metal props over the side of the main trench. Of Tom there was no sign.

It was barely light. Away across the line of trenches, he heard a laugh, then the rattling sound of shells being loaded.

'Where's Tom?' he hissed at Jack's bent back.

Jack nodded towards No Man's Land. 'Taken the first load out. He'll be back in a minute for the rest.'

Looking out into the swirl of mist, Ben had that same sense of unease again and swallowed hard. A gun chattered suddenly, breaking the silence, followed by two loud explosions. Something landed in front of them, out in that grey area near the opposing trenches. He heard the thud as it impacted against the damp earth. A soft hissing sound came on the air, brought by a faint breeze. Gas!

There was no movement through the mist. No

familiar looming figure came towards him, no sound of boots.

'Tom?' he called softly.

There was no reply.

A bubble of fear rose through his chest. Determinedly he pushed it away. Engrossed in his task, Tom couldn't hear him, that was all. Any moment now he'd be back, hoisting himself into the trench, a silly grin on his face.

Someone tapped him on the shoulder. Turning, he saw it was Jack, a puzzled expression on his face. In one hand he held a gas mask. 'It's Tom's,' he said. 'The stupid bugger forgot to take it.'

'Shit! Shit! Shit!'

It was lachrymatory, or tear gas, Ben realised, feeling the first sting of it against his own eyes. Pulling his mask over his face, he scrambled up the tiered layer of sandbags. Hoisting himself over the trench rampart, he lay prostrate on the ground, peering into the gloom. There was no knowing which way his mate had gone.

'Tom?' he yelled, now careless of the noise.

A German gun spluttered into life in reply to his voice.

'For fuck's sake, answer me!'

'Ben?'

Tom's voice, muffled by the mist, came from his left, and he felt a surge of relief. 'Yes, mate. We're over here.'

'I can't see. The gas ...' Tom gave a choking sound as a violent fit of coughing ended his words.

For a moment the mist cleared and Ben could see clearly. Tom was feeling his way towards them, hands outstretched like a blind man. Before him lay a roll of wire. 'Christ!' he muttered, knowing there was no way Tom could avoid it. 'Stay there,' he yelled. 'Don't move. I'm coming.'

But Tom took another step forward, as though he hadn't heard. His trouser leg caught against the barbs. Reaching down, he tried to disentangle himself, plucking uselessly, frantically at the wire. 'BEN!' he screamed, staring blindly back in the direction of his own trench system.

Behind Tom, out of the mist, loomed the figure of a soldier. He was German, Ben knew, by the uniform and the metal spike just visible on the top of his helmet. Kneeling, he trained his gun on the trapped man.

'NO!' Ben tried to wriggle forward, trying to bring his own gun round at the same time. But it was too late. The German crouching against the ground took steady aim and fired.

One shot.

Tom's body jerked forward, hands flinging themselves defensively into the air. The gun fired again, two short bursts of flame. Tom's body rocked with the impact, then slowly crumpled, pleating itself into folds until he lay slumped over the roll of wire.

A terrible noise was coming from Ben's own mouth, a moaning scream that built somewhere in his chest then worked its way upwards. He could hear it echoing inside his mask, distracting him, though it came of its own accord and he was powerless to stop it. Tom! He had to get to Tom. Clumsily he levered himself into a crouching position. The German soldier was turning, swinging his gun in Ben's own direction. One step, two. The man's movements seemed laborious, cumbersome, but perhaps it was himself operating in slow motion?

The mist was swirling back in again, wisps of it blotting out the scene. His own hands were like lead, refusing to co-operate. Now! He should run to Tom now. Fuck the German!

A heavy tackle about his legs brought him crashing to the ground.

'Are you crazy?'

Jack's voice, urgent and loud, in his ear. He heard the words but they made no sense. Crazy? He couldn't leave Tom out there. It would be light soon. The sun would beat down on him, the flies would come, swarming in their thousands to feed off the blood.

He struggled under Jack's grasp, kicking out at the restraining arms. 'Let me go! For fuck's sake, let me go!'

'You stupid bastard, do you want to get yourself killed, too?'

Other hands were on his legs now, pulling him back into the trench. Lying pinned against the duckboards, he hit out at them. Someone ripped the mask from his face and slapped his cheek, hard. He stared upwards, seeing Jack's concerned face. 'Ah, Christ, Ben! Don't do it, mate!'

Tom lay out there, unretrievable until nightfall when, under the cover of darkness, Ben and Jack crawled forward and disentangled his body from the wire. Miraculously he was still alive.

'Sorry, mate,' whispered Ben, hearing the ragged groans as he lifted his friend easily into his arms.

'We'll get you to a doctor. Just hang in there. You'll be all right.'

Back in the trench he held water to Tom's mouth, but his lips barely moved. Blood streamed from a wound in his abdomen. Under the smears of grey clay and blood, his skin was already darkening.

At the dressing station, the doctor shook his head and drew Ben outside. 'He's suffered massive internal wounds. There's nothing we can do except ease his pain.'

It was Spud all over again, and Will. Except, this time, the grief lay closer to home. Tom had been part of his life before all this. They had shared good times and bad. Most of all, they had shared Hannah's love. He *couldn't* die.

'There must be something!'

Even as he said the words, he knew how useless they were, but he owed it to Tom to say them.

'I'm sorry.' The doctor shook his head again and moved away. There were others requiring his attention, others who might be saved.

Ben sat by the stretcher and waited, counted each rasping breath, noted each rise and fall of Tom's chest. Inside he felt leaden, full of hate.

Tom slipped away at dawn. No last goodbyes. No final regaining of consciousness. Simply one long shudder, one last exhalation of breath, and his shattered body was still. Ben sat there, not believing, not wanting to. Lowering his forehead, he pressed his knuckles against his brow as the tears finally came.

Numbed by grief and exhaustion, he stumbled from the tent. Outside, the countryside resembled an ancient ash heap, grey and bleak under an equally grey sky. Next to the trunk of a tree, he sank to the ground, his back against the rough bark, and buried his face in his shaking hands.

He was losing control. He could feel it slipping away, taking him to the boundary of his sanity. All that was precious was being snatched from him. Not all at once, though. Oh no! It was happening slowly, insidiously.

Blankly he stared ahead. A throbbing had started, deep inside his head. His brain seemed at bursting point, a pressure building there that made him bring his palms to his temples, as though to stop them from exploding. Questions, dozens of them, coursed through his consciousness, each one jumbling and overlaying the next. When would the nightmare end? What were the limits of human endurance? At what point would his body, his mind, simply refuse to function?

Surely his time here was finite, measured by a further predetermined number of days, weeks. Years ...

Years?

Not years, surely.

He shook his head, pressing the thought away.

The war couldn't go on that much longer!

CHAPTER 29

It was the early morning breeze coming through the open window that woke her. Callie stirred and stretched on the sofa, aware suddenly of the smell of fresh paint. She lay there for a minute, remembering. Then, when she opened one eye, the stack of boxes in the centre of the room came into vision.

The sight of them made her think of Hannah's relocation from the boarding house into the tiny cottage, decades earlier. It hadn't been so different from this, according to the letters she had read. Yellowing, curling pages, brittle now with age, that detailed Hannah and Nick's move into that strange place, suddenly finding themselves cast adrift from familiar things. Just like herself. How long had they stayed there? she wondered. So far the letters hadn't led her any further, and she'd had no time to delve into them during the past week.

Now that the flat was repainted, she should get up, put on the jug for coffee, start unpacking. But it was nice lying there, watching the curtains shuffle back and forth in the breeze. Nice not to be disturbed, she thought, surprised. And nice to have the whole day to herself, with no interruptions.

The past week had been tiring, both emotionally and physically. Now, mentally sifting back through the days and accompanying emotions, she was surprised to realise that she was handling it all better than she had expected. The relationship with Stuart was over, she had accepted that. Now it was time to move on.

Lazily her thoughts drifted back to Hannah. What had it been like all those years ago? Callie wondered. Praying that the war might end. Desperately waiting for Ben to return. But he hadn't, had he? Or if he had, there had been no wedding. Instead Hannah had married Uncle John and, in Callie's lifetime, there had never been any mention of a baby called Nick. Perhaps the child had died? Infant mortality was high back in those days, especially during the post-war influenza epidemic ...

'Stop it,' she reprimanded herself, sitting up and leaning on one elbow. No amount of imaginings would reveal the truth. Only the letters could do that, and they seemed to be taking an age to decipher. And whatever had happened, whatever sadness and misery her great-great-aunt had endured, she had survived, Callie reminded herself sternly, and had lived to a ripe old age.

The unpacking didn't take long. First she levered the barbeque onto the balcony. Then she arranged her desk near the window in the living room and set up the computer. With the books neatly arranged in the bookcase next to the filing cabinet, she pushed the chair under the desk, as though ready for work.

The hi-fi system took a little longer to put together. Faced with a tangle of leads, she carefully separated them and guessed at their destinations. After a couple of false starts, the radio hummed into life, so she put a selection of CDs onto the turntable and crossed her fingers. It worked.

She pushed the outdoor setting into the other corner, near the kitchen. Until a proper dining table and chairs could be purchased, it would have to suffice. The room, she thought, looked passable. Certainly the shampooed carpets and freshly painted walls were a huge improvement. Standing back, she surveyed her handiwork before tackling the kitchen.

There was still the matter of Hannah's painting of the wattles at the bottom of the Brunswick Street garden. The only picture hook in the whole flat was in the bedroom, above the spot where the bed — when she got around to buying one — would stand. So she hung it there, pleased that the tones roughly matched the primrose-gold walls.

Then, happy with the overall result, she took the Suzuki from the tiny garage at the rear of the flats and headed towards the supermarket.

Bonnie and Freya arrived at six o'clock. They dutifully inspected the flat, pronounced it bright and cheerful, though a little bare.

'Well,' began Callie tentatively, 'I thought perhaps I could buy some of the pieces in the Brunswick Street house.'

Bonnie and Freya had been talking about buying new furniture when they moved. Their prospective unit was much smaller than the house, and their large old-fashioned pieces would be too bulky for the modern interior.

'Oh, dear,' exclaimed Bonnie. 'With all that's happened, I quite forgot to tell you. We've sold the house!'

'And we got our price,' interjected Freya.

'A little more than we expected, actually,' added Bonnie. 'The new owner wanted to buy the place fully furnished so we worked out a reasonable deal. Thought it would save us the trouble of trying to sell it privately, and the pieces *do* suit the rooms.' Bonnie looked concerned. 'But if I'd known you wanted some of it, love ...'

So, at last the old place had sold. 'Never mind,' murmured Callie, attempting a smile. The surge of disappointment was almost palpable. She could feel it working its way down her chest, leaving a heaviness she couldn't explain. There was a moment's silence. 'That's great,' she added at last. 'I'm pleased for you.'

Through dinner the conversation continued along general lines, the two older women filling her in on the planned settlement date of the sale, in two months time. 'It'll give us plenty of opportunity to pack and clean out the junk up in the ceiling,' said Freya. 'Pity. We were hoping Stuart would give us a hand —'

She stopped suddenly, halted by a warning glance from Bonnie, who interjected: 'I'm sure we'll find a way around it'.

'What about that young man of yours, Michael?'

Young man of yours! The inference that she was somehow involved with Michael rankled. Well, in a way she was, but it was simply friendship, a mutual interest in the old letters and diary. Besides, it was none of Freya's business, and how dare her aunt assume ...

'He's *not* my young man, Aunt Freya,' she replied firmly. 'And I'm certain he's got more interesting things to do in his spare time.'

'Lovely meal, Cal,' said Bonnie, diffusing the situation.

After insisting on helping with the washing-up, the two women left, Freya muttering something about old buildings being infested with cockroaches and mice, and undesirable types living along the beachfront. Relieved, Callie stood on the balcony and watched them go, the old Vauxhall chug-chugging down the street, leaving a cloud of exhaust smoke in its wake.

Despite herself, she smiled. They were harmless, really, if a little tactless. And, their remarks notwithstanding, they had her welfare at heart.

Pity about the furniture, though, she thought wistfully. They were nice pieces and well looked after. The new owner of the house in Brunswick Street had made a wise purchase.

On Monday morning she drove to the furniture warehouse on the edge of town and ordered a bed. Then it was on to the electrical store, where she bought a small television, fridge and microwave.

At the kitchenware shop next to the supermarket, she dawdled over a set of glassware and a collection of knives in a practical wooden block. Bags bulging, she headed for the car, and home.

Thankfully she had kept her own bank accounts. There was a small amount saved, and the remainder of the advance for the latest book would soon come through. Bonnie had offered a small loan the previous evening but she had rejected her mother's offer. 'Thanks, Mum. I think I've got enough to get by.'

Stuart, she remembered as she lugged her purchases up the stairs and into the kitchen. She should ring him and discuss what was to be done about the unit. Half the deposit had been hers, and the earnings from her writing had paid alternate monthly payments. Property values had gone up a little in the last couple of years, so she would receive a fair sum once it was sold.

For several days she postponed ringing, not wanting to talk to him after the fiasco of the previous Saturday. And what if Primrose answered? What would she say then? She had a momentary vision of herself hanging up the phone, Primrose standing on the other end of the line, peering suspiciously into the receiver. Despite herself, she gave a reluctant laugh.

In the end she rang him at work. Since he shared his office with two others, he was less likely to start an argument.

'It's Callie. We need to discuss what's to be done with the unit,' she stated matter-of-factly when he answered.

'I'm busy this weekend,' he said abruptly.

With Primrose, she wanted to say, surprised that the thought had no effect on her at all. No jealousy, no regrets. Merely a sense of relief that it was over.

'Through the week then. We need to get it sorted out.'

He hung up without another word. Callie held the phone against her ear, listening to the buzz that came from the receiver. Several words filtered into her mind, words that her mother would not have approved of.

But it didn't matter what she thought of him.

'Goodbye, Stuart,' she said, instead, to the disconnected line and firmly replaced the receiver on the hook.

The week consisted of a mountain of paperwork, which Michael hated. It was the downside to the job, a necessary evil. Cataloguing negatives, arranging for copies of photographs to be sent on to the appropriate departments. Meetings with the art director, the lighting people. Writing up reports for the various companies who had ordered shoots. Planning the next assignment, booking accommodation. Some days he scarcely seemed to leave the phone.

As he sat at his desk, his thoughts turned randomly to Callie, remembering her as he had seen her last: pale oval face, blob of blue paint on her nose, grey solemn eyes.

It would have been so easy to kiss her. He had wanted to, desperately, but the timing wasn't right. Then, halfway down the esplanade on his way home, he had fought against a sudden need to turn the car around and race straight back to her. But he couldn't. He had promised to take Tim to the movies and he was already late.

Now there was the urge, every time he glanced at the phone, to dial her number. Hi, he could say. Casually. Nonchalantly. Just wanted to know how you're getting on. But somehow he summoned the strength and resisted. Leave her be, said an inner voice. She's too vulnerable right now, her hurt's too raw. Give her time. Besides, from the scene he had partly witnessed the previous Saturday, she wasn't about to patch up her relationship with Stuart.

His thoughts drifted to the time when he and Gaby had gone their separate ways. There were days, and nights, when he had wanted to call her, his wife, his *ex*-wife, the need born of that terrible loneliness and depression that engulfed him after she had taken Timmy and gone. But he hadn't then, either, a combination of masculine pride and stubbornness and sheer misery making him reclusive and uncommunicative for weeks.

The grief, the heartache that the relationship was finally over had been overwhelming at the time. He experienced, as he had once told Callie, an acute sense of failure. Why hadn't he been able to make his marriage work? What had gone wrong? He could pinpoint little things, but on the whole, he had been happy, hadn't he?

When, months later, he had been able to review the whole thing rationally, he knew Gaby had been right. They had survived without each other, grown, in fact. Luckily their friendship had endured, thanks to Gaby's good nature and their combined concern for Timmy's happiness. A divorce was bad enough on a child, without parents warring. And there had been no need to worry, he reflected now. The split had been amicable, the property divided satisfactorily. He had regular access to his son, though in many ways he'd like to see more of the boy.

He flicked over the pages on his desk calendar and circled Saturday's date, then he flicked the pages back again, counting the days. 'Oh, God, Paterson,' he groaned, bringing his palms up until they cupped his chin as he stared morosely through the window.

Saturday. Three days until he would see her again. And this time, unlike all the other times, he wasn't sure that he could keep his feelings to himself.

'I'm like a hormonal bloody sixteen-year-old, and that's a fact,' he informed Bess, the Labrador, as he let himself in the front door later. 'No, don't say anything,' he laughed, waggling a finger at the dog. 'It's all true. I admit it. This is worse than the crush I had on Miss Smith in Grade Six.'

Bess followed him inside. He opened a can of dog food while she stood next to the back door, waiting, her head tilted enquiringly, brown eyes following his every movement.

'By the way, Bess, how do you feel about cats?' he added as he moved towards the back door, bowl in hand. 'A big black-and-white cat, to be specific, who goes by the name of Oscar?'

Bess simply thumped her tail in reply.

Callie tried to work, but the words refused to come. Turning on the computer, she sat before the screen, her mind strangely blank. Weeks earlier she had been full of enthusiasm, telling Michael about the new book she planned to write. She had even managed to put down a few initial thoughts and ideas. But now, in hindsight, the whole concept was daunting. Ben. Hannah. The war experience revealed by the letters. How could she possibly recreate that on paper? And where to start?

Tentatively she typed in the word 'Hannah', followed by a colon. A multitude of scenes raced through her mind. Hannah waving Ben off at the station. Hannah discovering her pregnancy, giving birth. The first time she had held her son.

She, Callie, had never experienced childbirth. Certainly she had read of the wonder of it all, the pain, followed by the moment of pure joy when the child is placed in its mother's arms for the first time, the surge of relief at finding fingers and toes all intact.

But they were other women's experiences, not her own.

Then there was Ben. Through his eyes, his words, she had witnessed the vagaries of war. How could she describe the constant never-ending noise on the front line, the lack of sleep, the cold, gut-wrenching fear of going into the trenches?

'Okay,' she muttered. 'Be disciplined. Think.'

Hesitantly she typed a few words. Then, frowning, she deleted them all.

From the dusty pages of the letters, it was Ben's words, and Hannah's, that had made their characters come alive. Now, eighty years on, it was those on-the-spot descriptions that evoked previously unknown emotions within her own mind.

'I know!' she exclaimed, a sudden idea forming. Her first thought had been to fictionalise the whole account, turning it into a novel. But it wasn't fiction, was it? Why not use Ben and Hannah's words? Why not create a book that was part autobiography and part biography?

Suddenly the ideas poured forth. She could combine the letters and the entries in the diary, then add some factual information on Ben's engineering company. The Australian War Memorial in Canberra would surely be able to provide records and official photographs. There were also the photos in the trunk and the array of wartime memorabilia: postcards, eulogy cards, and so on. They would provide a good visual display for the book and a little relief from solid margin-to-margin text.

Once decided, the words came easily: a condensed background history on the Cordukes, followed by the little she knew about Ben's family, into a file she named Chapter One. A visit to the local genealogy society might unearth some more information on the Galbraith line, and she made a mental note to follow up that lead the following week. Meanwhile, she worked steadily for several hours, hands flying over the keyboard with a sudden urgency, emerging mid-afternoon to discover that she had quite forgotten lunch.

She worked happily for the remainder of the week, typing in the contents of the first few letters and visiting the local library, ordering several books on World War I. The days flew past, so caught up was she in the project that, before she knew it, it was Saturday.

She had barely made the bed and tidied the flat when Michael knocked on the door. He stood there, a beach towel flung over one shoulder, a grin slapped across his face. 'Hi. Thought I'd come down early and get some serious swimming in, before the day gets too hot.'

They spent the next few hours at the beach, coming back to the flat a little before lunch. Callie made sandwiches and iced tea, and Michael produced a small brown-covered book.

'What is it?' she asked, her interest aroused.

'History of the 11th Field Company Australian Engineers,' said Michael, reading from the front cover. 'I knew from Ben's diary what company he served with, and I managed to borrow this through the local library service. It's the relevant potted history, written somewhere in France after the war had ended, while the men were waiting to be shipped back home.'

'Can I borrow it for a few days? I've started on Ben and Hannah's story in earnest, and it's just the sort of research material I'll be looking for.'

The conversation shifted to Callie's writing and she explained the form that the book was taking. 'You see, I just don't think I can do justice to their story by fictionalising it. Something is certain to be lost in the translation. I want it to be as stark and real as the letters.'

Michael sounded disappointed. 'I thought Ben's and Hannah's story would make a great novel.'

'So did I at first, but it wasn't working for me. This way I get to use their own words.'

'Well, you're the writer, so I'll have to place my trust in you,' he said, and they both laughed.

'You know, war was something that never interested me until now. I always thought of it as being a male thing. Macho blokes going off to kill or be killed, heroes to the last dying breath. Ben's letters have shown me it wasn't like that.'

'No.'

She glanced up at him, regarding him steadily for a moment before continuing. 'Some of those blokes, Ben included, hated being there. It was a living nightmare for them. Reading his words, I can almost imagine how terrible it must have been.'

'You know, we see the photographs and we try to understand,' Michael agreed, 'but until you've lived through it, I don't think you could ever fully imagine the horror.'

'That's precisely why I want to present the book this way,' Callie broke in. 'You *do* understand.'

The afternoon passed pleasantly, sitting on the balcony. Callie opened a bottle of wine, and Michael produced a pack of cards. They played snap and euchre, and a few rounds of canasta, which Michael won. Finally, purple shadows stretching across the expanse of once-golden beach, Michael suggested dinner.

'I brought some good clothes, on the off-chance. They're in the car, if you're in the mood for going out?'

'Sounds like an invitation too good to refuse.'

They drove down the coastline, stopping eventually at a small restaurant that overlooked the sea. It was cosy, reasonably priced, and the food superb. Afterwards, as he dropped her at the flat, she invited him up for a nightcap.

'I'd like that,' he accepted.

In the kitchen she set the percolator bubbling before pouring two small glasses of port. Then, loading it all onto a tray, she headed back into the lounge room.

Michael was standing on the balcony, looking down at the street below, his figure outlined against the darkness by the light spilling outwards from the room. Placing the tray on the table, she joined him, noting that the sea breeze was cooler now.

'Coffee's ready.'

She went to walk back inside, but he reached forward and took her hand, staying her. 'How *are* you, Callie?'

'I'm fine, really.'

'You're not just saying that, putting on a front? People do that, you know.'

'No,' she laughed. 'Truly. Everyone keeps asking the same question and, to be honest, I'm feeling much better about it all than I expected.'

'It's always difficult to end a relationship, no matter what the circumstances are. And it's a scary feeling, stepping out of what we perceive as our comfort zone.'

'Even if we are unhappy,' Callie added on a deep breath.

'And were you?'

'Unhappy?' She thought for a moment, staring down at her own hand held so firmly within his. Should she withdraw it or simply wait and see what happened next? 'Yes and no. It wasn't *all* bad. It just takes time adjusting to being alone again. Thinking as a single, not a couple.'

'I missed you through the week.'

Startled, her face came up to meet his. 'You did?'

'Yes. There were probably fifty times when I wanted to pick up the phone and dial your number.'

'Why didn't you?'

He stared at her, his mouth curving into a sheepish smile. 'This is silly,' he laughed, shaking his head. 'We're acting like sixteen-year-olds. Why can't we come right out and say what we feel?'

She could see his mouth moving, heard his words sliding silently into the abyss that had become her mind. Words waiting to be acknowledged, drawing them onto a new and uncharted level of intimacy.

'And what *do* you feel?'

'Oh, God!' He gave a mock groan and brought her hand upwards, pressing his mouth briefly against her knuckles, staring at her all the while.

In that brief unexpected moment, he bent his head and kissed her.

It seemed so inevitable, his mouth on hers as he drew her close, arms sliding around her shoulders, cradling her in his embrace. His mouth tasted sweet, like honey, and sent a dizzying rush of emotion surging through her chest. Tiny pinprick shocks radiated from his touch, a slow spread of tingling heat that reminded her of the need to be held, the urge to touch, to feel.

Little flickers of awareness, a sense of familiarity, touched the soft core of her. She was conscious of her own hands moving at the back of Michael's neck, kneading, pulling his mouth hard against hers. Conscious also of a sudden tension, a sexual urgency, lying between them like a coiled spring, and she was inordinately aware of Michael's needs, and her own surprising acknowledged desire to satisfy them.

Abruptly he pulled away, the sudden movement almost like a physical blow. She took one step backwards, the night air cold against her skin where his arms had rested. 'I've got to go,' he whispered, his breath ragged as he cupped her chin in his trembling hands.

She turned blindly away, hearing the front door close in his wake. Oh, God! she thought, pressing her knuckles against her mouth. What was happening? She hadn't wanted to feel this way, not about anyone. It was too early. Much too soon. Yet there was an undeniable response, a sudden indisputable reaction that he had stirred within her, which she was unable to ignore.

Later, lying in bed, the room lit by the streetlights below, the disappointment coursed an agonising path through her chest, lodging eventually into the ball of her stomach. It sat there, a tight pain, reminding her that it had been weeks since that last time with Stuart, and she was a red-blooded mature woman and needed more.

CHAPTER 30

Stuart arrived unannounced on Monday evening and thrust a bundle of letters into Callie's hands. 'Thank you,' she replied graciously, mentally making a note to go to the post office first thing the following morning and have her mail redirected.

Uninvited, he made a quick tour of the flat. 'At least it's a little more presentable than when I saw it last.'

She bit back a retort, and the urge to tell him, not so politely, to leave. But the problem of the unit needed sorting out, and the sooner they squared everything away, the sooner she could cease to have further contact with him.

'I'll get some more furniture,' she said instead.

'I see Bonnie and Freya have sold the house. There's a big 'Sold' sticker over the sign on the front fence.'

'What were you doing around there?'

Stuart shrugged. 'Just popped in to say hello on my way here.'

'*Really*?'

Try as she might, she couldn't disguise the cynicism in her voice. Stuart had never gone out of his way to involve himself with her family, so what was going on?

'I called in to apologise, if you must know. I told your mother what an arsehole I was, though I didn't use that exact word. I told her how much I needed you and wanted you back —'

Incredulously: '*You what*?'

'Come home, Cal,' he said, moving towards her and taking her hand. 'We can work this out.'

Shock rendered her speechless. She stood, unmoving, staring at him, trying to assimilate the odd words coming from his mouth.

'We could get married, start a family, if that's what you want,' he went on. 'I wouldn't mind.'

'No!'

She wrenched her hand from his. The touch of him made her skin crawl.

'Prim doesn't mean a thing to me,' he insisted, his voice rising. 'It's you I want. It's always been you.'

'You're unbelievable!'

'I love you.'

She walked away from him then. Across the newly cleaned carpet she went, towards the window, where she stood, propped against the timber ledge, looking back across the room. Her hands were shaking, uncontrollably so. Quickly she brought them up, folding her arms across her chest like a barrier, tucking her wayward hands under her armpits. 'I'd like my share of money from the unit.'

'What if I don't want to sell?' His tone was suddenly angry, belligerent.

'You can buy me out. Look, I don't really care either way. The choice is yours. I'll arrange for a real estate agent to call around for a valuation. Now, I think I'd prefer it if you left.'

Stuart stared hard at her for a moment, his mouth a tight thin line. He was, Callie realised, furious at her easy dismissal of him. 'Have it your own way, then,' he snapped. 'But don't say I didn't try to patch things up.'

For several minutes after he left, she fought to control her anger. Silver-tongue! How dare he come here, expecting her to drop everything and go running back to him! He must be mad! Or stupid!

I love you.

There were days, in the past, when she would have given anything to hear Stuart say those words. But now they were too late, too easily said, and meant nothing.

The week's weather had started badly, overcast and plagued by light intermittent rain. The sea matched the colour of the sky, all grey, and the line of the horizon was lost in a haze of salt spray. Peering through the lounge room window, past the rain-wet balcony and row of tossing pines along the esplanade, Callie wrinkled her nose in dismay and settled to some serious writing.

Michael's book, detailing the formation and activities of the 11th Field Company Engineers, proved to be a goldmine of information. Ben's letters to Hannah, written according to the strict censorship guidelines of the day, usually carried the notation 'Somewhere in France', giving no clue to his actual whereabouts at the time. Now, using the official handbook and relevant dates, she was able to place him, firstly around the Armentières area, then Ypres in Belgium, eventually moving south to Amiens and along the Somme for the final battles of the war.

At the local bookshop, she purchased a current Euro-Map of northern France, which took in most of the Flanders and Picardie regions. One whole afternoon was spent marking with a highlighter the route taken by Ben and his company. It was time-consuming work. Though the map was very detailed, many of the tiny villages that the soldiers had passed through during the war either no longer existed or were too small to mention. Nevertheless, by the end of several hours, she had a basic idea of his movements.

The need to fill her hours with work was a compulsion and, so far, between the letters, the maps and the book, Callie had plenty to go on with. At varying hours of the night, unable to sleep, she turned on the computer, typing away until the words on the screen became black dancing dots. With this new book coming so close on the heels of finishing the other, she knew she was working too hard, pushing herself, trying to blot out the events and memories of the past few weeks.

From time to time, her thoughts stumbled back to the previous Saturday night and to Michael, to that brief unexpected moment of sensual awareness and to the stab of disappointment, almost like a physical pain, when he had left. She had wanted him, she admitted to herself, and not simply as a friend.

Bonnie rang through the week. 'I'm up to my armpits in packing,' she said with a laugh. 'You know, I hadn't realised how much junk we've managed to collect over the years.'

'The joys of moving. Good excuse for a throw-out, Mum.'

501

'That's what Freya said. So, what are you up to?'

'Writing.'

'I thought you were going to have a few weeks off?'

'I was. Then I had a brilliant idea.' Callie went on to detail the concept of the new book: Hannah's and Ben's letters, the inclusion of the diary entries backed up by the official company records. 'The thing is, I was so keen to get started that I gave up the idea of a break.'

'I don't know,' broke in Bonnie hesitantly. 'I wonder what Hannah would think of your turning her letters into public property. They were private correspondence, and I know I haven't seen them, but it all seems kind of personal somehow.'

'I know. That's what I thought, too, when I first started reading the letters. It was like treading on sacred ground, spying, some kind of voyeurism. And you're right. They *are* personal and intimate.'

'Why go on with it, then?'

'Because this is more than the sum of the letters. It's the story of Hannah and Ben, and thousands of other couples. It's a story of love in desperate circumstances, of hope and strength and utter belief in what is good and true and right.'

'You certainly sound passionate enough about it.'

'Perhaps my finding the letters and diary happened for a reason. Maybe I was *meant* to write this book. Hannah could have destroyed the contents of that trunk before she died, but she didn't. Why?'

'I don't know, Cal,' replied her mother faintly. 'And somehow, all these years later, I wonder if it really matters.'

502

They moved on to general topics, Bonnie enquiring after Michael and Timmy, the flat, and promising to pop round later in the week with a box full of surplus kitchenware. 'So I'll see you then. Bye, love.'

The phone call had interrupted her writing. Distracted, she wandered through the flat, straightening a cushion here, a rug there, before boiling the jug to make a cup of coffee. Then, mug in hand, she paused in front of Hannah's trunk.

Though she had been busy transcribing the contents of the previously-read letters into the appropriate computer files, it had been several weeks since she had made any new advances with those piles of crumbling correspondence, and she missed the intrigue of it. Michael, she knew, had been busy, too, and had had little chance to work on the diary. What was happening to Hannah and Ben? Curious, she picked up the unread pile of letters from the top of the trunk and settled on the sofa in front of the window.

The first envelope contained a postcard that bore the title, 'Kaiser Wilhelm II im Felde' and depicted an austere German wearing a fur-collared cloak and a domed metal helmet. On the back were printed verses of 'Das Kaiserbild'.

There were several others. She flipped through them casually: another severe-looking gentleman, General von Kluck; groups of soldiers in full military regalia; and German seaplanes flying low over an English fleet.

Carefully she drew out Ben's accompanying letter. The paper was thin and breaking away at the edges.

Written in pencil, the words were barely legible and she went in search of a pad and pen, planning to copy the letter as she went.

Dearest Hannah,

I think all the time about coming home to you, and how lucky I will be to have such a loving wife and beautiful wee son. We shall have a houseful of children, playmates for Nick. What do you think?

They say the war will end soon. Fritz is on the run, and we are close behind. He is destroying everything in his path as he retreats. Houses, woods, roads. What utter waste!

I often think about Tom and Spud, and all those other mates who are never coming home, buried in the soil of the country they were fighting to save. Especially I think of all those unmarked graves, those shallow ditches carrying unknown mother's sons, women's sweethearts and husbands.

I was lucky enough to receive two of your letters this week. They are the only things that keep me sane in this mad, mad world. Tell me everything that happens to you both, my darling, however small and insignificant it may seem to you. The comparative normalcy of your life seems to counter every gross indecency that we are witness to here.

I will love you always,
Ben.

I will love you always: the words on the horseshoe.

Callie went to her desk and took the two halves from the top drawer, slotting them together as she stared at the engraving. Words written over eighty years earlier, a declaration of absolute love.

The horseshoe, a mystery still. How had Michael come to possess Hannah's half? How had it come to be mixed up with his late father's belongings?

She shrugged, not knowing. The important thing was that it had led Michael to the house in Brunswick Street, bringing them together, two people who would otherwise never have met.

On Friday morning her agent, Anthony, rang with a publication date for the recently finished book. 'And that's not all,' he added. 'One of the leading women's magazines is considering serialising a condensed form of it.'

'Great. I could do with the money.'

'There's also a chance that a nationally syndicated radio program may want to do a live interview. It'll be on a Saturday afternoon in a few weeks' time, but I'll have to get back to you on the exact date. They've been focussing on one Australian writer each week. It's a wonderful chance for some pre-publicity now we've got a release date.'

'Sounds wonderful. When will you let me know?'

'Look, I'll get back to them, see if I can find out a few more details, and I'll ring you tonight.'

No sooner had she replaced the receiver, than the phone rang again. It was Michael.

'Thought I'd pop down after work this afternoon. I've had a good go at the diary this week and there are a few things I think you'll be interested in. Only if you feel like it,' he added, 'or if you'd rather, we could go out to dinner.'

'I can't,' Callie replied, marginally disappointed at having to refuse the offer of a night out. 'I'm expecting a call from my agent. But why don't you come down, anyway? I'd love to go over your notes and we can send out for pizza.'

'Sounds good. See you about six.'

It was six-thirty by the time he arrived, carrying two bottles of wine and a briefcase, and denouncing late afternoon Friday traffic on the highway. She met him at the door and he kissed her lightly on the cheek. 'Good week?'

'Mmmm. Pretty frantic, actually. I started on the book in earnest and I'm really enjoying it. How about you?'

Michael grinned. 'Oh, you know, the usual. Can't complain. No-one listens.'

He opened a bottle of wine while Callie set out a tray of nuts and chips. Together they sat on the living room floor, and Michael pulled forward the briefcase filled with sheets of paper that soon lay scattered across the carpet.

'This will be of interest with the new book,' he said. 'It's a 1917 street map of Ypres. And I also found a trench map of Ploegsteert Wood. They were tucked away at the back of the diary.'

Callie brought out the Euro-Map, showing Michael the highlighted route of Ben's company. 'According to the booklet you left behind last weekend, they ended up near Ypres at the end of the war.'

'Almost back where they started,' mused Michael.

After what seemed merely minutes, Callie glanced up at the clock, surprised to see that it was after eight and dark outside. Quickly dialling for a home delivery pizza, she put a clean cloth on the dining table and took another bottle of cold wine from the refrigerator.

Michael appeared beside her. 'Here, I'll open that,' he said, taking the bottle. For a fraction of a second, their fingers touched, and when she moved away to rinse the glasses, she was surprised to find her hands shaking.

The pizza was good, the wine numbing. Callie opened a third bottle, then they moved on to an unopened flask of port and coffee. Diligently she went over Michael's notes from the diary, and the maps. The latter were in surprisingly good order, printed on good quality, heavy-duty paper, and would make a wonderful inclusion for the book.

Stopping to take another sip of coffee, she glanced up to find him watching her, a bemused expression on his face. 'Yes, I know,' she returned his smile. 'I'm like a kid at Christmas. But finding all this stuff is just incredible, after all this time. Don't you agree?'

'Definitely. And it was worth bringing it here tonight, just to see the expression of delight on your face.'

'Really? I mean, is it that obvious?'

He laughed and, with that sense of shared intimacy, Callie fought back an impulse to go to him, to wrap her arms around him. Instead, she cradled the coffee cup in her hands, peering intently into its lukewarm depths. Later, taking the empty cups to the kitchen, she paused at the bench and took a deep breath. Relax, she told herself sternly, willing herself calm as she walked back into the lounge room.

Michael had moved out onto the far end of the balcony. He stood, tanned forearms outstretched, hands firmly gripping the balcony railing as he stared out at the darkened mass of sand and sea that lay beyond. It was windy and his shirt billowed against his body, the fabric lifting and settling against the nape of his neck and the square set of his shoulders.

She stepped quietly across the carpet, out onto the balcony behind him. The wind caught at her own hair. She felt it lift up about her face, caressing her cheeks with the softest touch. The tang of salt lay in the air, bringing with it a layer of damp. From further down the esplanade came the sound of a car horn, a jangling of noise.

She paused, leaning back against the opened doorway, suddenly unable to go on. Ten steps and she would be beside him, yet her feet refused to move. For some inexplicable reason, her hands had started shaking again, and she folded them across her chest, tucking them between the sides of her breasts and forearms.

As though sensing her presence, he turned, an amused, yet puzzled expression on his face.

'Callie?'

Somehow, her feet responded and she walked towards him. One step, two, each one leading her closer. She laid her cheek against his shirt and his arms folded about her, crushing her to his chest. The faint aroma of aftershave rose up to meet her, mixed with the tang of salt, as he pressed his mouth against her hair.

With a sudden shiver, she raised her face, her fingers moving automatically to the nape of his neck.

His hands cupped her chin as he brought his mouth down to meet hers, raining kisses along her brow, her cheek, her lips.

She was aware of little details: the sweet taste of him; the aftershave; the wind bringing sounds of a band playing in the pub further along the street; the deep bass of the drums matching her own erratic heartbeat.

The wanting had become an ache, deep in her belly, and the intensity of his response told her he felt the same. There was a sense of being caught up in something, of being uplifted, carried along. A shudder ran along her spine as she clung to him, feeling the heat of his body through his shirt.

'Oh, Callie,' he whispered, and his voice was a drawn-out sigh, filled with longing. It came from a distant past that was somehow caught up inexplicably with the present, and now the future. It came on the wind and wrapped itself around her, assuring her that whatever happened next was right, for she knew with certain finality that she was powerless to stop herself, even if she wanted to.

Callie woke later, the bedroom lit faintly by the streetlights on the esplanade below. Michael lay curled, spoon-like, against her back, one arm thrown across her hip, palm resting against her abdomen.

She stirred and stretched, rolling onto her back.

'Awake?' He propped himself on one elbow.

The air felt cold against her skin where his hand had been. 'Mmmm.' It was an effort to speak — her body, muscles, every minute part of her was lethargic with sleep. Lazily she raised her hand, wanting to retain some of that unaccustomed intimacy, tracing the outline of his mouth with her fingers in the half-light.

'What are you thinking?' he asked, voice low, that same amused expression on his face.

A bubble of laughter rose to her mouth. 'Any regrets, is that what you mean?'

'Already you know me too well,' he sighed in mock dismay, leaning forward and kissing her firmly on the mouth. 'But I do believe,' he added, after a moment's hesitation, 'that somehow you instigated all this.'

'Did I hear a cry of protest, however small?'

'No.'

Michael smiled and a wash of tenderness surged over her, a warm flooding of delight mixed with a happiness that settled somewhere in her chest, making her feel magnanimous. The window was open and a breeze blew the curtains about. Below, in the street, a group of teenagers passed, full of bright chatter and laughter which wafted upwards.

'Do you wish you were that age again?'

His question surprised her, caught her off guard. 'No. Not really. Do you?'

'Sometimes. There are days when I look at Timmy and I wish I were that innocent, that unworldly. No cynicism. No distrust. Just a naive acceptance of life.'

'I think the best part of being young was not having any responsibilities. Letting others worry about all the dreary things in life, like paying the bills and wondering when the next pay cheque will arrive — that sort of thing.'

She was inordinately aware of him, his mouth, his maleness, the sandy-coloured shock of hair that fell across his forehead. Aware too of his nakedness, of the rumpled sheets pushed to the far end of the bed, that bore silent witness to their frenzied lovemaking only hours earlier.

'But it's hard to predict, in hindsight, what I would do differently if I had the chance,' he added, brushing an errant wisp of hair from her cheek.

It was the most tender of touches, barely felt, yet it reflected the intimacy between them. 'I'm not sorry I married Gaby,' he went on. 'It wasn't all sadness and tears. There were lots of happy times, too. And without that marriage there would never have been Tim.'

'He's very important to you, isn't he?'

'Yes. And so are you.'

The air caught in her lungs, making it momentarily difficult to breathe. She and Michael had shared that most intimate, most tender of unions, yet there had been no declarations made by either of them. Pure lust, Jill would have said and, on the surface, she had to agree.

She had *wanted* Michael, craved the touch of him, but for what reason? Love? The need to feel wanted, desirable? Or did she want him to erase those last awful images of Stuart from her life? But there were other less tangible emotions involved, feelings lying submerged, not acknowledged, caught up somehow with Hannah and Ben, the diaries and letters.

What was it she felt for Michael?

Undecided, she bit her lip. 'In what way?' she replied at last, regaining her composure.

Michael was silent for a moment, as though gathering his thoughts. 'You know, ever since I met you, that first day at the house at Brunswick Street, I felt I belonged, as though I were coming home. You, the house ...'

He paused and smiled at her. Such a lovely smile she thought, kissing his mouth.

Then: 'I thought you were witty and intelligent and pretty. In a moment of madness, I thought you felt something towards me, too.'

Again, that same sense of uncertainty. Exactly *what* did she feel? She drew back and nodded in agreement.

He laughed, pulling her close. 'You probably think I'm crazy. And when you think about it, bringing that half horseshoe back, thinking there may have been some connection between us — it was all so insane. But I don't care,' he added, as he kissed her again, playful little nips along her bare shoulders, that made her skin tingle. 'It brought me to you. Perhaps it was meant to, like some master plan, coincidental but fateful.'

He stopped and regarded her thoughtfully. The shock of hair that fell across his forehead made him appear suddenly boyish and unsure. 'You want me to be honest?'

'Yes,' she confirmed, nodding in agreement.

'Since Gaby and I went our separate ways, there's been no-one special. I'm lonely, and I feel something for you. Don't ask me to define it, simply know that it's there. I want more than just a platonic friendship. And now that we're both unattached, it seems pointless to try to hide it any longer.' He raised his palms, a gesture of surrender, and smiled ruefully. 'I can't be any more honest than that.'

Slowly he moved his hand upwards, tracing across her belly, her breasts. Instantly, her body responded. Trails of fire burned where his fingers had touched, and she turned to him, cupping her own hands around firm buttocks, drawing him hungrily towards her.

CHAPTER 31

A procession of local townsfolk called at the Brunswick Street house to offer their condolences. David and Enid Corduke sat woodenly in the darkened parlour, blinds drawn as a mark of respect. The telegram, neatly folded and placed back in its envelope, sat on the mantelpiece: evidence of Tom's death.

Hannah thought Enid's reaction rather contrived. She had made a great fuss about Tom's joining up, and Hannah had expected to hear 'I told you so' over and over. But Enid was thin and pale, withdrawn, and Hannah thought she had lost weight. She showed little interest in the house, and the garden was in an abandoned state. Flowerbeds were overgrown with weeds. Shrubs needed pruning. Even the wattles seemed drab, hanging listlessly along the creek bank.

David seemed distracted, too, not his usual self. Finally, several days into the visit, he drew her aside while Enid was resting, propelling her into the parlour. 'There was another baby,' he said, bringing his hands to his chin, and Hannah could see they were shaking badly. 'But it came early and there were problems. A little girl. She only lived a few hours. Enid's taking it very badly, I'm afraid.'

'I didn't know.'

'No.'

What to say? There seemed few words that could ease her brother's pain. At that moment, death seemed all around them. Yet it was not Tom for whom Enid mourned, Hannah now knew, but her own lost child.

Thank God she still had Nick.

In the kitchen she occupied herself by making endless scones and pots of tea. Thoughts of Tom, mixed somehow with the imagined image of that tiny baby, Enid's lost daughter, wove themselves randomly through her consciousness, reducing her constantly to sudden tears. She smiled graciously at the visitors when required, and accepted the commiserations, casseroles and lamingtons. 'So good of you to come home and take care of David and Enid,' they murmured. 'They'll be needing you now.'

Outwardly she coped, making the correct replies and being the dutiful sister. Inside, part of her lay dead, too, missing Tom unbearably. 'Go away!' she wanted to scream. All the solicitous words in the world wouldn't bring her brother back. He was gone, never to be seen again. Buried in foreign mud. No nearby grave to lay flowers against. No place to mourn, to weep.

So she locked the tears away, dusted and swept, and cooked meals that no-one had the inclination to eat. Hannah: capable, in control. Keeping the wheels of the household turning, functioning. 'She's a godsend, that sister of yours,' she overheard one woman confiding to David.

David and Enid's daughter, Lily, was a delight, too young to understand what had happened. Of

Davie, there was little sign. He was thirteen now, grown long and lanky during the past year. In some ways he was like Tom physically. Dark hair, same shape of face and unconscious gestures. Shocking, startling reminders.

He was remote and uncommunicative, and kept mostly to himself, either lying on his bed staring at the ceiling or disappearing in the direction of the creek. Hannah felt a certain guilt at her neglect of him, but there was so much to do in the house. By the fifth day, the activity had slowed and, finding herself at a loose end one afternoon while Enid rested, she went in search of him.

He was sitting on the creek bank, arms wrapped around his knees, staring into the water. He seemed aware of her approach, tightening his grip on his knees, though he didn't turn.

'Davie?' she said, squatting down beside him. 'What are you doing?'

He shrugged, raising his shoulders in a resigned way. 'Just sitting here keeping out of everyone's way.'

'I've scarcely seen you since I've been back. We've had so little time to talk,' Hannah went on.

His mouth momentarily compressed, and his forehead furrowed into a frown. '*Talk*! What's there to *talk* about? Tom's dead and nothing's going to change that!'

His voice was harsh and she sensed an anger there, barely concealed.

'No,' she replied softly. 'But sometimes it helps to remember the happy times. There are so many *good* memories.'

'Are there? Its all right for you,' he blurted, his mouth becoming lopsided, unmanageable. 'You haven't been here. All Mum's interested in is her Comforts Fund and Red Cross. Dad's forever busy at the bank. And it's always Lily, Lily, Lily! There's never any time for me. I might as well not be here. And now Tom's dead! No-one cares how I feel, but he was my uncle, too!'

He turned towards her then, and she could see his eyes brimful of tears.

'Oh, Davie.'

Her words came as a drawn-out sigh, a regret for things unsaid. He came into her arms, sagging against her shoulder, his body wracked with sobs.

Why hadn't anyone seen?

Back in the city, the bleeding started again, random floodings that left Hannah exhausted and pale.

'For goodness' sake, go and see a doctor,' remonstrated Lottie.

Instead she went to the chemist, returning home with a bottle of iron tonic.

Life seemed to be running at breakneck speed. Always chores to be done, bedpans emptied, bedding changed, constant grumblings from everyone. Men coming and going. Her only escape was Nick, the provider of unquestionable, absolute love

It was two weeks since she had seen him. Already, in that short time, he seemed to have grown. Laughing, he came towards her the following Sunday on sturdy legs, arms thrown back. Unable to stop the tears, she scooped him up, raining kisses over his face.

517

A letter from Ben arrived the following week. In parts it was lucid, in control. In others, she could make little sense of the words, as though the battle were being fought in his own mind.

I can't believe Tom is dead. Yesterday he was alive, speaking to me. In fact, we talked of going home, and the day the war would end. I wonder if I was only dreaming though. Perhaps we did not speak of this at all, and it was merely an imagination on my part. Sometimes I think the war will never end and we will go on like this, killing and slaughtering each other until there is no-one left ...

Tom's death was a turning point, a climax, a moment when, in many ways, Ben ceased to care. There were days when the war seemed all-consuming, and the intensity of it began to blot out the final traces of that other previous life. Sometimes Hannah and Nick seemed unreal, simply a figment of his own fertile imagination. Did they really exist? Certainly her letters were proof of that, and the photograph, he thought, taking it from his pocket once more. It was creased slightly, the corners curling. Hannah holding her son, *his son*, propping him against her hip as she smiled uncertainly into the camera lens.

But that part of his life seemed far away now, scarcely remembered. This was real. War. Killing. Maiming. Rats rustling through the straw at night, scampering up the earthen trench walls. Rats feeding off the bodies of the dead. Corpses of soldiers strewn on the ground, lying as they had fallen because no-one had the time to bury them.

Coming away from the front line at last, back along the ridge they trudged, careless of the view westwards through to the cathedral at Amiens. It was a fine day, the sky dark blue, marred only by the presence of two German observation balloons hovering further back, near the river.

They set up camp in an open valley west of Heilly. Once it had been a productive orchard. Now it lay untended, with grass and weeds flourishing around the bases of the trees. It was late May. Pears and apples ripened on the few remaining branches. A wild tangle of gooseberry bushes yielded up plump fruit. Above the tent a nightingale perched on a rotten bough, singing, and the sound almost made Ben weep.

He was reminded of all the men who were no longer there, either buried in almost-forgotten battlefields or repatriated back home. Men missing arms or legs. Men hideously gassed. Muttering jumbled wrecks of men, barely recognisable when he had seen them last, compared to the laughing full-of-bravado soldiers who had arrived in this country almost two years earlier. He tried to remember their names, but his mind was blank, a wall of pain. How quickly we forget! he thought.

Or did he really want to remember?

On the rare occasions that sleep came, he dreamt. Strange images stayed in his mind long after he woke, lines of men filing past, ghostly figures barely formed, huge gaping holes where their mouths should have been. No lips to cry out in pain. No tongues to voice the horror. Silent men marching, though he could hear no fall of boots against the chalky earth of his dreams.

On and on they marched, passing without a glance in his direction, as though he were invisible, a ghost perhaps. Or, he wondered, were they the ghosts, souls of the men who had already gone?

Days were spent cleaning and repairing stores, and painting lorries. The company was full of talk about the infamous German airman, Von Richthofen, whose bright red aeroplane had been shot down by a Lewis gun belonging to an Australian Field Artillery, crashing quite spectacularly close to a party of sappers.

A chateau near Heilly became the new company headquarters. One section of the slate roof had been bombed, though the rooms below were, in the main, habitable. Miraculously, the cellars underneath yielded up a good supply of wine.

There was a piano in what had probably been the ballroom, covered in dust and cobwebs. Gingerly Jack lifted the lid and fingered the keys. Surprisingly, they were still in tune.

'Play us something, then,' suggested one of the men.

So they squatted on the floor and lounged against the shredded wallpaper, singing 'Pack up Your Troubles' and 'It's a Long Way to Tipperary', and other songs which, hours later, Ben could not remember, though at the time they seemed to bring back unbearably painful memories.

He wandered away from the group, glancing idly into the rooms. In one bedroom a broken mirror still hung on the wall. A central hole, as though the mirror had been pierced by a bullet, radiated jagged lines towards its chipped edges. Confused, he studied his own reflection. Sunken eyes stared back, sandy hair longer than he usually wore it, cheek bones prominent. He supposed he must have lost weight, certainly his belt now fastened a few notches tighter. He moved his hand tentatively across his jaw line, feeling the rough stubble, and the hand in the reflected image did likewise.

Dazedly, he stumbled outside into the ruins of the garden. Poppies and cornflowers ran riot against the edges of the overgrown path. A jumble of rubble nearby had probably once been a barn. The bricks were weathered, the gashes in them faded to grey. The rubble was overgrown in places by weeds and creepers and clumps of pink peonies.

Nature reclaiming its own, he thought numbly.

An avenue of trees led from the lopsided back gate to the nearby wood. They had passed that way earlier, through the big firs that had mostly been lopped by the bombs. On the edge of the line of trees, bordered on one side by a small copse, was a soldiers' cemetery. Even from this distance, he could see the white crosses.

That night they watched a picture show in an old barn. It was a rowdy affair, the bottles of local wine being consumed with abandon. After it was over, Ben wandered outside and looked at the sky. It was dark above, with tiny pinpricks of winking stars. A moon, blood red, was sidling over the nearby ridge, shedding orange light across the bare fields.

Confused, he stared at the landscape, his mind empty, refusing to form thoughts. And later, when he consciously tried to bring his attention back and focus on something, *anything*, he couldn't remember one single scene from the movie.

The feeling stayed with him as they marched back towards the front line, the weather glorious under the cloak of late spring. Along the straight dusty road between Albert and Amiens they went, past the place where the road curved unexpectedly around the chateau at Querrieu, alongside deep inviting lagoons where he longed to strip his clothes from his body and dive into the cool water.

At night, sleep eluding him, his mind replayed those last exquisite agonising hours in Tom's flat over two years earlier. Hannah sitting before the fire, its light highlighting the curve of her back, belly and breasts, the cleft of her buttocks. Hannah, soft and pliable in the narrow bed, opening herself up to him, offering her body like a sacrifice. The remembering brought an ache to his chest, in the place where his heart might be. An ache for the past, for the future, for something, *anything*, better than this.

CHAPTER 32

Too soon it was back into the trenches, into living hell. Back into dirt and filth and human excreta, and an exploding shell that sent Ben diving for cover, rolling awkwardly down a steep embankment. When he finally reached the bottom, after the dust and debris had cleared, he tried to move, but excruciating pain stopped him.

Jack came sprinting down, sending a shower of gravel in his wake. Carefully he rolled up Ben's trouser leg. Already a dark purplish bruise covered most of his shin, and a large lump pressed the flesh out into an odd shape.

'I'll be right.' Optimistically Ben tried to struggle to his feet. 'Just help me up.'

With Jack's aid he stood. The pain was so severe he thought he might faint. His world momentarily slipped sideways, then righted itself. He took one step forward, letting the bad leg take his weight, and collapsed with the strain.

'Bloody hell!' he gasped as Jack eased him into a sitting position on the ground. 'I think it's broken.'

He was taken to the closest dressing station under cover of darkness. There were dozens of men queueing outside. Ben waited his turn, only to be given the news he had expected. The leg *was* broken and would require weeks, perhaps months, of rest.

'Lucky bastard,' pronounced Jack, looking envious. 'It's a Blighty one. Back to England for you, old chap.'

Ben attempted a smile through gritted teeth. 'Well, you make sure you keep everything under control until I get back, okay?'

'Yair, sure,' grinned Jack. 'We'll keep the bastards on their toes.'

The fracture was set and a shot of morphia given to ease the pain. A jolting ride at dawn in a field ambulance took him to a casualty clearing station at the nearest rail head, and from there by train to Boulogne.

Escorted by two destroyers, it was a several-hour trip across the English Channel, or 'The Creek' as it was fondly referred to, and regulations meant that every man on board wore a lifebelt even though the sea was calm. Looking back as they left Boulogne, Ben was struck by the view. The town was framed by softly rolling hills, a wireless station just visible on top of the highest. Brightly coloured bathing boxes lined the beachfront esplanade. To the right lay the breakwater and harbour entrance, guarded by the harbourmaster's office. Several cranes on the wharf lay idle, baking under the hot sun.

On the way over, they passed several other steamers bringing troops back to France from leave, resulting in much cheering and waving of hats between the boats. At Portsmouth the wounded were carried onto the hospital train bound for Waterloo Station in London, then transferred to the No. 3 General Hospital at Wandsworth by a fleet of cars.

He was there for almost two months, incapacitated by the bulky plaster. At first he found himself sleeping for what seemed like extraordinarily long hours. Making up for lost time, he convinced himself, the memory of those sleepless days and weeks in the trenches a raw reminder.

Time passed slowly, mindless and boring, a dawdling sequence of minutes and hours. There was a ready supply of books but he could not settle to reading. His mind was jumpy and overactive, unused to relaxation. Begging a supply of paper and envelopes from an obliging ward-sister, he wrote endlessly to Hannah instead. They were lengthy missives, filled with plans for their lives: his, Hannah's and Nick's. *After this is all over* was a much-used phrase. As the weeks progressed, he became adept at the crutches, swinging himself along the hallways with practised ease, and across the wide sweeping lawns.

Nights were the worst. At odd hours he woke, drenched in sweat, vaguely remembering the fading images of some nightmare. The mouthless men still marched through his dreams, bringing him suddenly and unexpectedly to wakefulness. He lay there, unable to conjure up sleep, listening to the sounds of the city and the slow chug-chugging of the passing trains.

At last the plaster was removed and he spent the next few weeks at the divisional training headquarters at Codford, followed by several days' leave in London. How he would have loved to have brought Hannah and the boy here! he thought, watching the city mothers pushing high perambulators along the pavements, full shopping bags hanging from spare arms, despite the wartime shortages.

There seemed so many empty hours to fill, so he did the usual tourist activities, thinking how different it was since he had been there last, with Spud and Tom and Jack. Hiring a taxi, he saw Trafalgar Square, St James Park and Buckingham Palace, and drank copious quantities of Peter Dawson Scotch in smoky pubs that seemed patronised more by women than men.

He wandered through Hyde Park, enviously watching the couples strolling across the grass. He was homesick, he admitted to himself, though he had no home to return to. It was all gone: Da, the forge, every single aspect of his former life except Hannah. Even then some days he had to take her photograph from his wallet, to remind himself of her features, that she was real. There was a sense of loneliness despite the continual pressing throng, and a feeling that he was only marking time. Until what, though? he wondered. His return to France? Possible death?

It was a dull day, bleak and dismal, when he made his way to the dock at Folkstone. Departure time had originally been scheduled for nine o'clock, but they were forced to wait, shivering in the uncharacteristically cold summer morning for two hours until the tide had risen. It was foggy, a slow mist rising upwards from the water, and vision was merely a few yards in any direction.

The boat was brimming with men returning from leave. Most were dressed haphazardly, some wearing overcoats, others carrying sheepskin jackets. Their faces, although they had been out of the lines for two weeks, were still lean and curiously drawn. Amongst them, in his new uniform — his old one had been destroyed after his admission to hospital — Ben felt conspicuous and old.

He rejoined the company in Amiens, where the men were enjoying a few days' leave. So many faces were new. Sergeant Hayes was finally gone, missing in action after one particularly bad night's bombing. Ben was surprised to feel a momentary sadness for the man, despite the ongoing antagonism.

Jack was pleased to see him, slapping him heartily on the back and shouting him several drinks at the Hôtel du Rhin. Afterwards they mooched around Madame Carpentier's bookshop, Ben purchasing a new supply of stationery while Jack thumbed covertly through the latest copy of *La Vie Parisienne*.

Too soon they were heading back to the front line, marching along country lanes beside undulating fields thick with heavy-eared wheat and interspersed with scarlet poppies and blue cornflowers. The air was full of birdsong: blackbirds and larks, magpies and partridges. Tiny hedge sparrows flitted in the ditches at the side of the roadway. Always at the periphery of their vision lay the Somme, its course denoted by dark clumps of trees, and beyond that the chalk hills reclaimed by the 3rd Australian Division months earlier.

In parts the landscape seemed unnaturally lifeless, somnolent under the searing sun. Old, long-deserted trenches were weaving lines of white thrown-up earth, straggling through emerging crops and under rusting tangles of barbed wire. It was hot and Ben's leg ached as he marched, but he went on uncomplainingly, though each footfall became sheer agony.

As they came closer to the lines, there were men moving everywhere. Cumbersome tanks clanked across the debris-strewn earth. They were noisy and smelly, Whippets and Mark V's mostly, kicking up dust as they ground past.

The men were kept busy tunnelling dugouts into the white chalky soil. The weather was fine and warm, and they worked with their shirt sleeves rolled up, grateful for the slouch hats which kept the worst of the sun from already-burnt faces. Alongside a company of Australian Pioneers they toiled, shoring up dugouts with timber slabs, fitting bunks and gas-proof doorways. In Villers-Bretonneux they strung barbed wire among the shattered buildings of the ruined town. The 3rd Australian Division held the line there, along with the French. Relations between the two nationalities were very cordial, the Australians happily swapping cigarettes for a share of *pinard*, the French wine issue.

He took to walking in the wood behind the billets at twilight, amongst the elm and white poplar. The occasional owl swept overhead, making no sound except for the beating of its wings against the warm air. The sky was golden, the same colour reflected in the solitary wheatfield away to the left. In the distance he could hear the muffled boom of the guns.

It was here that he usually took a piece of paper and a pencil from his pocket, intending to write to Hannah. Sometimes the words came. At other times his mind was only filled with images of the dead, the dying.

Today he already had the words planned. He had thought about them for hours, forming and re-forming them in his mind. No longer could they be pushed into the back reaches of his consciousness. They *had* to be written so, in the event of anything happening, she'd know.

My darling Hannah,
We are going back into the lines again. Things are pretty rough and we are all trying not to be afraid, although sometimes the fear itself is almost too much to bear. Death is part of life here. I see it every day, in every form. Sometimes, when I feel I can no longer go on, I almost wish it would take me from all this. Then I think of you, my love, and I remember my reason for living.

Memories of home came to me often this week. The forge. Pa. The house in Brunswick Street. I suppose the wattles will be out now. Little balls of yellow fluff. By the time they bloom again, I pray that this agonising madness will be over and I'm home with you and our darling son, a family at last. Missing you and loving you always.
Ben

He sat on the hill, re-reading the words as the light faded to pink, then grey, then disappeared altogether, and the only illumination was a shuddering flicker on the eastern horizon.

Only then, letter tucked safely in his pocket, did he make his way back down the hill towards the camp.

The town of Albert, re-captured by the British in August, was deserted, reduced to piles of red rubble. The allied armies were out of the trenches now, advancing across the broad open country to the east of the town, hard on the heels of the retreating enemy. Ahead of them moved the engineers, checking bridges, water supplies, roads and signboards.

Extra supplies came from the most surprising places. German dugouts yielded up maps of the area and extra bales of fodder for horses. A derelict quartermaster's store contained quantities of new underclothes and boots. Abandoned German wagons were loaded with timber, steel girders, barbed wire, corrugated iron and malthoid.

It was the old enemy trenches that Ben quickly learned to avoid. Thin layers of dried mud disguised bodies buried below; unwary boots sank unexpectedly into putrid flesh, disturbing thousands of fat white wriggling maggots. Feet or hands protruded from the ground, blackish-blue and grotesquely swollen. Here and there lay the occasional shinbone wrapped in the remnants of a rotting puttee.

Despite all this, despite the disgusting, vomit-inducing remnants of the war, for the first time in ages, Ben experienced an exhilarating sense of optimism. The enemy was on the run and there was a feeling that it would soon be all over. Life would return to normal and he would be on his way back to Hannah and Nick. Nothing, no-one, could touch him again.

There were times when he regretted sending that last letter, written in one of his bleakest moments.

Hannah would worry over the words, misconstruing his feelings, for how could she really know what he meant?

Death is part of life here ... Sometimes I almost wish it would take me from all this.

How could anyone who hadn't experienced this place ever *know*?

Further along the Somme. Suzanne, Curlu and Cléry: towns and villages with only the shells of buildings remaining. Streets littered with rubble, almost impassable. A town hall, once a source of local pride, reduced to a few remaining archways and large blocks of stone lying nearby. Senseless, needless swathe of destruction.

At night the eastern sky was lit by the glow of many fires. By daylight, the long columns of smoke ahead indicated that the Germans were burning everything in their path as they retreated.

September. Mont St Quentin. Peronne. Pushing forward on the heels of the enemy across a countryside dotted with old disused trenches and barbed wire. More deserted villages. Buire. Tincourt. Roisel. Following the trail of destruction, sabotage. Bridges had been destroyed, pumps left broken. Wheels on vehicles were smashed and trees lopped. Mine craters, deliberately positioned, dotted most road junctions. The large houses that lined the roadways had been mercilessly shelled. Glassless windows offered up smoke-blackened interiors to view, and roofs were crisscrosses of rafters outlined against the sky.

Nights were spent sleeping in barns, in earthen shelters. Curling his body against the hardness of the floor, Ben's dreams were light-filled and airy, full of Hannah and Nick. Hannah appeared to be floating towards him, holding out his son. He heard laughter behind his closed lids and woke feeling a sense of happiness he hadn't known for years. Lying there in the darkness, holding onto the last remnants of the images, Ben heard the rats rustling through the straw and knew they were not part of that same dream. But it didn't matter. *Nothing* mattered. Soon he would be heading home, and all this would be nothing more than an evil memory.

Unexpectedly they were directed north in late September, back towards Ypres. Movement was slow, owing to the congestion on the roads. A convoy of lorries took them through the shattered countryside, past piles of broken bricks and timber where houses, even whole villages had once stood, alongside splintered stumps that were the remains of woods.

The weather changed and became very cold, and the deteriorating condition of the road meant the vehicles could go no further.

'I don't give a shit,' laughed Jack happily as he clambered onto the roadway and hoisted his kit bag over his shoulder. 'I'd gladly walk from here back to Australia if I could.'

'Silly bugger,' grinned Ben.

'You would, too,' Jack retorted, 'if it meant getting back to your Hannah any sooner. Fritz is on the run and it's only a matter of time before this whole god-damned mess is over. With a bit of luck, we could even be home for Christmas.'

Christmas with Hannah and Nick! The thought, unimaginable two months earlier, now loomed temptingly close. Ben slid his hand inside his coat pocket and fingered the remaining half of the horseshoe. It felt solid, and cold.

They marched, boots thudding against the damp earth and breath issuing as a white cloud before them. Jack whistled a jaunty tune that raised their spirits even further. Ben glanced about the countryside, taking in the scene. If Jack was right, they'd be on their way home soon. No more marching into unknown territory. No more guns and bombs. Perhaps this might be the last time he ever had to walk along this road. Any road. *Au revoir*, France.

He had been so engrossed in his thoughts he failed to see that the men in front had come to a sudden halt. Awkwardly he cannoned into the soldier in front, acknowledging the 'Watch it, Galbraith,' with a murmured apology and a slight frown.

Further along, from the corner of his eye, Ben saw a movement in the ditch that ran alongside the road. 'What do you reckon's going on?' he asked, nudging Jack with the butt of his rifle, indicating with the tip of his bayonet.

'Don't know,' muttered Jack, peering ahead. Then: 'Crikey! Is that what I think it is?'

It was a small party of Germans, three in total. Two were dead, lying sprawled in separate pools of blood. On closer inspection, the lone survivor, waving a piece of white cloth, was suffering from leg and stomach wounds and unable to walk.

'We'll have to carry him, then,' said the acting sergeant, after the man had been searched for weapons.

'Fuck that! I'm not carrying any bloody German,' came a voice from the rear. 'He can sit here and bleed to death for all I care.'

'Officially he's a prisoner of war and under the convention —'

'Bugger the bloody convention.'

No-one seemed inclined to agree with the sergeant and they all stood around, waiting. The sergeant spoke with the German, using a few halting phrases, promising to send a Red Cross cart once they reached the next clearing station.

One of the other Germans lay sprawled on the ground, face down, his right arm caught underneath his body. Curious, Ben watched as one of his own men casually nudged the man's shoulder, turning him over, and the thought struck him, as the soldier's head rolled back, that he wasn't dead at all.

As though in slow motion, Ben saw one eye lazily open. He watched transfixed as the soldier's hand moved forward. The fingers were dirt-stained and pudgy. He was aware of them, curling around something dark and metallic, scattering a blazing trail of light and sound towards him.

There was a sudden pressure inside his head, followed by a pain so intense, so agonising, that involuntarily he brought his hands up, pressing his palms against his temple. Around him, an eerie assortment of fireworks exploded, each one louder than the next. Skyrockets, bungers and Catherine wheels spun trails of blue light towards the place where the sun might have been, as the pain abruptly, miraculously, disappeared and he pitched forward into dark nothingness.

Jack turned to see the gun discharge, saw Ben's head gush bright blood, his hands coming up, too late, as his legs folded under him.

'BEN! NO!'

A sound, somewhere between a scream and a high-pitched moan, came from his own mouth. He took several steps forward, aware of the shocked faces of the other men. Slow moving steps, one foot after the next, hand forward, his fingers closing around the butt of the rifle that lay slung over his shoulder. Pale sunlight glinted on the attached bayonet, though he scarcely registered the agonising scream as he drove the metal through living flesh, impaling the German soldier on the moist earth below.

Merely images, not comprehended. Sluggish, unhurried scenes that he would remember forever. And over all, Ben's body lying twisted in the dirt, a crumpled heap, and blood sprayed out over the dry earth. Dark ropey drops, red, like rubies, glistening under the pale sun.

Two of the men moved towards Ben, but Jack sprang between them, arms outstretched, pushing them back. 'No! Don't touch him.'

'He's dead,' one of the men intoned.

'We'll have to bury him,' another reasoned. 'Come on, Jack. You can give us a hand.'

He stood looking at the pair. They were new recruits, only arrived in the company a few months earlier. 'You don't *understand*,' he said, emphasising the word. 'We've been mates together from the start, Ben and I. Through the worst of it, I thought we were, only ...'

Thinking suddenly of Hannah and Nick, his voice faltered and stopped. Oh, Christ! How could he bring himself to tell her, to pass on the terrible news?

He felt his mouth, lopsided and suddenly uncontrollable, and the scene blurred before him. Stiffly he hunkered against the cold earth, scrabbling in the dirt with his bare hands. Someone produced a small shovel and he stood, pressing the blade downwards.

Singlehandedly he dug the grave, refusing all offers of help, excavating an old shell hole at the side of the road several feet deeper. As he worked, it started raining. The drops wet his face, mingling with salty tears, plastering his hair to his scalp. Reverently he took the half horseshoe from Ben's pocket, along with a partly finished letter to Hannah and a few loose coins.

One of the sergeants helped him lower Ben's body into the hole. 'Come along,' said the man gruffly, raising his eyes towards the rain. 'We've orders to move on. Mark the grave and make a note of the location. We'll send a message through to headquarters tomorrow.'

The rain was coming down harder now, sending muddy rivulets rushing across the ground. Numbly Jack shovelled the earth back into the hole, tears blurring his vision as the clods showered across Ben's face and chest. Finished at last, he pushed a rough wooden cross into the centre of the mound.

A lone clump of poppies grew by the side of the road. They were dark red, like blood, and wet with raindrops. Picking several of the blooms, he sprinkled them across the freshly dug grave. One he kept back. He would press it in Ben's unfinished letter and send both to Hannah.

Only then was he ready to leave. He gave a cursory glance at the dead German as he passed, numbly noting the pale waxy face dotted with beads of moisture and the head hanging backwards against the mud. The man's eyes were open, staring unseeingly towards the grey drizzling sky, and his mouth lay agape, a cavernous void, expressing a suffering that had long since passed.

The rain fell harder, saturating everything in its path. Some time during the night, Jack's rough cross teetered and fell, the water nudging it inch by inch along the muddy ground. A group of soldiers splashed through at dawn, picking their way across the boggy ground. They were followed by a team of horses pulling ambulance carts, and the cross was pushed deep into the mud.

Ben's grave, like so many others, was lost forever.

CHAPTER 33

Gaby called by on Sunday morning, as they had arranged earlier in the week, bringing Timmy. Michael was sitting on the back verandah when they arrived, sipping his first cup of coffee for the morning. He heard his son's excited galloping through the house.

'Hi, Dad!' Tim exclaimed, throwing his arms around his father's neck.

'Hi, yourself. What's happening?'

'Nothing. Mum wants to talk to you, though.'

As though on cue, Gaby poked her head around the corner. 'Got a few spare minutes?'

'Sure.' He patted the seat next to his. 'Come and sit down. Coffee?'

It never ceased to amaze him the friendship they maintained. Several of his colleagues often arrived at work on Monday mornings full of ex-wife woes, which he found hard to understand, given his own circumstances. His relationship with Gaby had become, during the past few years, more of a brother-sister thing, a comfortable association, with Tim as the main focal point. They never intruded on each other's private lives and, though Tim occasionally let slip about some new male friend of his mother's, he was comfortable now with the arrangement and the thought no longer bothered him.

'What's up?' he asked, after making Gaby a cup of coffee and shooing Tim in to watch a video.

'Bit of a dilemma, really. I've been offered a work transfer to America for twelve months.'

'That's great! When do you leave?'

'I haven't decided to take the job yet.'

'What's stopping you?'

'Tim.' She placed her cup on the small cane side table and rose to her feet, pacing along the verandah. 'Look, as much as I want this job, I just happen to think it's a bit unfair on him, that's all. He'll miss all his friends and I know he'll miss you, and it doesn't seem worth uprooting him for a year.'

'He could learn from the experience. And it'd be a great chance for him to see another country.'

'I know, I know.' She gave a forced laugh and raised her hands in mock defeat. 'I've considered all the pros and cons and still can't make up my mind.'

'So you want me to help make it up for you? Come on, Gab. Don't do this, hey? What if you go, on my say-so, and hate it? I'll be blamed forever.'

'Don't be silly.' She bent, picked up a cushion, and threw it playfully at him. 'I just want your opinion, that's all. It affects you, too.'

'There is another option,' he reminded her quietly. 'Tim could stay with me.'

'But you're away so often with your work. And there are the long hours ...'

He rose, joining her at the verandah railing as he stared down into the yard below. It was a mess, really, long grass and overgrown gardens, but he could raise little enthusiasm about the place. 'I've been thinking about going out on my own for a while now,' he said, rubbing his hands along his jaw line. 'Totally freelance. I think I can make a go of it. It'll mean a bit less travel and I know my sister Anne will help out, if necessary.'

'So, you think it's a good idea that I go and Tim stays with you?' Gaby asked tentatively, her voice edged with a tinge of disbelief. 'You wouldn't mind?'

'Mind! We'd have a great time, Tim and I. We're good mates, you know.'

'Yes,' she replied softly. 'I know.'

Michael spent a busy day with his son, mowing the lawns and washing Bess. Later, when the shadows were long on the ground, they went down to the corner pub and had a quick meal, but it wasn't the same as that other time, when Callie was there. Somehow she completed their circle, made them whole.

Walking home again, down the darkened street, Tim took his hand, swinging happily along. 'It's great, isn't it, Dad, Mum going to America? She's been so excited about it.'

'You don't mind staying behind with your boring old Dad?'

'You're not boring! We do cool things together.'

'But it won't be like that all the time. I can be a mean old ogre about things like school and homework and keeping your room clean.'

'Sure, Dad.'

'What if we bought our own place?' he said as they came back through the gate.

'That'd be even better.'

After Tim was in bed, Michael wandered into the study, his gaze falling on the large manila envelope that sat on the far corner of his desk. 'Australian Archives, World War I Personnel Records Service', read the insignia on the bottom left-hand corner. It had arrived on Friday and, until now, he had had no opportunity to open it.

It contained Ben's war record. Michael had said nothing to Callie about its arrival, wanting both to surprise her and go through the information first. Why, he hadn't known, but having read most of the diary, having witnessed first-hand the words Ben had written over eighty years earlier, there seemed some common bond between them, some link through the years that he was powerless to describe, let alone understand.

He slit the envelope open tentatively. There were a dozen or more sheets of paper inside. Application to enlist, attestation papers, medical certificate. There was quite a bit of information: Ben's father's name, Harold; Ben's place of birth; his age at enlistment. Another sheet detailed his physical features: eyes brown, dark blond hair, height 6'2". Strange, Michael thought, how many features we shared. In some ways, he could have been reading a description of himself.

There was one sheet of paper marked WILL.

In the event of my death, I, Benjamin Harold Galbraith, bequeath my entire property to Miss Hannah Corduke ...

Casually Michael flicked through the pages, eventually coming to one marked 'Statement of Service'. At the bottom of the sheet the stamped words, larger by far than all the scrawled handwritten notes, stared back at him: KILLED IN ACTION. Accompanying it was a typewritten letter, brief yet concise:

> *No. 18171 Dvr Galbraith, B.*
> *11th Field Co Engineers, A.I.F.*
> *Killed in Action 30.9.1918*
> *After passing Zillebeke, Driver Galbraith was hit by a bullet and was buried by his mates. The grave is approximately 1 mile north-east of the outskirts of the town, on the left-hand side, near the steep bank of the gully that runs along the side of the Menin-Ypres road. Battalion cross erected.*
> *Signed H Bainbridge,*
> *Chaplain for C. O.*

Ben was dead! The enormity of the revelation registered with a sudden pain, and Michael thrust the pages away, unable to read further. Cautiously he took a deep breath, retaining it in his lungs for several seconds before exhaling, then brought his hands up, pressing them against his temples as though to stem the sense of grief welling up inside. The pages, desk, even his own hands blurred, swimming together into a formless mishmash of colour as he squeezed his eyes closed, trying to erase the memory of the words.

> *Buried by his mates.*
> *Battalion cross erected.*
> *So final. So ...*

Yet he *had* suspected, hadn't he, that Ben had died during those last few months of the war? Callie had already told him that her great-great-aunt Hannah had married someone called John, and that, in itself, was an ominous sign that Ben hadn't survived. In some ways, he had tried to prepare himself, having already flicked ahead through the diary and discovered that the entries had stopped suddenly in late September. But now, with the finality of the words facing him, he knew the preparation had not been enough.

And why should he feel such grief for someone he had never known? Six months earlier he had never heard of a man named Benjamin Galbraith. It wasn't as though he had been part of Michael's family, or even vaguely connected with them. So why did the news bring such a sense of utter desolation?

A sudden movement at the doorway made him turn. Timmy stood there in striped pyjamas, propped against the woodwork, blinking in the unaccustomed light.

'What's wrong, Dad? I heard you call out.'

Had he voiced his pain aloud? Michael couldn't be sure.

'You were probably dreaming, son. Come on, back to bed.'

He led Tim back into his room and tucked him in. Pausing by his son's bed, he bent and kissed that warm forehead. Already the boy's eyes were closed, his breathing even and deep.

Back at the desk, despite his inner caution, he took up the pages again, letting his eye wander tentatively down the lines. There might be more information

543

about how Ben had died. Callie would want to know for her book, and it was best that he check the details before handing the information on to her.

There was an additional testimony from the company sergeant, and another from someone called Donaldson: words elaborating on the manner of Ben's death and the general surprise of the other men at his untimely end, so close to the final days of the war. Michael's eyes flew over the handwritten words, small personal details that evoked and strengthened his own sense of loss.

> *... caught a bullet in the forehead ...*
> *... died instantly, painlessly ...*
> *... he was a mate to everyone in the company ...*
> *... despite an intensive search and directions from the company chaplain, the deceased's grave could not be later located ...*

At the bottom of the page was a typewritten notation. *The actual whereabouts of the grave of the deceased is unknown.*

It was the last statement that brought with it a flood of disappointment. In death, Ben had been denied the right of a proper military burial, complete with marker and cross. Instead, somewhere along the side of a road thousands of miles away, his body still lay undetected, eighty years on.

Wearily, Michael put the papers back into the envelope. He would pass them on to Callie, and she could make of it what she would.

He showered and cleaned his teeth, padding naked into the bedroom and sliding between cool sheets. Somewhere outside, a night bird called, and he could hear the wail of a distant siren. Unable to settle, he tossed and turned for an hour. Unwelcome words danced behind his closed lids. His mind acted out scenes long past, ones he would rather forget. Ben, Hannah. Himself and Callie. Relationships intertwining, becoming confused in his tired mind.

Some time during the night, a shower of rain fell. Waking, he heard it drumming against the roof and trickling noisily along the gutters. And sleep, when it came again, was not filled with scenes of war and destruction as he had expected, but with a house quietly sleeping in the sunshine behind a mass of plumbago shedding a carpet of mauve.

CHAPTER 34

Several weeks of debilitating bleeding and constant pain finally sent Hannah to a doctor's rooms in the inner city. He examined her, rubbed his hand across his chin, frowned, then ordered her into hospital for tests.

'What sort of tests?' demanded Lottie later, back at the Kangaroo Street house.

Hannah, who had been too surprised to ask and too weary to care, shook her head. 'I don't know. He said something about exploratory surgery.' She raised her face, staring at her friend. 'I don't mind what they do to me, as long as they fix whatever's wrong. It's Nick I'm worried about. I could be off work for weeks and there's so little money saved to pay for his upkeep at the home.'

'Go and talk to them,' suggested Lottie. 'Tell them your circumstances. I'm sure you could come to some arrangement.'

She went the following Sunday, taking him a bag of rosy apples and a handful of sweets. 'Mam!' he exclaimed, seeing her approach, a huge smile lighting up his face as he ran to her.

Those same old feelings of inadequacy rose in her heart again, the wanting to have him with her. Every day, not just for a few snatched hours once a week. But lately Ben's letters were hopeful of a quick settlement to the fighting.

*They say the war will end soon. Fritz is on the run
and we are after him.*

Soon he would be home and they would be a family,
the three of them. Never ever would she have to
come back to this place again.

She played with Nick for an hour outside on the
grass, throwing a brightly-coloured ball and
rationing out the sweets she had brought. Every so
often he toddled over to her and sat on her lap,
resting for a moment, throwing his sturdy arms
around her neck. She buried her face in his hair,
taking in the still-baby smell of him, and he laughed
and touched a hand to her cheek.

'Come on,' she said at last, scooping him up into
her arms, where he wriggled and demanded to be
put down. 'Ball! Ball!' he repeated, so she blew
bubbles of air against his neck with her mouth until
he squealed with delight at this new antic.

The matron of the home received her in a
room off the main office. It was sparsely furnished
with a large table, several filing cabinets and
two chairs. Hannah sat tentatively on the edge of
hers, while Nick settled on her lap, munching an
apple.

'So,' the older woman said, glancing at a copy of
Nick's records, which she had taken from the file.
'What you're asking is that we keep Nick here free
of charge?'

'No,' replied Hannah quietly. 'I intend to pay you
back, every last penny.'

'And how long might that take?' the woman
asked crisply.

'I — I'm not sure. It depends on how long I'm off work. A few weeks. A month, at the most.'

The woman closed the file with a snap and sat staring at Hannah, who felt uncomfortable under her gaze. 'I do have a more sensible solution,' she said at last. 'I know a couple who are willing to foster —'

'No!' interrupted Hannah emphatically. 'I want Nick to stay here with the other children.'

The older woman's voice rose an octave. 'Even though you have no money to pay for his upkeep?'

'I said I'd pay you back.'

The possibility had not occurred to her that her request would be denied. What other options would be open to her, then?

The matron shook her head. 'I really believe this is a much better solution. What harm can it do?'

Hannah tried to picture her son as part of a different family. Another mother to snuggle his chubby frame against. A father. Perhaps brothers and sisters.

'This couple,' she began cautiously, 'do they have other children?'

'Unfortunately, no. But Nick would be well looked after.'

The offer of delaying Nick's fees was not raised again and there seemed no other alternative. 'I'll have my secretary prepare the necessary forms. Pop back in a few days' time and sign them,' the matron added briskly, rising to her feet. As Hannah walked towards the door, the woman laid a reassuring hand on her arm. 'You'll see. In the long run, this is the most practical solution. I'm sure you want the best for Nick.'

Despondently Hannah walked back down the drive, towards the main road. Surgery and now temporarily losing Nick in yet another subtle way. It seemed every step she made took him further and further from her.

Halfway along the footpath on the route back to the tram stop, she paused and blew her nose. 'Goodness,' she chided herself, attempting a smile. 'What's wrong with you, girl?' Nick was being well taken care of. Soon her own health problems would be solved and, according to Ben, the long, long war was almost at an end.

'It's a long way to Tipperary, it's a long way to go. It's a long way to Tipperary, to the sweetest girl I know! Goodbye Piccadilly, farewell Leicester —'

Lottie paused in her singing, glancing up at Hannah as she came across the front verandah. 'Mrs Worthington wants to see you in her office,' she said, standing the broom next to the front door.

'What's wrong?'

Lottie shrugged. 'Don't ask me. I was just told to send you up the minute you came back, that's all.'

No more information seemed forthcoming so Hannah climbed the wide stairs that led to her employer's study. Mrs Worthington stood near the window, an envelope in her hands. 'Ah, Hannah, there you are. The telegram boy brought this earlier, but Lottie said you had gone to visit Nick.'

A telegram? Hannah swallowed, her mouth suddenly dry. An ache of despair had begun, a small pain, radiating from the base of her skull. Her first thought was to turn and run. Telegrams usually meant bad news and she wanted none of it. Things were already depressing enough. But Mrs Worthington was already walking towards her, holding the envelope out.

Wordlessly she took it, her hands shaking badly. Inserting her fingernail under one corner, she peeled the flap back and drew out the contents. In disbelief, her eyes skimmed over the words, black smudges against white paper, a momentarily meaningless jumble of letters that sat on the periphery of her consciousness waiting to be acknowledged.

We regret to inform ...
Benjamin Galbraith was killed ...
Single bullet ...

'No.'

Her voice came as a whisper, barely heard. Mrs Worthington turned towards her, a frown creasing her usually placid features. As though to stem the surge of unwelcome pain, Hannah crushed the paper in her hand and brought it to her mouth, pressing it against her lips in case she should cry out.

'It can't be true! It *can't* be!'

Had she said the words aloud or were they simply repeating themselves in her mind? Ben dead? It wasn't possible. Only days earlier, she had received his letter telling her the war was almost over. Only the formalities were left, hadn't he hinted? That he had gone through so much and survived, only to have life snatched away now seemed incomprehensible.

'There must be some mistake!' she blurted, knowing as she said the words that they were futile. A denial of sorts, an unwillingness to believe.

Blindly she turned, feeling her way towards the door.

'Hannah!' Mrs Worthington's anxious voice. 'Hannah, what's wrong? Come back!'

She was running now, frantically, along the hallway and down the stairs. Running with quick agitated steps away from those ugly cruel words that had destroyed everything meaningful in her life. Running from the knowledge that nothing would ever be the same again. Across the tiled foyer and through the front door she went, no destination in mind.

At the front door, someone caught her around her waist. 'For God's sake, Hannah! What's wrong?'

Panting, she came to a sudden standstill, staring into Lottie's concerned features. How could she say the words? How could she utter them, knowing they were the truth, when a part of her still fought against their existence?

'Ben's dead,' she said woodenly.

She took a step forward, trying to pull away from Lottie's grasp, but her legs buckled beneath her. She allowed Lottie to lead her to a chair on the verandah, sinking gratefully onto the firm seat.

It was there, Lottie's arms around her, that she buried her face in her hands and let the racking sobs consume her. She cried not just for Ben, but for all the others who had died. Tom. The Spuds and Wills of Ben's letters. Other unknown men. Mothers' sons. Sweethearts. Husbands. Fathers. Wasted, wasted lives.

But most of all, she cried for Nick, a little boy who would never know his father's generous heart, and the loss of a future she now knew she and Ben would never share.

Hannah packed the few remaining clothes of Nick's that she kept at the Kangaroo Street house. The weather would soon be warming, and there were several new summer suits she had bought. She placed them into a small suitcase, given to her by Mrs Worthington. 'Don't worry if it's not returned at once,' said her employer kindly. 'It's only an old one. And if there's anything I can do ...'

Hannah shook her head.

Later she picked up the white shawl that Ben had sent from France. Heartbroken, she brought it up to her face, laying her cheek against its softness. The thought of him sent her scurrying for the remaining half of the horseshoe, her last tangible link. The metal felt cold against her palm. Through the ever-present tears she studied it, running her fingers along the etched surface. At the top of the J-shaped object was the word 'Ben'. On the bottom of the broken arc were the words 'you always'. The back bore her own faint, familiar, hand-scratched message — 'Hannah Elizabeth Corduke, Brunswick Street. 1915'.

The other half of the horseshoe, the one she had handed to Ben at the railway station all those years ago: where was it? Had it been buried with him? He always said he kept it in his pocket, close to his heart.

She placed the object on the table before her and picked up the shawl again. In her despair, she didn't notice the extra weight of the fabric, the jagged edges of the horseshoe caught in its fringe. Carefully she laid it in the suitcase, then closed the lid.

When she looked later, the horseshoe was nowhere to be seen.

The following morning, Mr Bonham drove Hannah to the hospital, detouring past the Children's home so she could leave the small suitcase of clothes for Nick and sign the foster forms. She was hoping to see her son, even if only for a few minutes. It would probably be weeks before she could travel out that way again.

'I'm sorry,' said the woman at the reception desk. 'He's already with his new foster parents.'

Even Nick had gone. With a heavy heart, Hannah left the suitcase with instructions that it be passed on. Another woman came from the office behind, carrying several forms. 'Before you go,' she said, 'Matron says these have to be signed.'

Quickly she added her signature to the paperwork, seeing the words as a blur through tears she fought hard to control.

The bleeding, the doctor later told her, had been caused by an infection incurred during or after Nick's birth. The internal damage had been so severe that the only option was a full hysterectomy.

He was quite apologetic, stressing the lack of options open to him. 'If I'd known the full extent of it, I could have prepared you,' he said brusquely. 'But as it was ...'

He let his voice trail away, his hands coming up in defence. Hannah looked away, staring at the white hospital wall. No Ben. No more babies. How could she possibly go on?

If it wasn't for Nick, she thought later, she would wish herself dead, too.

Suddenly it was Armistice Day. The long war was over at last. At the Kangaroo Point house, hearing the unaccustomed tolling of the bell from the little church around the corner, Hannah hobbled out onto the upstairs verandah. 'What is it?' she called to the postman who was passing on his bicycle.

'It's all over!' he called. 'The war's over! Now the boys will be able to come home!'

She turned and walked inside, part of her unable to share the joy. For Ben and thousands of other Australian men, their war had long since ended. There would be no homecoming, only sadness.

Peace marches were held in the inner city. Hannah accompanied Lottie and Mrs Worthington, taking the ferry to the Alice Street wharf. It was her first outing since leaving hospital and she was soon weary. Crowds surged along the pavements like a moving sea. There was much waving of flags and banging of tins. Women alternately cried and danced, and children wore tricolours in their buttonholes. Bells rang and whistles blew. In one of the nearby parks, a large bonfire was lit and an effigy of the Kaiser was burned.

Hannah watched the victory parade move down Queen Street, still too numb from the news of Ben's death to properly take it all in. It's another chapter of my life ending, she thought, as though someone had closed the pages of the book. But the pages were old and thin, falling around her in disarray. Like her life. Smashed. Ruined. Like the crumpled remains of the telegram she had thrown in the kitchen fire, watching the paper as it curled and blackened and shrivelled to nothing.

The parade, the noise, seemed to be happening to someone else, going on around her, but somehow distant. She saw mouths open and hands clap, yet heard none of it. Instead her thoughts were with Nick. Now that she was back on her feet, she would visit the Children's Home, ask to have him brought back there. Somehow she would find a way to have him permanently with her.

'There seems to be some mistake,' said the woman at the main desk.

'What mistake?' asked Hannah, feeling inordinately tired after the tram ride and the lengthy walk. A small pain had started in her stomach, near the vicinity of the scar, throbbing with each successive step. All she wanted to do was arrange Nick's return from his foster family and hold his sturdy body in her arms once more.

'Wait right here. I'll just get matron.'

The woman hurried away, returning shortly with the matron in tow. 'Let's just pop along to my office, shall we?' said the older woman, taking her arm.

Apprehension settled like a cloak. 'What's wrong? Where's Nick?'

Matron steered her into the office and closed the door. 'Please sit down.'

She felt the edge of the chair behind her knees and sank gratefully onto the seat. 'I — I don't understand. I want my son.'

'Nick's not coming back, Hannah.'

He couldn't be dead! Not Nick! He was so healthy the last time she had seen him. What had they done to him, the married couple who had been entrusted with his care?

'Why not?' Her own voice sounded wooden, leaden to her ears.

'The forms you signed, the last time you were here — did you read them?'

Cautiously. 'No.'

The woman stood behind her desk, arms folded, a frown on her face.

'Was I supposed to?' Hannah went on desperately, hating the momentary silence. 'You said they were forms to allow Nick to stay with foster parents while I was in hospital. You said he would come back here, as soon as I could afford the fees. You said —'

She stopped, realisation dawning. 'The couple who took Nick, they're not bringing him back, are they? They want to keep him.'

'By law they are legally allowed to. The forms you signed were permission to adopt.'

It took several seconds to digest the words, make sense of them. Her hands flew at the woman then, battering her chest, her arms. 'I want my son! Bring him back! Oh, my God!'

As suddenly as she had begun, she stopped, stepping backwards. The room seemed miles wide, filled with cotton wool, dipping and swaying alarmingly. Suddenly the view telescoped, rushing towards her with alarming speed. She sensed the older woman's arms clutching at her, supporting her weight, then a dark void from which no more heartache came.

The envelope arrived the following week, bearing a French postmark. Listlessly Hannah sat it on the dresser in her room, unable to bring herself to open it. France. She would always hate that name. Both Tom and Ben were buried somewhere in its soil. The flower of Australian manhood lay interred there, and no amount of victory marches and trumpet playing could ever bring them back.

Lottie picked up the letter on the fourth day, waving it at Hannah. 'Aren't you in the least bit curious?' she asked.

'No.'

Wordlessly she took the envelope from Lottie's hand, tearing it open, bringing out several folded sheets of paper.

'Go on,' prompted Lottie. 'Read it.'

'Dear Hannah,' she read aloud.

'Who's it from?' interrupted Lottie.

'I don't know,' she replied crossly. 'Do let me get through it, Lottie, then I'll know.'

She sat on the bed, the letter spread before her.

I hope you don't mind me referring to you in such a familiar tone, but I feel as though I know you, although we have never met. Ben was a mate of mine, a good friend, and we had been together since the early days in the barracks in Brisbane. Just days before he died, we spoke about the war, our lives, how much he loved you and your little boy, Nick. He was also a good mate to every one of us, and will be sorely missed.

Hannah paused and raised her face, blinking back tears, pressing the pages back on her lap. Lottie's arms were instantly around her. 'You can finish it,' she said.

> *This will be our third Christmas in France and I know the chaps are keen to see their families once more. When I get back, I would like to call on you, return the letters you sent to Ben, his diary and personal effects, etc.*
> *Kind regards,*
> *John (Jack) Deacon*
> *P. S. You will see a poppy pressed in this letter. I took it from a clump growing near Ben's grave, thinking you might like to have it.*
> *J.*

As Hannah spread the pages on her lap, the crushed remnant of a flower fell onto her skirt. She stared at it in surprise. The petals were faded, not bright red as she had imagined. Carefully she picked it up and slotted it back inside the folded pages, inserting them back into the envelope.

It was a flower, nothing more. It held no meaning. Ben was dead, the poppy was, too, and the sight of it rekindled the pain.

During her bleakest moments, it seemed to Hannah that her life had been neatly divided into three uneven parts: before, during and after the war. She, herself, used such phrases, catching herself too late. It was easy, she thought, to categorise time. Before the war was a great stretch of seasons echoing back into infinity. The war had been a nightmare interval, when she had lived each day as though on a knife's edge, forever fearful, tense, as though waiting for a coiled snake to strike.

And afterwards?

The future loomed ahead, vague and formless without Ben and Nick. What would they hold, these years to come? Sorrow? Happiness? Regret? Hannah could not say; in her grief, she predicted nothing. She never once said the words, 'after Ben's death', could not even bear to bring herself to say his name. Along with Nick he was, however, always in her thoughts.

Ben's deferred pay had been sent on, as per the instructions in his will. The money, Hannah thought, was no compensation for the emptiness she felt inside. Christmas came and went, and suddenly it was a new year, bringing with it the beginnings of the 'Spanish Flu' epidemic which had already been raging in Europe since last April.

She stayed on at the house at Kangaroo Point, helping with the last of the repatriated men. The memories were there, in that city, and she was not ready to be parted from them. She nursed a dream that one day she would see Nick. Anxiously she studied small children as she hurried along the city streets or through some park, searching for the mop of tousled blond hair. But the sight of him never materialised before her. Where was he? Was he well, happy?

It was late winter before Jack Deacon called. In the city parks, the acacias had begun to bloom, boughs laden with gold. The sight of them rekindled the words from one of Ben's last letters. Something about wattles, she remembered, the memory jolting suddenly back at her: *little balls of yellow fluff*, and the fact that he hoped to be home before they flowered again.

It was a disheartening time. A cold wind blew through the city, depressing her further. A deep sense of loss, combined with an immeasurable sadness, consumed her every waking moment. And the thought of Jack Deacon's impending visit, the imagined effort of having to discuss all that had happened, of resurrecting all the memories, was almost too much to bear.

She found Jack standing at the front door, looking uncomfortable in his uniform, one windswept August morning. Two years older than herself, she later discovered, he was a tall red-headed farmer from Roma in the state's west, in the city to attend to his final discharge from the army.

'You must be Hannah,' he said. 'I recognise you from Ben's photograph.'

'Won't you come in,' she replied faintly, holding open the door.

Once inside, he held out a medium-sized box. 'The letters you sent Ben, and his diary,' he offered by way of explanation. Suddenly he cleared his throat and went on, obviously overcome in some way by the words he was about to say. 'Hannah, I understand what you've been through. Ben loved you and that baby, even though he never saw him.'

She nodded, unable for a moment to speak. Her voice, when it came, was soft, close to breaking point. 'Would you care for some tea?'

Over a plate of scones and several cups of tea, she told him about Nick, the way she had lost him. 'They assured me it was a mistake. Someone had prepared the wrong forms, adoption and not foster. I agonised over it. I *had* signed them, I wasn't forced into it. I should have read them but it was so soon, so soon after losing Ben. I couldn't think properly. Mrs Worthington, my employer, tried to help but they said nothing could be done. So I had to let him go, just as I had to let Ben go. I tell myself he is in good hands, with a mother and a father who truly love him. But no-one could love him as I did.'

She wiped the tears from her eyes with a clean white handkerchief supplied by Jack and they continued their tea, chatting about this and that. When it was all over, when Jack had gone, she knew she had found a kindred spirit, someone who understood. After all, he had been through it all, too.

Later, going through the box of Ben's belongings, she found the other half of the horseshoe.

Jack came to the city every month or so, never failing to call on Hannah. Though a smile lit her face and she seemed pleased to see him, her features were drawn and her eyes held a measure of sadness he was unable to erase.

He took her to various places about the city on her days off. It seemed a natural thing to spend his spare time with her. Getting back into civilian life was hard, and he found it difficult to talk to his parents, his sisters about the war. How could they ever hope to understand? With Hannah he didn't talk about these things either, but she knew, she *knew*. It was an unspoken bond between them, the sharing of something much more than friendship.

She wouldn't call him Jack, saying it reminded

her too much of what had happened, the war, how Ben had died, his letters. So she called him John, his real name, and it became a password between them, a small sign of acceptance and trust.

Almost twelve months passed before Jack asked her to marry him. He had purchased a ring in anticipation, the jeweller offering to exchange it if it was not the correct size. Hannah was visiting the house in Brunswick Street at the time, and he went directly to the bank before visiting her, to ask David Corduke's permission.

Elated by her brother's consent, he called at the house, suggesting a walk down by the creek. There he took the ring from his pocket and slipped it into Hannah's folded palm. She stared at it for a moment, a puzzled expression on her face.

'I want to marry you, and I think Ben would have approved,' he said simply, reducing her to unexpected tears, which he felt bound to mop up as he clumsily kissed her.

He knew there could never be any children. Hannah had told him the full story, the problems she had had after the birth of Nick, the subsequent hysterectomy. In truth, he didn't care. It was her he wanted.

'Yes,' she said at last, awarding him a shy smile. 'I'd like that.'

Almost unable to believe his luck, Jack took her in his arms and kissed her. Against the backdrop of bougainvillea and wattles, he felt her mouth move against his, felt those first tender stirrings, and knew that everything would be all right.

'I love you, Hannah,' he whispered, and the

sound mingled with the breeze, uniting the past and the present, and offering him a future he'd hardly dared hope for.

The day of the wedding dawned bright and clear, with just the hint of cloud on the horizon. Hannah was up early, wanting the ceremony to be done with, anxious to catch the later train to Brisbane, where she and John would take a short honeymoon before settling on the Deacon family property out west.

The church arrangements had been made. David Corduke would lead his sister up the aisle, while Davie was full of excitement at the prospect of visiting the soon-to-be married couple 'out back' during the next school holidays.

Before dressing, she sat at the desk in her room and took a single sheet of paper from the drawer. Today she would move on to a new life, but first she had to let go of the old. That much she owed John. Biting her bottom lip, she picked up the pen and began to write.

My darling Ben,
Today John and I are to be married. His friendship has been good for me, and during these last few months he has taught me how to smile again. We share the pain of the past, he and I, and it seems right that we should also share the future, whatever it may bring. Take care, my love, wherever you are, and watch over me. Tonight, when I look up at the sky, I will think of that bright star and, behind it, I will see your smiling face.
Forever yours
Hannah

It seemed official, now it was done, the severing of old ties, bringing a sense of finalisation and peace. Wiping a tear from her eye, she folded the paper and put it in an envelope, sealing it. On the front she wrote one word, 'Ben', and stored it with the others.

There was a knock on the door. It was Lottie, who had come down from the city for the occasion.

'Ready?' her friend asked, face beaming.

Hannah nodded. The sun was shining, a good omen. The wattles were in bloom. Today was hers, hers and John's. The future was theirs, too. She would make it bright and welcoming, and not let the past intrude.

Well, not too much, anyway.

CHAPTER 35

Callie shed several tears over the accounts of Ben's death enclosed in the official records, as Michael had known she would. In many ways, he wished he could have spared her, yet he sensed her grief was an outward sign of mourning. Ben was gone; Hannah, too. And the story of their lives, as told through the letters and diary, was finished.

The information was all there. Ben's correspondence to Hannah, carefully preserved. Hannah's letters to Ben, returned by Jack after the war. Several notes written by Jack, and that one last letter written by Hannah on her wedding day. Reverently Callie had taken the crumbling remains of the poppy and had it laminated, preserved from further deterioration between two see-through sheets of plastic. The photographs from the trunk were all slotted into a specially-purchased album.

It was seeing the full signature on the end of that first letter from Jack that helped tie up all the loose ends.

'The Jack in Ben's letters', Callie said later, planning to hunt through her own family album for a copy of Hannah's wedding photo, 'was Uncle John. I never realised.'

They were sitting at the table on the balcony, sipping their first-of-the-morning coffees. Michael was wearing a pale blue bathrobe that fell away at the neck, exposing his tanned chest. Callie wore a bright kimono, a present from Michael the previous evening. The sun was a red ball rising over the sea.

'Do you think they were happy after all that happened?' he asked, taking another sip of coffee. 'I wonder how Jack really felt about Hannah's relationship with Ben, and the baby.'

'Maybe that's what drew them together, that shared grief. Jack had lost most of his mates in the war, too.'

'I suppose so.'

'When you think about it, Hannah lost almost everyone who was important to her during that last year: Tom. Ben. Nick.'

'Even the ability to bear more children,' added Michael. 'That must have been difficult to accept, especially after losing her son. And as the years passed, there must have been lots of days in each year that she found hard to bear — the anniversary of Ben's death, Nick's birthday.'

Callie nodded. 'She experienced things that would have us running for counselling today. But, in the end, she simply put it all behind her and got on with life. She must have been a very resilient woman.'

'With our modern propensity for counselling and all the associated brouhaha, does that make us weaker?'

'Weaker?' Callie thought for a moment. 'Perhaps it just made her stronger,' she offered.

'Witch! Stop playing with words.'

Callie chuckled, then grew serious again. 'The other thing that amazes me is the fact that, through all that happened, Hannah never felt she could go to her brother, David, for help. I always had an impression that ours had been a united family. But that wasn't the case. I never knew my great-grandfather but, from looking at his photograph I always had the impression of great strength.'

Michael nodded in agreement. 'It's the name, I suppose — David — and his profession. Accountants always give that impression of being in control.'

'I realise now that he was an incredibly weak man. Quite dominated by Enid.' Callie paused for a moment. 'There's something else that's been niggling, too. I think I remember Lottie.'

'How? Where?'

'After Uncle John died and Hannah was living with Mum and Dad at the house in Brunswick Street, an old woman came down from the city to see Hannah a few times. Miss Lucas, that was how Hannah introduced her. Later she said her name was Charlotte.'

'So what happened to Lottie after the war?'

'Obviously she never married, hence the 'Miss', but I seem to remember that she was a nanny or governess, something like that. She was a lively old lady, full of wit and good humour. Funny, I never realised, never connected until now that she was the same person.'

'So they kept in contact then,' mused Michael. 'When you consider that Lottie was there for Hannah every time she faced a crisis in her life, the two women must have shared a very strong bond.'

They were quiet for a while, Callie mulling over the newfound revelations. She stared out over the sea, which was calm, with tiny waves lapping at the sand.

'In the end she *did* love Jack. I stayed with them a few times when I was young — you know, holidays in the bush, that sort of thing. They were a very devoted couple and always seemed so content together.'

Michael nodded and drew her close. 'Life works in strange ways,' he whispered in her ear. Then: 'Happy?'

'Yes.'

'Then come up to the city with me for the day. We'll take Timmy out somewhere.'

'Sounds good.'

He paused and grinned at her wickedly.

'On second thoughts, perhaps I should just take you back to bed.'

The envelope, bearing the crest of the Queensland Department of Births, Deaths and Marriages, arrived late the following week. With all the ensuing problems, Callie had forgotten about applying for it. Eagerly she tore open the envelope, spreading the sheet of paper on her study desk.

The details were all there. Hannah's name, Ben's. Nick's birth date, the address of the house where he had been born, and the name of the attendant nurse. Stamped across the centre of the document were the words 'NOT TO BE USED FOR OFFICIAL PURPOSES'. A typed notation on the side advised the reader that 'the child whose birth is herein registered has been adopted' and went on to name the appropriate Adoption Register.

She sat for a while, rereading the words. It was the final sum of Hannah's grief, she thought, trying to imagine how her great-great-aunt must have felt later, after Nick and Ben had both gone.

Michael rang on Thursday evening and she filled him in on the week's events.

'Any chance of your taking a few days off?' he asked when she had finished. 'I've got a photo shoot up on one of the islands next week. It's a private commission and I'm taking some of my holiday leave to fit it in. I thought you might like to come.'

'How long will you be away?'

'Allowing for the drive either way, at least a week.'

Callie hesitated for a moment, the invitation catching her off-guard. Her relationship with Michael was still testing new boundaries. Sex and sharing weekends was one thing, harmless really, not requiring long-term commitments. No obligations. No responsibilities. An immediate matter fulfilling immediate needs. But now ... She took a deep breath. *Now* he wanted her to travel with him, wanted to involve her in his work and the separate life he had, taking their relationship onto a different level altogether.

Should she accept or decline?

Slowly, slowly, warned an inner voice. *Back off. Don't get too involved.* Her independence from Stuart had been hard-won and traumatic. There was no way she wanted to get too involved, too soon, with anyone.

'No strings, Callie,' Michael said, as though sensing her hesitation. 'Come on, it'll be fun. A little sunshine, good food, wine, great company —'

'Whose? Yours or mine?'

'Both,' he laughed.

What was there to lose? She'd been feeling pretty tense lately, and a few days away from the town, and Stuart, might put things back in their proper perspective. 'Sounds great,' she replied, feeling a surprised tingle of anticipation. 'I'll make a phone call and see if Mum will look after the cat.'

'About this weekend. It's my turn to have Tim, and we usually do something special; otherwise, we just seem to end up sitting staring at one another.'

'What did you have in mind?'

'I thought we'd go fishing. Interested?'

Fishing! Her thoughts scrambled back to childhood, and she and Bonnie and Alex out in the wooden dinghy. Three of them lumbering through the water, the old motor chug-chugging along, the smell of the fuel and salt blending in her nostrils. How long since she'd been out in a boat? Years. 'Try keeping me away.'

'That's that, then. Come up Friday and we'll have the weekend with Tim. Then we'll head north, first thing Monday morning.'

Saturday morning dawned bright and sunny, typical mid-March weather. Michael packed a picnic hamper and, after collecting Timmy from Gaby's, they headed south on the highway. It was still early and traffic was light. They passed the occasional truck, interstate rigs mostly, with Timmy trying to guess the makes of the vehicles from a distance.

'Reminds me of myself when I was that age,' Michael laughed. 'I was going to the Territory to drive the big road trains.'

'Why didn't you, Dad?' queried Tim from the back seat. 'That would have been cool.'

Callie flashed Michael a challenging look. 'Yes, why didn't you?'

'Because I decided to stay here in this equally wonderful part of Australia and take photographs instead,' he replied with a grin.

After twenty minutes they turned off the highway and headed east, towards the sun. Canefields rose out of the flat expanse of land, green tips waving in the breeze. Here and there were dotted old farmhouses. The occasional bird hovered high overhead, dark smudges against an impossibly blue sky.

At last Michael pulled into a small car park in front of a ramshackle boatshed. Above the door was a faded sign that read, 'Smith's Bait and Tackle. Boats For Hire. Hourly or Daily Rates'. Callie extricated herself from the front seat, stretched her legs and took in the briny tang of the water.

Gear settled in the boat, Michael guided the craft away from the jetty. Callie sat next to him, aware of little details. Michael's tanned hand resting against the throttle of the motor. The thud and lurch of the dinghy as it headed into the choppy water, causing his thigh to rub against hers. Pleasurable details, she thought happily, watching lazily from under a broad-brimmed hat as Timmy hung over the stern of the boat, trailing his fingers in the water.

A few minutes from shore, a large cruiser approached, sending out a foaming wash in its wake.

'Look at that, Dad!' yelled Timmy excitedly, pointing. 'Hey, Callie, have you ever seen anything as big as that? Cool!'

Callie laughed and felt the pressure of Michael's hand around hers. As Timmy stared back at the approaching boat, he lifted her fingers to his mouth.

'Happy?'

'Yes. And you?'

'Ecstatic.'

'Oh, silly!' She gave him a playful push and he pretended to overbalance. 'You say the most ridiculous things.'

'I do not,' he said in mock indignation.

Words lapping around her, lulling her like the wash of the tide and the slow movement of seagulls that hovered further out. Playful bantering. Relaxed, easy conversation. And it all seemed so natural, as though she had always known him, making those years with Stuart seem worlds away.

Michael pulled the boat up on a sandy beach, and they spent a few pleasant hours swimming and exploring the rock pools around the nearest headland. At lunchtime Callie spread a blanket in the shade of a stand of trees and brought out the contents of the esky — fresh bread rolls, cold chicken, salads, cheese, and fruit. A bottle of cold chardonnay completed the meal.

Too soon the day was ended, shadows long on the ground as Michael steered the dinghy back towards the wharf. Tired and a little sunburned, despite the sunscreen Callie had liberally applied, they retraced their route through the canefields and merged with the highway traffic heading back towards the city.

Fish and chips seemed a sensible dinner option for the two adults, with Timmy almost nodding off in the middle of a huge hamburger that Callie was certain he would never finish. Finally, with Timmy bathed and tucked in bed, they had the house to themselves.

She was standing under a steaming shower when Michael let himself into the cubicle behind her. Tenderly he soaped her back, her breasts and belly, moving his hands down.

'Nice?'

'Mmmm.' She turned and slid her arms around his neck, pulling his face towards her own. 'But this is much nicer,' she murmured, kissing him.

'I've been waiting patiently all day for you to do that.'

'Patience is a virtue.'

'And at the moment I'm all out of it.'

With one seemingly fluid movement, he flicked off the water and scooped her up, carrying her squealing and dripping wet from the ensuite bathroom. The bedclothes were already turned back, the bedspread folded at the end. Laughing, he deposited her on the sheets and rolled onto the mattress beside her.

He was loving and tender, taking the time to attend to her own needs as well as his. A kiss. An embrace. Touch of hand, of mouth. All senses leading to that one explosive moment that left her momentarily breathless, gasping with delight.

Later, when she turned towards him, only partly awake, he reached for her and held her close, burying his face in her hair.

573

'This feels so right,' he whispered, his voice sounding loud against the silence of the night. 'You. Me. I suppose I have to thank that mysterious old horseshoe for leading me to you.'

'Fate,' she replied, drowsy with sleep. 'Perhaps it was meant to be.'

'So,' added Michael, propping himself on one elbow and staring down at her. 'Where does *fate* lead us to from here?'

Two days of almost non-stop driving brought them to their north Queensland coastal destination by late Tuesday. The two-bedroom accommodation was very modern, across the road from a shingled beach. Cassowaries wandered in the garden, their brightly plumed red, yellow and blue heads bobbing amongst the foliage.

The following morning they caught the motor launch across to the island. Callie helped Michael carry his photographic equipment up from the wharf, and then sat under an umbrella by the pool while he discussed concepts with the resort manager who had commissioned a series of photographs to be used in a new glossy advertising brochure. After a while she wandered along the beach, watching as the tide slowly receded, leaving an expanse of mud flats in its wake.

Too soon the days passed, a haze of cameras and angles, buffet lunches served under the palms on the flat expanse of lawn around the resort pool, and making love as the moon rose over the water, leaving a shimmering myriad of light reflecting off the calm sea. On impulse, on their last night, they wandered along the beach at midnight, water lapping at their feet and tiny crabs scuttling across the sand.

'You know,' said Michael as they came to a halt at the rocky headland and she rested her cheek against his shoulder, 'it hasn't seemed like work with you here. More like a holiday. Just knowing you're waiting, that we can be together at the end of the day, makes it all worthwhile.'

He cupped her chin and raised her face towards his, kissing her. 'In fact, I haven't felt so alive for ages.'

Slowly they walked back along the beach. For Callie the holiday was almost over, but it had been a special time, just her and Michael. Tomorrow they would head back to the city, back to humdrum routines and work, to other lives no longer shared.

Michael felt himself tense as the car wove in and out of the city traffic, that old familiar tightening of the shoulder and neck muscles that left a dull ache. The week was over, days blurring and merging so successfully that already he was unable to separate them in his mind.

Small details stood out, however, each one distinct from the rest. Callie dancing along beside him on the beach at night, the lights from the island reflected back in the inky water. Callie running naked from the shower, beads of moisture clinging to her arms and her breasts, pulling him urgently towards her. Later, lying on the bed, moonlight shafting through the open balcony door, their bodies a warm tangle of arms and legs from which he felt loath to extricate himself.

Remembering, he glanced sideways at her. She was staring morosely out the window as the grey lines of buildings flashed past. 'Welcome home,' she grimaced, looking up, awarding him a sad smile.

Bess was there to greet them as they pulled up at the house. Seeing the car, the neighbour who had been feeding the dog wandered over, returning one unopened can of dog food in the process. By the time Michael turned his attention back to Callie, she had unlocked the Suzuki and was busy lugging her own bag from his car. 'Here, I'll do that,' he said, taking the heavy case from her and stowing it in the rear luggage compartment.

'I'd better be off,' Callie replied, standing back. 'I told Mum I'd be back tonight to collect the cat.'

'You could ring,' suggested Michael hopefully. 'Tell her you'll be an extra night.'

'And delay the inevitable?' Callie shook her head. 'Thank you, Michael. I've had a lovely week, but now it's back to reality.'

'Yeah. Reality. Thanks for reminding me.'

She moved forward as though to kiss him, but stopped suddenly, regarding him with serious grey eyes. 'Don't you wish it never had to end?'

'It doesn't have to,' he responded. 'We could easily make every day a holiday, you and I.'

She stood regarding him for a few seconds, a quizzical expression on her face. 'We could?' she answered at last, taking a step back and running her tongue along her bottom lip. He saw a momentary flash of hurt in her eyes. Had Stuart once said those same words? Had he made promises he had been unable to keep?

He could have told her then, blurted the words, but something held him back. Slow down, Paterson, said the inner voice. Things are going along fine. On a physical level, the relationship is merely weeks old. Don't spoil it by getting too serious too soon.

He took her arm instead, steering her towards her car. 'You're important to me. We go well together, you and I. Like yin and yang, according to Chinese legend.'

She smiled at him then and kissed him goodbye. *I love you*, he wanted to say, *you're my every breath, my being*, but the words wouldn't come. They died in his mouth, halted by the barricade she had put up, that questioning look, that expression of hurt that had, for one brief moment, made him want to smash Stuart into oblivion.

He watched gloomily as her blue 4WD headed down the road, away from him, and felt an emptiness he was unable to dismiss.

The house had a stale odour. Quickly he flung open the windows and loaded a few CDs into the player, before dumping a load of washing in the machine. When he came back past the table later, munching on a toasted sandwich, the envelope caught his eye. Callie had left it on Friday, a collection of photocopied documents and letters she thought he might like to go through. Curious, he brought the contents out, casually flicking through them.

One in particular drew his attention. It was Nick's birth certificate. He knew Hannah's son had been born in January 1917. Callie had told him so, although there had been no reference to the actual day in Ben's diary. By the time Hannah's letter had arrived telling him he was finally a father, weeks had passed, and Ben had simply recorded the fact on the day the letter had arrived.

Michael let his eyes wander down the document, noting the details. Strange, he thought, suddenly realising that his father and Hannah's child had shared the same birth date. What a coincidence!

His gaze travelled further down the document, a faint niggle of unease threatening, as he paused over the typed notation at the side: 'The child whose birth is herein registered has been adopted. See adoption Register #544. G Hanlon Registrar-General. 5 October 1918.'

5 October 1918.

Michael stared at the words, some inconsistency jarring at his mind. He wasn't certain why, but he had the oddest sensation that something was wrong. Nick and his father sharing the same birthday. His father's own birth registration, well after his birth. Nick's adoption in October 1918, at nineteen months of age.

He halted suddenly, the air catching in his throat; it seemed a thousand alarm bells were ringing inside his head. Abruptly he rose and went to the desk where he kept his personal papers.

The copy of his father's birth certificate in hand, he compared it to Nick's. Same birth date. Same place of birth. Even the same attendant nurse. Everything identical, except for the parents' names and the date of registration. Nick's had been only a few days after the birth. His father's had been nineteen months later. The 5th of October, to be exact.

There was only one logical implication.

Stunned, he sat staring at the sheet of paper, dozens of questions racing through his mind. If his own suspicions were true, had his father known he was adopted? No mention had ever been made of it. Probably not, he decided, mind whirling. And he, himself, growing up believing that he was a Paterson. But he wasn't, not really. He was a Corduke, part of Callie's family.

Callie! His attention was diverted by a jumble of impressions. Callie the lover juxtaposed against Callie the blood relative. Second cousin? Third? Mentally he tallied the generation spans and his own scant knowledge of family history. The connection was certainly not close enough to be a major concern, but it added a new slant to their relationship. And the Brunswick Street house? That sense of belonging, the first time he had been there. That faint impression that he had known the house well, although he had never before set eyes on it.

He smiled then, thinking about the house, the gardens. They were part of him, his heritage. He belonged there.

Needing to share the discovery, he glanced at his watch, surprised to find it was after eleven o'clock. He should ring Callie, but she would probably be in bed. 'Damn,' he cursed softly, glaring at the telephone. But she would want to know, he reasoned, desperate also to hear the sound of her voice. Without further hesitation, he picked up the receiver and dialled her number.

'I know this sounds incredible, but I think my father was Hannah's son,' he said in answer to her sleepy voice.

The Department of Family and Community Services was able to provide some information. 'There are not a lot of existing records,' said the young man at the counter, 'but we can certainly tell you about the children's home where your father was placed, provide you with dates, etcetera.'

Michael's sister Anne had been most surprised. He rang her early in the week with the news, and there had been a momentary stunned silence on the other end of the phone. 'So you mean to tell me we have a whole new family out there that I never knew about?'

'Yes.'

'Do you think Dad knew he was adopted?'

'I don't think so. He certainly never said anything about it, if he did.'

'Just as well there's plenty of disk space left on my family tree program,' she replied pragmatically. 'So when do I get to meet them?'

He made a tentative date, several weekends ahead, hoping that Callie would be able to talk Freya and Bonnie into coming up to the city. Anne had offered to open her house for the occasion. 'It's easier with the baby,' she said. 'I can just put him to bed if he gets tired and grizzly. Come for lunch. I expect we'll have heaps to talk about.'

'Heaps,' he grinned, anticipating Freya's reaction.

Armed with the relevant information, Michael headed down the coast to Callie's on Friday evening. She met him at the door, a bundle of excitement. 'I can't believe it,' she said, throwing her arms around his neck. 'This is amazing. Wait until we tell Freya, the old doubting Thomas. Remember all the fuss about the horseshoe and you wanting to know how it had come into your father's possession? Muckraking, I think she called it. Well, she was wrong. That shoe had everything to do with you.'

'So you haven't said anything to Freya or Bonnie yet?'

'No. I thought I'd wait until you came down, and we could tell them together.'

'Chicken!'

He had missed her though the week, and the house had seemed unbearably quiet. Even the radio or television had failed to dispel the feeling. It was human company he needed, he finally acknowledged, not a voice emanating from a set of speakers.

'Anyway,' he added, taking her in his arms. 'I didn't come down here to discuss Freya tonight. Tomorrow will be soon enough.'

'So,' she grinned. 'Just what did you come down here for?'

'This.' He kissed her on the mouth. 'And this,' he added, kissing her again. 'Unless you've any objections.'

'No,' she murmured, running her hand along his jaw line. 'I guess it's just fine with me.'

CHAPTER 36

Standing in front of the Brunswick Street house the following morning, the knowledge that sometime in the past Hannah had lived there washed over him. Hannah — the grandmother Michael had never known, never suspected existed.

Opening the gate, he had that same sense of *deja vu*, of having done this before. And he had. Twice. But this time was different. He was coming back armed with the knowledge that he was one of them, linked by blood and genes, and a love affair that had been cruelly cut short by a single bullet almost eighty years earlier.

Six months had passed since he had first visited the house. It was autumn now, not spring, yet little had changed, apart from the FOR SALE sign attached to the front fence and the large red-and-white SOLD sticker plastered diagonally across its surface. Still the house slept in the sunshine behind the sprawling mass of plumbago, beyond the flagged pathway and wide verandah, and paint-peeling front door.

Callie had gone ahead, walking purposefully up the path, but he had hung back for a moment, absorbing the ambience of the place. The house had soul, he decided, created and moulded by the people who had once lived there. John and Elizabeth

Corduke, Hannah, Thomas and David. Even the unyielding Enid. Davie and Lily. They were all long gone, yet Hannah's letters had somehow brought them alive, made them real.

If he closed his eyes, he could almost imagine them there, Elizabeth tending to the flower garden, John mowing the lawn. The children would be running on a patch of freshly cut grass, throwing a ball. A laugh. A giggle. Had he really heard them? he thought, suddenly opening his eyes. But it was merely Callie calling him as she waited on the verandah, Bonnie holding the screen door open beside her.

Bonnie and Freya listened, their eyes wide with surprise, as he and Callie filled them in on the details, backed up by photostat copies of the official forms.

'So,' said Bonnie, when they were done, 'great-aunt Hannah was your grandmother. That must make you and Callie distant cousins, right?'

'Right. Second, I think, though I'm not sure.'

'What about grandfather David?' asked Freya, a frown creasing her brow. 'Do you think he ever knew about Hannah's baby?'

Callie shook her head. 'From what I've managed to make out through the letters, the only family she ever told was Tom, and that knowledge died with him.'

With the connection established to the satisfaction of the two older women, Bonnie went in search of the old family photograph albums. They had already been packed, in preparation for the move, but Callie's mother, with her usual orderliness, knew exactly where to find them.

They were all there. Elizabeth and John. Thomas in his soldier's uniform. Hannah and David. Enid, dour-faced and glaring towards the camera. Davie and Lily standing next to a waist-high column topped by a potted plant. There was even one austere portrait of Hannah and Jack on their wedding day. Then Callie's own parents — Bonnie and Alex — running hand in hand down the front steps of the local church years later, a shower of confetti hanging suspended over them, their smiles captured forever on bromide.

It seemed to Michael he could see a mixture of his father's features in all of them. Here a nose, there a tilt of eyebrow, the curve of a mouth. In turn, he brought out a collection of his own photographs: his father, mother, sister Anne.

'Tell us about your dad,' prompted Bonnie after they had admired them all, commenting in turn on the various similarities.

'He grew up in the city, as you know,' explained Michael. 'And spent a bit of time up in New Guinea during the war. He never talked about it much and I suspect it affected him badly.'

'Davie, Callie's grandfather, was up there too,' broke in Bonnie. 'Wouldn't it have been a coincidence if they'd known each other?'

'After the war he joined a large engineering firm, ended up being the manager. He was almost forty when he met my mother. Love at first sight, that's what he always said. Anyway, they married six months later and I was born the following year. My sister Anne came along three years later.'

'Isn't it strange?' mused Callie. 'How he ended

up in a career similar to Ben Galbraith? Like father, like son.'

'And, like Ben, he was an easygoing popular bloke. Everyone loved Dad. His funeral was one of the largest I've ever attended.'

'Speaking of Anne,' Bonnie cut in. 'When are we going to meet her?'

'Oh, sorry. I almost forgot. Anne has asked me to invite you all up to her place for lunch in a few weeks' time. In her own words, she's dying to meet you all.'

It was mid-morning before they left, Bonnie shooing them out the door so she could re-pack the photo albums in peace.

'Where to now?' Michael asked. An odd deflated feeling had settled over him, a sense of anticlimax. The clues had been there, the same route waiting to be taken all those months ago, yet somehow he'd almost missed it. What if he'd never found out? What if Hannah's secret had been lost, never to be discovered?

They parked the car at the top of the hill overlooking the ocean and Callie guided Michael in the direction of the cemetery. 'I don't know why I didn't think to bring you here before,' she said, leading him along the neatly-clipped pathway between the graves.

At last they came to a halt in front of a collection of headstones, the names of long-dead Cordukes staring back at him. Callie had brought a small bunch of flowers, roses and carnations mostly, picked from the Brunswick Street garden. Solemnly she handed them to him, nodding towards Hannah's grave.

Hannah Deacon, nee Corduke. 1896 — 1978, read the epitaph. *Wife of John.*

Wife of John. The sum of Hannah's life reduced to three small words. But she had been more than that, Michael thought. Lover of Ben. Mother of Nick. His own grandmother. Yet no-one had known, had they? And if it hadn't been for the horseshoe and his own dogged determination, the secrets would have been lost for all time.

Reverently he laid the flowers against the marble slab, which was warm from the sun, and bowed his head for a few moments. In his mind he could see Hannah as she had been, in the photograph Callie had found amongst the old letters. Dark hair curling about her face, pretty in an unconventional way, a ready smile. One arm cradling Nick, his own father, who was perched on her hip. A young woman. Not an old lady. Somehow he couldn't picture her *old*.

Frowning, he turned, aware of Callie standing merely metres away. Instantly his thoughts weren't of Hannah. Seeing her there, grey eyes narrowed against the glare, concerned expression on her face: it was Callie who filled his senses. The weekends weren't enough, he thought abruptly. Their enforced separations were beginning to grind, badly. He missed her, damn it, during those long drawn-out weekdays. And it wasn't just the sex, he acknowledged silently. That had been an unexpected bonus. He missed *her*, as a person, warm and funny and witty and caring; he craved her bright company, her easy manner.

Soon Gaby would be gone, and Timmy would be coming to stay. His own life was changing and he couldn't allow his relationship with Callie to stagnate. He couldn't let her go, that much he knew. So what were the options? Go on as they were? Move in together? Unconsciously he shook his head at that. 'Too old-fashioned,' he muttered to himself, 'and too bloody-minded.'

So what was the alternative? Marriage?

The thought had flickered through his mind a few times but, until now, he had quickly dismissed it. Marriage was a major emotional undertaking. What if they made a mistake, like he and Gaby, but didn't find out till years down the track? He couldn't bear that kind of heartache again.

What he had told Callie, that first night they had made love, had been true. He *had* been lonely and looking for something more than just a platonic friendship. And he *did* feel something towards her.

Don't ask me to define it, simply know that it's there.

Why couldn't he say the words? What was he afraid of? Another failure? Rejection?

So, Paterson, he thought grimly. What does a man do? He was almost forty years of age. Some days he felt life was passing him by. Didn't he deserve some chance at happiness?

'Michael?'

The word interrupted his train of thought. She was watching him with a curious stare, hands in the pockets of her jeans. 'What's wrong?'

'Nothing,' he shrugged. How to explain when he wasn't certain himself?

She moved towards him, breaking the mood. As she wrapped her arms around his chest, he could feel the solid warmth of her through the fabric of his shirt. 'I'm sorry. Perhaps we shouldn't have come here. It's upsetting.'

'No. I'm fine, really.' Michael swept one hand sideways, indicating the ragged rows of headstones. 'It's just coming here, seeing all this. I guess I'm reminded how quickly my own life is passing.'

Pausing, he took a deep breath. 'I love you.'

She pulled away, staring in amazement, as though she hadn't heard him correctly. 'What did you say?'

The words had already been said, and there was no going back, whatever the outcome. 'I said *I love you.*'

Her eyes crinkled in an expression of bewilderment. 'I don't understand.'

'Marry me, Callie. We can make a life together.'

She took one further step backwards, bringing her arms across her chest as she shook her head. For a second her mouth wavered, and he wondered if she were about to cry. 'Don't do this, Michael.'

'Do what?'

She shook her head again.

'Callie! Don't you understand? *I love you.* I've just asked you to be my wife. I want to spend the rest of my life with you.'

Her voice, when it came, was soft, almost inaudible. 'I can't.'

The reaction was so unexpected that he was momentarily at a loss what to say next. Confused, he brought a hand to his forehead, resting his palm against his brow for a brief moment. 'This is crazy. We're playing word games, getting nowhere. What do you mean, *can't?*'

She turned and walked away from him, her voice muffled. 'You don't understand.'

'Try me.' He was at her side, pulling her around to face him. '*Try* me, Callie, god-damn it!'

'I'm very fond of you, Michael, truly I am.'

'I thought there was something between us. For my part, it wasn't simply meaningless sex. What about last night?'

'Please!'

As she pulled her arm from his grasp, he was suddenly aware that he had been holding her very tightly. 'I'm sorry,' he said, staring down at his own hands, which were unsteady.

She was crying, he realised, tears welling in her eyes. With a jerky movement she brushed them away, leaving spiky wet lashes resting against her skin. He had an urge to press his lips to them, but there was something about the set of her mouth, determined and unwavering, something about the way she held her rigid body, that stopped him.

'Can we talk about it?' he asked softly.

She gave him a wavering smile, but it was forced, he saw, and her face like a brittle mask. 'The last few weeks have been wonderful, Michael. Truly. But *marriage*? I'm not ready to make that kind of commitment. This is all happening too quickly. Don't let's spoil what we have.'

The disappointment was almost palpable, yet what had he thought? That she would fall willingly in with his plans? That her own feelings would mirror his? Foolishly he had already begun to organise his own life around her. Ideas for a new house, new job. Timmy coming to stay. Yet now, the weight of her rejection stinging, it all seemed unimportant, a mockery of sorts.

Fools rush in ...

He had broken his own cardinal rule.

The scene stayed with her for days. Blue sky. Soft swish of breeze through the pines that lined the cemetery fence line. The distant cawing of a crow. Michael bending over the grave, laying the flowers against the slab. Unbidden, a lump had formed in her throat, similar to the day Bonnie had told her about selling the Brunswick Street house. Even now, recalling the memory, Callie felt her eyes mist over with suppressed grief.

Her writer's mind had taken it all in, that conflicting panorama of sights and emotions. Taken it in and filed it away, to be extracted later and studied, dissected, analysed. Michael with his back to her, head bowed. What thoughts had run through his mind at that precise moment?

She had walked away, waiting under the shade of a nearby tree, leaving him to his silent contemplation, feeling as though she were intruding on something private and personal: a belated, yet spiritual, meeting between a man and the grandmother he had never known.

Then he had turned, his face a reflection of thought, and she had gone to him, holding the solid warmth of him in her arms. Through the shirt she had felt his heartbeat, steady and strong.

I love you, he had said.

Marry me.

And spoilt it all.

The horrid memories of Stuart had come flooding back, unbidden. Stuart kissing Primrose in the street, his hand moving down the curve of her back in a familiar way. That same hand, later, lashing out towards her own face. In her mind she could still hear the crack as her head flew back, could feel the stinging blow across her cheek.

Stuart standing in the lounge room of her new flat. *We could get married, start a family . . .*

It's you I want . . .

It's always been you. I love you . . .

Words. Meaningless words. Lies and pretences. She had given him two years of her life, only to have them thrust back at her, used, soiled. Wasted.

For a moment she hadn't been able to speak, her mouth and lips refusing to move. Michael had waited expectantly, smiling hesitantly.

Suddenly she had found her tongue. 'Don't do this, Michael.'

'Do what?'

The smile had faded, replaced by a frown as Callie shook her head. She had wanted to make him understand, but how could she? Her own feelings were a confused disjointed mess. Though she had known Michael for months, had been attracted to him right from that first meeting, the acceleration of their relationship had come hard on the heels of her break-up with Stuart. Her independence had been hard-won, and she was loath to surrender it.

And Michael? Had she given him the wrong indication of her feelings? Her thoughts scrambled frantically back over the times they had been together. There had been no declarations made by either of them, of that she was sure. And he'd said nothing, given no indication of the way he felt.

Another thought had occurred to her, disturbing in all its implications. She and Michael had been drawn together by the horseshoe, the letters, the old diary, and an eighty-year-old story of love and grief that had affected them all. Was he, she wondered, in some bizarre and unintentional way, trying to provide a happy ending to the story, years later?

The questions and possibilities had spun dizzily inside her head, requiring answers, to which she had none. It was all too sudden, too soon. She needed time. Time to sort out her own priorities, how she felt about Michael. In some ways they scarcely knew each other. She simply *couldn't* allow herself to be drawn into another relationship. Not yet.

'Look, just forget it,' he had said brusquely, turning his face away, and she knew she had hurt him beyond words.

The rest of the day had passed in a series of awkward silences, punctuated by strained conversation, the morning's events an unspoken barrier between them. They had tried a few hands of canasta, but Callie's heart had not been in it. Michael looked so wretched, she had finally put down her cards and gone to the study, scooping up a scrap of paper she had placed on the desk the previous day.

'I want to read you something,' she had said, coming back into the lounge room. 'It's a poem. 'Lament.' Written by a soldier, Gibson his name was, in France in 1917.'

Michael had laid his cards on the table, not looking up at her. 'Callie, I'm not really in the mood for poetry. It's been a tough day, one way or another.'

'Please, it won't take a moment.'

He had raised his face, and she had plainly seen a small furrow of tension across his brow. The thought had occurred to her that she was the cause of those lines.

Momentarily, she had closed her eyes against the sight of him, then stared at the words on the paper, unable to go on. If she spoke the words, she'd cry, she had known she would. Stand there and bawl like a baby, or like a child whose ice-cream has fallen off the cone and into the dirt.

Stop it! she had told herself sternly. Somehow she'd be strong. Somehow she had to make Michael see what was happening. To herself. To them both. Carried away by the aftermath of all that had happened, struggling to make sense of it all. The awfulness of the war. Hannah losing Ben, Nick. Secrets too long kept and only now revealed. Made more upsetting by the absolute senselessness of it all. Her own life seemed so pathetic, so … so trivial in comparison.

On a deep breath she had begun:

We who are left, how shall we look again
Happily on the sun or feel the rain,
Without remembering how they who went
Ungrudgingly, and spent
Their all for us, loved too the sun and rain?

A bird among the rain-wet lilac sings—
But we, how shall we turn to little things,
And listen to the birds and winds and streams
Made holy by their dreams,
Nor feel the heart-break in the heart of things?

Her voice had wavered on the last word, the emotion catching rawly at her throat. 'I just wanted to read it to you,' she had whispered, slipping the paper into her jeans pocket. 'It sort of summed up how I feel at the moment. Everything that's happened lately — it's all been too much, too soon. After what happened to Hannah and Ben, I can't even begin to imagine the rest of my own life.'

'Okay, so it's upsetting. And going to the cemetery today ...' He had paused and glanced down at his hands, interlacing his fingers.

'Don't you see?' she had continued, wanting him to understand the random frailty of her own mind. 'You and I, we're caught up in all of this, whether we like it or not. It's affecting our judgement. We can't complete the circle. We can't provide the happy-ever-after ending to what should have been Hannah and Ben's life together. *We're* not Hannah and Ben.'

'I never imagined we were,' Michael had replied wearily, running a hand through his hair. 'Look, it's all in the past and we have to move on. We can't put our lives on hold while we contemplate something that happened over eighty years ago. It involved my father, too. When you think about it, we've all been through so much. But no matter what's happened in the past, we have to take chances sometimes, make a grab for happiness.'

She had gone to him, kneeling on the floor by his chair and laying her head in his lap. 'I'm sorry, Michael.'

'No, I'm the one who should apologise,' he had replied brusquely, pushing the chair back and rising to his feet. He had picked up his keys and wallet from the kitchen bench and given her a perfunctory kiss on the cheek.

'Michael!' she had protested.

'No, you're right,' he had said, one hand on the front door handle as they stood, facing each other. 'The last few weeks *have* been wonderful, but we obviously had different expectations from this relationship. Forget what I said. I won't mention it again. Now, if you'll excuse me, I think I'll be off. As you can see, I'm not very good company right now.'

And he had gone, sprinting lightly down the stairs.

Callie had run to the balustrade, staring down the vortex of the stairway, seeing his tanned hand sliding along the railing as he went, finally disappearing from view as the entrance door banged shut, two floors below.

'Michael, please,' she had cried, begging him to understand, but it was too late.

Despondently she had walked inside, slamming the front door in her wake. Damn! Damn! Damn! It was their first argument and she hadn't meant the day to end like this. If only she'd been more prepared, more aware, perhaps she could have diffused the situation.

That night, Callie couldn't sleep. The scenes kept repeating themselves in her mind: Michael's declaration, her own almost-hysterical reaction. His hasty exit from her flat seemed so final, so irrevocable, and resembled something out of a bad dream.

Padding through the silent rooms, she made a cup of coffee and turned on the computer, watching as the screen slowly came to life. Oscar, disturbed by her nocturnal wandering, jumped onto her lap, purring loudly.

She sat for a while, chewing the end of a pen, a mixture of thoughts running through her mind. Michael. A man who had simply walked into their lives, her life, revealing secrets so long kept. Michael, opening his heart to her, taking her back into those other lives, Hannah's and Ben's, letting her see what it had been like during those years of the war, helping her understand.

Understand what? she thought. That she missed him unbearably when he was away? That he had turned her life around, helped ease her over the trauma of Stuart's betrayal?

And, in return, she had sent him away.

She let her mind wander, projecting itself through the months ahead. Would she be satisfied with these weekend flings, a month, a year down the track? She was almost thirty-three. The old biological clock, to use the trendy phrase, was ticking away. One day she wanted marriage, children! Was Michael the one to share that part of her life?

As she stared at the keyboard, a series of disconnected words surged through her mind. She started typing, the sentences flowing rapidly onto the screen.

Dear Michael

Yesterday, as you stood by Hannah's grave, I felt your pain, and your anger. I'm sorry if I hurt you. It wasn't intentional.

Callie paused and dabbed the back of her hand across her eyes. Silly, she admonished herself, letting her emotions get in the way. Nevertheless, it was true. She *had* felt his pain, his anger, but neither emotion was hers. She could not assume them, or assume anything that had passed between Michael and herself in the cemetery, the previous day. All she knew was her own private hurt, and the sense of finality, of wishing things undone, although that could never be.

Angry at herself, she kept at the task doggedly, then turned on the printer and typed in the appropriate commands, watching as the newly inked paper slid out the bottom of the machine. Leaning forward, tiredness overwhelming her, she re-read the words.

Dissatisfied, annoyed with herself at the waste of time, she pushed the paper away. What a load of sentimental rhetoric! The events were all in the past, long gone. So why was she letting herself get caught up in the emotive aftermath?

Because I love him.

The words rose in her mind like a phoenix flapping its mythical wings, and she closed her eyes, shutting out the sight of the paper and screen. She was simply aware of the weight of the sleeping cat on her knee, and the hot tears that threatened at the back of her lids, as the possibility snaked its way towards her.

What if she never saw him again? What if she had hurt him so badly that he never returned? The prospect manifested itself as an ache in her chest, a slow spiralling pain that made her momentarily catch her breath.

'No! I won't think about it,' she muttered furiously, screwing the paper into a tight ball and lobbing it into the wastepaper basket with an expert throw. That would never happen. Michael would come back the following weekend, as usual and, somehow, together they would work out this mess. One small argument didn't signal the end of their relationship.

Meanwhile, there was the following week to be dispensed with. Work. That was the only answer. If she pulled out all stops, she could probably transcribe most of the letters onto hard disk before the following weekend.

With a sigh she turned off the computer and went to bed.

CHAPTER 37

Never, ever, had a week passed so slowly. Michael had given notice the previous month, and there was the usual round of farewells at work. The normal loose ends had to be tied up, his office cleared out in preparation for his successor. Carrying box after box down to his car, he was surprised at the accumulation of effects, even after twenty years.

His leaving brought with it a sense of sadness, and a feeling that perhaps he had rushed into the decision. Pulling away from this comfortable close-knit community, he felt a loss that he was, at times, unable to explain. And his reason for doing so — Callie — seemed as remote as ever.

He resisted calling her. An argument over the phone was the last thing he needed. Give her time, said that old familiar voice inside. Back off!

On Wednesday evening, the chaps from the art department took him to the local pub for a meal, where he succeeded in getting himself very drunk. He barely remembered the cab ride home, and Bess greeting him at the door. Barely remembered sitting on the edge of his bed, holding the now-framed photograph of Hannah and Nick, aware suddenly of an anger building inside him. Anger at the waste of it all, the senseless grief and lives wasted. His own father. Ben. The grandmother he had never known.

For one furious moment, he wanted to smash the frame against the wall, to hear the glass shatter. And for that one brief moment, he wondered if the old ghosts should have been left undisturbed, hidden for all time. In hindsight, had he really wanted to know the secrets revealed by the diary, the letters?

But it was too late.

A phone call on Friday morning meant a sudden change of plans. Minutes later, when he had had a chance to take it all in, he rang Gaby.

'About having Tim this weekend, something's come up.'

'Oh?'

'Well, I let it be known around the traps that I was leaving the newspaper and looking for more freelance work. One of the national women's magazines is doing a feature article. Eighty years after the last Battles of the Somme and the end of the First World War in France, that sort of thing. The photographer who was supposed to be covering the story is laid up in hospital with appendicitis. So I've been offered the job.'

'That's great.'

'It's the chance of a lifetime,' he went on, barely able to conceal the excitement in his voice. 'My first commission. France. Pity about the two weeks I was going to have off. But that can wait.'

'Then it's a wonderful opportunity. When do you go?'

'The plane leaves first thing in the morning.'

'Tomorrow?'

'Like I said, it really was a last-minute change of plan.'

'How long will you be away?'

'Three weeks. But,' he cautioned, 'I'll be well and truly back before you jet off for America, and before the date for moving into the new house.'

'What does Callie think about all the changes?'

'She doesn't know!' he said abruptly. 'They were meant to be a surprise.' Then, taking a deep breath: 'Look, I've got to go. Work beckons and there are a million ends to tie up here. I'm sorry about all this. Tell Tim I'll make it up to him when I get back.'

'You'll have plenty of time to do that.' She laughed, and he could hear the warm tones echoing down the line.

All afternoon he deliberated over ringing Callie. No communication had passed between them since that last abortive meeting, and he wondered if she were expecting him for the weekend. There were, as he had just told Gaby, lots of loose ends at work that had to be attended to before he left, and a meeting with the magazine executives later this evening. He'd be lucky to get home before midnight, and there was still the packing.

Three weeks until he could see Callie again!

'Absence makes the heart grow fonder,' he muttered with a wry grimace. The time apart might be a bonus, letting them both take stock of their priorities. Yet, no sooner had the words left his lips than another phrase crowded in.

Out of sight, out of mind.

Suddenly it seemed very important to hear her voice.

Dialling her number, he listened to the repetitious buzzing, only putting the receiver down when the dial tone cut out. 'Damn and blast!' Where was she?

601

He tried again at various times, frustration mounting as the phone continually rang out. Callie was either not home or refusing to answer. Finally, after eight o'clock, with the hour rapidly approaching for the executive meeting, he turned on the computer and typed a short note. Then, rummaging in his wallet, he pulled out the crinkled business card on which Callie had added her fax number, months ago.

Stuart was sipping his third bourbon and coke for the evening when he heard the shrill ringing of the fax line. Puzzled, he ambled into the study. The machine sat on the carpet, a solitary piece of machinery, a stream of off-white paper sliding from its interior.

Who could possibly be sending him a message? The machine had been used by Callie mostly, sending letters and articles to her agent or publisher. His own paperwork was attended to at the office. There was a chopping sound from somewhere inside the machine and the paper, neatly severed, slithered onto the carpet. Curious, he bent down and retrieved it, frowning at first over the words.

Dear Callie,
I'm sorry about last weekend, the way it ended. It wasn't meant to be like that. I'm not sorry, though, for the things I said. I do love you. It wasn't something I planned. It just happened. You're warm and funny, and smart and witty, and I find you one of the most comfortable people to be around. Somehow, I thought you liked me, too.

I wanted to explain all these things to you in person. The problem is, I won't get the chance for another three weeks. A job has come up, unexpectedly, and I'll be out of the country. France! Can you believe that? How coincidental! I'll be taking photos for a feature article on the Great War, perhaps walking in Ben's footsteps.

I'll miss you like crazy, but I suppose it'll give us a chance to spend some time apart, to rationalise our own feelings. I'll be back on the ninth of next month. Qantas flight, around midday. It would be nice to see you at the airport. And if you change your mind, the offer still stands.

What offer? Quickly, Stuart scanned the last few sentences. 'Love from Michael,' he mimicked at the end. 'Love from your ever-loving precious Michael!'

'What's that?' asked Prim, emerging from the bathroom, wearing nothing but a towel. Stuart scowled. Blonde bimbo. Already she bored him. He wanted Callie back. She *was* all those things Michael had said. Interesting and fun, smart and witty. He must have been crazy to let her go. What was the old saying? The grass is always greener ... Well, in Prim's case, he had to admit the old adage had been right.

He had tried to persuade Callie to come back, all but gone down on his knees to her. Bitch! Couldn't she learn to forgive?

'Nothing,' he replied to Prim's question, slapping her a little too hard on her naked rump as she passed.

In the kitchen he screwed the paper into a ball. There was no way Callie would ever see Michael's fax. It was finally pay-back time.

'Have a nice trip, Michael!' he said with a smile, as he dropped it neatly into the bin.

Paul, the journalist who would be researching and writing the editorials to accompany Michael's photos, was waiting at the main desk in the Qantas terminal. He was a studious-looking man in his mid-twenties. Michael had seen him at a few industry functions over the years, and at the meeting the previous evening, and was on nodding acquaintance.

'Been to France before?' asked Paul conversationally as they found their seats in the aeroplane and stowed the overhead luggage.

'No.' He'd done the mandatory tripping around over the years: New Zealand, Bali, Fiji and India. He and Gaby had once spent a month trekking through Nepal. But the Continent? Somehow it had never interested him, until now. He turned towards Paul. 'You?'

Paul shook his head and pushed his glasses back along his nose. 'Nope. This is my first trip overseas. Brand new passport, I'm afraid. You've got a pretty raw recruit here.'

'Oh well, it'll be an experience for both of us,' added Michael, settling back and letting his mind turn to Callie once again.

Paul, with his nose thrust in a book of handy French phrases, didn't reply.

There was a three-hour wait at Heathrow for the connecting flight to Paris. Headache threatening, Michael took a couple of Panadol, sprawled in a seat in the waiting lounge and tried to sleep. At Charles de Gaulle airport, visas and passports were inspected. While Paul went to the money exchange counter, Michael organised a Hertz rental car and purchased a Paris road map. Then, registration documents and insurance papers in the glove box, photographic equipment and luggage in the boot, they set off.

It was agreed that Paul would take the first turn at driving while Michael navigated. Paris! It all felt so strange, so foreign, especially the custom of driving on the right-hand side of the road. Glancing through the car window, he felt an urgent need to distance himself from the frenetic pace, the hustle and bustle. He was tired, probably suffering the effects of jet lag. And, knowing he was weeks away from seeing her, already he missed Callie.

After an hour's drive, darkness approaching, Paul pulled up outside a Formula 1 motel and turned off the motor, pleading exhaustion. 'Don't know about you,' he said, 'but I'm stuffed, and tomorrow's another day.'

There was only one room available, containing two single beds. 'We'll take it,' said Michael quickly, tired beyond all reason, as the door opened behind him and a young couple entered.

Although the restaurant was closed, the manageress offered to make them a plate of sandwiches. The room was bland and characterless, but at least it afforded a hot shower. Exhausted, he collapsed into bed and slept until the first pale rays of dawn brightened the room.

After a quick shower, they were on the road, stopping a few miles further along at a roadside café for breakfast. There were croissants and hard-boiled eggs displayed on the counter, so Michael ordered several of each, along with espresso coffee. He was ravenous, and the food was surprisingly good, hot and filling. He helped himself to another coffee: while Paul studied the French guidebook he had purchased at the newsagent next door.

'So, what are the plans for today?' asked Michael, as he sipped his second cup of coffee.

Paul brought out the map of France and spread it on the table. 'At the moment we're here,' he said, pointing towards a small dot, 'heading towards the town of Albert. We'll base ourselves there for a few days. Most of the 1916 fighting happened around there. Besides the town itself, there are a whole host of tiny villages nearby to investigate.'

He went on to name several of them, but they were unfamiliar to Michael. Ben had still been in England training at that time and had not been part of those bloody battles.

'We'll be mainly photographing the old cemeteries in the area. There were originally five types. Many soldiers were buried on the battlefields where they died. These graves were emptied after the war and bodies relocated to larger cemeteries for easier maintenance. Did you know that no Australian bodies, as far as we know, remain in battlefield cemeteries on the Somme?'

Michael shook his head. 'No, I didn't.' The subject wasn't something he had researched; however, he suspected that Paul was about to set him straight on that issue.

'First there was the front-line cemetery, small usually, beside a laneway or walking track, and then there were communal village cemeteries which housed a mixture of civilian and war graves. There were also the dressing station and casualty clearing station burial grounds.'

'That's only four types, or have I lost track along the way?'

'No, you're right on the ball. The other type are the base hospital cemeteries, but we won't find any in this area. They're found further towards the coast, around Boulogne and Calais mostly, where the large hospitals were situated.'

Michael couldn't resist a friendly jibe. 'You seem to know an awful lot about a country you've never seen before.'

'I've done a mammoth amount of research. And unlike you, I've had plenty of time to prepare for this trip. I've read heaps of books.'

'I've been reading a few books myself,' said Michael quietly. 'It turns out that my grandfather served over here during the war. I have his diary back home.'

'Oh?' Paul leaned forward, interested, folding the map. 'What company?'

'11th Field Engineers. They were stationed around Armentieres and Ypres at first, then down around the lower Somme during the last battles there. He was killed towards the end of the war, near Ypres.'

Back in the car, from the autoroute there was an occasional glimpse of a cemetery or monument silhouetted against the sky. 'This is no good,' Paul frowned, slowing to take the next exit. 'We've got to get off here, take the slower country roads. We'll never see a thing at this rate.'

Albert was a red-brick town, rebuilt after the war, according to Paul, and bearing little resemblance to the original. They had lunch in a small café: *potée auvergnate* — cabbage and meat soup — and bread rolls, washed down with a bottle of crisp chablis.

'You are staying in town?' asked the waitress in halting English.

'*Oui*,' Paul nodded, practising his textbook French with a grin. 'Several nights, in fact. Can you recommend a hotel?'

'Ah,' the woman replied, smiling at Paul's clumsy attempt. 'Perhaps the Royal Picardie. You want to try our wonderful cuisine, yes? The dining room there is very good.'

After booking two rooms at the hotel, they wandered about the town, Michael taking a few rolls of film as he went. He was especially intrigued by the local church, which was topped by a golden statue of a woman.

'La Basilique of Notre-Dame de Brebières, otherwise known as Our Lady of the Ewes,' said Paul knowledgeably, while Michael prowled the perimeter of the building searching for the best photographic angles. 'See the Madonna?'

Michael slipped the camera onto the tripod, peering through the lens at the statue that seemed to be wavering against the blue sky and scudding clouds. 'She's a beauty.'

'The original was partly toppled by German shelling early in the war. French engineers temporarily secured it from falling, and a few superstitions grew up around it. The British and French believed that the war would end on the day it fell; however the Germans believed that whoever knocked down the statue would lose the war.'

'And?' Michael asked, curious.

'Well, neither proved true. The British eventually destroyed it while the town was under German occupation. And we all know who won the war.'

'Right,' said Michael, nodding. But Paul's remark was ambiguous. History had recorded an Allied victory, but was there really such a clear-cut definition between winning and losing? In a way, they had all lost. German, British and Australian, to name but a few. The flower of Aussie manhood had been decimated. Scarcely a single family had been left unscarred during those four years of bloody fighting. It was a sobering thought.

They packed up at dusk, returning to the hotel and a tasty meal. Paul chatted amiably about his wife and small son, and Michael felt a momentary pang of homesickness. Tim. Callie. The two most important people in his life, and already he missed them unbearably. How would he ever get through the next few weeks?

Afterwards, back in his room and at a loss what to do next, he switched on the television. It was a movie and the words were in French. Frustrated, he turned it off, not bothering to understand the gist of it or change channels, and picked up a magazine, abruptly flicking through the pages. Nothing of interest there.

Taking a bottle of *Kronenbourg* beer from the mini-bar, he sprawled on the bed and gazed morosely at the ceiling. Lying there, in that strange room, he felt oddly detached, even disorientated. Had it been like that for Ben, all those years ago, travelling under the threat of war, not knowing where he was going from day to day, whether he was ever going to see Hannah again and his baby son?

Michael shook his head and ran a hand through his hair. Though the trip had loomed excitingly, there was now a curious need to finish the job as quickly as possible and get home.

Callie sat staring dejectedly at the phone, listening to its muted bleat, her mind racing with a mixture of despair and pain. The prospect of hearing Michael's voice, for the first time in days, had been welcome, but there was no answer.

There had been no communication between them since the day of the visit to Hannah's grave. Several times she had telephoned, with the same result, and the weekend had come and gone, with no sign, no contact at all. Was he that upset with her? she wondered. What had she thought, that last day together, when he'd left, obviously upset, his masculine pride wounded by her refusal?

Callie paused. 'Yes,' she said aloud. 'Be truthful! Just what did you think?'

That he would come back? That they would take up where they left off, pretend the argument in the cemetery had never happened? But how could he? she reasoned. He had made that absolute declaration of love and she had taken one conclusive step away, distancing herself from her feelings, and his.

What if he didn't want to see her again?

The thought was almost too much to bear. She hadn't meant to fall in love again so soon, especially after Stuart. Hadn't meant to lose herself so completely, but there, it was done. Now it was up to her to undo the mess, extricate her emotions as cleanly and completely as possible.

Finally she replaced the receiver, further severing the already-severed contact. 'Bloody hell!' she said glumly to the cat.

By morning the mood had passed him by. Aided by several more beers and a solid night's sleep, Michael and Paul spent four days exploring the area north-west of the town.

He was kept busy taking photographs, checking the quality of the light, angles. Everywhere he looked, there were overwhelming reminders of the war. The memorial at Thiepval recorded the names of over seventy thousand men who had 'disappeared' on the Somme. Cemeteries, bearing row upon row of white headstones, were meticulously maintained by the Commonwealth War Graves Commission. Between the villages, carefully preserved, were the remains of leaf-covered concrete bunkers and deserted observation posts, shell holes, and moss-covered limbers hidden away in woods, down overgrown paths. Grassed-over trenches at Beaumont-Hamel had been preserved as a memorial, showing the world, years later, how terrible it had all been.

'While most people are familiar with the names of the villages connected with that first series of battles in 1916,' said Paul over dinner on the last night, 'everyone tends to forget about the area to the south and east of here, where the main fighting went on in 1918. In many ways it was the Allied victories there that brought about the end of the war.'

'So where are we heading next?'

'Amiens. We'll base ourselves there for a few days. Roam about the lower Somme. Isn't that where you said your grandfather was stationed during the last part of the war?'

'Yes.'

'The city itself was a fairly safe rear area during that time. There are a few interesting memorials and cemeteries. In the Cathedral of Notre Dame there's a memorial to the Australian Imperial Force.'

They arrived during the late afternoon rush hour. At last Michael felt he was in familiar territory. According to the diary, Ben had been here shortly before his death, after his return from hospital in England.

Curiously Michael glanced about the streets, trying to equate the neat orderliness with the descriptions in Ben's letters. Perhaps little had changed, he thought later, training his camera towards the skylarks winging above the cemeteries, the Roses of Picardy in full bloom, and the poppies, bright red, thrusting bobbing faces between the graves.

They parked the car near the cathedral and wandered about the old port area along the river. In an outrageously expensive gift shop, Michael bought Callie a bottle of French perfume. He couldn't help remembering that last time he had seen her, that last day. She had seemed reserved, tense, as though a barrier had come down between them, a shutter of sorts. Unintentionally his words had upset her, that much he knew, perhaps rekindled memories of other lovers and other hurts that she was not willing to repeat.

His last-minute decision to send the fax had been a wise one. Minimal intrusion, he considered wryly, giving her space while at the same time letting her share his news. At least she knew where he was, and the reason he had not made contact.

Perhaps some time apart would do them good. Let things slide for a while, allow them both to evaluate what was happening. And when he got back, after these few weeks away, maybe they could pick up where they had left off, resume that easy familiarity.

After Amiens the names of the towns were familiar to Michael, like old friends: Villers-Bretonneux, Corbie, Bonnay, Mericourt-l'Abbé — unprepossessing and rebuilt with a quiet charm. Along roadways, they unexpectedly came across cemeteries, either small collections of white crosses tucked away in the corners of fields, or vast sites containing row upon row of identical headstones constructed of Portland limestone, marking graves both known and unknown. Michael could never have imagined, not in a million years, the sadness it brought, the despair at the waste of life and the utter senselessness of it all.

He and Paul joined a few tours but his heart was not in that kind of structured information. Instead he let the group wander ahead, happy to absorb the atmosphere by himself. His presence there was like a pilgrimage of sorts, a way of acknowledging what had happened then and since. The hours and days blurred into dozens of rolls of film, the details of each shot meticulously recorded in his notebook.

Where possible they followed the river Somme. Sunlight reflected from its surface, a thousand mirror images; it was lost to view occasionally, until they rounded a bend in the road and there it was again, spread out below.

The countryside itself had changed. Here it was more open, quiet, dotted with fewer small villages and towns, cut by the north-south motorway. There were no mine craters or preserved trenches. Michael knew from Ben's diary that the fighting here had been on a grander scale, attacks made in wide sweeps, mostly not from the confines of trenches.

'It's hard to imagine what went on here,' said Paul as they pulled to the verge of the road on the outskirts of one of the villages. Fields of barley grew where once there had been tangles of barbed wire. Birds twittered in the trees overhead. On a far rise, several cattle grazed, their heads lowered to the sweet-smelling grass. 'The countryside almost exudes a sense of peace. I didn't expect that.'

'What *did* you expect, then?'

'I don't really know. A sense of something terrible happening, I guess, some sort of bad vibes. But there are none. Or if there are, I'm quite impervious to them.'

Piles of shells were neatly stacked at the edges of fields, waiting for collection by the military authorities. 'Even after all this time, farmers are forever digging them up,' commented Paul. 'They call it the 'Iron Harvest'.'

To prove his point, he stopped the car and they ferreted around in the soil at the edge of a nearby paddock until Michael found the remains of two .303 bullets and several round shrapnel balls.

At Heilly, Michael spent several reflective minutes beside Tom's grave, remembering the photograph Bonnie had shown him of the young soldier with a ready smile. He took several photos of the headstone, planning to give them to Callie for her book.

Mericourt-l'Abbé. The 3rd Australian Division Memorial at Sailly-le-Sec. Curlu. The Australian Digger Memorial outside Bullencourt. Peronne. Towns and villages, memorials and cemeteries blurring into one another, merging the past with the present. In Peronne he spent hours in the Historical de la Grande Guerre, photographing the uniforms, equipment and weapons, before leaving by the N17, climbing up to Mont-St-Quentin to see the Memorial of the 2nd Australian Division — a bronze digger mounted on a square plinth.

They crossed the Somme and wound their way back through the southernmost villages, heading towards Villers-Bretonneux. There, high on a hill north of the village, reached via the D23 road to Corbie, stood the Australian National Memorial on a large grassed area at the rear of the Villers-Bretonneux Military Cemetery.

Sombrely Michael climbed the memorial tower, amazed by the view. To the north lay the valley of the Somme. Westwards, across cleared fields, sprawled the city of Amiens, denoted by the spire of the cathedral. Even now, eighty years later, the zigzag outline of the old German trenches could still be seen in the tilled fields below, the white chalk discolouring the brown soil.

Everywhere he looked, he was faced with reminders of the past. Road signs pointing to cemeteries, museums, study centres. The soil still yielding up bullets. Only now that he was here could he visualise the enormity of it all. Tanks clanking across the ground, sweeps of armies advancing, waves of men thronging eastwards. And, in the middle of it all, Ben and Callie tangled oddly in his mind.

In reflective moments, he acknowledged the journey had been like a catharsis of sorts. It had taken him from the immediacy of her, given him time to think, to put the separate compartments of his life into proper perspective. He and Gaby were finished. There was never going to be anything between them, other than friendship and the mutual concerns for Timmy. He had spent enough time grieving over the end of his marriage. It was time to move on.

And Callie?

Through it all, past the stirring of memories and recollections from the diary — the knowledge that Ben had been here — walked these same paths, Michael's thoughts were never far from her. Relaxing in a coffee shop in a small village square, drinking *café au lait*, he caught himself thinking, Callie would love it here. But she was thousands of miles away, on the other side of the world. And sitting there, cradling the mug in his palms, scarcely aware of the aroma of roasting coffee, fresh bread and cakes, he was aware of only one thing. He missed her unbearably.

CHAPTER 38

It rained through the night, heavy falls that splattered against the closed windows. Dawn was grey, the ocean too — to match her mood, Callie thought, as she stared out the lounge room window at the sodden pines and wet stretch of sand below. Not even the diehard surfers were lined up in the water off the point.

After a snatched piece of toast and coffee at the kitchen bench, she turned the computer on and worked solidly for a couple of hours, until the ringing of the phone roused her from her task.

It was Bonnie. 'Just thought I'd give you a quick ring, love,' she said. 'Have you heard from Michael?'

'No.'

It was two weeks since she had seen him and a gnawing doubt had begun manifesting itself. Perhaps something was wrong? Maybe he was ill, in hospital? But Timmy would have let her know, surely.

They chatted on, discussing, for the umpteenth time, the looming move from the house in Brunswick Street. Afterwards, her writing interrupted, she threw caution to the wind and rang Michael's newspaper.

'I'm sorry, he doesn't work here any more,' said the anonymous voice on the end of the line.

'Are you sure?' asked Callie incredulously. Michael had been with the firm for twenty years and had said nothing about leaving.

'Look,' said the woman on the other end of the line. 'I'm only new here and I didn't know him all that well. But I think someone said something about him going overseas. France, I think. If you'd like to hold, I can ask.'

'No!'

Overseas! And he hadn't even let her know! For a moment she was speechless, hurt beyond words. 'I love you,' he had said, yet he hadn't even given her the courtesy of a phone call, just one, to tell her his plans. Obviously, she thought with a bitterness that surprised her, he had changed his mind, reassessed his own feelings.

Somehow, during the days that followed, Callie managed to lose herself in work, sitting at the computer, transcribing the contents of the diary. Periodically hunger drove her to the kitchen, and even when her eyes began to blur with tiredness, she still pushed on. She spent a weekend at the house in Brunswick Street, helping Bonnie pack the last of the books and knick-knacks in the living room. And after several hair-raising trips up and down the rickety ladder, most of the personal belongings were taken from the space under the roof.

Daily her emotions seesawed between missing Michael unbearably and promising herself, with quiet resolve, to sever all feelings. Vast swings of sentiment brought her to a standstill at odd moments, as she tried to fathom what she really felt. Had the relationship begun on the rebound from her break-up with Stuart? Had their common interest in the diary and letters led automatically to something more? Were they unconsciously acting out some modern-day replica of Ben's and Hannah's relationship?

'It was only a fling,' she told Jill morosely.

'Then why do you look so god-damned terrible?' Jill raised her eyebrows. 'You look like you haven't slept or eaten in a week. Come on, Cal. You can't fool me.'

Briefly she explained the chain of events leading to that last day. 'He asked you to *marry* him?' asked Jill, incredulously. 'And you said no?'

'He went overseas. He didn't even bother to tell me,' Callie went on. 'So what do you think of that?'

Jill shrugged. 'Beats me. Have you ever thought there might be a logical explanation to all this? Perhaps he tried to ring, let you know.'

'If he'd tried to telephone, then I'd know, wouldn't I?' replied Callie quietly. 'Anyway, that's not the real issue. It's not the explanation that bothers me, it's the lack of trust. *My* lack of trust. It's all *me*, Jill. Sometimes I lie awake at night and all I see is Stuart walking down the road with his hand on that woman's bum. I can't go on like this, feeling like a suspicious old shrew. And if I can't trust Michael, then it's not much of a relationship.'

'If you'll excuse my prying, exactly what *sort* of a relationship are we talking about here?'

Miserably Callie turned away, swallowing hard. 'I don't know,' she shrugged. 'For the past few weeks it seemed almost perfect.'

'Perfect!' snorted Jill. 'You stand there and tell me you have —'

'Had!' interrupted Callie.

'*Have*,' corrected Jill, 'a perfect relationship and you're going to throw it all away because of some imagined comparison between Michael and that slimy creep, Stuart!'

Callie compressed her lips. 'It's not that simple.'

'So you're going to punish yourself, and you're also going to punish Michael. You're going to deny any involvement with this man, with whom you say you *had* a perfect relationship, because of something Stuart did?'

'I just don't think I was ready for this so soon. Rebound romances are usually doomed,' she replied gloomily.

Jill threw Callie a scornful glance. 'Bullshit! This was no rebound romance. You and Michael have known each other for months. You've been attracted to him since the first day you met. Stop making excuses. Admit that you're exercising a little self-preservation instead. *Don't get involved, so you can't get hurt*, is that it?'

'It's too late for that.'

Jill sighed and raised her hands in defeat. 'God, Callie. I thought writers were supposed to be sensitive, astute, intelligent people.'

'Meaning?'

'Meaning the truth is staring you in the face, but you're blind to it. You're overreacting to something that has absolutely no bearing on this at all. Michael and Stuart are two totally different men.'

'Look, it's over! Finished! I don't need the hassle of previously married men, complete with emotional baggage. I don't need ex-wives and children, and I certainly don't need you to make me feel worse than I already do!'

'Emotional baggage? From what you've told me, and the one time I met him, Michael seems to be the most together male I've met in a long time.'

'Well, perhaps it's me carrying the emotional baggage. Either way, I just don't need to be involved right now. Not with Michael! Not with anyone!'

After Jill had gone, Callie took the photograph from the dresser. She had taken it on the island, during those few perfect days. Michael had been studying a brochure by the pool as she advanced along the path with the camera. 'Smile,' she'd said, and he had glanced up, grinning at the sound of her voice, as the shutter clicked.

Unblinking, she stared hard at the features — sandy hair, curved mouth, eyes crinkled against the sun. She almost said it then, those three words: I love you. Almost voiced them aloud, unable to contain them any longer. But she checked herself, remembering her resolve. It was Stuart. He'd turned her life upside down and there was no way she'd let Michael do the same.

'I am an independent woman. I will not let him hurt me,' she steadfastly told herself later, studying her reflection in the bathroom mirror.

Grey eyes stared back at her, and a face that was paler than usual. Her hair needed a decent trim so, wanting a pep-up, she bypassed the computer and took herself off to the hairdresser in High Street.

They had three spare days before flying out again, and Paul suggested a quick run up to the Belgian border and into Ypres. 'It's called Ieper now,' he explained. 'Quite a few of the Belgian towns have had fairly recent name changes. I thought you might like to have a look around the area where your grandfather was killed. Then we can make arrangements to fly out from Brussels, instead of taking the car back into Paris.'

'That'd be great. I'd love to see the place.'

'Do you know where he's buried?'

Michael shook his head. 'Somewhere near Zillebeke, according to the official documentation, though the actual grave site is unknown.'

They headed north on the A1 autoroute, detouring at Lille and continuing west to Armentières. Laughing, they sang 'Mademoiselle from Armentières', very loudly and decidedly out of tune. On the outskirts they had to wait at the level crossing for a train to pass, then took the D22 through the main part of town along the rue de Béthune, past the new residential areas. It was a red-brick town, mainly rebuilt since the Great War and once famous for its linen, according to Paul, who read snippets of information from his tour guide as Michael manoeuvred the car along the streets in what he hoped was the right direction.

They took the back roads, enjoying the scenery and the slow pace. At Le Bizet they crossed the border into Belgium, stopping to show their passports and adjust their watches. Then came the trail of familiar-sounding villages again. Ploegsteert, where both Spud and Will had met their end, Neuve-Eglise and Kemmel.

After Kemmel there were views of wooded slopes, before the hilly land began to flatten out. Clumps of poppies grew along the roadside, interspersed with patches of yellow charlock and white chamomile.

In Flanders Fields the poppies grow
Between the crosses, row on row,
That mark our place, and in the sky
The larks, still bravely singing, fly
Scarce heard amid the guns below.

'In Flanders Fields,' written by the Canadian doctor John McCrae, who himself had died during the war. A doctor so moved by the sight of poppies growing amongst the graves that he had penned those most poignant words in the spring of 1915. How long since Michael had heard them? Five years? Ten? He wasn't sure. Yet they had stayed, firmly entrenched in some dark recess of his mind, easily remembered.

'Flanders' fields,' said Paul reflectively. 'Can you imagine fighting here? No hiding places, just flat barren land. No wonder they had to exist in trenches during the war.'

Over a dry canal and through the crossroads at Kruistraathoek they went, into Ypres via Lille Gate, past the military barracks.

After booking into the Regina in the Grote Markt, the main central marketplace, Paul and Michael ate lunch in one of the nearby cafés: crusty *baguettes* with ham and cheese, washed down with a couple of glasses of red wine. Then, feeling more like an afternoon siesta, they wandered about the main part of the town.

623

The most impressive building was the Cloth Hall, a rebuilt replica of the original which had been destroyed during the war. It housed the offices of the burgomaster and his staff, a tourist office, council chamber or *Raadszaal*, and the Salient 1914–1918 War Museum.

Michael spent several hours in the museum, Paul opting to wander about the marketplace, insisting that, despite his interest in the war, if he saw the inside of another museum he wouldn't be liable for the consequences. 'After the past couple of weeks, I'm all historied out. It's been pretty full on. You don't mind, do you?' he added.

'Of course not.' Ben's visits to Ypres had been well documented in the diary, and Michael was keen to see photographs of the place as it had been then. 'I'll see you back at the hotel later.'

There were displays of equipment, weapons and uniforms of all armies, both allied and enemy, badges and posters. Maps and photographs of old Ypres showed in graphic detail how the town had deteriorated under the ravages of war, highlighting the suffering not only of the soldiers, but of the civilians as well.

Michael paused in front of one photograph in particular for several minutes. In the foreground, a column of Australian infantry marched past a solitary street lamp, though there was no sign that a road had ever existed alongside. Piles of debris and rubble littered what must have been part of the original roadway, while a group of covered wagons waited behind the line of soldiers. In the background loomed a ruined shell which he barely recognised as the tower and perimeter walls of the Cloth Hall, the huge archways framing a grey sky.

How could it be, he wondered, that the town had been rebuilt, like the mythical phoenix rising from the ashes, after such complete and total devastation? What had motivated these people to start again?

He was lost in thought when a figure appeared at his elbow, startling him. It was one of the attendants. 'I am sorry, sir,' the woman said apologetically. 'It is five-thirty, and we are closing now. You could come back in the morning.'

'No, no thank you,' said Michael, stepping back. 'I think I have seen enough. Good day.'

Suddenly he was out on the pavement, blinking in the sunshine, surprised to see that the streets were still crowded and life was going on as normal.

Callie was surprised to find Stuart waiting on the front steps of the flats when she returned from the hairdresser. 'Thought you were never coming home,' he said with a smile as he took the stairs in front of her, two at a time.

He seemed in an uncharacteristically good mood, taking the key from her and holding open the front door.

'What do you want?' she asked, dumping her bag on the kitchen bench, aware of the ungracious tone of her voice, but having little control over it. These days Stuart seemed to bring out the worst in her.

'Nothing much,' he replied airily. 'Just popped over to see how you're getting on.'

'Well, as you can see, I'm getting on with my life,

getting on with my career. In short, I'm *getting on* just fine.'

'And how's the big romance?' Stuart went on, ignoring her last comment, a saccharin tone to his voice. 'Just how are you *getting on* with Michael?'

'It's none of your business!'

He stepped back, his eyes raking over her, an amused indulgent leer turning the corners of his mouth upwards. 'Touchy! Touchy! Don't tell me the two of you have had a falling out?'

'I don't know what you mean! And if you're quite finished with whatever you came here for, which obviously isn't much, then you can leave.'

She walked grimly towards the door, pointedly holding it open, as she tapped the heel of her shoe against the tiles.

'Okay, okay, I'm going,' he agreed, holding his hands up in a gesture of surrender. 'My attempts at friendship are obviously wasted here. Don't say I didn't try, though, to keep it all amicable and nice.'

'Nice!' snorted Callie, too incensed to reply further.

Stuart moved past her into the hallway, leaving a trail of expensive aftershave in his wake. At the last minute he turned, leaning lazily against the stair rail. 'Oh, by the way. That old fax machine you left behind. I put it out with a box of things for the Salvos. You didn't want it, did you?'

Callie replied by slamming the door.

The following afternoon they were due to fly out from Brussels, and plans for their last day were made over a simple breakfast of croissants and strong black coffee.

'I've kept the best till last,' offered Paul, smiling mysteriously.

'Such as?'

'Well, you said your grandfather was killed near here. If he has no known grave, then by rights his name should be recorded at the Menin Gate Memorial. The building with the huge archway we can see from our rooms,' he added, in answer to Michael's puzzled expression.

Although the memorial was only a short walk east from the hotel, Michael's photographic equipment meant taking the car. Curious now, he loaded the camera gear into the boot, thinking that Paul's new piece of information was a bonus, indeed. It had been playing on his mind during these last few days: the fact that he had come all this way, yet there was nowhere he could pay his respects to the grandfather he had never met.

They parked the car and Michael unloaded his equipment, carrying it under the cover of the archway that spanned the road. On the top of the southern arch of the gate, a stone lion watched over the traffic along the Menin Road which, he knew from studying the local maps, led towards Hooges and Polygon Wood. Underneath the lion was the inscription, 'To the armies of the British Empire who stood here from 1914–1918 and to those of their dead who have no known grave'.

'Pretty impressive, eh?' said Paul, standing back and folding his arms, a bemused expression on his face. 'Just the sheer size of this place is amazing.'

Michael took several steps forward, noting the Portland stone panels that lined the arches of the gate, the sides of the staircases and the walls of the enclosed loggias. A closer inspection revealed names of soldiers, listed firstly under their National force, then the appropriate unit.

'So, you think my grandfather's name will be here?'

'In theory, yes. This memorial was built to the soldiers whose bodies still lie on the old battlefields around here.'

That information digested, Michael left Paul to mind the equipment and jot a few notes, while he scoured the walls, eventually finding the Australian data on several separate panels. Slowly he traced his way around until he came to the appropriate company: 11ᵗʰ Field Company Australian Engineers. Following the names, he found Ben's easily.

B. H. Galbraith.

Dark lettering juxtapositioned against pale beige stone.

He stopped in sudden awe, his breath catching in his throat, surprised at his own calm. What had he expected to feel? Sadness? Anger at all the needless deaths, the suffering, the pain that those names depicted? A sense of helplessness?

He thought about Ben's body, resting in its lonely grave, somewhere along the side of an old road. A body buried in mud that had long since dried, cracked, pulled away from the soft flesh. It could have been easy for the French and Belgians, he thought as he stepped back, lowering his head, to forget the men who had paid the supreme sacrifice and given their lives. Hadn't they wanted, after the war, to wipe all traces of it from their daily existences? But someone had cared enough to record the names here, and in hundreds of other memorials and graveyards across the countryside.

Slowly Michael raised his hand, tracing the tips of his fingers over the etched characters, and the stone felt cool and smooth beneath his touch. 'Thank you,' he whispered.

Noting the spot, he hurried back to tell Paul. Then he set up one of the cameras and spent an hour or so taking photographs. He had several good ones that he thought might be useful for Callie's book. A few close-ups of Ben's name plaque, shots of the staircases and loggias.

'That'll do for today,' Paul said, tucking his notebook back into his pocket and turning towards Michael. 'It's lunchtime and I'm starving. Ready to go?'

Michael lowered his camera and glanced at his watch, surprised to see that it was after midday. 'Just a few more minutes. I want to get a couple of long-distance shots. If I pace back a few hundred metres along the road, I'll get a good wide-angled view of the memorial itself.'

'Okay,' said Paul, gathering up one of Michael's equipment bags and a tripod. 'I'll get this lot loaded. See you back at the car, then?'

For some unknown reason, his appetite had deserted him. Over a *Pils* beer, bread, sausage and cheese in a nearby café, Michael thought about his departure the next day, and all the changes waiting to happen in his life. Gaby going overseas for the next year. Timmy coming to live with him. Moving. He hadn't said anything to Callie. Perhaps he should have, he considered in retrospect. Perhaps if she had known how totally he had planned his life around her ...

'Stop it, Paterson,' he muttered. What was done, was done, and there was no going back. Callie or not, he had already decided it was time to move on, change his life's patterns.

After lunch, he wandered along the Grote Markt, finding himself eventually at the window of a jewellery shop. Pausing, he went inside and asked the assistant about the availability of gold charms.

'What sort of charms?' she asked in halting English. 'We have several kinds.'

She brought a tray from one of the display cases. There, nestled against a bed of felt, were several dozen, all shiny gold. One design in particular caught his eye: a small horseshoe.

'That one,' he said, pointing to it. 'Do you have any more?'

There were six in total, brought from surplus stock at the back of the shop. Next he asked to see the selection of bracelets, finally choosing one that was outrageously expensive, though simple in design.

'I need them fitted this afternoon. Can you arrange that?'

'That will not be a problem. Come back in one hour and the bracelet will be ready.'

While the charms were soldered onto the bracelet, he cooled his heels by shouting himself to another beer at the café and flicking through a local newspaper. Then, after he had collected the finished article, neatly gift-wrapped at his instruction, he went back to the hotel to pack his suitcase, in readiness for their early start in the morning.

Later, lying on the bed and staring at the ceiling, he felt unsettled. Thinking about seeing Callie again and giving her the bracelet made him suddenly edgy. The purchase had been impulsive, a peace offering. But what if she refused to accept it?

Restless, he slid from the bed and knocked on the connecting door to Paul's room. 'I'm going back to the memorial. I wouldn't mind some sunset shots, and the light will be about right in a few minutes.'

'Mind if I don't come?' asked Paul, who had settled in front of the television with a can of beer.

'Of course not.' Wanting suddenly to be by himself, Michael felt a sense of relief. 'I'll be back in an hour or so, and we'll go out for dinner. Our last night. We've got some celebrating to do.'

Under a slowly darkening sky, the exterior of the memorial was floodlit, the lights turning the stone to butter-gold. Michael parked the car and sat behind the wheel for a few minutes, taking in the size of the structure and the enormity of all it stood for. According to Paul it bore the names of fifty-four thousand men whose remains lay scattered around the countryside in nameless graves, and over six thousand of them were Australian. He tried to imagine that number of men, tried to picture them crammed into an auditorium or hall, and was overwhelmed by the thought.

He suddenly felt loath to take the photographic equipment from the vehicle. Somehow it didn't seem necessary. Instead he locked the car doors and crossed the road, walking back under the enormous archway to the place where he had found Ben's name earlier in the day.

There was a seat there, a rough wooden bench, and he sat, staring up reflectively at the plaques. A wreath lay against the bottom row of names. Michael was certain it had not been there earlier. He would have noticed it. *I* should have brought flowers, too, he thought, silently berating himself. How could he come all this way and not bring *something*? But it was too late. The florists would have all closed.

Drawing his gaze upwards from the wreath, he was suddenly aware of an old man limping towards him, dragging one leg painfully behind. He was wearing a cap and a scarf. A Frenchman or a Belgian, no doubt, thought Michael as, with difficulty, the man lowered himself onto the opposite end of the seat.

'Good evening.' Michael met his gaze and smiled.

'You are Australian?' the man replied in a ragged voice, heavily accented.

'Yes.'

The old man glanced away for a moment and, when he looked back, Michael could see his eyes were bright with tears. 'You Australians helped save our county, yes?'

'Yes,' Michael replied simply.

'I was too young for that war. But my older brother, he's out there somewhere ...' He paused for a moment, then smiled. 'They have a saying at Menin Gate: "He is not dead, he is not missing. He is here".'

'It's a comforting thought.'

'You are paying your respects to someone?'

'My grandfather. He was killed near here towards the end of the war. I found his name up there today.'

'It feels strange to be in this place, yes?'

'Very strange,' answered Michael slowly.

Gnarled fingers reached out, grasping Michael's hand. 'Do not feel that way. There are no strangers here, only friends. Your family's blood is mixed with our soil. You are one of us.'

Simple words, for which Michael had no answer. As the old man withdrew his fingers, he stared down at his hands, surprised to find them shaking. When he looked up again, the old man had risen and was ambling away.

It was dark now. As he returned to the car, he noticed it had been raining, a light shower that had been and gone while he was inside, and the golden glow of the stone monument was reflected in the pools of water lying along the pavement.

Settling himself in the car, he wound the window down, letting in the rain-fresh air. As he started the engine, he glanced at his watch. Eight o'clock. Time to collect Paul and go out somewhere for dinner.

He had just pulled away from the footpath and was heading towards the archway that straddled the road when a policeman stepped from the curb, holding his hand out to indicate that Michael should stop. His first thought was that he had broken some rule. Had he put his indicator on? He couldn't possibly have been speeding, not in that short distance.

But the policeman stepped aside as two men descended the steps of the memorial. They were dressed identically in some kind of dark uniform, complete with brass buttons that caught the light, hats and white gloves. As they came to the centre of the road, they faced the main section of town and brought something metallic to their lips.

They were bugles, Michael realised, hearing the first strains of the 'Last Post'. Notes rising and falling, caressing the loggias and stairwells of the monument, floating out into the night air. Notes bringing a sense of sadness mixed with hope, glory and jubilation. Notes dying away on the breeze, melting into that dark infinite space above.

He sat, mesmerised, each pure desolate sound bringing with it exquisite pain. It rose inside him, beating its way across his chest, swamping him with its weight. Ben! he thought, with sudden realisation. In a sense Ben *was* here, not buried away beside some forgotten roadway, but remembered and revered by all who came to this place, by the men who raised the bugles to their lips and played the songs, gathering old ghosts.

Too soon it was over. Their performance finished, the buglers slowly ascended the stairs and disappeared into the interior of the monument. Michael glanced in the rear-vision mirror. There was no-one else about, simply his own solitary car parked in the centre of the roadway. Of the policeman there was no sign.

It seemed the presentation had been for him, and him alone. An individual farewell, a goodbye of sorts. A special moment, one that might happen once in a lifetime, when he sensed his past and future merging, becoming one. Ben and Hannah, the child they had lost: his own father. Tom and all the others who had died, buried in that foreign soil.

He is not missing. He is here.

Ben — a victim of the war, in the worst possible way. But now, being here, feeling that sense of ... belonging, Ben was no longer some smudged writing in a diary or simply a name on a wall. Not a ghostly spectre or decaying bones, but part of him, his own flesh and blood. He thought of his son, Timmy, sashaying off into the future, carrying genes from all of them. Hannah and Ben, Nick, himself and Gaby. A continuation of sorts. Ben's death was not an end, but part of a new beginning, leading them all forward, not back.

The knowledge brought with it wave after wave of engulfing heartache. Bittersweet anguish, newly discovered, blotting out his own miseries and indecisions. An anguish that he almost welcomed, which brought an accompanying sense of release, and realisation. All that had happened in the previous six months had been for a reason, leading him from an uncertain past.

It was then, knowing what he wanted the future to hold, for himself and Callie, balanced against the futility of all that had happened during those terrible far-off years, that he laid his head against the steering wheel and wept.

CHAPTER 39

Callie called in at the Brunswick Street house, helping to pack the remainder of Bonnie and Freya's belongings. As promised, Bonnie had passed on several boxes of kitchen utensils that were no longer needed, and the small removalist van was booked for seven o'clock on Friday morning.

They had all gone over to the new townhouse, in the Vauxhall at Bonnie's insistence, and organised the telephone connection and a dozen or so other trivial matters that Callie was certain could have waited until they moved. She was impatient lately, lacking tolerance. It was all to do with Michael, she acknowledged privately; his absence swung her from one extreme mood to another.

The book was progressing well. By Thursday, the diary entries had all been typed into the appropriate computer files, and she was a good way through the letters. From time to time she stopped and stared impatiently at the telephone, willing it to make a sound, any sound, but it remained obstinately silent. Every day she was certain it would ring, telling her of Michael's whereabouts.

But the awaited phone call never came.

Turning off the computer, Callie paced up and down, past the large lounge room window, oblivious to the view, before coming to an abrupt halt. 'Stop it!' she told herself angrily. 'It's over, remember?'

No matter how many times she said them, she knew the words were not true. How could she wipe the past few weeks with a few well-chosen phrases? What had Jill said? *Don't get involved, so you can't get hurt.* That was pretty much how Callie saw it, too. Self-preservation, the need to close off her emotions, not leaving herself vulnerable.

Teatime came and went, and she nibbled on a sandwich, her appetite non-existent. Later, walking into the bedroom, her attention was caught by Hannah's painting of the wattles hanging on the wall above the bed. It was there, below that framed watercolour, that she and Michael had first made love. Remembering that sense of wild abandonment, she felt the pain of grief. Was it all for nothing? She had driven him away. Why? Why? Why?

The painting, she thought reflectively, staring hard at its muted colours through a wash of sudden tears, had come to symbolise the tragic losses they had all endured. And under those bright daubs of yellow paint, the flowers had assumed a pathetic air of sadness, mirroring her own despair. Michael was gone, along with the house in Brunswick Street. She was losing control of all that was comfortable and familiar in her life.

It was almost midnight before the plane landed, after an agonising twelve-hour delay in Singapore. Exhausted, Michael staggered through customs.

Paul's wife, Linda, was waiting outside. She threw her arms around her husband and kissed him soundly, which only served to highlight Michael's own sense of abandonment. He was acutely aware that Callie was not there to meet him. *It would be nice to see you at the airport*, he had written in the fax. Despite the plane's delay, she could have easily checked the airline's schedule. One phone call, he thought morosely.

He was scarcely able to stay awake during the taxi-ride across the city. Wearily he lugged the suitcase and camera equipment inside, leaving them in a pile in the centre of the lounge room, as he stumbled under a hot shower.

Never, ever, had he felt so jet-lagged. Back in the bedroom, towel wrapped around his waist, he glanced at the luminous face of the bedside clock. Two a.m. He should ring Callie, let her know he was safely home, but she would be sound asleep by now. Besides, in his exhausted state, his conversation was likely to make little sense. Better to leave it until the morning. His first priority now was sleep, blessed sleep. The following day was shaping up to be a long one.

He was woken by the shrilling of the phone. Groggily he fumbled at the receiver, bringing it to his ear. It was his solicitor. 'Thank God you're back. I need you down here first thing this morning to finalise a couple of signatures.'

'Mmmm.'

'You were supposed to call me yesterday afternoon. You haven't forgotten that the house sale is going through today. I need those signatures now.'

'Oh, shit!' Michael exclaimed, sitting abruptly upright and bringing his watch close to his face.

Nine-fifteen. Hell! 'The wretched plane was delayed last night and I've slept in. Give me half an hour.'

'Cutting things a bit fine. See you in a while, then.'

Callie was at the Brunswick Street house by the time the furniture removalist arrived. She watched morosely as the men carried the boxes down the front path, depositing them in the confines of the truck. After they had gone, unable to bear the silence in the house, she took the Suzuki and headed north.

In low spirits, she turned off the highway after a few kilometres and guided the car through the cane fields, towards the water. It was the place Michael had brought her to before, with Timmy. Fishing boats tied up alongside the rickety wharf. The small shed with a sign 'BOATS FOR HIRE'. Two pelicans bobbing on the choppy waves that lapped at the shoreline.

Sitting in the car, watching, the memories rushed back. Determinedly she brushed them away and opened the door, her senses assailed by the tang of salt air. A stiff breeze was blowing, whipping up small white caps further out. She ambled down to the water's edge, the sand damp between her toes. It was late April, well into autumn, and the wind was cold against her face. Seagulls wheeled overhead, diving at random into the blue water.

Head down, hands pushed deep into the pockets of her jeans, she made her way along the beach. It's over, she thought bleakly, wondering how she could bear the thought. Michael had left his job and gone away, and he hadn't even bothered to let her know.

It had all been her fault, she concluded, angry with herself. If only she hadn't reacted so badly to his offer of marriage. If only she had been able to talk about it, be open.

But she hadn't, and Michael had gone.

She had come to the end of the beach. Ahead lay a rocky bluff, impassable. Slowly she turned in the direction from which she had come. In the distance, the hills to the west were a haze of blue-grey. Her little car sat forlornly in the far-off car park, a blue speck. It was time to go home, get on with the rest of her life. Somehow, things would go on. It wouldn't, simply couldn't, get any worse than this.

It was eleven o'clock by the time Michael emerged from the solicitor's, scrambled back into the car and threaded his way through the traffic. Coming back, looking constantly at his watch, he was impatient to be out on the highway. He would turn the radio up loud, pretend he was twenty-something. Then he grinned at the absurdity of it all. Here he was, almost forty yet, whenever he thought of Callie, he felt like a teenager again. She had that sort of effect on him.

Suddenly the traffic ahead ground to a halt. There had been a minor accident, a car running into the bumper of another at low speed. Nothing serious, but enough to block the road for a further twenty minutes until the police arrived and moved the vehicles. Jammed in from behind, Michael thrummed his fingers against the steering wheel in annoyance.

Why was it, when things were at their lowest, she couldn't face going back to the flat? Instead, Callie found herself pulling up in Brunswick Street for the second time that day.

Bonnie stood at the front of the house, hosing down the path. 'Hi, Mum.' Callie gave her mother a kiss on the cheek. 'Where's Freya?'

'Over at the new place, starting on the unpacking. I suppose I should be there, too, helping, but I had promised to stay and hand over the keys when the new owner arrived. In a funny kind of way, I suppose it's just a means of delaying that final moment of leaving.'

Incapable of answering, Callie wandered inside. The rooms smelt of beeswax and camphor and, devoid of the usual knick-knacks, seemed rather bare. There was a hollow, echoing sound to her footfalls. In the living room, she ran her finger lightly over the writing desk that had once belonged to her grandfather, a feeling of absolute grief welling up inside. Why had she come back this last time? She should have stayed away, letting Bonnie attend to the last final details. Why was she torturing herself like this?

A car pulled up in the street outside. A door slammed and there was the muffled sound of voices. Bonnie and some unknown male. The new owner obviously. Oh, hell! She didn't want to be a witness to this, watching as strangers took over all that was familiar and comfortable to her.

She fled into the yard, striding purposely towards the back fence. Tears blurred the colours of the garden to a faded wash. How could she bear to leave? There was so much history in this house, history she had only recently discovered. Hannah's and Tom's. David's. Even Ben's. Old ghosts that refused to die.

The voices came closer, invading her own private space. Go away, she wanted to call out. She didn't want to meet the new owners. How could she, wanting so badly to keep the house herself?

'Callie?' Her mother's voice.

There was, it seemed, no escape. Halfway down the yard, she rubbed a hand across her eyes, ineffectually wiping at the tears as she glanced up towards the rear of the house. 'Yes, Mum. I'm down here,' she answered resignedly.

Bonnie was standing at the back door, at the top of the steps. 'Someone to see you, love,' she said. Even from that distance, Callie could see her smile.

As Bonnie turned and walked inside, a tall shape loomed beside her. It was Michael, she thought with surprise. What was he doing here?

Heartsick, she turned away and continued walking towards the rear fence. The roses nodded to her as she passed, heads bobbing in the breeze behind neat ordered rows of agapanthus and lilies. There were hydrangeas and cyclamen, clumps of alyssum with tiny white flowers: quaint old-fashioned flowers of her childhood. As she bent down to pick a flower, a damp moist smell, of blood-and-bone, manure and moss, rose up to meet her.

It was then she turned and looked back at Michael waiting uncertainly on the step. 'Callie,' he called as he bounded towards her with long, loping strides. He was smiling, an infuriating mysterious twitching of the corners of his mouth that he was obviously fighting to control. For herself, Callie could see nothing to smile about.

'Come to say goodbye?'

She hoped her voice sounded casual. Inside her chest, a dozen drums banged in union. She could hardly breathe. Oh, God! She wiped a hand across her face, trying to blot out the sight of him. Please get it over with quickly, she prayed.

'No.' A brief expression of bewilderment creased his brow, then smoothed. 'Yesterday's flight didn't get in until almost midnight. I know I did ask you to meet me, but we were delayed at some god-forsaken place en-route. I had planned to ring you this morning, but I slept in, and then there was an unexpected dash to the solicitor.'

She looked at him blankly. What on earth was he talking about? 'I — I don't understand,' she stammered. 'What flight?'

'The fax,' he said. 'I told you all about it in the fax.' Then, cautiously: 'You *did* get my fax?'

Callie shook her head. 'I don't know anything about a fax.'

'But I sent it. Three weeks ago. Before I left.' He rummaged in his wallet and brought out the small white card. Her business card. Her *old* business card. 'Here. That's the number.'

'Not any more,' she replied faintly. 'It's Stuart's.'

He was silent for a moment, staring disbelievingly at her. 'I sent your fax to Stuart? He took my message and didn't let you know?'

'Know what?'

'That I had resigned from work, had picked up an overseas assignment at the last minute. I tried to call and let you know, but there was no answer. In desperation I sent the fax. Sent it to the wrong bloody number!'

Anger winged its way across her chest. Stuart's possession of Michael's fax, the fact that he had not forwarded the information — the act had been deliberate, of that she was certain. Stuart! Of all the lowdown ... A multitude of adjectives crowded her mind.

'It doesn't matter now. I'm back and so pleased to see you again,' Michael smiled, bringing forward a small package. 'Something for you from Ypres.'

'What is it?'

'Open it and see,' he teased.

Carefully she drew back the layers of tissue paper, surprised to find a gold bracelet with several charms attached. On closer inspection she could see that they were all identical: tiny replica horseshoes. 'At the risk of being labelled a hopeless romantic, I thought it was appropriate.'

'Oh,' she whispered, holding it towards the light. 'It's beautiful.'

'And so are you. I love you.'

She looked up at him in amazement, wondering if she had heard correctly, not knowing whether to laugh or cry as he bent his head and kissed her. One long lingering kiss, mouths and noses touching, that told her things were as they had been, as they should be.

'I love you, too,' she said, pulling away at last. 'Since that very first day you came here, I felt something.'

'Then say you'll marry me. Help me fill this wonderful old house with children. Our children. Yours and mine.' He tucked one hand under her chin, raising her face towards his again. 'I think we'd make beautiful babies together.'

She stared at him in astonishment, her mind scarcely registering the words. 'Wh-what did you say?'

Michael took a deep breath and straightened himself to his full height. 'Callie, I bought the house. I'm the new owner. I know I should have told you before this, but I wanted it to be a surprise. Bonnie and Freya were sworn to secrecy, and Timmy, too.'

He took her arm and led her back up towards the house, telling her of his plans. 'There are a few other things you should know. The local paper here is keen to take some of my work, and it'll mean less travel. Then there's Gaby. She's going overseas for at least twelve months, so Tim will be coming here to live. It means you'll be taking on two of us.'

'I don't mind.'

'You haven't answered my question. Will you marry me?'

'Yes,' she replied simply, pausing at the top of the steps to glance back reflectively towards the mass of shrubbery below. In the moving shadows she imagined she could see them all there — Hannah and Ben, Thomas, Enid and David, Davie with his jar of tadpoles. Lily. Nick. Her own father, Alex. Ghostly lives winding through the generations, part of her, and part of Michael, too.

'Do you feel it?' she asked, tightening her grip on Michael's hand and giving an involuntary shiver. 'It's as though they're all there, watching, giving us their seal of approval.'

'And so they should. In a way, they brought us together.'

'With a little help from a silver horseshoe,' she broke in.

'But we're not Hannah and Ben,' he added, hugging her fiercely to his chest. 'Maybe our love is simply a replica of theirs, simply caught in a different loop of time.'

'Circles of time,' she mused, swinging open the back door. 'Do you believe in reincarnation? I was thinking of writing a book about it one day ...'

'Callie! Be serious.'

'I am,' she laughed, kissing him again and linking her arm through his. 'About that wedding. We could have it here, in the garden —'

The door slammed in their wake and the garden lay quietly sleeping, somnolent and drowsy in the early afternoon sunshine. The mulberry tree cast its mottled shade on the neatly-trimmed lawn. From above came the sound of a bird singing, its pure sweet notes filling the air. Bees hummed around a bed of daisies, busily carrying pollen back to their hive.

Without warning, a breeze blew up from the creek. It swayed through the wattles like a whisper, a drawn-out sigh. Through the long years it came, bringing with it a soft murmuring sound, like rain falling on leaves. With a faint rustle, it scattered a layer of rose petals, making a carpet of bridal white across the damp soil.

EPILOGUE

South Coast Times
Tuesday August 18, 1998

Last Saturday, local author, Callie Corduke, married
South Coast Times *photographer, Michael Paterson,*
in the garden of the old Corduke family home. The
bride wore an ivory guipure lace gown and carried a
bouquet of wattle. Attendants were Jill Gordon, a
friend of the bride, and Timothy Paterson, the
groom's son. The happy couple are honeymooning
in France. On their return, they will make their
home in Brunswick Street.

South Coast Times
Saturday 19 June 1999

Critics are hailing local writer Callie Corduke-
Paterson's recently released biography, Circles of
Time, *as the latest Australian literary success. The*
book spans the years of the Great War, between the
city of Brisbane and war-torn France. It is believed
that Warner Roadshow has already purchased the
film rights for an undisclosed sum.

And for first-time mother, Corduke-Paterson, the
timing couldn't be better. Last week, she and her
husband celebrated the birth of their first child, a son
named Benjamin Galbraith Corduke Paterson ...